G. R. LINDEN

Magic, Masks, & Monsters

First published by Book Krewe Books 2019

Copyright © 2019 by G. R. Linden

All rights reserved. No part of this publication may be reproduced, stored or transmitted in any form or by any means, electronic, mechanical, photocopying, recording, scanning, or otherwise without written permission from the publisher. It is illegal to copy this book, post it to a website, or distribute it by any other means without permission.

This novel is entirely a work of fiction. The names, characters and incidents portrayed in it are the work of the author's imagination. Any resemblance to actual persons, living or dead, events or localities is entirely coincidental.

Second edition

ISBN: 9781999381714

Cover art by CJ Boucher

This book was professionally typeset on Reedsy. Find out more at reedsy.com

Contents

I   Magic, Masks, & Monsters

A Time for Reflections	3
Where Have All My Heroes Gone?	34
Oasis	69
Remedial Spellcasting	96
Intermezzo	128
The Climb	136
No Refuge	161
Fight Night	187
The Coming Flood	222

II   Lagniappe

The War of Eight	293
Time to Dance	299
Selected Six-Word Stories	303
Selected Playlists	304

I

Magic, Masks, & Monsters

A Time for Reflections

*(This story first appeared in **Never Fear: Christmas Terrors**)*

December 22nd, 1881

While he would never admit it to himself, Lewis was frightened. He was about to enter a brand-new world and he had no idea what to expect. Already he felt things changing: the white snow on the banks giving way to brown drudge, the crisp, chill air becoming a warm, wet blanket that seemed to engulf you no matter where you were. It was December, and if the weather here was so decidedly odd, what would the rest of his new home be like? Not for the first time Lewis wished his pa was there with him.

But Pa was dead, and Mother didn't want him around anymore. So here he was, shipped off to stay with his mother's brother, a man he had never met before.

The breath left him as he caught sight of the strange cityscape he would be calling home. It was dirtier than St. Louis had been, busier too. But for all its grime, there was a beauty to it, an unquantifiable mystique that made him forget the apprehensions that had gripped him only moments ago. Not for the first time he wondered what his new life in New Orleans would entail.

The sharp shriek of the steamboat whistle shocked him, causing him to nearly jump out of his shoes. He fought to regain his composure as his cheeks turned red under the condescending looks of the adult nearby. Clearly they thought he should not be about without proper supervision. Lewis ignored their looks and gathered his luggage. It was almost time to disembark.

As the steamboat sidled into the dock, Lewis tried to get a better look at his new habitat. But his vantage points were all blocked by people much larger and much more important than he was and they were not about to move for the likes of Lewis. One man even knocked over his luggage before yelling at Lewis to stay out of the way of his betters and muttering something about pathetic orphans and being underfoot. That man would find his pocket watch gone the next time he went to look for it.

Pickpocketing wasn't something they taught good lads at school. Lewis had learned it from some kids he'd met after Pa died, what his mother had called a "bad crowd." It was part of the reason she'd sent him away.

It wasn't that Lewis didn't know stealing was wrong. He was simply of the opinion that being mean was wrong-er.

When the boat was finally moored, Lewis had to fight tooth and nail just to remain upright against the throng of disembarking humanity. His knuckles turned white from his efforts to hold on to his luggage. He managed to fight himself free and get to a quiet place on the docks.

His eyes darted through the crowd, looking for someone who was looking for him

The problem was that Lewis had no idea who he was supposed to be looking for. He'd never met his uncle and had only an old photograph his mother had given him to identify the man from. Standing on his tiptoes did little to help matters. Why did adults have to be so tall?

"Lewis! Lewis Everhart!" The sound came roaring out of the crowd like an orchestral overture. It took Lewis a second to locate the source of the booming bass that called his name, but only a second.

The voice belonged to a man of mixed origin who stood a hand above the rest of the multitude. The top hat he wore accentuated his height in the same way his too-tight sky-blue vest highlighted his portliness. His suit was blood-red, and where his tie should have been hung a loose collection of what looked to Lewis a lot like bones. Lewis dismissed this thought as merely a trick of the distance. No civilized man wore bones around his neck.

Like Moses parting the Red Sea, the crowd gave way before him. Lewis had never seen white men give way to a mulatto before. He thought it was rather grand. Lewis also thought that Mother wouldn't approve at all, which made the whole thing doubly grand.

The man locked eyes on him as if he had known where Lewis was all along. When Lewis said the man was big, he didn't just mean that he was tall or wide; he meant that this man was big in a way that people felt in their souls. There was a presence about him.

A young couple shyly held up their baby to the man as he passed. He stopped, said a few words, and traced something on the baby's head. The child's parents seemed overcome and began kissing his hands, but he gently waived them on their way and he continued toward Lewis.

Now that the behemoth of a man was standing in front of him, Lewis could see clearly that he was indeed wearing a necklace made of bones.

Lewis gulped as the man opened his mouth to speak.

"Ah, young Master Everhart, you've got de same energy as your uncle about you. I'd recognize it anywhere. Allow me te introduce me self. I am Doctor Antoine Laveau at your service." Doctor Laveau removed his top hat and made a deep, formal bow.

"It's a pleasure to meet you, Doctor Laveau." Lewis tried to match the bow and almost fell over.

"Please call me Antoine." The burly man picked up Lewis' luggage. "Come now. I will take you te your uncle. He wanted ta collect you himself, but he has much work still te do if he is ta succeed dis night."

"Succeed?" Lewis had absolutely no idea what Antoine was talking about and the man's strange accent wasn't helping.

"You have arrived on an evening dat is most auspicious. Tonight your uncle means ta see beyond de veil and in ta de realms beyond."

"Oh." Not really knowing what to say to that Lewis simply fell silent. His new home made less and less sense to him by the moment.

As their carriage made its way through the crowded cobblestone streets, Lewis struggled to pay attention to the history lesson that Antoine was offering him. Rather, his focus lay with the marvelous and strange architecture that surrounded them.

They passed a beautiful cathedral that looked like nothing Lewis had seen before, and the streets were lined with balconies where he could see a wide array of peoples relaxing and looking out on the people below.

Perhaps what struck Lewis the most were the Christmas wreaths he saw on every gas lamp. To him it was the most incredible oddity to see a city covered in holly and wreaths with no snow on the ground.

As they moved out of what Antoine had called the French Quarter, the wrought iron facades and colorful two-story buildings gave way to larger, more American-looking buildings. Antoine had stopped his history lesson and gone back to talking about Lewis' uncle.

"Gideon is a brilliant man, but he is misunderstood by many. Dey laugh at his theories and ask for proof. When he brings dem proof, dey decry it as a fabrication. Dey mock what dey do not understand. But dough dey may ridicule his theories, dey respect your uncle. Some of dem even fear him. You know how I know dis?"

Lewis did not. He indicated this by staring blankly back at Doctor Laveau, who by the speed with which he carried on, apparently meant the question to be a rhetorical one anyway.

"Because when dey speak of your uncle, when dey speak of de foolish Professor Gideon Giles and his far-fetched experiments, dey do so in a whisper." Antoine's words were laced with menace but were not as off-putting as the laughter that followed them.

Lewis wasn't sure what Antoine meant by telling him all this. He knew that his mother was not overly fond of her brother and considered him an embarrassment. In Lewis' mind that was a point in his uncle's favor. The truth was he knew very little about his Uncle Gideon, other than he had fought in the war and was now a professor of some kind.

Their mud-spattered carriage pulled up to a mansion that would have been described as palatial if not for the general sense of foreboding it exuded.

Where the other estates they had passed looked bright and classical in their design, his uncle's was more Gothic in nature. It would have been far more at home in medieval Europe than modern America.

Antoine walked him to the door as the footman collected Lewis' baggage. The knocker looked comically small in his gargantuan hand as he banged it three times.

The door opened and a small, matronly looking woman appeared. She gave a quick glance at Antoine before taking a long look at Lewis.

"Ah, Doctor Laveau, you have delivered our weary traveler. The professor will be most grateful to you. You'll find him in the laboratory. He was anxious that you attend to him immediately upon your return." The woman's words were sharp and clear, enunciating each word with clipped precision.

"Den I leave you in Mrs. Dunham's capable care, young Lewis." Antoine gave Lewis' back a pat and made his way into the house.

"Right this way, Master Everhart. Your uncle had me fix up one of the upstairs rooms for you." Lewis followed Mrs. Dunham closely, certain that he did not want to become lost in this place. Myriad stuffed animal heads were mounted on the walls. Some he recognized easy enough: bears, lions, alligators, and the like. But some were decidedly strange: the impossibly large head of a spider, the impossibly small head of a bull, and a just plain impossible head that looked to be an elephant with antlers and an extra eye. Lewis thought the shadows must be playing tricks on him because he would have sworn that the heads were watching him as he climbed the stairs.

"Here we are. Prepared especially for you. You'll find your luggage in the corner. I'll let you get settled. Dinner is at six." Lewis simply nodded as Mrs. Dunham went through her checklist. His attention was engaged by the small firearm that was resting on his pillow, a firearm that Mrs. Dunham seemed to be taking no notice of at all.

The housekeeper left him, and Lewis walked slowly toward the bed. He was certain that if he moved too quickly, the pistol would disappear, proving to be a figment of his overactive imagination. When he finally reached it, Lewis took it carefully in his hands. He could tell by the weight that it wasn't loaded.

He examined it carefully. It was a beautiful piece, silver-plated and balanced perfectly. Lewis hadn't held a gun since before his pa had died.

"My father gave me that gun when I was your age."

Lewis turned with a start. Standing in the doorway was his uncle. The man was older than he had looked in the photo Lewis' mother had given him, but he was still possessed of a wiry frame and a certain air of youthful sophistication. It was the eyes that gave him away, dark brown eyes that somehow managed to be hard and curious at the same time.

"Truth be told, I almost killed your mother with that a few times. Fortunately for you, I was a rather awful shot back then." Lewis couldn't tell whether or not his uncle was joking. "Consider it an early Christmas present. I assume you know how to shoot?"

"Pa taught me a little, but Mother forbade it once she found out." And Lewis hated her for it.

"That sounds like my sister dear. Very well. I'll take you out for target practice starting tomorrow. No sense you losing an appendage out of ignorance." His uncle pulled a whistle out of his pocket and put it to his mouth. "I have one more present for you."

Gideon blew the whistle twice and looked expectantly down the hallway. A few seconds later a rather large Border collie came bounding into Gideon's arms. Lewis' uncle dropped to one knee and petted the exuberant dog for a few seconds before commanding him to sit.

"Lewis, I'd like you to meet your newest companion. I'm afraid I've never been particularly good at naming things, so it's up to you to decide what to call him." Lewis needed less than a moment to answer.

"I'd like to call him Will, if that's all right. After my father."

"I think Will is a fine name for a dog." His uncle smiled then gave a sharp cough. "There, that's done then. I've always said there are three things a boy your age needs: a gun, a dog, and an education. I've taken care of the first two, and tonight we'll get to work on the third. Dinner is at six sharp and Mrs. Dunham abhors tardiness. I'll leave you to get acquainted with your new friend."

Dinner came too quickly for Lewis, but not wanting to make a bad impression on his first night in his new home, he pulled himself away from Will and managed to get dressed and downstairs in time.

Dinner consisted of pork chops smothered in some kind of gravy, a new species of pepper Lewis had never seen, stuffed with cheese and beef, and a serving of what Antoine had called jambalaya. It was all delicious and a vast improvement on the disappointingly small portions of soup Lewis had been eating on the way down the river. It was safe to say that the food on Lewis' plate had his undivided attention.

Which was good because he had only a fleeting comprehension of what Gideon and Antoine were discussing.

"I accept that there are things beyond the current understanding of science, but I will not accept that this will always be the case. To the first cave dwellers fire seemed to be a gift from the gods. The sun, the moon, and the stars were all worshiped before we came to understand them for what they really are. Gravity itself baffled the scientific community and was held to be merely an extension of God's will until a man of intellect proved otherwise. What you call mysticism is merely a state of natural laws that we have yet to unravel."

"Science is a powerful ding, Professor. 'Dis is true, but it does not solve all de mysteries of God's creation. De spirits are here te guide us, but dey will not be chained by man's laws."

Gideon guffawed at Antoine's assertions. "God is a myth. These spirits of yours are no more than apparitions. Imprints of consciousness left behind. No more than energy trapped between our reality and another." His uncle said in rebuttal.

"God is all around you, Professor. You simply choose not te believe. Tonight you will have de proof you need." Antoine spoke with supreme confidence.

"Yes, I very much believe I will."

The conversation continued but became increasingly more technical and centered on the specifics of this great experiment that was to occur after supper. And thus it was increasingly beyond Lewis' ability to comprehend.

Lewis let his thoughts dwell on his uncle's statement that God was a myth.

He had never heard anyone speak such a thought out loud. While it was true that his mother had been more interested in church activities than his pa, his father had been able to quote his Scripture by chapter and verse and had insisted that Lewis be able to do the same.

But with his father dead and his mother run off to San Francisco in search of a rich husband, he wondered if there really was a God after all. And if there was, why was everyone so certain he was benevolent?

After dinner Lewis, with Will now at his side, was ushered down to what he presumed to be his uncle's laboratory. He could only presume because, while it seemed unlikely to be anything else, it also looked nothing like what Lewis thought a scientific laboratory should look like.

Incense burned throughout the room, combining with the odd bits of steam that various gadgets and doodads were popping out, to make the lab's atmosphere heavy and difficult to breathe. Where Lewis would have expected to find the shelves lined with beakers and sundries, instead they were lined with hollowed-out skulls and other, more unfamiliar oddities. The far wall was perhaps the most surprising as it served as a rack for a variety of heavily modified firearms.

Lewis highly doubted that this room was typical for a university professor.

"Stand by the door. If you see fire, ghosts, or any unnatural atmospheric occurrences, run and get Mrs. Dunham. Understood?" The oddness of his uncle's command was overshadowed by the severity of its delivery.

"Yes sir," Lewis responded fairly bewildered.

Gideon double-checked his equipment while Antoine drew a circle and some other markings on the floor. From his spot in the doorway it was difficult for Lewis to see what they might be. When he was done, he positioned himself in the center of the circle, sat down cross-legged, and began mixing various herbs and liquids. Gideon paced impatiently and looked over the equipment twice more before Antoine spoke.

"I am ready te begin, Professor. May de spirits smile upon us." Antoine produced a flask from his pocket and took a swig before handing it to Gideon.

"Here's to not blowing ourselves up." His uncle took his own long tug on the flask and threw the switch attached to a large piece of machinery. Cords ran from the machine to two separate brackets that stood on opposite sides of the room.

The machine and Antoine began to hum in unison as the lights flickered and dimmed.

"Come on, work, damn you, work," came his uncle's quiet imploring. Antoine ceased his humming and began chanting in a powerful voice and blowing some sort of white powder into the air.

The laboratory crackled with energy. Sparks flew from various pieces of equipment. Will whined and barked from behind Lewis' legs, the poor creature frightened out of his mind. Gideon cackled as Antoine continued his chanting, calling to unknown spirits. Madness had taken hold of the room and only Lewis seemed to notice or care.

Colors began to swirl as the energy coalesced at the center of his uncle's contraption. A horizontal funnel of electricity and fire appeared out of thin air, boring a hole through reality itself. Wind rushed around the room, sending papers flying all around.

A maddening cacophony of unholy shrieks attacked his ears. Lewis tried to cover them, but to no avail. The screams reached him no matter what he tried, drilling through his every defense and straight into his soul.

The cyclone expanded until its edges were touching Gideon's machines. Suddenly the funnel snapped back and locked into place, creating a wall of electricity and fire at the center of the lab.

Distorted images began to appear in the brackets, flickering fragments of creatures and people that should have been impossible for them to view.

The images came into focus and the room calmed. Before them, bracketed by his uncle's invention and humming with the power of Antoine's spirits, was a vision of an unearthly wasteland.

"It worked," was Gideon's breathless reply to the successful culmination of his maniacal endeavor.

Leaving the safety of the doorway and a still whimpering Will, Lewis stepped toward his uncle's experiment. In a voice of awe and wonder he spoke his first words since this lunacy had begun. "What is it?"

"That," smug satisfaction filled his uncle's words "is another dimension."

"Your uncle has built a window into de mind of God." Antoine pronounced solemnly.

"Nonsense. It's not a window. It's a mirror. A mirror that shows us the reflections of all our might-have-beens. Observe." Gideon walked over to one of the brackets and began adjusting dials. As he did, the image changed.

A group of children were playing a game of baseball in a park. The children were from all different backgrounds: black, white, mixed, even a few Chinese boys among them. Standing by the foul line, watching over everyone, was grey-haired Antoine smiling from ear to ear.

"Not a bad find for de first attempt," said Antoine, wearing the same exact smile his mirrored-self wore.

"You don't even like baseball," was Gideon's teasingly gruff reply.

"No, but I do enjoy seeing de little ones enjoying demselves," Antoine pointed out with a hearty laugh.

"If I wanted to watch a baseball game, I'd go to the park. Let's see if we can't find something a bit worthier of our genius, shall we?" Gideon turned the dials and a new moving portrait came into focus.

A man walked across a field of corpses, dressed in gray and blue. He moved frantically, searching the faces of the bodies. When he found the one he was looking for, he fell to his knees and began to weep uncontrollably. Lewis realized the man they saw was Gideon, only much younger. Younger even than the picture his mother had given him.

Gideon shifted the dials and the picture changed again.

Lewis gasped. The new image showed Lewis sitting in front of a Christmas tree, digging through his stocking. His mother was there, laughing and handing Lewis more presents to open. In the corner of the room, sitting in a rocking chair as if he didn't have a care in the world, was his father.

He felt Antoine's firm grip on his shoulder. He couldn't tell if it was meant to be reassuring, or if it was there to keep him from running headlong into his favorite dream.

"It's not real, Lewis. It's nothing but a mirage." His uncle's words rang hollow in is ears. It wasn't a mirage. His father was right there. Close enough to touch.

He didn't realize his hand had been reaching out to do just that until Antoine knocked it away. Gideon quickly reset the dials on his machine and the image became a wall of red and blue energy.

"I think that's enough for tonight. Antoine, why don't you take Lewis up to bed while I clean up down here."

Numbly, Lewis allowed himself to be led away from the life he had always wanted.

***

Just before midnight, after everyone else had gone to bed, Lewis snuck back down to his uncle's laboratory. The blue-red wall still hummed, its glow lighting the otherwise darkened room. Carefully, he moved the dials the way his uncle had until he had again found the image of his family. He sat there for hours, watching them open presents, play with his new toys, eat Christmas dinner. Smiling and laughing. Being a family.

Sometime after he had run out of tears, but before dawn, Lewis heard a noise coming from down the hall. Not wanting to be caught playing with his uncle's experiment, he rushed out of the laboratory and back to his room, completely forgetting to reset the dials on the mirror.

***

December 23rd, 1881

Lewis didn't see his reflection reach for the mirror's edge. He didn't smell the skin burning as his doppelganger's hand crossed the portal's threshold and entered our world. He didn't know that the happy life he had seen for himself had been a lie, a fabrication concocted by a creature so desperate to escape Hell that it would endure the flesh melting off its bones to be liberated from its torments. Nor did he know that after the demon had suffered through such an ordeal, it would hunger. No, Lewis was ignorant of all these things and one more. Lewis also didn't know that Mrs. Dunham always awoke in the early hours of the morning to bake fresh bread for the day.

* * *

After a night of unsettling dreams, Lewis opened his eyes at Will's insistent nuzzling. The Border collie was whimpering with some urgency. Lewis dressed quickly and followed his new pup down the stairs.

The first thing to hit him was the smell, a layer of stench that coated the entire first floor of the house. Vile, putrid air filled his nostrils and roiled his insides. Lewis blocked out the smell as best he could and continued down the stairs. If Will could manage it with his canine sense of smell, then so could Lewis.

Further and further into the house they went, finding more and more signs of distress. Bookcases and end tables were strewn about, haphazardly knocked over by some unknown force. Fingernail scratches laced the walls, marring the beautiful woodwork Lewis had been introduced to only the day before.

Finally they came upon his uncle. Gideon stood like a statue in the doorway, oblivious to their approach. Still whimpering, Will stayed in the hallway as Lewis moved past his uncle and into the kitchen, a decision that he immediately regretted.

Horrifying could not begin to describe the tableau of gore that lay before him. Mrs. Dunham's body lay in front of the stove. She had been ripped open and unburdened of her internal organs. The few ribs that had not been broken were now protruding from her hollowed-out corpse at an angle of ninety degrees. Her head lay a few feet away. It was only missing its tongue. Mrs. Dunham's eyes remained open, forever imprinted with the terror of her final moments. Lewis' stomach heaved. He managed to swallow down the vomit, but the taste of bile lingered in his mouth. He stepped out of the room, fearing that he would be unable to keep control of another such outburst.

There was a heavy knocking at the door and unseen chimes began ringing throughout the house. Will barked at the noise, and Lewis was sure that his pup shared his master's fear and discomfort.

The noise jolted Gideon from his dire contemplations, and finally he too stepped away from the terrible scene.

"That will be the police. Perhaps it's best if you took Will to the library, keep him out of the way while they're here. I'll join you shortly."

Lewis knew that the task was meant to keep them both out of the way and he would normally bristle at being condescended to, but in this particular instance he was grateful to his uncle for the opportunity to get as far away from this horrid scene as possible.

Lewis only took three wrong turns on his way to the library. The further from the smell they got, the more Will seemed to perk up, though his new pup was still quite rattled from the experience.

They sat in silence in the library as the police did their work. Nearly an hour had gone by when his uncle stepped through the door, with Antoine trailing in his wake.

"Yours were not de only ill words ta reach me doorstep dis morning. Der were two other poor souls ta share Mrs. Dunham's fate last night."

"Tell me," was Gideon's cold response to the disturbing news.

"Remi St. Croix was found in de basement of Touro, ripped te shreds, and pieces of Walter Jackson were found in tree different rooms of de iron works on Tchoupitoulas. Der be no coincidence about dis Professor. Dis be the work of Loa. We have unleashed de evil spirits on our home. Dis blood be on our hands." Antoine trembled as he spoke the last words.

"What exactly we've unleashed is yet to be assessed. But I do agree with you that this is no coincidence and the burden of guilt is ours to bear."

Lewis felt a sinking feeling in his gut. If these murders were a result of his uncle's mirror, then they were Lewis' fault. He'd been the one to sneak back down and play with the dials. Lewis wanted to say something but held his tongue. Gideon was his uncle, but he'd only met the man last night. What did one say at a time like this? How could he tell his uncle that he was responsible for these people's horrible deaths?

"Three murders in three different wards. Even if we lucked upon a group of honest officers, they won't know what they're truly up against. How could they if we don't even know? Without our involvement there is no chance that this does not become a bloodbath of Biblical scale. Besides which is the matter of a debt to be repaid." Gideon paused for moment. "Lewis, grab your pistol. We're going out."

"Out" by Gideon's definition was the crime scene closest to his residence, a hospital called Touro Infirmary. Lewis' first full day in New Orleans was not going as he had expected. It was shocking to him that his uncle could be so untouched by the gruesome murder of his housekeeper, but if the man felt any emotion at all, he was keeping it buried deep inside.

The approach to the hospital was clogged by a crowd of gawkers and hysterical citizens. A line of stalwart officers had their batons out and were quite literally beating the mob back with a stick. With a mix of contempt and frustration, Gideon instructed their driver to keep moving.

"Maybe we have more luck at de Ironworks?" said Antoine.

"We'd better," was his uncle's terse reply.

The additional half-mile ride was more than a frustrating annoyance for Lewis, as it left him with time to dwell on the horrible deaths multiple people had suffered because of his own weakness. The thought ate away at him as they arrived at their secondary destination.

Gideon was a striking sight as he climbed out of the carriage. His hat was slightly askew, and he had removed his jacket and rolled up his white shirtsleeves. His maroon vest was accentuated by a purple cravat that was the color of royalty. The silver-plated pistols that hung naturally on each of his uncle's hips and the dark glasses that covered his eyes gave his cultivated aura of refined casualness a lethal seriousness.

Gideon handed Lewis his black medical bag and started giving orders.

"Lewis, stay here and out of trouble. Antoine, work some of that voodoo doctor charm and get us in to see that body." Lewis' stomach revolted at merely the thought of seeing another sight like Mrs. Dunham, and for once he was glad to be left holding the bag.

From where they exited the carriage, they could see the police carrying three different black bags from the building. The sight of three body bags sent Lewis into panic spiral. Antoine had said that there had been only one death here. His heart ached and his breath shortened as the weight of two more deaths crushed down upon his soul.

Lewis was not the only one shaken by the thought of two more bodies. Antoine's voice cracked as he spoke to the officer impeding their path.

"Excuse me, constable, but I was told der had been only de one man killed."

"That's right," the constable replied coarsely.

"Why den tree bags?"

"He was killed in a very nasty way." The constable paused to let the words sink in.

"If you'll allow me, my name is Professor Gideon Giles. I'm with the university, and I'm doing some research. I was hoping I might get a look at the room where the unfortunate man was found." Gideon started to walk past the officer, but he was stopped with a firm hand.

"I don't care who you're with. No one's getting in here without a badge. Now get moving before I haul you down for irritating an officer." The officer stared them down until, reluctantly, Gideon walked away.

"Damn. I need to know what happened in there. I wouldn't even need to see the scene. Just a look at the detective's notebook would be enough," his uncle complained once they were out of earshot.

Lewis could see the head detective giving orders to various officers and had an idea.

He dropped his uncle's medical bag and ducked away from Gideon and Antoine. Making sure his path would take him right by the detective, he took off at full speed toward the body bags, screaming "Daddy" at the top of his lungs.

"Whoa, lad, slow down. What's the matter?" Sure enough the detective stepped in front of him to block his way.

On command, Lewis began to bawl his eyes out.

"That's my daddy." Lewis called upon all the anguish he had felt at his father's death to sell it.

"What's your daddy's name?" The detective was dour, but there was genuine concern there. Lewis' plan would work.

"Joe. Joe King." Sometimes Lewis was too clever for his own good.

"Then that's not your daddy. Now why would you think it was?"

"He works here. I haven't been able to find him all morning."

"Well, if I was your daddy, I'd need a drink after seeing a sight like this. He's likely at the saloon and will be home later. Best if you go home and wait for him there."

"Okay. I'm sorry, sir. I was just scarred it might be him." Lewis reduced the waterworks to a light sob and let his teary, eye contact work its magic.

Feeling awkward and unsure of what to do, the detective bent down and gave Lewis a hug to reassure him. Lewis took the opportunity to carefully slip his hands into the man's breast pocket and remove his notebook. When the detective broke the hug, he was none the wiser. Lewis rubbed his eyes dry and thanked the man for both his knowing and unknowing assistance.

"Thank you, sir, I feel better now."

"I'm glad to hear it. Run along then, lad. This is no place for a boy your age."

Lewis did as he was told. He was well away from the crowd of gawkers by the time Gideon and Antoine caught up with him.

"What the devil was that all about?"

"You wanted a look at the detective's notebook." Lewis produced the notebook from his pocket and handed it to his uncle.

"Impressive," said Antoine.

"Most," said Gideon with a nod of approval. "Now let's see what we have here. The victim is Walter Jackson. He comes in early to get the smelter heated up for the day. He was found when the first shift came in. Or rather, his devoured, mostly to the bone, legs were found in the front office. Then his arm was found by the changing station, and finally the rest of him by the smelter. Ripped open like the others. Missing most his internal organs along with his eyes and his tongue. The detective's current working theory is animal attack."

"He was a good man," Antoine bowed his head and said a silent prayer.

"Der is nah'ting der we didn't know already."

"No there isn't." Gideon must have seen the disappointment on Lewis' face because he quickly added, "Not right now at least, but every bit of information helps. This was a good get, Lewis. Well done."

"What do we do now?" he asked bypassing his uncle's patronizing remark.

"Now we search all of Uptown and pray we get lucky," was Gideon's uninspired response.

And so they hunted. They spent hours walking the streets, checking every building and alley, canvasing the neighborhood, looking for any sign of the foul, murdering beast they had set loose upon the world.

They were still patrolling well after sunset when a Creole woman came running down the street in a fit of hysteria.

"A demon! A demon from hell! It killed him! Ripped him apart. Loa! Loa!!" The words came rushing out of the woman in a jumble, barely audible between sobs.

"Calm, sweet sister. It will be alright. Where did ya see de beast?" Antoine spoke in a melodic, soothing voice, but the woman refused to be slowed by their questions. She continued to scream and flee, leaving her direction of origin as their only clue.

They hurried toward the source of the woman's fright. Will must have sensed his fear. The Border collie was never more than a foot away, constantly searching the shadows for threats to his master. Maybe that was why the pup was the first to locate the demon's latest meal.

Lewis was horrified to find yet another mangled corpse but was more than a little relieved to discover the creature already gone. From the looks of it, the victim was a lamplighter in the middle of his evening rounds. The man's equipment and the lack of light on half the street made that much obvious. Faced with his imminent doom, he had run back toward the light, perhaps hoping it might provide some discouragement to his attacker. Or maybe he was just following that primal instinct that made human beings identify darkness as danger and light as safety. Whatever his motivation, he did not make it far.

The man had been slashed open just like the others. His throat was torn out, and of his limbs, only the left arm remained attached to the body. Bits of flesh and bone were scattered about like debris from a sunken ship. Blood pooled beneath the body, the dark-red looking black underneath the moonlight. This man's death had not been a humane one. Indeed it had been about as horrible a death as Lewis could imagine anyone ever having.

Gideon cautiously stepped around the various pieces of corpse and bent down low to examine what remained of the man's upper torso.

"The teeth marks are different here than on the other three bodies. Those were definitely human or at least a close approximation. These are more canine in nature," was his uncle's assessment.

"Dogs, or maybe der be more den one creature?" Antoine put forth as an explanation. The thought of more than one of these horrible monsters roaming the streets sent shivers down Lewis' spine.

"No, the attack patterns are too similar, and if more than one of these things was loose, I think we'd have seen more signs of it at the house. There were no attacks during the day, but then the sun goes down and another body shows up." Gideon paced as he considered the problem. He stopped when he reached a conclusion. "It's hibernating during the day, using its victims as food to fuel some sort of metamorphosis."

"Dat is a long leap, Professor." The incredulity in Antoine's tone was light, but it was there.

"Perhaps, but it fits the evidence. There's nothing else we're going to learn here." Gideon nodded to the police officers who were beginning to arrive on the scene. "Let's leave the police to their work while we tend to ours."

Casually they moved away from the body and melted back into the gathering crowd of onlookers. When they were clear of the crowd, they found themselves standing on the edge between the lighted streets behind them and the darkened path before them. If Lewis hadn't been so completely terrified, he might have found the setting rather literary.

"No lamplighter ta finish de rounds." From the tone in Antoine's voice Lewis could tell he wasn't the only one who was ill at ease, not that a little bit of nighttime would faze his uncle.

"That's unfortunate. You'd think there would be redundancies for things like this. Lewis, hand me my bag."

Lewis did as he was told. His uncle pulled out three lengths of cloth and a thermos. Carefully he soaked each piece of cloth with whatever liquid the thermos contained. Gideon then broke off three lengths of wood from a nearby tree and wrapped the ends with the soaked cloth. He handed one to each of them and used his lighter to light each one in turn. At the end of two minutes' time they each held a brightly burning torch. "I'll take point, Antoine guard our rear, Lewis stay between us and stay close."

As they moved into the unlit section of the city, Lewis could feel the darkness increase around them despite the fire they held in their hands. The blackness weighed on him, an outward sign of the shadows that now marred his own soul. Envy was one of the deadly sins, and his envy of a mirage had cost four people their lives already. Maybe his mother had been right to get as far away as possible from him. Maybe he really was good for nothing.

A woman's high-pitched scream cut through the night, freezing the party in its tracks.

"Whe…" Lewis started to ask where the scream had come from but held his tongue at Gideon's raised hand.

Another scream came, cut off abruptly by some unknown horror.

"This way," was all his uncle said as they rushed toward the cry for help, knowing they would not get there in time.

A few minutes of sprinting through a maze of side streets brought them to two partially consumed corpses. To Lewis they had the look of a young couple, or at least the remnants of one. The man lay face down in the street. His spine had been removed, and most of his right side had been eaten away. His gnawed-upon legs had been haphazardly discarded a few feet away.

The woman looked to be lying face-down as well until Lewis got closer and saw that she was in fact right-side up. It was simply her head that had been twisted all the way round. Her rib cage had been ripped open in the same fashion as Mrs. Dunham's, though her insides were not entirely missing but rather lay next to her, half eaten.

Lewis looked at the scene and made a mental inventory of the items surrounding the bodies. He tried to stay cold and detached like his uncle, pushing down his guilt and focusing on the problem at hand. He could deal with the additional blemishes on his soul later, after they'd stopped this demon. Somewhere inside him he registered the fact that he no longer wretched automatically at a sight such as this, and that worried him immensely.

"It appears we interrupted the beast. On your guard. It may still be lurking about." Gideon emphasized his point by drawing his pistol. Lewis imitated his uncle, though he doubted he'd be much good with his in this light.

A shadow moved in the corner of his eye. Lewis turned, raising his pistol, but saw nothing there.

"Top hat, bonnet, cigarette case, lighter, and a walking cane. That's it. Nothing that tells us why these people. Damn it all to hell I'm missing something." Gideon's voice was tight and full of rage. Lewis wanted to tell his uncle that this was his fault, but shame stopped him from confessing his role in all of this.

Again something stirred at the edge of his vision. Again Lewis turned with his pistol raised only to find nothing waiting for him. He took a few steps forward to be certain, but his torch revealed nothing but an empty sidewalk. His guilty conscience had him jumping at shadows.

"Lewis, what de ya see?" Antoine asked.

"Nothing. Just a figment of my imagination." He started to walk back toward his companions when Will began barking in earnest. The collie's warnings were soon joined by a deep, guttural growling noise.

"Down boy!" screamed Antoine as something leaped out of the darkness at Lewis. The shape was intercepted in midair by Will. The pair fell back into the night. A few seconds of barking and growling and the collie burst back into the light with a shadowy figure hot on his tail. Gunshots rang out as Gideon unloaded into the figure with his pistol.

The shots did nothing to slow the creature down. Indeed, the only evidence that it had been hit at all were the bits of blood that flew from it as Gideon's bullets struck flesh.

It was only a few paces from Lewis now.

The beast snarled with its wolfish snout, its beady, scarlet eyes burning with hate.

Lewis raised his pistol to fire, but his finger froze on the trigger. Fear and guilt gripped him. He didn't want to die, but maybe it was the fate he deserved for unleashing this demon on the world.

At the last possible moment Antoine stepped between Lewis and the beast. The creature's teeth sunk into the large man's arm, causing him to drop his torch. Lewis cowered as Antoine brought his own pistol to bear, firing multiple rounds into the creature's belly.

The beast released its grip on Antoine as it howled in rage and pain. Antoine's dropped torch flickered on the ground next to the beast, alternatingly draping their foe in darkness and light.

The beast stood upright like a man, just short of six feet in height. The demon's skin was a patchwork of oozing blood-red bits and charred, cracked pieces as black as coal. Its hands were closer to claws in description and it possessed long, spindly talons for feet. Blood dripped from its teeth and ran down its naked form. Lewis didn't know if this was the Devil, but if it wasn't, it was certainly one of his spawn.

Gideon had reloaded his pistol and wasted no time in unleashing another torrent of gunfire. The beast let out an unearthly scream and took off into the night.

"Report!" barked Gideon.

"Alive," came Antoine's rueful call.

"Lewis?" His uncle's voice had a note of worry to it. Lewis was still too stunned by the events of the last few minutes to find his voice.

"Lewis!... Lewis!" The second shout finally snapped Lewis out of his stupor.

"I'm all right." Lewis felt like he was the farthest thing from all right he could be.

"Antoine, you're injured." His uncle spoke the words as cold assessment rather than caring inquiry.

"It be no ding." The blood soaking the voodoo doctor's sleeve suggested otherwise.

"We have to go after it." That was not what Lewis wanted to do, but he felt that he had a responsibility stop the creature before it could kill again. Whatever the cost.

"Nonsense. Between us we put a dozen bullets in the monster and we hardly slowed it down. If we give chase, we'll end up like those two there." Gideon pointed to the disemboweled couple, and Lewis needed only a quick glance to lose his will to continue the hunt. "Come on. Back to the house. With any luck the demon will be dormant again until tomorrow night. We need to regroup and come up with a plan, one a little bit more advanced than our previous shoot-and-pray strategy. Chin up, everyone. We had a bad night, but tomorrow will be different."

"Why is that?" Lewis didn't understand why his uncle didn't share his own despondency at the beast's escape.

"Because now we know what we're up against. And once you understand your enemy, you can beat your enemy."

* * *

December 24th, 1881

By the time Lewis awoke, it was already approaching midday. Will lay next to him on the bed, looking worriedly at his master. After he dressed, he found his uncle and Antoine in the dining room, poring over maps and books and the policeman's notebook he had stolen an eternity ago. They looked haggard. Lewis doubted they had gotten much sleep, if they had gotten any at all. Another thing to feel guilty about. At least Antoine's wounds had been dressed.

"There's something I'm missing. Something that connects the attacks that I'm not seeing." Gideon's voice was strained, and his frustration was visibly boiling over.

"You said last night that you knew what we were up against." Doubt filled Lewis.

A TIME FOR REFLECTIONS

"I do. The problem is that I don't know what I know yet. All the information is here. I just have to piece it together." His uncle spoke with what Lewis considered to be an unearned confidence. "We have to go over the other murders again. What connects them?"

"Tree before dawn yesterday. None during de day. Den tree more last night," Antoine recapped for them all.

"Then none again today. It hibernates during the day. We'd already soused that out. No, I mean the individual victims. That thing covered a lot of ground the last two nights in what could hardly be called a straight line. Why that route? Why those people?"

"It was looking for the easiest kills?" Lewis posited.

"Hardly. It completely bypassed the orphanage. And why go to the basement of the infirmary, kill an able-bodied man, then leave again when you have plenty of tasty, immobile human snacks above you?" Gideon paused pensively "List every victim in order for me, telling me where and how they were found."

"Mrs. Dunham was in de kitchen baking de morning bread. Remi was in de basement at Touro Infirmary working on de building boiler. Walter Jackson was getting ready for de day at de Ironworks. Dey found him by de—"

"By the smelter! That's it! The missing piece! Right in front of me the whole time. How could I be so stupid as to miss it? It's so obvious. Can't you see it?" Lewis looked to see if Antoine understood what his uncle was going on about. It was a comfort to him that the large man looked as lost as he was. "The heat! It's drawn to heat! Mrs. Dunham had the oven going. St. Croix was stoking the boiler at Touro. Jackson was working a smelter—"

"—De lamplighter had a torch wid him…" came Antoine's wide-eyed comprehension.

"There was an open cigarette case and a lighter by the couple." Lewis excitedly chimed in.

"Now put it all together. Everything we know about this monstrosity. It's nocturnal, it's drawn to sources of heat, it's hiding somewhere in City Park, and bullets merely seem to annoy it." Lewis could see the gears turning in

25

his uncle's head now.

"Dat seems te be de long and de short of it," Antoine affirmed.

"So if we can't kill it, we'll have to send it back to where it came from."

"Ain't no easy ding to trick de Devil back to Hell Professor."

"We'll need some sort of heat source, something large enough to lure the beast to us. We won't be able to get it to the lab. We'll need some place wide open in or near the park." His uncle was pacing again.

"Den it's a good ding Papa Noel rides tonight." The words stopped Gideon mid-stride. A smile broke out all over his face.

"Antoine, you're a genius. Can you make the arrangements in time?"

"It shouldn't be a problem. Can you say de same?"

"Are you asking if I can build a portable generator capable of powering an extra-dimensional portal between now and sundown? Antoine, please, I'll be done with an hour to spare."

"Best be to it den." Without further discussion Antoine headed out the door.

Gideon was about to do the same when the need to confess suddenly overwhelmed Lewis.

"Uncle..." The words stuck in his throat. "Uncle Gideon, there's something I have to tell you."

"Lewis, I need to get to my laboratory." His uncle looked at him and his facial expression went from stern to concern in an instant. "Lewis, what is it?"

"It's just that..." Lewis forced himself to tell his uncle his shameful secret. "The truth is that this is all my fault. I snuck back down to your laboratory after everyone had gone to bed. I know I shouldn't have, but I couldn't help it. I just wanted to see him again. I turned the dials back to where you had them before. I swear all I did was watch them. I didn't touch anything other than the dials, honest. They're all dead because of me." Tears filled his eyes and he began to sob uncontrollably.

"Is that what's been eating at you this whole time? Lewis, I'm going to say something now, and I want you to listen very closely because it's important that you believe me. None of this is your fault. It can't be because the fault lies with me. I tampered with the natural order of things. More than that, I did so in the most cavalier way possible. There should have been nothing for you to find when you snuck back down. It was the height of arrogance and idiocy to leave that connection open and unmonitored. I have no idea what possessed me to do so, especially in light of the obvious temptation it offered you. Everything that has happened has been a result of my hubris and not your innocent desire to see your father alive and happy again. You are a good lad, Lewis, as good as I've seen."

"But mother said—"

"My sister is a ghastly woman completely unable to look beyond her own petty needs. What your father saw in her I'll never know. How she could send you down here alone to stay with a stranger, at Christmas of all times, absolutely boggles my mind, but I'm damn glad she did. Now, there'll be time for feeling feelings later, but right now we need to get to work. We have a beast to slay and honor to regain. Are you with me?"

"Yes sir," Lewis said. Will barked his affirmation as well.

The work took most of the afternoon, but Gideon was good to his word. They finished loading the equipment onto the wagon while the sun was still two fingers over the horizon. Gideon, Lewis, and Will rode to the park in silence. Lewis assumed that his uncle was too preoccupied with going over the plan in his head to speak, and Will was too preoccupied with sticking his head out the window and barking at passing streetcars to pay much attention to his master.

Their destination was well into the park, a clearing somewhere along the bank of the Mississippi. They found Antoine waiting for them when they arrived. Lewis was still completely in the dark about what the plan was. If he had to guess, he would say the giant, twelve-foot-high stack of wood they were setting up next to them was going to be involved in some manner or another. But something about the demeanor of the two adults made him think it was best not to ask questions at the moment. He simply got to work unloading the wagon.

Gideon had not just brought with him a stack of lab equipment. He'd also loaded the wagon with a small armory. Lewis pulled out a gun with a single long barrel and some kind of pumping mechanism attached to the bottom. He had never seen anything like it before although, given the frequency at which he had been making that observation lately, he supposed his uncle's custom firearm was apropos. While he was admiring it, his uncle came up behind him and snatched it out of his grasp.

"What is that?"

"It's a shotgun."

"It doesn't look like any shotgun I've ever seen."

"That's because it's a repeating shotgun, one of the many tricks I have hidden up my sleeve and years ahead of anything that bastard Browning's come up with. Any other questions?" His uncle meant it as a dismissal.

"Who's Papa Noel?" Lewis asked immediately

"Cajun Santa Claus. Every year on Christmas Eve people light huge bonfires to guide him in. Now back to work." Suddenly their plan made much more sense to Lewis.

By the time they had set up the equipment to Gideon's satisfaction, the sun had sunk long past the horizon and given way to the black of night. The general apprehension Lewis had felt all day was now completely gone, replaced by a more palpable sense of doom.

"The generator has limited power. Once you turn it on, we'll have less than five minutes to drive the demon back to whatever hell it came from. Stay out of sight, and don't throw the switch until you hear me shout for it. Understand?"

Lewis nodded at his uncle's instructions.

Across the river, giant pillars of fire came roaring to life as families began to light their bonfires in celebration of Christmas.

"Dey light de way for Papa Noel," came a jubilant shout from Antoine.

"Then we'd best do the same," was the gruffer response from his uncle as he lit the pyre next to him. Antoine had long since chased off any other revelers on their side of the river, so when Gideon started their specially chosen bonfire, it stood out like a fiery beacon against the dark. If they were right about the demon's attraction to heat, it would be impossible for the creature to resist the bonfire's lure.

A TIME FOR REFLECTIONS

"What now?" Lewis asked

"Now we wait for the Devil to show himself," was his uncle's intense reply.

They did not have to wait long.

The ground trembled under their feet, alerting them to the demon's approach. The beast let loose with a horrible cry as it stepped out into the moonlight. This was not the same creature they had faced the previous evening. In its day of hibernation it had grown almost six feet and now stood over twelve feet high. Massive leathery wings had sprouted from its back, each one as wide as the beast was tall. Its skin was the deep black of the void, making the demon almost impossible to see.

"Bigger than I remember. And with wings. That's certainly an unfortunate development." His uncle spoke the words casually, showing defiance through his nonchalance.

Gideon opened fire with both pistols, unloading shot after shot into the demon's chest. A roar of anger escaped its throat.

"I tink you got its attention," Antoine called out, staff in one hand, pistol in the other.

"Yes, I think you might be right," Gideon responded as the beast increased its speed from a lumbering stride to a quick gallop.

The demon closed the distance between itself and Gideon in mere moments. Lewis cringed as the boom of gunfire turned into the hollow clicks of an empty chamber.

His uncle let his now useless weapons fall from his hands, diving toward his right to escape the beast's slashing claws. Lewis watched his uncle repeat the tactic twice more, each escape narrower than the last, the creature allowing Gideon no time to do anything but dodge.

Eventually Gideon's luck gave out and the demon's claws found flesh. His uncle cried out, instinctively reaching out for the newly formed gash in his thigh.

The creature raised its hand back to strike, ready to deliver the deathblow.

"Gideon! Roll!" Antoine bellowed while unleashing his own barrage of pistol fire. The bullets did minimal damage, succeeding only in puncturing a few holes in the creature's leathery wings, but they did manage to distract the beast long enough for Gideon to roll clear.

The creature swept its wing back at its attacker. The wing struck Antoine with incredible force and sent the large man flying through the air. He landed in a heap, clearly dazed by the blow.

The demon turned its attention back to Gideon, who was struggling to get upright.

Lewis pulled his pistol from its holster.

His uncle had told him to remain hidden, but if Lewis didn't act now, the monstrosity was sure to devour both Antoine and Gideon. Lewis was old enough to know that sometimes doing what is right means not doing what you're told.

He inhaled deeply, aimed, and pulled the trigger as he exhaled. The shot exploded from his gun with a thunderclap, the recoil nearly ripping his arm out of its socket. The bullet struck home, burying itself in the creature's shoulder.

Its howl cut through the night. The beast turned, its fiery red eyes locking in on Lewis.

"Lewis, run!" He did not need to hear his uncle's advice to heed it.

The ground rumbled underneath the demon's lengthy stride. Lewis' legs pumped up and down with the fury of a railroad piston, but he was quickly losing his lead. A loose branch sent him tumbling to the ground, and Lewis knew he was about to die.

Or at least he would have if not for his faithful pup. Will came sprinting out of the shadows, letting out a howl as the collie launched itself into the creature's knees. The demon bellowed and toppled over, mirroring Lewis' fall of only moments before.

The monstrosity's flailing hands caught Will with a glancing blow that sent the dog flying through the air.

Lewis scrambled to his feet, and it was then that he realized his mistake.

In fleeing from the demon he'd led the creature too far away from Gideon's invention. Now, as the beast righted itself, it stood between Lewis and his companions and was headed toward him and further away from his uncle's trap.

Antoine and Gideon were running toward them, but both were injured and moving slowly. Lewis was on his own, and somehow he had to force the beast back in the right direction.

He could figure out only one way to do that. He just prayed that he was fast enough and small enough not to die.

The demon was fully recovered now, gaining momentum with every step. Lewis had seconds to act or be eaten.

Lewis did the only thing he could do to avoid being gruesomely devoured. He sprinted headlong toward the creature that wanted him for supper.

There was a moment of confusion in the beast's eyes, then a soul wrenching noise erupted from its throat. Lewis thought it must be laughter. Lewis responded with a war cry of his own, screaming manically as he rushed forward to impending doom.

When the beast was only steps away Lewis, raised his pistol and fired.

The demon pulled up, covering its face while Lewis ran between its enormous legs.

Lewis didn't dare slow down or look back. He made a beeline for the generator, hoping he had bought himself enough distance to make it in time.

The trembling earth beneath him told him that his time was quickly running out. He pushed his young legs harder than he ever had in his life.

Lewis could clearly see his companions now.

Gideon stood ready with a shotgun as Antoine retook his position in his chalk circle.

Strange, ethereal shapes began to form around Antoine as he pointed his staff to the heavens and mumbled incantations to the wind.

Lewis rushed past Antoine and Gideon, feeling the demon's hot breath on his neck as he pushed to cover the last few yards between himself and his uncle's generator before the beast could consume him.

The explosion of a shotgun blast was followed by another howl of rage from the demon. Lewis was almost to the generator now. He went into a baseball slide, gliding across the dewy grass and coming to a stop with the generator's switch in his hand.

"Now!" his uncle screamed.

Blue sparks of electricity started flying out of Gideon's machine, supercharging the air while simultaneously blackening any bit of earth they touched. Reality began to twist as colors became fluid and commingled. The same horizontal funnel of electricity and fire that had appeared in his uncle's lab two nights ago began to form, tearing a hole in the fabric of the universe. A chorus of infernal shrieks poured forth from the opening, cutting through Lewis' defenses like a dagger to his soul.

The wind howled and thunder bellowed as lighting rained down all around them.

Antoine slammed his staff into the ground and shouted something indecipherable. The phantoms that had been gathering around him went flying toward the creature, harrying it in a way that Lewis did not understand.

The demon staggered backwards as Gideon unloaded shotgun blast after shotgun blast into its chest, delivering on the deadly promises of its maker.

Lassos of light and fire emerged from the portal, wrapping themselves around the demon's limbs. It howled in pain as it was pulled unwillingly toward the red-blue wall that had spawned it.

With one last swipe of its massive claw, the beast seized Gideon by the ankle and yanked him to the ground, trying to pull him with it into the awaiting abyss. Lewis could only watch as his uncle's specialized shotgun went flying out of his grasp and out of his reach.

Lewis knew he was too far away to reach his uncle before he was pulled through the gateway. He looked to Antoine but saw that he too would be unable to close the distance in time. Gideon had only moments before the hell beast dragged him through the gateway.

With a flick of his wrist Gideon produced a pistol from his coat sleeve. Taking no time to aim he fired off a shot at the generator.

There was a blinding flash of light, and a deafening blast ripped through the air as the generator exploded and the portal collapsed upon itself.

Scorched equipment and spent shotgun shells littered the earth. It was quiet. Not a sound to be heard except for crackling of the bonfire's flame.

And at the center of it all sat the severed right hand of the demon.

**

December 25th, 1881

His uncle stood up, dusted himself off, carefully replaced his hat on his head, and said in a uniquely unflappable voice, "Well, I think it's safe to say we missed Midnight Mass. I'm not sure about the rest of you, but I think could do with a spot of breakfast. Doctor Laveau, I believe your wife is hosting Reveillon this year?"

Antoine let out a hearty laugh and Lewis joined him. Will came running into his arms, covering his face in kisses. Lewis decided that Christmas with his uncle was vastly preferable to spending the holidays with his mother.

Where Have All My Heroes Gone?

Hostage Situation

Location: *Hollis Building. Forty-Second Floor.*
 SitRep: *Five shooters. Twelve hostages. Six potential entry points.*
 Tactical Assessment: *Thirty-seven outcomes with an occurrence probability above one percent.*
 ....*Eliminating scenarios resulting in civilian casualties.*
 ....*Nine possible plans of action.*
 ....*Selecting plan of action with highest remaining probability of success.*
 ....*Plan of action selected.*
"Heh," She snickered. "Looks like I'm going through the ceiling."
Her lips drew back into a smile.
"Again."

Selecting the appropriate arrow from her quiver, she took aim, and let fly. The bolt soared gracefully across the night sky, a dark cord of Teflon rope trailing tight behind. It took only seconds for her delivery to cross the few hundred-yard chasm between her and her objective. As always, she found her target.

She pulled the rope tight and secured it.

Adrenaline flowed through her as she zip-lined from skyscraper to skyscraper; the red and blue of police lights far beneath her.

Cushioned boots muted her landing, the rooftop giving her plenty of room to safely run off her momentum. A rock propped open the roof's access door, saving her the precious seconds it would take to pick the lock.

Thank you, lazy smokers.

Now she had a choice: elevator shaft or stairs. Taking the elevator shaft would be faster, but it also had a higher chance of exposing her presence. She chose the stairs.

The hostages were on the forty-second floor. She stopped on floor forty-three.

Closing her eyes, she accessed the buildings architectural plans from memory. It was amazing how productive a night of hacking into the city manager's files could be. She hadn't memorized the plans for every building in the city, just the commercial ones.

Quickly and quietly, she set her pair of charges and prepared to breach.

A single click on the detonator and the first charge exploded with all the sound and fury you'd want from a high-powered explosive. Plaster and insulation flew everywhere.

A second click of the detonator and the second charge blew; this was the quieter, subtler charge. Now she had her entry point.

Paralytic darts of her own design left her hands before her feet touched the ground. They buried themselves in baddies one and two, who were too busy aiming their guns at her decoy explosion to appreciate her dramatic entrance.

Only two seconds had passed from the time of the first explosion to the thud of their unconscious bodies against the floor.

Baddie Number Three was the first to notice her arrival on the scene.

It didn't help him all that much.

The thing about assault rifles is, in tight quarters, they're awfully hard to get pointed in the right direction.

She caught the barrel of the rifle in her right hand as it was coming around and kept it pointing down and away as she sent her left fist careening into Baddie Number Three's face.

It wasn't enough to knock him out on its own. This wasn't television after all. But it was enough to get him to slacken his grip on his weapon, allowing her to disarm him. It was also enough to break his nose.

A sweeping kick took Baddie Number Three to the ground. Stabbing him in the neck with a paralytic dart made sure he'd stay there until this was all over.

Baddies Four and Five were staring at her in wide-eyed shock. She had a small window to end this before it turned into a bloodbath.

Twenty feet lay between her and the remaining baddies. If they were on the streets that wouldn't be a problem; but that twenty feet contained six desks, eight chairs, and an overturned copy machine.

Instead, she ran at an angle towards a point in the wall three-fourths of the way to them.

Her feet moved as her brain did the math.

The element of surprise was gone now.

Gunfire erupted from the muzzle of Baddie Number Four's automatic rifle.

She vaulted over one desk before sliding under another, using the obstacles in front of her to change the eye-line of the shooter.

Right foot office chair, left foot desk, right foot wall. Her momentum changed suddenly as she used the wall to ricochet back towards Baddie Number Four.

Bullets ripped through the plaster wall behind her as he unloaded his automatic rifle in her direction. But she was too fast and his reactions were far too slow.

The click-click of his empty clip was quickly followed by the sound of her steel-reinforced boot cracking his collar-bone.

Stumbling backwards, he smacked his head against a large, metal filing cabinet and fell to the floor.

Given the concussion Number Four just picked up, her dart seemed like overkill. Still, better safe than sorry.

Now it was down to Number Five.

"Stay the fuck away from me, bitch. I swear to fucking god I'll blow her Goddamned head off."

Five's Beretta was pointed at the head of a middle-aged woman, using the frightened executive as a human shield.

There was no clear shot. At least not one that ended with everyone walking out of there alive. She put her hands up and tried to engage the man.

"Listen, there's no need for any of this. It's over. You know that. The only thing that can change now is if you've got the chair waiting for you when you walk out of here. So far nobody's died. I think we'd both like to keep it that way."

"That's where you're wrong bitch." Number Five pulled his hostage with him through the door as a small, round object left his hand. The falling pin registered with her at the same moment the tell-tale lever did.

A grenade. Heading directly towards the remaining hostages.

Time slowed. Her mind took over.

Time to Detonation: *Three Seconds*
Blast Radius: *Five Meter Kill Zone/Fifteen Meter Casualty Zone*
.... *Calculating Ballistic Trajectory of the Projectile*
.... *Calculating Height for all points along the curve*
.... *Calculating Velocity for all points along the curve*
.... *Calculating changes in Angle and Velocity needed to minimize Casualties*
.... *Rendering Action Plan*

Her muscles tensed as she leaped into the air. The top of her foot struck the bottom of the grenade as it hit the apex of its arc, altering its trajectory and sending it darting through the large hole opened up by her initial entrance.

"Everybody down!" she screamed only to have her voice drowned out by the ensuing explosion.

The room shook and pieces of ceiling fell on top of them, but when she checked for injuries no one appeared to be seriously harmed.

She herded them towards the stairs before heading to the roof in the hopes of ending the night without any loss of life.

She drew her bow and nocked an arrow. Slowly, she pushed the door open with her foot and stepped on to the roof.

Five was there with his human shield. Her shot wasn't any better here than it had been below.

"It's over. You've got nowhere to go. Put the gun down and you don't end up in a body bag." She tried to reason with the armed thug.

"Fuck…fuck…fuck. Fuck! Back the fuck off cunt. I mean it. You may not die like you're supposed to but this bitch sure as shit will." Five was losing his cool. This needed to end soon.

She kept her breath steady waiting for Five to make a mistake and give her an opening. The faint sound of a helicopter's roto-blades let her know that she was about to get her chance.

The police helicopter came roaring over the edge of the roof, directing its spotlight directly on her target. Blinded, he raised his hands to shield his eyes.

Her arrow left her bow and flew true, severing the nerves in Five's right wrist. The Beretta dropped from his hand as he cried out and fell to his knees.

It had been a dangerous shot to take. If she'd been off by a centimeter in either direction her arrow would have severed an artery. It was a shot she'd made a thousand times before.

Baddie Number Five moaned in pain as she approached. Kicking away his pistol, she bent down and locked her eyes onto his.

"How the fuck did you think this was going to end asshole?" She figured a paralytic dart was a bit too gentle for this particular prick. Instead, she gave him a swift kick to the temple and rendered the last of the night's hostage-takers unconscious.

She turned to the police helicopter in order to give the pilot the all clear signal. It was hard to tell with the chopper's spotlight shining directly in her eyes, but she almost thought its snipers had their guns trained on her.

Her unasked question was answered by the booming sound of the chopper's public address system. "Attention unidentified masked female. You are in violation of federal law. You are ordered to cease your current activities and surrender yourself for processing and registration."

The roof's access door burst open and over a dozen members of the city's elite S.W.A.T. unit surrounded her in a semi-circle with their weapons drawn, effectively trapping her against the roof's edge.

"I repeat: Unidentified masked female. You are in violation of federal law. You are ordered to stand down and surrender yourself for processing and registration. Interlock your hands behind your head and lie face down on the ground."

She'd known it had been coming. All the signs had been there. She'd prepared herself for it. But still, now that it had happened she was disappointed. In them. In herself. In the world. Things were about to get a whole lot worse and there wasn't a damn thing she could do about it.

Her hands went back behind her head as the officer instructed, but instead of interlocking her fingers she slipped them into her glove and pulled out a small black ball. She threw it to the ground and smoke filled the air around her.

By the time it cleared a few seconds later, she was gone.

That was the night the Russo Act passed. The night they made wearing a mask a capital offense. The night they came for them all. Heroes and villains alike. They rounded up the powers and put them in their camps. Some went quietly. Some did not. Some, the costumes without real powers, they never found. Some just faded back into the shadows that had birthed them.

It was the last reported sighting of the hero known as Artemis.

* * *

Ten Years Later

"Police. Hands in the air, asshole!" Diana had her gun up, but she kept her finger off the trigger. Her perp might be an asshole, but he was a small-time asshole. Making him a dead asshole would mean all kinds of paperwork. Paperwork that was a major league pain in her ass. That was why, as a rule, she tried to only shoot major league assholes.

She'd hoped to surprise this prick by busting down the door to his apartment, all loud and forceful like, while he had his pants around his ankles. That would have made all this a whole lot easier.

But the patrolman watching the place for her had been made. So instead she stood here, on some godforsaken side street, ten feet from the out-of-breath asshole who'd just made her run seven blocks.

He stared back at her in some effort to show the poor, little girl cop that he was a tough guy and she knew that the asshole was going to do something incredibly stupid.

It was the body language. Small time assholes always telegraph when they're about to do something stupid. They can't help themselves.

In contrast, Diana always made a concerted effort to never telegraph her next move.

Which explained why she was prepared for her perp to lunge at her with the small blade he'd pulled from his jacket pocket, but he was not prepared for her to subtly step out of the way of his clumsy attack before smacking him on the back of the skull with the butt of her pistol.

When she got back to the precinct she threw the shithead in for processing and headed to her desk. On the way she was reminded that assholes came in cop flavor as well as traditional perp.

"What the fuck Diana? My case. My collar. Why are you stepping on my turf?" Detective Dietrich was a chauvinist pig and a Grade-A douchebag, but that wasn't why Diana hated him. She hated him because he was shit at his job. And him being shit at his job tended to get people killed.

"Maybe if it didn't take you three months to follow up on a lead I wouldn't have to clean up your messes. You got a problem with me solving your cases take it up with the captain. It was her call."

Dietrich made an obscene gesture as she kept walking. Ten years ago she would have broken all the bones in his hand for that move. Hell, five years ago she would have had to break her own fingers just to keep from breaking his jaw. But she'd learned to keep her temper in check. Keeping a cool head was necessary to her continued survival.

One wrong move and she'd spend the rest of her life in a maximum-security facility. Chained up and left to rot by the same people she'd risked her life time and time again to save.

The thought annoyed the fuck out of her. So much so that she considered turning around so she could punch Dietrich in in the mouth to console herself.

"What'd ya do to the prick this time?" As he usually did, Detective Bill

Sanders spoke up at just the right time to keep her from doing something rash.

"Solved the Richmond killings." She shrugged.

"Oh yeah? Good work. What broke it?" Diana noticed Sanders lean in to hear her answer. He was starting to lose his hearing. Another reason to hang it up.

"The babysitter was a lying bitch with an ex-con ex-boyfriend." She shrugged, "If Dietrich had been able to stop staring at her tits long enough to take a good look at her, he would have found it too."

But he didn't." Her former partner had a grin a mile wide.

"No, he didn't." Diana wasn't one to seek out the approval of others. That she felt a swell of pride at the older detective's words of approval spoke volumes of the man and what they'd been through together. Sanders had been her partner for six years before he'd transferred to desk duty to close out his last sixty days before retirement. Now that sixty days had become five it was beginning to sink in that her biggest ally on the force was about to be gone for good.

"Captain wanted you. Said to send you in as soon as you got back." Diana immediately turned her attention to her captain's office. The door was closed and the blinds were shut.

That was never a good sign.

"Well, then I guess I'd better not keep her waiting."

Captain Eve Thorne was an intimidating woman. Not physically. No, in that sense she was actually quite frail, coming in at five foot three inches and maybe one hundred pounds soaking wet. But that didn't keep her from scaring the shit out of every man and woman under her command.

Her reputation came from her cold, blue eyes. She had a way of staring at you that could chill you to your bones and make you want to tell her all your darkest sins. There were tales told around the precinct that she'd closed every case she'd ever worked with a confession.

Many of Diana's fellow officers resented her because they thought she was the Captain's favorite, a brown-nose, and while it was true that the Captain often gave her the juiciest assignments it was also true that she was harder on her than any of her other detectives. Trips to the Captain's office where seldom pleasant.

Diana took a breath and opened the door to Captain Thorne's office. She was surprised to find it held an additional occupant.

"Detective Graves. Good of you to join us. Please, take a seat."

Diana did as she was told, doing her best to maintain eye contact with the captain while sizing up their guest with her peripheral vision.

It was tough to be accurate with him sitting down but she made him for about six-one, six two. An athletic muscular build put his weight in the two-twenty range. Short-cropped black hair with a slight greying at the temples indicated late thirties, maybe early forties. His straight posture and rigid demeanor screamed ex-military. All that, added to the fact he was here, made him law enforcement of some kind. Most likely a fed.

"Detective Graves meet Agent Lambert of the FBI's Masked Criminals Unit. Agent Lambert why don't you fill the detective in on what you just told me." The Captain's voice was tense; whatever Agent Lambert was here for it was serious business.

"This morning at approximately oh-three-hundred hours Richard Cutter aka "The Dick" was scheduled to be transported from Mamertine Correctional Facility here in New Delt City to the Greyhill Federal Supermax Facility for the Dangerous and Super Powered. His convoy was attacked and overpowered shortly after picking up the prisoner, killing seven members of the security detail and freeing Cutter. It is the belief of many of my colleagues in the Bureau that Cutter is headed for the border." The agent spoke with clipped precision.

"You believe differently?" Diana asked, already certain that he did.

"Given his fanatical obsession with settling scores with those he's believed to have wronged him and his history with the vigilante know as Artemis; I believe he's going to attempt to draw her out. I believe he is still here in the city and that he's planning something big." Lambert had answered Diana's question, but he'd really been addressing the Captain. Thorne stayed silent. She expected her subordinate to ask the tough questions for her.

So Diana persisted.

"But nobody has seen Artemis in ten years. How does he expect to lure her out? She could be dead for all we know."

Lambert barely let her finish speaking before launching into his rebuttal.

"Artemis is one of the few notable masks to avoid being rounded up under the Russo Act. Doesn't matter if she's around or not. There's still going to be blood on the ground if Cutter decides to call her out. If she's long gone then we need to be prepared to stop him on our own. If she's not, well then we take them both in." The man was incredibly sure of himself. Diana found it annoying.

"And just how exactly do you think he's going to call her out?" This time the question came directly from the captain.

"I don't know. But if Cutter's history is any indication, it will be bloody and it will be public." He was right. And with a single look, the two women confirmed that they both knew he was right. That was what finally made up the Captain's mind.

"Graves you're assigned to Agent Lambert until Cutter is back in custody. Knock over some rocks and see what crawls out. I want hourly status updates on what you find. The last thing I need is another…"The Captain was interrupted by a clearly rattled Sanders bursting through her office door.

He didn't bother apologizing for his interruption but rather stated simply. "Captain, you need to see this."

There was a tremble in his voice Diana had never heard before. Not one time in the six years they'd been partners. He was spooked and she was fairly sure she knew why.

He left the room without waiting to see if its three occupants were following him. They were.

The breaking news banner was rolling across the department's television screen.

Sanders grabbed the remote from a young patrolman and cranked up the volume.

"We're coming to you live from the corner of Twentieth and Barrone where just a block away on an unknown assailant has been attacking customers and staff at a Jupiter's Coffeehouse location. This is breaking news as police are only just beginning to arrive on scene."

Diana's eyes went to her captain.

"Go." The words were hard as steel and meant only for her. When the captain repeated her orders a few seconds later for the rest of the precinct Diana was already in the elevator headed to the garage, Fed in one hand keys in the other.

It was a six-minute drive to the coffee shop. Diana made it in four. It didn't matter. By the time they arrived Cutter was long gone, leaving nothing in his wake but madness and tragedy.

Blood covered the coffeehouse. Arterial spray spread out over the walls to create frightening designs of horrible consequence. Small, wet drops fell from the ceiling to coalesce with the dark red pools of sadness forming on the ground beneath Cutter's victims.

Those victims came from every walk of life. The young, Latina barista who'd had her throat slit running to the back room. The middle-aged white guy in an expensive, tailored suit who'd had his belly slit open. The elderly black couple whose severed hands were still holding each other. Massacre was too polite a word for what had happened here.

Agent Lambert barked orders at the officers already on site, flashing his badge and screaming about setting up a perimeter. They both knew it was just for show. That the cameras were on them and the good folks at home needed to be reassured that the police were doing something to keep them safe. That everything was under control.

It was all a lie. Cutter was just too good. They wouldn't find him again until he wanted to be found. All they could do now was pick up the pieces and figure out what game he was playing. So that when he did show his face again they'd be ready to break his nose.

"Fuck." It was the first break in the stoic façade she'd seen from Agent Lambert since they'd meet all of thirty minutes ago. He went up slightly in her esteem.

"How long you been chasing costumes?" She asked, trying to get more of a feel for the man.

"About six months. I transferred from counter-terrorism. Thought I could do more good here than monitoring signal traffic in some desert." Agent Lambert paused and looked pensively around the room. A look of understanding came over his face before he asked her "Do you recognize the building?"

"Of course. My old partner loved the hot chocolate here. Why?" She replied, pretending not to know what he was getting at.

"Twelve years ago this building housed the central branch of Atlantic National Bank. This was where they finally took Cutter down." His kept his eyes looking up. Surveying the architecture rather than the bloody mess lying at their feet.

"You mean this is where Artemis finally took Cutter down." She had been hoping that Lambert would be a bit slower in putting that connection together. "Could just be a coincidence."

"No. It's a message. It says 'I remember.'"

They didn't speak on the way back to the precinct. There wasn't anything to say. Instead, she left Agent Lambert to his thoughts and concentrated on her own.

It was a horribly kept secret that crime was up across the board since the Russo Act had come into effect. Most of the good guys had turned themselves in, accepting the law as the will of the people, a mandate dictating they stand down. The bad guys just kept on doing what they had been doing, except now there was no one standing in their way except America's police departments. Departments that were, by in large, outgunned and underfunded. Some thought this was by design. To keep the people too busy watching shit shows like Tacoma and Cedar Rapids unfold on their televisions to pay attention to the fascist policies coming out of Washington.

For ten years she'd kept her head low, fighting back the urge to put on that mask and answer her city's nightly cries for justice. How many monsters had she let run wild rather than putting them down? But this was different. None of those monsters had called her out. How many people would she let Cutter kill before she gave him what he wanted?

The elevator doors opened, and they walked into a circus. The Feds were everywhere; the bullpen, the conference room, they'd even appropriated the Captain's office. Pandemonium was the order of the day as phones rang off the hook and city maps and known associates were plastered all over the walls.

Captain Thorne called them into her office with a wave of her hand. She was still shooing out federal interlopers when they squeezed through the door. Quickly and methodically they ran through everything they had learned at the crime scene. There wasn't much to report.

"Okay, Agent Lambert what next?" Lambert tilted his head quizzically at the Captain's inquiry. "I talked to your boss, Special Agent Thompson, she said this is your show to run as far as the Feds are concerned. And given how spot on you've been up to now, I think letting you run point is the best chance we've got at catching Cutter. So what's his play? What do we need to do to get ahead of this bastard?"

"Honestly Captain, I'm not sure. Cutter has always been a bit theatrical. This afternoon was almost like an opening act. An overture if you will. He's foreshadowed the fact that he's going to call Artemis out, but in his mind, he'll still need to make some sort of grand proclamation to that effect. And do that he'll want a big stage with some high-value targets."

"The MOMA opening." Diana blurted.

"Sorry, what?" Lambert asked, obviously confused by the outburst.

"The Museum of Modern Art has it's grand reopening gala tonight after being closed for renovations for most of the last year. It's the hottest ticket in town, even the mayor is going to be there. The same mayor who prosecuted Cutter back when he was in the DA's office." She explained, articulating her thoughts a bit better on the second attempt.

"That's our target. How long till the gala starts?" Lambert asked. His hands already fumbling through neighborhood maps looking for the museum's location.

Diana pulled out her phone and did a quick search. "Event starts at eight. That gives us about four hours to secure the building and come up with a plan to catch this bastard."

Diana and Agent Lambert quickly got to work mobilizing the resources they'd need. Luckily, since the gala was going to play host to a slew of city dignitaries and V.I.P.s, the department already had a security team on site and a complete set of floor plans and architectural layouts ready to go. While they were busy formulating a plan the captain took the time to brief the troops.

"Attention everyone, this is now a joint NDPD and FBI task force. Agent Lambert will have command in the field while I coordinate operations from here. Detective Sanders knows Cutter the best. I've asked him to brief us all on what to expect." The Captain stepped aside, and Sanders took her place at the dais.

"Your target is one Richard Cutter a.k.a. The Dick…"

"Heh. Dick Cutter." One of the patrolmen interrupted with a snicker. Asshole probably hadn't seen the crime scene photos from the coffee shop yet. Still, no excuse and Sanders lit into him with the proper amount of rage and disgust.

"Yeah rookie, real funny. There were some guys a while back who thought of that one too. Some of the old crews when Cutter was on his way up. He didn't care for it too much. So you know what he did? He cut off all their dicks and let them bleed to death. Took pictures too. Sent them to all the papers. Since then nobody's thought that name was all that funny." The room was silent and Sanders continued with his briefing. "So far he's killed nine people since his escape early this morning. Add that to the seven officers who were gunned down when his crew busted him out and we're looking at sixteen dead and another dozen in critical condition. The worst part is he's probably just getting started. We believe this afternoon's attack was staged as an attempt a message to the masked vigilante Artemis who has not been seen or heard from since the passage of the Russo Act ten years ago."

"For those too young to remember this is not the first time that The Dick has terrorized the streets of New Delt City. Twelve years ago Cutter and his crew ran the drug trade this town. Or at least they did until Artemis systematically took apart the whole operation brick by brick. Desperate for money to keep his supply moving Cutter perpetrated a series of bank heists that left a lot of innocent folks dead. He'd already hit four banks when we got a tip Atlantic National was next on his list. The tip was a setup. Cutter just wanted to kill himself some cops. The whole thing went tits up and more than one good officer lost his life that day. Me and my partner were done for when Artemis burst through the ceiling and put that son of a bitch down.

Now I don't care what revisionist hogwash the folks at city hall want to peddle; we were not about to apprehend Cutter when Artemis interfered with a lawful arrest. We were about to die. If Artemis hadn't of shown up when she did Cutter would have stuck me like a pig and that's a fact. Cutter is big and mean and fast. He will not hesitate to slit you open from ear to ear. Do not underestimate him or you will die. Got it."

A collective "Yes Sir" came from the mouths of cops and feds alike. Even the captain seemed a bit shaken by Detective Sander's speech.

"Now that you know who we're up against I'll tell you what we're looking for. Suspect is approximately six foot six inches, two hundred and sixty pounds, bald with numerous tattoos on his arms and neck……."

While Agent Lambert gave a detailed description and handed out assignments Diana went over to talk to Bill. Catching up with him as he headed towards the coffee machine. "I didn't know all that. That Artemis saved your life. You never talk about those days all that much."

"What's there to say? It was a different time then. I'm not very political and I'm sure they had their reasons, but I think that whole Russo Act was a bunch of crap. No one's ever going to convince me that Artemis wasn't good for this city. That she wasn't a hero." Sanders stopped walking and looked Diana dead in the eye. "If she did decide to come back and face off with Cutter I sure as hell won't be the one arresting her. I don't care what the law says. And what's more, I know a whole lot of cops who feel the exact same way."

Diana appreciated her partner's sentiment. But she knew that this time the NDPD would have to catch Cutter on its own.

* * *

Opening Night

The New Delt City Museum of Modern Art was the centerpiece of the Harbor District Reclamation Project. In addition to the nine-month renovation of the main building, two new annexes had been constructed to house various traveling exhibits. Tonight's gala marked the first time these annexes would be open to the public.

Under other circumstances, Diana would have appreciated the architect who had so seamlessly melded the industrial aesthetic of the museum with the gentle waves of the harbor that lay behind it. But for the time being, all she could consider was just how much ground he had left them to cover.

The plan was to subtly beef up the gala's pre-arraigned security while peppering the party with undercover members of the task force. Bill had wanted to flood the place with an army of cops, but the Captain and Agent Lambert were in agreement that they didn't want to spook Cutter. Diana didn't think Cutter could be spooked, but she was a good detective and followed her Captain's orders.

Which explained why she was wearing a six-hundred-dollar evening gown. The white, sleeveless number was her go-to outfit for this kind of undercover work, meaning she'd worn it exactly twice since she'd bought it four years ago. The dress' slit ran high up her thigh, revealing far more skin than Diana would ordinarily be comfortable with. Unfortunately, modesty was the price she paid in order to maintain her legs' full range of motion. Still, it didn't run so high as to reveal her garter and the small blade it kept strapped to her leg. The other advantage of this dress was its hem, which was high enough off the ground she'd be able to ditch her heels and run without tripping over herself if the night went sideways. In a bit of girlish indulgence, she'd even bought a matching handbag that fit her gun and makeup perfectly.

She grabbed a glass of champagne from the bar and worked the crowd. Cutter wouldn't be here yet, he was too easy to identify, and he knew it, but there was a good chance that some of his gang had already infiltrated the proceedings. Identifying those men was the first stepping in stopping whatever Cutter had planned for the night.

She gave no reaction as Detective Dietrich, dressed as a waiter, passed by her.

"Ohh…Detective Graves, you are looking good tonight. How about a later we get together and play a little game of 'Hide the Gun'?" Dietrich's comment came in on her earpiece, she was certain she could feel the man's eyes on her ass.

"You keep running your mouth Dietrich you're going to end up playing 'Dodge the Bullet,'" Diana whispered into her mic as she pretended to take a sip of her champagne.

"Cut the chatter people. Assume Cutter has eyes everywhere." Agent Lambert ordered. He stood on the other side of the room from her, feigned fascination with a sculpture that looked an awful lot like a ceramic doughnut.

Diana's eyes moved past the FBI agent to the wall behind him. There a row of coffins had been put on display. A coffin, she'd learned at the school of the blatantly obvious, was a pretty good place for a bad guy to hide.

Casually, she worked her way across the room, making sure to give a few of the other works in the room a cursory examination in order to make her real interest less obvious. One of the coffins was draped in a bloody American flag, another proclaimed to hold the corpse of Lady Liberty. The rest were similarly decorated with the standard symbols of anti-war, anti-government rhetoric. The pieces seem a little cliché and on the nose to her, but their message fit right in with the exhibit's other works.

"What's the report on these coffins?" She asked, discreetly whispering into her comm unit.

"They were checked out by the security team when they arrived. The lids are welded shut. There's no way to open them." Lambert reported back.

Over the course of her long career fighting crime the one thing that had saved her life more than anything thing else was her compulsive need to be thorough. That compulsion meant she would never just take someone else's word on something when she was perfectly capable of confirming the facts for herself.

The lids were sealed, just as Agent Lambert had described. Diana glanced around and made sure no one was looking before running her fingers along the edges. She felt no seams or spots of wear. Stepping around, she checked the back side of the metal box. This time she did feel something, a latch of some kind. Carefully, with a hand on the gun she'd hidden in her purse, Diana pressed down on the latch.

The back of the coffin swung open like a door. The inside was empty.

"Dammit, the coffins had trap doors on the back. We have hostiles in the building. I repeat we have…" she did a quick count of the coffins "… six hostiles lose in the building."

"Do you have a visual?" Lambert asked over the radio.

"Negative, but this is no coincidence. Cutter is here." Diana insisted.

"All right, this changes nothing people. All it does is confirm what we already suspected. That Cutter is planning an attack and his thugs are here in the building already. At least now we know how many we're looking for." Lambert's reassurances did nothing to dispel Diana's uneasy feeling that they were already too many steps behind.

A round of applause erupted from the crowd. Diana's head snapped to the sudden noise. The mayor was walking to the dais to address the gala attendees and unveil the centerpiece of the new entrance hall.

"Please tell me somebody checked underneath that curtain." Diana tried to position herself to get a better look.

"The guys checked it three times its clean." Lambert responded.

"We're these the same guys who checked the coffins?" She asked already knowing the answer.

"There's nothing underneath that curtain except a sculpture made out of mangled car parts." The FBI agent insisted.

"Mangled car parts?" She asked skeptically.

"Don't ask me. I don't go in for Modern Art. I prefer landscapes and fruit bowls. The point is its solid, crushed steel all the way through. If Cutter is going to make an appearance, he'll have another point of entry." Lambert didn't sound entirely convinced himself anymore.

The mayor was concluding his brief remarks. They were out of time. Cutter was going to make his move when that curtain came down, she could feel it.

Taking his time so as to give the photographers every opportunity to capture him doing his civic duty, the mayor reached for the long yellow cord attached to the velvet curtain and pulled.

The curtain fell to the floor and the junk car sculpture was revealed to be almost exactly as Lambert had described it with two major difference. The first difference being that it was not solid steel all the way through as he had put it but rather a mish-mash of smashed car parts; doors, headlights, leather seats and most germane to Diana at the moment a car trunk. A trunk that had been popped open.

The second difference stood six-feet six-inches, was armed with two curved ten-inch blades and looked disturbingly well-suited to the jet-black tux he wore.

"Thank you for the kind introduction Mr. Mayor."

It took Diana sixth-tenths of a second to pull her gun out of her purse and point it at Cutter. Her shout of "Freeze" joined a chorus of similar demands from her colleagues.

Cutter was unfazed by the half-dozen guns suddenly pointing in his direction.

"Now, now, let's all take a deep breath. There's no need to be rude. Gentlemen, show them what happens if they're rude."

Flashes of steel revealed Cutter's men around the room. No longer hiding in plan sight among the other guests, their long, sharp blades were now pressed firmly against some of the more prominent necks in the room.

Despite the imminent threat to civilians, not a single one of the drawn guns changed its target.

"So which one of you fine, upstanding lawmen is in charge here?" Cutter queried with unnerving politeness.

"I am." Agent Lambert declared through gritted teeth.

"And you are?" Cutter idly meandered about the podium as he asked his questions. Being sure to frighten as many hostages with his devilish grin as possible.

"FBI" Lambert stated curtly.

Cutter directed his smile back at Lambert.

"Masked Criminals Unit I'd wager?"

Agent Lambert gave no response to Cutter's query. Cutter signaled to his men and they pressed their blades tighter against their hostages' jugulars. Drips of blood began to roll down several necks. Lambert broke.

"Yes, I'm M.C.U." the angry Fed answered.

Cutter nodded and his men relaxed their holds.

"A cape chaser, excellent. Order your men to lower their weapons and I promise you most of the people in this room will live."

"What assurances do I….." Agent Lambert was interrupted by Cutter's raised hand.

"I'm sorry to cut you off agent. Mr. Mayor, I suggest you keep still. I have a tendency to stab anything I see moving in my peripheral vision." Caught in his attempt at subtly slinking away, the mayor froze in his tracks. "Please continue agent."

"How do I know you'll keep your word?" Lambert asked.

"You don't. But a man smart enough to make it into the FBI's most elite unit must realize his options are limited." Cutter stated plainly. His brutal logic impossible to argue with.

Diana could see the resignation in Lambert's eyes as they scanned the room. Any decision he made was going to end in a body count, but he had to at least try to negotiate. Slowly he put his gun on the ground and motioned for the rest of them to do the same.

Reluctantly Diana followed his lead. Bending all the way to the floor to set her own piece aside. While everyone was watching her right hand, her left carefully pulled the blade out of her garter and palmed it.

"Kick them over here please, all of you. Yes, thank you, that's it." Diana kicked her gun toward Cutter as she was instructed taking the opportunity to kick off her heels as well.

"You there with the camera." Cutter gestured to one of the news crews covering the event. "Are we recording?"

The cameraman nodded. Even on the other side of the room, she could tell his hands were trembling.

"Good, because I have a message for Artemis." Cutter looked directly into the camera. "Twelve years ago, without provocation, you came after me and mine. But you didn't finish the job. Now I'm back and I'm going to make you bleed. I'm Going To Make You And This Entire Fucking City Bleed!!! YOU HEAR ME BITCH?!? IM GOING TO CUT OFF YOUR TITS AND FEED THEM TO MY DOGS!!!!" Cutter was practically rabid as he screamed the last words into the camera. He took several deep breaths to regain his composure before he continued. "I'd hoped you'd be joining me tonight, alas it seems you need a bit more coxing. I'm sorry Mr. Mayor I'm afraid you won't be getting that second term you were hoping for." The blade left Cutter's hand as he turned from the camera, Diana's blade left her hand a fraction of a second later. She prayed it would hit its mark but didn't stand around waiting to find out.

She sprinted towards Cutter, who was still marveling at the flight of his own blade. Too late he saw her in the corner of his eye. He swiped at her with his remaining knife, but she was already underneath his guard. She heard the clanging of their blades mid-flight collision as her first punch struck Cutter's ribs. She completed the combo with another shot to the body and a powerful uppercut to Cutter's jaw. The murderous asshole staggered back at the shock of her blows.

"Who the fuck are you?!?" Cutter shouted in surprise.

But Diana wasn't paying attention to him. Instead, she did a backflip, picking up her own piece while kicking Lambert's and Dietrich's firearms back toward their respective owners. The two men picked up their weapons on the move. Agent Lambert slid across the floor and put a bullet between the eyes of the closest goon to him. Dietrich dropped to a crouch and shot another henchman in the thigh. The bastard dropped his blade and fell to the floor clutching his leg, screaming in agony.

Diana brought her own gun to bear on Cutter and pulled the trigger without hesitation. Cutter's blade deflected her bullet, the ricochet catching one of the hostages in the arm.

Cutter snarled. His eyes full of savage bloodlust.

"Kill them all." But the other members of the task force had not stood idly by while Diana had made her move. Every one of Cutter's men was now engaged in close combat with an officer of the law.

Cutter came charging at her, knowing she wouldn't risk another ricochet hitting a civilian. Dropping her gun, she set herself in a fighting stance.

Cutter slashed wildly at her head. Diana stepped back, allowing the blade to pass within inches of her face before stepping into a high kick aimed at Cutter's chest. The kick connected, but Cutter was unfazed. With his free hand, he grabbed Diana's ankle. His blade came down at her again. This time she blocked the blow with a forearm to his wrist.

Using Cutter's mass against him, Diana launched a spin kick that caught him square in the jaw. His grip slackened and she fell to the floor.

She rolled on instinct, bracing herself to absorb a follow-up blow.

It never came.

Raising her eyes, she saw Cutter hustling towards the back exit.

"He's headed out the back," she shouted to no one in particular. She picked up her gun and gave chase. Cutter knocked over several exhibits as he ran, ducking and weaving so as to prevent her from getting a clean shot. The alarm went off as he burst through the fire exit, viciously debilitating the officers posted on the other side.

A few seconds later Diana slammed open that same door. She didn't stop to check on the downed officers.

Cutter was about a hundred yards ahead of her, sprinting towards the harbor. Suddenly he dropped from her view. She knew why. There was an eight-foot ledge between them and the water. Diana didn't slow down as she approached the drop.

She planted her right foot and leaped. Forever passed as she hung in the air, then the illusion was broken, and the ground came rushing towards her.

She landed in a roll and came up in a sprint, barely losing any of her momentum.

Behind her, Dietrich screamed. Diana turned back to see what had happened and found him grabbing his ankle, clearly in pain.

"I'm fine. Go!" Dietrich yelled, waving her on.

Cutter was almost to the water now.

She could see a speedboat waiting for him.

Throwing knives left Cutter's hands with deadly speed. The dock's guards fell without even getting their weapons up. Diana poured everything she had into her stride, willing herself to close the gap between her and Cutter. But the bastard's feet were as quick as his hands and his legs were just too long for her to make up the distance.

She fired pointlessly at the boat as it sped away from land and past the inert Harbor Police boat whose job it had been to secure the waters behind the museum. Later they would find the crew of the patrol boat with their throats slit. Another three victims to be added to Cutter's total body count.

Agent Lambert finally caught up with her at the edge of the water.

"Cutter?" he asked, clearly out of breath.

Diana pointed at the fleeing boat.

"Fuck." Lambert said to no one in particular before taking to his microphone to scream instructions. There was no point. Cutter was long gone now. They'd had their shot and they'd missed. She'd missed.

* * *

Escalation

Diana finished her debriefing sometime around one. Her head hit the pillow just before two. The ringing of her phone woke her at exactly twelve to five. Begrudgingly she picked up.

"Go for Graves." Diana answered with her eyes half open.

"We need you back at the precinct asap." A crisp, far too awake Fed spoke on the other end of the line.

"Lambert? Jesus. Don't you ever sleep." She responded resisting the urge to swear profusely at her temporary partner.

"I'll sleep when Cutter's back in custody where he belongs. Rise and shine detective, we've got a lead." Lambert informed her then hung up without any further conversation.

Diana rolled over and forced herself out of bed. Thirty minutes later she walked into the precinct and took the cup of coffee offered to her by one of the rookies without comment. The rest of the cops in the room looked as haggard as she felt. Lambert's Feds looked as if they'd been at it all night.

Once everyone was gathered and suitably caffeinated, Agent Lambert started his briefing.

"At approximately Zero Four Thirty this morning we received an anonymous tip informing us of a warehouse being used by Cutter and his men to stage their attacks. The tipster gave details of the previous two attacks not yet released to the public that would indicate this is for real." The FBI agent relayed the information with all the emotion of a granite slab.

"For real? You can be sure as shit it's a trap. Pulled the same damn stunt twelve years ago." Bill interrupted from the back. Diana shared her former partner's assessment. And they should know, she and Bill were the only ones who were there. Although nobody else in this room knew about her participation in that particular arrest.

"By for real, I meant it clearly came from someone with first-hand knowledge of the attacks. I agree with Detective Sanders that this is almost certainly a trap. But if it is a trap at least we know Cutter will be there and we have a shot of taking him down away from civilians." Lambert reasoned.

"I concur with Agent Lambert's assessment." Captain Thorne put in her two cents. "The plan is to establish a solid perimeter around the warehouse while a heavily armored s.w.a.t. unit enters the building and triggers the trap. When Cutter shows himself we collapse the perimeter and close the net."

"Captain, Cutter has to know that we know it's a trap. He'll see us coming a mile away." Diana tried to plead her case. She had a feeling this whole thing was a very bad idea.

"And he knows that we know that he knows that we know. We can play that game all day long detective. The bottom line is that we have an opportunity to take Cutter out before he strikes again and we're going to take it. This is the plan people. Let's do our jobs and come home alive. Report to Agent Lambert for your assignments." The Captain's tone conveyed that she was no longer open to persuasion on the topic.

While Lambert attended to his responsibilities, Diana decided to sort through the stack of reports on her desk, Bill was waiting for her there. One look and she knew she what he was going to say.

"Diana, be careful out there." Coming from anyone else she would have found the fatherly tone patronizing. From Bill, it was touching, though still rather annoying.

"I always am, Bill." She replied solemnly.

"I'm serious. I've got a bad feeling about this one." There was an earnestness to his fear she found disturbing.

"Hey, it's you I should be worried about. If I'm out there who's going to protect you from all the splinters your ass is going to get sitting around worrying about us?" She tried to tease him, but her heart wasn't in it.

"Diana…" Worry covered his face like a funeral veil.

"I know Bill. I'll watch my ass." She shouted back over her shoulder as she grabbed her jacket and keys and headed for the elevator.

"I'll watch that ass for you Graves" was Dietrich's inappropriate interjection into the conversation.

"I prefer men who can get up without any artificial aids" Diana snapped back gesturing to crutches Dietrich was now sporting as a result of his fall the night before. "I think you're just faking it to get out of doing any real police work."

"You're the expert on faking it, honey." Dietrich retorted.

Diana flipped him off and kept walking.

Agent Lambert was waiting for her at the elevator. "You ready to roll?" she gave him a nod and he hit the down button. "All right let's do this."

The warehouse was in the city's aptly named Warehouse District and covered half a city block. It was possessed of no distinctive features to speak of and showed no outward signs of harboring a criminal mastermind.

Slowly the various task force units rolled into position, using unmarked vehicles to avoid tipping off their presence to Cutter and his goons. Officers went building to building, evacuating any civilians they found to a safe distance.

With the perimeter established, Agent Lambert checked with his rooftop snipers to confirm that there were indeed hostiles in the building.

"Report, do we have eyes on target?" He barked into his radio.

"Sniper One. I have movement on the second story. Looks to be a sentry." Sniper One reported.

"Sniper Two confirms." a second disembodied voice affirmed over the designated frequency.

"All right that will have to do. S.W.A.T. ONE move into position." Lambert ordered.

"Wait a minute. That's it? There's absolutely zero indication that Cutter is in that building." Diana's incredulity was too great for her to remain silent.

"Detective Graves, I'm not sure how many of these operations you've been in but this is as good as its going to get. We've been tipped to a location and we've confirmed a hostile presence. Back in the Sandbox, we would have called in a drone strike and not given it a second thought. If anything goes wrong, we've got most the cops in the city out here to handle it. I'm giving this operation a green light" The agent told Diana with conviction. Lambert's walkie cut Diana off before she could press her argument.

"S.W.A.T. ONE in position." A third disembodied voice reported.

"S.W.A.T. ONE you are green for breach." Agent Lambert responded, completing his mental transition from cop to soldier.

"Confirmed S.W.A.T. ONE is green for breach" The third voice verified.

Diana didn't like it. Everything was moving too fast. Her gut told her that Cutter was playing them. She moved away from Agent Lambert's makeshift command center and found herself a better vantage point. She only needed a few steps to find the shape the snipers had identified as a probable sentry. She didn't trust it. There was something off about the silhouette.

"Ready. On my count." Agent Lambert's voice came over the radio.

Diana pulled out her binoculars and gave the figure a hard look.

"THREE!"

The tinted windows made it impossible to see anything more than shapes.

"TWO!"

But there was something unnatural about the way the figure moved.

"ONE!"

Not like a real person.

"GO!"

More like a mannequin on a string.

"IT'S A TRAP!" She screamed into her radio.

She was too late.

The first explosion killed the city's best S.W.A.T. team in a fireball that could be seen for miles. The second explosion finished what the first one started, demolishing the building and killing anyone still trapped inside.

A cloud of dust and debris engulfed them as chunks of brick and steel rained down around them like industrial hail. Screams filled the air only to be cut short by coughing fits.

The blast had knocked Diana off her feet. A quick inventory told her she had some scrapes and bruises but no major injuries. She'd gotten lucky.

A realization struck her.

"Lambert listen to me! We have to get back to the precinct right now!" She shouted, her ears still buzzing.

"What are you talking about? We've got men inside. We need to find Cutter." The FBI agent was dazed and pale. Trying to push himself to his feet so he could try and rescue his men.

"Those men are dead. Cutter's not here. Think about it. He likes his kills to be personal. He wouldn't use explosives unless this was all a distraction." Diana insisted.

"He lured us here." Lambert stated with a fair amount of self-recrimination that he'd been played.

"No. He lured us *away* from the precinct." Diana explained.

"Where there's nothing left but a skeleton crew of desk jockeys." Now the realization was beginning to dawn on Lambert as well.

"What better statement than to hit the police on their home turf." Diana was already stumbling toward their vehicle as she finished her thought.

Lambert flicked on his walkie. "I WANT EVERY ABLE-BODIED OFFICER BACK TO THE PRECINCT NOW!!!!" The officers nearby looked at the agent in confusion. "I SAID NOW GODDAMIT!"

Frantically, Diana put her keys in the ignition as Agent Lambert slammed the passenger door shut. The engine revved to life and she slammed her foot on the gas. Dread filled her as she raced through the streets of New Delt City.

She was halfway out of the car before it came to a complete stop. Running desperately up to the precinct's front door. The same door she'd walked through for the better part of a decade. When she finally reached it she found a note, pinned there by a bloody knife. Her heart sank.

Dearest Artemis,

You've been playing hard to get and I'm done flirting now. Don't get me wrong I've enjoyed the foreplay, but I think its high time we came full circle, don't you? Meet me at nine o'clock tonight for our final date. You know the place.

Sincerely Yours,

Richard Cornelius Cutter

P.S. If you stand me up I'll personally rip the larynx out of every man, woman, and child in New Delt City. Bye for now.

For the second time today Diana knew she'd been too slow. Gun drawn she opened the door and pushed forward into the precinct. Agent Lambert was on her hip, his own weapon at the ready. She wanted to sprint up the two flights of stairs to the homicide department, but she fought off the urge. Instead, they went room by room. Bodies lay everywhere, a few of them even had pulses.

By the time they secured the ground floor more officers were arriving on scene. Lambert sent a group of uniforms to check the second floor while the pair of them secured the third. Diana tried to prepare herself for what she would find when she exited the stairwell.

It was a futile attempt. There is nothing that can prepare you to see such savagery perpetrated against a place and people you know so intimately.

Detective Dietrich lay closest to the stairs. Or rather his head did. The rest of his body had been impaled against the wall with the crutches he'd earned the night before.

She recognized many of the other bodies she saw. Officer Mendez had loved baking cupcakes for their birthdays. She'd been killed by blunt force trauma to the head. Detective Wilton had constantly tried to set Diana up with one of his cousins. She doubted they'd ever know for sure which one of the multiple stab wounds had been the fatal blow.

The Captain lay in front of her office door, an eight-inch blade lodged in her chest. Her weapon was still in her hand, the smell of gunpowder hung in the air. Diana checked the door. It was locked. A group of civilians, the office admins and a few random visitors, were huddled together behind the captain's desk. They were all still breathing. Captain Eve Thorne had died saving lives, a better epithet for a cop there would never be.

"Diana…" Bill's voice was faint. She turned to find her former partner propped up against his desk. Multiple lacerations covered his body but the wound that was going to kill him was the deep gash in his side that was oozing dark red blood.

"OFFICER DOWN!!! OFFICER DOWN!!! I NEED A MEDIC IN HERE NOW!!!" Diana's screams echoed in through the silent tomb the precinct had become. Bill reached out and gestured for her to come close. Diana clasped his hand tightly and knelt down next to the man who had been her mentor these last ten years.

"You've got to take this bastard down." Bill squeezed her hand as he spoke.

"We will Bill. We'll get him together. The whole department." Tears filled her eyes. She tried to put pressure on the wound, tried to stop the bleeding, but they both knew there was no point.

"Not as a cop…as Artemis" His eyes held hers. There was so much kindness in them, so much warmth and understanding. Mostly his eyes were full of hope.

"You knew?" the revelation only deepened Diana's grief.

"Of course I knew……. I'm a detective." The words came out haltingly, the effort clearly costing him.

"I can't Bill. Just be still. Help is on the way." She looked up from her dying partner and screamed her despair "HELP! CAN WE GET SOME HELP OVER HERE!!!"

Bill grabbed her shirt and pulled her close. His blood soaked her blouse.

"You've got to…… end this. Promise me." He started to cough, and more blood came trickling out of his mouth. "Promise me." His eyes went blank and he was gone.

Emotion left her. She knew she should feel rage or grief or something, anything at the loss of her mentor, her partner, her friend; but all she felt was empty.

It was shock, she knew. Knowing didn't change anything. The next few hours went by in a haze. Paramedics arrived to take the wounded to the hospital. The Coroner arrived to take the rest to the morgue. Witnesses were interviewed. Statements were taken. Procedures were followed. And everyone's eyes kept drifting to the clock. Everyone's eyes but hers.

All toll thirty-two cops were dead with another forty-seven in intensive care. In a single day, Cutter had effectively crippled the NDPD. She didn't know all the names on the casualty board, but she'd known enough. She'd known Captain Thorne. She'd known Bill.

"Listen up people. The bastard who did this to us is still out there and unless we do something about it he's going to kill a whole lot more people. There will be time to grieve later. Right now you need to get your heads in the game and focus on the task at hand." Lambert said the only thing he could say at a time like this.

Diana looked around the room at the faces of her fellow officers.

She'd hoped to find those faces full of steely resolve, unbowed and unbroken by the hell they'd been through, ready to fight back against the evil that had violated their home.

But that's not what she found. Instead, she saw fear and despair. Worse, she saw hopelessness. There was no way these people were going to be able to do what needed to be done.

Cutter had said that unless Artemis showed up to fight him tonight he'd murder every man, woman, and child in New Delt City.

She believed him.

Diana finally admitted to herself what she had to do.

* * *

The Return of Artemis

The suit still fit. Under different circumstances that might have pleased her. The lightweight, flexible, ceramic nano-composite polymer was designed to deflect most knife attacks and absorb small arms fire without being cumbersome. It didn't make her indestructible, but it made her a hell of a lot harder to kill. She slid on her custom steel-lined, cushioned-soled, knee-high boots and gloves before taking stock of her inventory.

In the old days, her base of operations had been her father's ancient underground bunker that had doubled as his secret lab. The same secret lab where he'd created the serum that gave Diana her abilities. That was the reason the government had never caught her with their power sniffers. Without her serum, she was simply a martial arts expert with a photographic memory. Not exactly your common girl next door but hardly super-powered. With the serum, her brain's processing power increased a hundredfold. It didn't make her smarter or stronger or even faster, but it did make her quicker. Her reflexes became inhumanely fast because her brain was absorbing and reacting to stimuli at a fraction of the time it took a normal human. She could run thousands of calculations and simulations through her mind in the blink of an eye, allowing her time to assess situations and decide on a course of action with the benefit of virtual hours to plan. For all that, the serum was also a drug. It was addictive and it had side effects. Quitting cold turkey ten years ago had nearly broken her. Injecting herself with it tonight was not going to be pleasant.

Along with her suit and her bow, she'd kept three vials of the serum in an anonymous storage unit on the outskirts of town. She'd paid cash, up front, one year at a time since she'd scuttled the entrance to her base and rented the unit ten years ago.

The unit didn't contain any trick arrows, smoke bombs, or her trademark paralytic darts. It did contain various sex toys and bondage paraphernalia. It had been her hope if the unit had ever been discovered she could have played everything off as an Artemis cosplay fetish. Unfortunately, she doubted a studded paddle was going to be much help against Cutter.

Knowing there was no more time to waste she injected herself with the serum. The effects began almost as soon as the needle left her arm. Thoughts moved through her active mind faster, she was suddenly aware of the position and composition of every object in the unit while simultaneously playing out their possible utility across a myriad of scenarios. Her head hurt and she braced herself against the pull-up door as information threatened to overwhelm her.

She practiced the breathing exercises she'd taught herself long ago and brought her mind to heel. Focus was her only tether. Without it she would spin out of control, losing herself in a deluge of thought. So she focused on Cutter's message.

He wanted to her to meet him and insisted that she knew where that meeting was supposed to happen. In his note, he'd talked about coming full circle. The bank heist had not been their first encounter. The first time they'd faced off had been in the Hallows on Bell Street. The cops didn't know about the encounter. Neither, she guessed, did the Feds. She grabbed her bow and headed out.

The Hallows had gotten its name from the copious amount of churches that occupied the neighborhood, effectively making the whole area hallowed ground. Most of these churches resided on Bell Street where their many bell towers sang out in unison at the top of each hour. Many of the churches were derelict, but the crackheads and squatters who occupied the buildings now made sure to keep the bells ringing. The reason for their labor was one of New Delt City's biggest mysteries.

At nine o'clock the bells began to chime. Artemis stepped into the street. At the other end of the block Cutter stood waiting for her.

They said nothing as they stared each other down. There was nothing to be said. No grand plans to be revealed. No stalling for time to get innocent bystanders clear. It was down to the two of them. And they were going to beat on each other until only one of them was left standing.

Cutter's face twisted itself into a macabre smile. That was all the warning Diana needed.

A trio of small blades flew from Cutter's hands before Diana's eyes registered he'd drawn them. It's didn't matter. She'd already let loose with an arrow of her own and had nocked another one. Her feet moved forward of their own accord. Everything was muscle memory now. Three arrows deflecting three blades as she ran headlong towards her destiny.

Cutter did her the courtesy of meeting her halfway. He led with a right hook, putting all of his weight behind it. He wanted her to block the blow or counter it. Either choice would put her at a disadvantage.

Diana decided on option three. She planted hard with her left foot and launched herself into the air. She landed behind Cutter and used her new position to direct a spinning kick right to the large man's kidneys.

Her strike connected but did nothing to slow Cutter down.

He turned his hips and swung his fist in a mighty backhand. Diana ducked and brought herself in close to her foe. Landing two quick jabs to the body before delivering an uppercut straight to Cutter's jaw.

Cutter staggered backwards before recovering and unleashing a massive chest kick, striking Diana and cracking her sternum.

She rolled on instinct as she hit the ground, narrowly avoiding Cutter's foot as it slammed into the space her head had occupied only moments before.

Coming up in a crouch she could feel panic seeping in. Cutter was too big, too fast. The last time they'd faced off she'd been in peak condition, at the height of her training. She'd had to use every weapon in her arsenal and she'd still barely managed to take him down. This time she was out of practice, unprepared, armed with nothing more than her bow.

Cutter's fists came at her like a pair of battering rams. Desperately she deflected his attacks, each block coming a fraction of a second slower than the last.

If she couldn't figure out a way to end this quickly, Cutter was going to win and she was going to die.

Diana moved with speed and fury. Relying on agility and acrobatics to avoid Cutter's meaty fists while her own appendages peppered his gargantuan frame with targeted strikes. Her hope was to slow him down, that the collective force of her blows would weaken him enough to make it a fair fight. But if Cutter was feeling fatigued it didn't show and the more she moved the more pain burned in her chest.

Cutter blocked a shin kick and countered with a right hook that sent her to the ground. She got her hands up in time to block Cutter's massive boot from breaking her nose.

Diana pushed upwards and managed to knock Cutter off his feet.

The two combatants each picked themselves off the ground and paused for a moment to catch their breath.

Cutter smiled at her.

"You made a mistake earlier. That combo you used. Two jabs to the body followed by an uppercut. You've used that move on me before. Isn't that right *detective?*"

Diana didn't respond. Didn't allow her body to react at all. Cutter pulled a machete from its sheath on his hip and charged her.

Reaching back into her quiver she let loose a pair of arrows at her oncoming foe. Cutter deflected the bolts with two quick swipes of his machete then brought the blade above his head in preparation for a massive overhead strike.

Raising her bow above her head to block the oncoming blow, she countered by ducking low into Cutter's body. Once she was in close she sprung upward, using Cutter's size and momentum against him. The bastard flipped over her and went flying through the air, landing on his back a few yards away.

Breath. Focus. Assess. She reminded herself.

Cutter got to his feet with a snarl on his lips. He screamed as he came at her again.

Time slowed and Diana's mind took over.

Time to Engagement with Hostile: *One Point Six Seconds*
Tactical Assessment: *Two Hundred Forty-Seven Ways to Intercept Hostile*
.... *Eliminating Scenarios Resulting Physical Harm to Self*
..........*Thirty-Eight Possible Ways to Intercept Hostile*
..........*Eliminating Scenarios Resulting in Hostile's Death*
..........*Seven Possible Ways to Intercept Hostile*

..........*Selecting Plan of Action with Highest Remaining Probability of Subduing Hostile*

..........*Plan of Action Selected.*

Diana nocked an arrow and took aim. Cutter swiped his machete at the incoming threat and deflected it. The diverted missile shot straight into his left foot. Cutter tripped while Diana pivoted and spun. As Cutter stumbled through empty air she brought down a heavy elbow, striking Cutter at the base of the neck and driving him to the ground.

Not waiting for him to get up she drew two arrows in rapid succession and put a shaft through each of his hands. The son of a bitch howled in pain as blood flowed from his wounds.

Cutter managed to get to his hands and knees. Diana walked over and slammed her boot down on his hand. He screamed and collapsed to the ground.

Straddling Cutter's back, Diana took his head in her hands and slammed it into the pavement. She did this two more times before putting his neck in a chokehold. Gasping, Cutter swiped at her. His hands still pierced with her arrows. Diana held her grip. Slowly Cutter succumbed to unconsciousness.

She pulled his limp body to the nearest lamppost and handcuffed the asshole to it. She watched from a nearby rooftop as her fellow officers took Richard Cutter aka "The Dick" into custody.

She stepped to the edge of the roof, letting the moonlight frame her silhouette. A few of the officers drew their weapons and shouted at her to freeze.

The rest began to clap.

She held the pose a little longer before disappearing back into the darkness. She wanted them all to know that once again this was her city.

It would be years before the Russo Act was repealed, and there would be many dark days before the light shone bright across the land. But the spark had been lit and in people's hearts hope once again stirred. Artemis had returned. In their darkest hour, she had come back to save them. And now they knew.

Everything was about to change.

Oasis

Arizona Territory, 1873

Moisture dripped down from his brow to his cheeks, the oppressive heat of the midday sun dampening his face while making a dry creek bed of his mouth. The air was suffocating. Every breath he took filled his lungs with fire. There was no breeze and no shade. Just the hot hell of the Arizona desert.

The land around him was hostile.

Given the opportunity, the desert would kill him.

It wouldn't think about it. It wouldn't construct some elaborate plot or suddenly decide to strike him down in a fit of violent rage. The desert would simply end him. And then it would continue on as it always had.

The desert was nature in her purest form; an unending, unyielding force of death and desolation.

There was no denying the desert was harsh, but so too were its inhabitants. They had survived, adapted, and learned to thrive. Here the strong endured and the weak died. The same as anywhere else in nature. The same as in any part of civilization. The desert was merely honest about it.

He wiped his face with his kerchief, the saturated cloth serving only to evenly disperse the dank sweat across his countenance. Squinting underneath the sky's harsh, yellow light his eyes scanned the horizon looking for a tiny speck of human civilization in the distance. When they finally found it he kicked his heels and directed his horse Agni towards it at a trot.

The town looked like every other town the west had to offer; hot, dry, and unimportant. The street was mostly empty, the few people he did see kept their heads down and avoided making eye contact with him as he rode by. The stench of fear filled his nostrils. Good. That meant he was in the right place. He stopped when he reached the town saloon, dismounted, and tied Agni to a post before heading inside.

The saloon had a few occupants: a card game in the corner, two passed out drunks at a table in the back and a trio of solitary drinkers scattered throughout the room.

He took a seat at the bar.

"Pour you a drink, stranger?" The bartender was a skeleton of a man, a white-haired old timer who'd clearly known better days. A strong breeze would have put an end to him. Probably why he came to the territories, out here the breeze hardly ever found you.

"Whiskey" he replied gruffly.

The bartender fished out a dirty shot glass and poured a disgusting looking amber liquid into it.

The stranger downed the liquid and tapped his now empty glass on the counter. The glass was refiled in seconds. The man served watered down swill and called it whiskey, but at least he kept it coming.

"What brings you to our little Oasis, partner?" The bartender inquired with a face stuck halfway between a smile and a grimace.

"Business" was all the stranger said in response.

"And what kind of business would that be then?" The bartender's follow-up question was friendly enough. But there was an edge to it that suggested the fellow wouldn't be satisfied unless the stranger elaborated further.

The stranger didn't elaborate. He raised his eyes to meet the bartender's and took another pull of his whiskey.

Sullenly, the barkeep took the hint and left the stranger to drink in peace.

It wasn't easy. He could feel the eyes of his fellow patrons burning into his back. This was not a town accustomed to welcoming guests it seemed. Then again, he had often found the pair of pistols he wore made all manner of people nervous.

Their unwelcome attention was soon redirected. One of the passed-out drunks had woken up and become quite lively, shouting at the saloon's various patrons.

"Gone. Just upped and vanished. Not that any of you sons of bitches gives a shit. Ain't right. My boy wouldn't have run off. Charlie wouldn't a done that. He ain't the only one neither. Y'all know it. Something dark has taken hold a this place. My boy wouldn't a just run off." The man stumbled about as he ranted, clearly still intoxicated despite his nap.

The stranger took stock of the drunk. Bags the size of craters hung beneath his eyes. His skin was devoid of all color. Energy was simply seeping out of him. Slowly draining him of his life force. This was a man who'd lost his will to fight. A man on the verge of losing his will to live.

The drunk took notice of the stranger's gaze and took it for an invitation. Making his way over to where the stranger sat.

"You're him right? The man I've been waiting for?" He spoke in a hushed voice. His breath reeked of whiskey. The stranger turned away.

Anxious questions from anxious men bothered the stranger. He considered them a sign of weakness. To display one's ignorance in such an agitated manner was an invitation to every predator within earshot to come hunting.

Where the stranger took offense was when the questioner included him in the invitation. He was a predator who hunted predators and the less his prey knew about him the better.

The drunk grabbed the stranger's coat and continued to wail at him about his troubles.

"I sent my boy Charlie after a wandering steer three weeks ago and haven't seen him since." The whiskey-soaked, wreck of a man began to weep.

"Nobody wants to hear your drunk ass ramble on today Rawls. You lost your boy and come tomorrow you're going to lose your farm. By my reckoning that makes you a loser twice over. I don't much fancy drinking in the company a losers, so why don't you get before I got ta make ya get"

A new man had entered the bar. Tall and lean. Early twenties by the looks of him. And a mean cuss if first impressions were anything to go by.

Thirty seconds in the same room and the stranger wanted to kill the man already.

"I ain't bothering nobody. People gotta right to know." Rawls sounded more like he was trying to convince himself of this than anyone of them.

"You're bothering me." The cuss grabbed Rawls by the shirt and tossed him to the ground. "Now get."

"Let him alone." The stranger did not raise his voice. And yet every head in the place snapped back to look at him when he spoke.

"Ain't none of your concern stranger." Again the cuss grabbed Rawls by the shirt. This time he raised back his hand to strike the man.

"I don't like repeating myself. I said let him alone. Don't make me say it again" The stranger's voice was as cold as the iron he wore on his hip.

"And I said this ain't none of your concern." But the man did let go of Rawls, turning his attention to the stranger instead.

The stranger turned to face the young buck but did not stand. With a lazy deliberateness, his hand settled on the hilt of his colt. Their eyes locked. The cold, steely blues of the stranger setting the upstart's angry brown on edge.

"You draw. You die." He paused for effect. "Your choice."

The stranger's words were spoken without emotion. Quiet and firm, his voice offered up not a threat, but a detached assessment of the facts.

The man's pupil's dilated and the stranger knew. It was always the case that young men let their pride get themselves killed.

Before the fool could draw, a well-dressed, well-fed man of middling years burst into the saloon.

"Gentlemen, gentlemen. Calm yourselves." The newest player in their little melodrama made a large show of waving his hands about. Once he was satisfied they weren't immediately going to shoot each other he addressed the younger of the two shooters.

"What seems to be the conflict? Terrance?"

The man may have been addressing Terrance, but his eyes never left the stranger's gun.

"This cocksucker doesn't know how to mind his own goddamn business, that's my fucking conflict." The young gun had quite the mouth on him. Just another reason for the stranger to shoot him.

"Language, Terrance. This gentleman is a guest in our town. It wouldn't do for us to give him the wrong impression."

Apparently, the big man shared the stranger's distaste for vulgarities. He guessed that was about all they shared.

"Sorry, Mr. Toomes." Terrance moved his hand away from his gun, but he didn't look happy about it. Whoever this Toomes was he clearly carried a lot of clout around these parts.

"Good now, why don't you go check on Lennox and Bertram while I get to know our new friend. Jim, can I get a couple of whiskeys down here?" Before sitting, the rotund man made a spectacle of addressing the frightened onlookers. "It's all right now folks go about your business. Next round is on me."

That proclamation would have gotten cheers in most any bar you could find, here it was met with meek nods of acknowledgment. The stranger took note; these people were afraid. Mr. Toomes wasn't just an important figure in this town, he was the main shot-caller.

"My apologies for my associate stranger. Youthful vigor has a way of making a man ignore the good sense God gave him. I hope you'll give our little frontier town the opportunity to make a better second impression than it did a first." He reached out a hand to the stranger as Jim the bartender poured their whiskeys. "My name is Toomes, Zachariah Toomes. I run the bank here in town. And you are?"

"Leaving." The stranger took his shot in a single, violent gulp and stood to go.

"Now I ask you is that any way to treat a man who just bought you a drink, might have just saved your life? You look confident with those pistols on your hip stranger but believe me Terrance is no snail. Could have been things didn't go your way today, but I was here and now no one ever has to find out. I think that's worthy of a little consideration don't you?"

This Toomes liked to talk. The stranger didn't much care for men who talked too much personally. But professionally he found them to be quite valuable, and often worth the irritation.

So the stranger sat back down and nodded for the man to continue.

"There now, that's the common ground I've been looking for to get us started. We don't get many visitors in these parts. In fact, I can't seem to recall the last time we had a new face here in Oasis. Pardon my assumption, but I don't take you for the livestock raising type. Might I hazard a guess that you are here investigating the rumored spat of disappearances we have suffered lately?" It surprised the stranger less that Toomes would make such a large leap in logic than that he would do it so casually.

"And if I was?" The stranger did not like when people he had just met involved themselves in his affairs

"Well, then I would welcome your investigation sir. I believe it will put to ease the minds of several of our town's residents." The impatient tapping of Toomes' fingers against the bar cast doubt on the banker's enthusiasm. Each thud of his silver ring against the wooden bar rang like an alarm bell in the stranger's ears. Even so, he kept his skepticism in check. Or at least he attempted to.

The bartender walked over and filled their glasses. The stranger waited until the man was out of earshot before resuming their conversation.

"Is that so?"

"It is indeed. You see I am quite confident that I already know what has transpired. I simply have been without the means or resources to prove it." Toomes stated matter-of-factly.

"And what do you believe has transpired?" The stranger asked, careful to show no more than a mild amount of interest in whatever answer he received.

"A series of simple coincidences. Farmhands and cowboys are a wayward lot by nature. Most of them probably just picked up stakes and moved on. Oasis is not exactly a bustling metropolis. We have few things to offer young men in search of adventure. If you understand my meaning." Toomes let the words hang just to make sure the stranger did. "The boys got a few dollars in their pocket and decided to chase their dreams elsewhere. I can hardly blame them."

"And the Rawls boy?" The stranger asked.

"That boy told everyone within earshot he wanted to see the big cities back east. Maybe he just got tired of looking after his drunk of a father, saw an opportunity to get free, and took it." The large man made a gesture that tacked on a 'and who could blame him' to the end of his matter-of-fact proclamation.

"Lots a maybes and probablys in that story of yours." The stranger noted.

"True. Like I said, hard to track down coincidences when I've got other things to attend to. Now that you're here the town will be able to put all this nonsense to bed for good. I think everyone will agree to have your investigation be the final word on the matter."

"Oh, I think it will be." The stranger had intended the remark as an ominous warning. If the stout banker took it as such he showed no signs. Indeed, he was all smiles as he stood from his stool and extended his hand. The stranger took it in his own. No point in being unnecessarily rude before he'd figured out who needed killing.

"Anything you need. Anything at all. You just come by the bank and I'll get you sorted." Toomes gushed on his way out the door.

The stranger had one more whiskey before following suit. He'd learned all he was going to learn in Oasis. It was time to go hunting.

He left Oasis with an ill feeling. There seemed to be more to this tale than a few missing men. He sensed conspiracy. What the nature of that conspiracy was he did not yet know.

But he aimed to find out.

The first step to getting answers was to find whatever had taken these men. Find it and put an end to it.

He rode for hours. Criss-crossing the open country surrounding the town. The stranger had no particular methodology in mind. That would require having some inkling of what he was looking for. He did not.

It was not completely impossible to hunt an unknown predator, but it was damn near. If the stranger wished to encounter the creature, he would have to be patient. He would also need to look like prey.

And so he wandered aimlessly through the desert. Doing his best impression of a lost and wayward soul. The stranger could tell that Agni didn't like it. She was not a horse accustomed to meandering.

A chill ran down his spine. Accompanied by an indistinct feeling of unease. It was a feeling he knew well. It meant he was on the right track.

Light faded from the sky above him. The sun lingering at the horizon. Overstaying its welcome. Twilight came, the time of hidden stars and awakened desire. A wise man was wary of what woke up at the end of the day.

The ridge crested, providing the stranger with a clear view of the valley in front of him. At its far end, he saw the flicker of a campfire. It wasn't much to go on but it was worth investigating just the same.

He coaxed Agni to a gallop and the pair covered the distance into time at all. As they got close the stranger pulled back on the reins and slowed his mare to a trot. No sense scaring whoever it was out here in the wilderness.

But upon reaching the campfire, there was not a soul to be scared. He dismounted and pulled one of his pistols from its holster. A fire didn't just start itself. Someone had been out here, perhaps another abductee. Or perhaps the abductor. Either way, better safe than sorry.

"Drop it!" The stranger whirled toward the voice, his gun raised. But when he turned he found no one there.

"Drop it or I shoot." It was a woman's voice. Scared but determined. The sound of a woman who would shoot him and cry about it afterwards. He knew the type. Best to do as she said.

"Alright." He said clearly, putting his pistol slowly on the ground.

"The other one too." He drew his second pistol and placed it on the dirt next to the first. "Good. Now kick them over here."

The stranger did as he was told.

His captor stepped out from her hiding place behind a large boulder and into the firelight.

She was a stunning creature, with hair as black as night and eyes the color of starlight. A descendant of the Amazons, with the air of one who had seen all the world had to see and had been unimpressed.

"You're a long way from civilization. Miss...?" The stranger kept his tone even. Under different circumstances, this woman would have been just his type. Hell, under these circumstances she was just his type. After all, who didn't like a woman who knew how to handle a gun.

"Ivy. Madeline Ivy. And yes, I am mister. Which is why it is so fortuitous for me that you happened along. I just don't know what I would have done out here in the dark, all alone."

His captor hesitated only for a moment before giving him her name. It wasn't much, but it was enough for him to tell she had to think about it. Meaning the name she gave him was a false one. He didn't mind. People never wanted to tell him their real names. He just had one of those faces.

"You look capable to me. I think you would have managed." The stranger said without a trace of sarcasm.

"Almost certainly." She flashed him a wicked smile. "But the night is so much better when you have someone to share it with."

The stranger tilted his head and raised his eyebrows. He was a bit out of practice, but he was fairly sure this woman was flirting with him.

"I suppose that means you're not gonna shoot me then." It was a statement, not a question.

"Maybe. Maybe not. I reckon I haven't decided yet." She stepped closer to the fire, allowing its light to further outline her exquisite figure. The heat of its flames causing her cheeks and bosom to turn red. It was enough to make the stranger feel the heat as well.

"Well while you reckon on that, how abouts I put my hands down?" Madeline shrugged at the stranger's proposal.

He lowered his hands. She didn't shoot him. He reasoned that was a good sign.

She gestured with the gun and he moved as instructed. Closer to the firelight he could make out that the boulder she had stepped out from was not a boulder at all. It was a dead horse. Someone had put a bullet in the poor beast's head.

"What happened?" He asked. Anger creeping into his voice. The stranger had always had far more compassion for animals than people.

"I was trying to reach town before nightfall, I pushed her too hard and she tripped. Broke her leg and nearly broke my neck. Poor thing. It was my fault; I should have known better." Ms. Ivy was almost in tears by the time she finished her story. She was distraught enough that she let her arm drop so that her pistol was no longer pointed at the stranger.

He chose to ignore this opening and focused on the horse corpse in front of him.

Closer examination clearly showed the animal had been lame and that it was likely an accident. It was hard to break a horse's leg like that on purpose. She'd been right to put it down. He'd have done the same for Agni. Still, if she was telling the truth it was a pretty stupid way to treat a horse.

"You're right. You should have known better." He stated plainly, offering her no sympathy or forgiveness for her foolish treatment of her animal.

They stood staring at each other in silence while she let her emotions run their course. The stranger had nothing to say and so he said nothing.

After she gathered herself, Madeline gave him a faint smile and raised the barrel of her pistol back in his direction.

"I like you. You're a straight shooter. Most men would have tried to coddle me. I mean I'm beautiful and holding a gun on you. You'd think you'd want to be in my good graces." She pulled up the hem of her dress so as not to trip and began moving towards him in a slow deliberate fashion.

The stranger, for his part, let her come to him.

"I'm not most men." He stated simply. It was a truer statement than people realized.

"Oh, is that a fact?" The space between them was nearly non-existent now. And that wicked smile had returned to her face.

"You move fast." He whispered. She was near enough to him now that to speak any louder would have been unnecessary.

"Life's short." She pressed her pistol again his skin, its cold steel sending shivers across his body. Her breasts heaved in her corset, inviting him closer. Her scent was intoxicating.

"A minute ago you wanted to shoot me." A fog had fallen over his mind. He wanted her. He needed her. He struggled to keep his mind clear.

"I still might." She teased. Her lips were so very close to his own.

Unable to resist any longer His hands gripped her and pulled her into his body. He could feel her breasts pressed against his chest. Her shapely curves contouring themselves to his embrace.

There was a tingling sensation as their lips touched. An emptiness began to pull at him, a void waiting to be filled. His body ached for her. Burned for her. All he wanted was to become lost in her forever.

Pushing the thing calling itself Madeline Ivy away, the stranger smiled and raised his empty right palm to face her.

"Darling, you are exactly the woman I've been looking for. *Electricus Incendia*" Strands of electricity exploded from his hand. Each strand laced with crimson fire.

The blast broke against a translucent red shield. The succubus stood unscathed behind it, eyes wide with surprise.

"Warlock!" she screamed.

Balls of fire and lightning flew from his hands in rapid succession as he back peddled. They too failed to reach their target, instead crashing against the succubus' protective conjuring. The collision of their magiks thundering like an artillery siege, destroying the quiet serenity of the valley. His blasts may not have done much damage to his hellish foe, but they did allow him to put some distance between himself and the demon.

The succubus' shield disappeared, replaced by a wall of flame. The warlock continued his barrage, but each new attack only enlarged the wall. He stopped firing his magic missiles and readied his shield.

The wall of flame collapsed into a ball. A wave of the succubus' hand sent the fiery sphere speeding towards him.

Crossing his arms in front of his face, the warlock whispered his ancient words and conjured. A shield of indigo energy formed as the succubus' rage crashed down upon him. Heat seeped through the shield. The warlock held on, knowing that to do differently would be suicide. Screams of pain ripped from his lungs as the flesh burned from his arms.

The succubus' assault lasted only a few seconds, but it was enough to take its toll. His sleeves had burned away and his arms had turned an angry red. Blisters ran from his elbows to his wrists. Mercifully, his hands had sustained only minimal damage. Meaning he could still shoot and he could still cast.

Two complex, subtle gestures collected the primordial energies he would need. His incantation set them free.

"Vis" He screamed, unleashing a blast of pure, invisible kinetic energy at his seductive foe.

The succubus took flight, and his attack passed harmlessly beneath her.She countered with her own blast of lighting and flame.

The warlock ran diagonally towards the largest bolder he could see with the intent of taking cover.

"Oh no, it's not going to be as easy as that moon-dancer." The succubus cackled.

The ground beneath him began to shake and tremor. Fissures opened as giant pieces of earth rose into the air. Eyes wide with manic glee, the succubus raised her arms and commenced conducting a symphony of geological mayhem. The rocks obeyed her every gesture, dancing in the air before careening towards the warlock at incredible speeds.

Dipping and dodging, the warlock fought to maintain his balance while he avoided being struck by the massive chunks of earth. A glint of silver caught the warlock's eye. His pistols, precariously perched on one of the succubus' floating boulders.

Distracted by the sight, the warlock almost didn't see the rocky missile headed straight for him. He jumped clear in time. But the near miss cost him his footing.

The demon cackled.

On instinct, he rolled left. Another flying rock crashing into the ground next to him.

He came up in a sprinter's crouch. Scanning the chaos, he again located the sheen of his gun. He ran towards it.

Craters formed at his heels, his legs pumping hard just to keep him one step ahead of the witch's earthy artillery.

The spurs on his boots rattled as he jumped from one rising rock to the next. One pistol fell before he could reach it, the second was sliding quickly from its perch.

Desperately he leaped for it, spinning in the air. His pistol was there, falling straight into his waiting palm. He gripped the handle, straightened out his aim, and pulled the trigger.

A new hole formed right between the succubus' eyes. She hung in the air for a moment. Then her lifeless corpse went crashing to the ground.

The witch was not the only one to suddenly rediscover gravity. The warlock too found himself rapidly falling towards the earth, along with all the chunks of rock and clay the succubus had pulled up into the air with her magiks.

He conjured a shield. It absorbed some of the impact of the fall, but not all of it. Pain engulfed every part of him

Knowing he had no time to waste, the warlock rolled and faced the sky, bringing his shield around with him. He held fast as an avalanche of earth rained down upon him.

It was a few minutes before the warlock could catch his breath, a few more before he felt able enough push himself out of what had become a somewhat shallow grave. Spellcasting was a taxing endeavor.

With very few exceptions, when a magic user dies their spells die with them. And so the death of the succubus revealed their surroundings to be a glamour, masking her real lair.

The warlock found that he was not in a wide-open valley as he had believed, but rather he was surrounded by a series of massive rock formations. They jutted out of the ground from a myriad of angles, forming a sort of geological cage that towered over him. It was beautiful and terrifying.

One of the formations was large enough to house a small inlet at its base. At the mouth of this inlet lay a collection of saddlebags and cooking utensils. It was a sight that would have put a great many in a state of unease. Not the warlock, he had been expecting to find a site like this since he arrived in the territories.

Cautiously, he approached the opening. While he was certain the succubus was dead and her magic dissipated, there was no sense in being reckless.

He'd been wrong to refer to the inlet as small. Upon closer inspection, the opening led to a full-fledged cave.

"Incendi" A faint light surrounded him. The dull glow of his spell giving his suspicions their final confirmation.

Piles of bones lay everywhere. Skeletons picked clean by the succubus' life-leaching powers. There was no way to confirm the identities of her victims, but it seemed clear there had been many.

A moaning sound came from the back of the cave. Gun drawn, the warlock stepped towards the noise.

What he found there filled every inch of him with rage.

The being before him could barely be described as a man. He was more an afterthought. An empty husk where once life had been. Unnaturally aged beyond human endurance, yet somehow still breathing. This was the end result of the succubus' feeding. Or at least very near the end.

"What's your name?"

"Charlie. Charlie Rawls." The rancher's boy had not been the last victim taken, but he had been the youngest. Likely she had left him here in case she needed a morsel to hold herself over until she found her next meal.

"All right Charlie. Hang in there. I'm going to get you out of here." The warlock was not normally one for platitudes. They only served to gloss over the harsh truths a man needed to face if he was to survive in this world. Charlie wasn't going to survive this. There was no counterspell, no cure, for what had happened to him. The warlock could not restore the boy's stolen life-force any more than he could turn a steak back into a steer. The best he could do was get the boy to his father so the two could say goodbye. And that required platitudes.

The warlock bent over and put his arms around the boy preparing to lift him out to Agni. Weakly, Charlie tried to push his hands away. The warlock stepped back. Looking at the agony in the boy's eyes.

"Kill me." His voice was hollow. Empty in a way that would haunt the warlock for the rest of his days. Charlie was dying. Every piece of him desperately fighting a losing battle with decay. The fire of his life now reduced to mere embers. He was not dying of old age. It was not a gentle surrender to the end of his days. His days were being violently ripped from him. A lifetime's worth of pain crammed into a single hour. It was an excruciating way to go.

And there was only one way to save him from it.

"Please. Kill Me."

The warlock pulled his pistol out of its holster.

"Thank you."

His hand stayed steady until the work was done.

He burned the succubus and buried the boy. It took a few hours to both dig a grave and build a pyre, but the boy deserved a proper burial. Turning the demon's corpse to ash was just good sense.

While prepping the succubus for her bonfire, the warlock took note of a silver ring she wore. It tickled his brain for some reason. Removing it from her finger, he gave it a closer examination.

"*Ostendi*" A quick revelation spell and the ring's purpose became clear to him. It had been enchanted to serve as a two-way communications device. With it, and the right incantations, the wearer could send and receive messages from its twin.

Its presence told him that the witch had been working with someone, a magic user, and he was certain he knew who. He'd seen one like it before, on the finger of that blowhard banker Toomes.

The warlock didn't believe in coincidences. In his line of work, things were hardly ever random. But in his line of work, it also paid to be certain before rushing in head first.

Plain silver rings were not all that uncommon. He needed more to go on.

He put the ring in his pocket and set fire to the demon. He stuck around long enough to make sure she burned, then turned and made his way back to an impatient Agni.

The question he needed answered was the why. Why bring a succubus all the way out here to the territories simply to kill a few farmhands? These men were of no importance, no significance. And what did that banker Toomes have to do with any of it?

The warlock needed to gather more information and he needed to gather it discreetly. So far only one person in this county had been straight with him and the warlock had just killed his son. He owed Clint Rawls a visit. If for no other reason than to tell him where his boy was buried.

For the average rider finding Rawls would mean stopping at every homestead along the way in the hopes of finding someone capable of giving directions. The warlock did not have that kind of time to waste. And he didn't have to.

Pulling Charlie Rawls' hat out of his satchel, the warlock closed his eyes and concentrated on what he wanted. When that image and no other was firmly rooted in his thoughts he spoke.

"*Sedis Loci*" the hat fidgeted in his grip. He released it. Rising in the air, the hat began to float towards the southwest. The warlock kicked Agni into a trot and followed.

He chased the hat for a long while before it dramatically stopped and dropped to the ground. The signal he had reached the Rawls property line.

The warlock climbed down from his saddle and retrieved the hat. No point in leaving it out there and he thought the boy's father might appreciate having something to remember him by.

A small structure lay a few acres from where he stood. There were men there. They appeared to be yelling at someone inside the house. The warlock was beginning to lose his patience with this assignment.

The closer he got to the house, the clearer the root of the disagreement became.

"It's moving day Rawls. Mr. Toomes has been mighty patient with you so far, but a debt is a debt. This place belongs to Reynard Savings and Loan now. You are trespassing. And the law says trespassers will be shot." Shouted one of the men outside the house

"If you're planning on shooting me Bertram, you best not miss. 'Cause my rifle sure as hell won't." came the response from inside. And suddenly the warlock had the final piece of the puzzle.

It really couldn't be as simple as all that could it. Toomes recruited the succubus to remove all the rancher's helpers so he could foreclose on their properties. It seemed far too petty a plot for a man with the power to bind a demon to his will. Still, he'd seen men do worse for less.

Toomes' man was holding a shotgun aimed directly at Rawls' front door. Upon hearing the warlock's approach, it notably changed its target.

"Who the fuck is you?" Bertram shouted, punctuating the question with an emphatic raising of his shotgun to eye level.

"Rawls and I have business." The warlock responded calmly.

"Not today you don't." Toomes' man stated curtly.

"You work for Mr. Toomes correct?" Time to try a different tactic.

"Bet your ass" Bertram responded proudly. The other two goons remained silent. Their hats shading their faces from the warlock's gaze.

"Well, your boss said I could count on him for any help I required while I was here. I assumed that included not getting shot by one of his boys. I need to speak to Mr. Rawls in there. I'd like to do that now before you all settle whatever other matter it is you feel you need to settle. Is that okay with you or do we need to go see Mr. Toomes?"

Bertram's mouth hung open, clearly wanting to say something but not precisely sure what that something should be. The warlock nodded to the man graciously inferring that he took his silence as consent. Then he promptly dismounted and walked towards Rawls' front door.

Agni neighed and stomped her feet. It was their signal for "turn around someone's about to try and kill you".

The mare's warning came just in time. The warlock turned and summoned up a weak shield right as a shotgun blast took him in the chest. The shield absorbed the scatter-shot, keeping the warlock from developing a few dozen new holes. However, it did not absorb the blast's kinetic energy. As a result, the warlock went flying backwards through Rawls' front door.

Spots filled the warlock's vision. He felt as if a mule had kicked him. Repeatedly. He tried to blink himself back to normal.

"You sons of bitches! I'll kill ya for this Bertram Coles!" He heard Rawls shout. His sight began to clear. He watched Rawls take aim at one of the men shooting up his place. The rifle barked. Its target lurched backwards for a moment then resumed its advance.

Rawls fired his rifle two more times. Again striking the advancing man in the chest. The bullets had no effect. The man kept coming.

Not a man. A golem.

Golems were dark magic. Soulless soldiers made of clay. Unthinking, Unyielding, Undying. Their presence here confirmed not only that Toomes was behind the succubus and her murders, but that he too was a mage of some skill.

The warlock lifted himself off the floor of Rawls' cottage. He picked up his hat, dusted it off, and returned it to his head.

Bullets continued to ricochet off the front of the house. Rawls ducked down to reload and caught sight of the warlock stalking towards the front door. His eyes went wide with shock

"You should be dead." The man cursed between shotgun blasts.

"Not dead." The warlock's fingers danced. Energy coalesced in his palm. "Angry."

The warlock stepped out on to the front porch. His targets spaced themselves out as they continued to approach. The man Rawls' called Bertram trained his gun on the warlock. The warlock did not draw. Instead, he spoke a single word.

"*Vis*"

Pure power erupted from the warlock's hands. A ball of invisible energy struck Bertram with the force of a locomotive, lifting him twenty feet up into the air before callously dropping him back to earth. The warlock almost winced at the breaking of the man's bones. Almost.

The two golems sprinted towards him. Closing the distance before he could draw his pistols. Just as well, the warlock was in the mood to hit something.

Golems didn't feel pain. At least not in the way real humans did. The mages who used them as muscle viewed that as an advantage. They were wrong. Pain made a man cautious, it made him clever, and it made him quick. Brute force might work when put up against the common man, but against a trained fighter it was easily neutralized. These golems bodies might not feel pain, but they could still be broken.

The warlock planted his left foot and spun. His elbow connected sharply with the base of the first golem's neck, altering its trajectory and causing it to crash into golem number two.

The two creatures would not stay on the ground long. Before they could recover the warlock pressed his advantage, sprinting towards his unnatural foes.

His right knee connected with the second golem's chin. The creature stumbled backwards at the impact. The first golem threw a haymaker at the warlock's head. He blocked it and counter-punched with a staggering right hook of his own.

The Golems had him bracketed, one on his left and one on his right. Which just so happened to coincide with the positions of his two holstered pistols. The warlock drew and fired.

The golems bodies burst into flame, writhing on the ground as they were consumed by white fire. The warlock's pistols were accustomed to dealing with unnatural creatures.

The warlock left the golems to burn out and went to check on the one actual human he'd faced. Bertram's eyes were wide with shock. Various bones jutted out from his body and differing angles. But the pool of blood underneath his head indicated that getting is skull cracked open on impact had been what did him in.

The warlock felt no remorse. He'd killed a killer. Their kind only died one way.

"That's the second time you backed me when you didn't have to stranger. I owe you." Clint Rawls stood next to the warlock. The pair stared down at their attacker's shattered corpse. Vultures began to circle overhead. "I suppose we ought to bury him. Bertram may have been a son of a bitch, but no man deserves to be bird chow."

The warlock nodded at the farmer's suggestion.

The two men dug in silence. The warlock could sense that Rawls had questions, but the farmer did not ask them. Perhaps afraid of the answers he would receive. Some things once heard cannot be unheard.

When the hole was suitably deep they shoved Bertram's body into it. Filling the hole went significantly faster than digging it. That was always the case. Something about a dead man's eyes staring up at them made men much quicker with their shovels.

They said no words over the grave, nor did they mark it in any way. Bertram had not been a man worthy of remembrance.

Upon their return to the house, Rawls poured them both a cup of coffee. They sat down at the kitchen table. Their muteness extending itself until their cups were empty.

Finally, Rawls asked the question that terrified them both.

"What happened to my boy?"

The warlock took a deep breath, then explained what he could.

"There was a woman. She was seducing the missing men. Leading them to their deaths." The warlock let Rawls absorb the information. Waiting for the inevitable follow-up question.

"And this woman she took my Charlie?'

The warlock nodded.

"You're certain?"

The warlock stood and walked outside to his saddle. When he returned he was holding Charlie's hat. He handed it to the boy's father. Tears ran down the elder Rawls' face.

"She was working with someone else, I suspected Toomes. Now I know." The scheme seemed petty for the amount of magical talent involved. Kill a bunch of farmhands in order to foreclose on a handful of parcels identical to a thousand others you could find along the frontier. The investment didn't seem near worth the payoff. But the pieces fit. The golems were more than enough proof all on their own.

"What are you going to do now?" The grieving father asked.

"I'm going to kill him." The warlock put his hat on his head and walked out the door.

Oasis was an hour's ride from the Rawls' farm. He left Agni on the outskirts of town. If for whatever reason he did not return by the time night fell the mare would return to the Enclave without its master, alerting the council to his failure.

He did not foresee that becoming an issue.

Walking with purpose down the town's main, and only, thoroughfare; he prepared himself for the battle to come. The revelation that Toomes was a sorcerer shook him. He did not fear facing another mage in combat. He'd done that many times before.

What troubled him was that he hadn't seen it coming. He should have sensed Toomes' power when they'd first met at the saloon. That he hadn't carried with it ramifications that went far beyond this assignment.

Realizing there would be no other assignments beyond this one if he didn't focus on the task at hand, the warlock cleared his mind of all distractions.

A half dozen men stepped out from the bank as he approached. To be precise it was only two men accompanied by four golems. The warlock recognized the one called Terrance from their encounter at the saloon. That made the other human Lennox, if he remembered Toomes words from their first encounter correctly.

The warlock didn't wish to waste his energies before facing another mage of unknown power, so he offered them an out.

"Gentleman," The warlock spoke his words calmly and clearly to the two humans. "I'm here for your employer. Take a walk. There's no need for you to die today."

Terrance smiled at him. "The Sun addle that brain of yours? There's six of us and one of you. Boss wants you dead, so you die. Simple. Can't say I haven't been looking forward to this."

A stillness settled upon them all. Their hands resting a few inches above their holsters, waiting to draw their guns. The warlock locked eyes with Terrance. The banker's lackey was sweating. The warlock was not.

His eyes twitched and Terrance went for his gun. Lennox and the Golems followed his lead.

The warlock drew but did not fire, instead, he used his free hand to project a shield in front of himself. Bullet after bullet impacted the shield.

The barrage ceased. The pronounced *click-click* of empty pistols filled the air. Dropping his shield, the warlock tilted his head, gave Terrance a grim grin, and calmly opened fire.

Six shots.

Six kills.

The blank, lifeless faces of Lennox and Terrance smashed into the dirt, while white flames consumed the bodies of the four golems.

"I told you once before. You draw. You die."

A blast of invisible force struck the warlock square in the chest, knocking his pistol from his hand. The massive blow took him off his feet and through the window of the town's general store.

The warlock lifted himself from the floor, shaking off the shards of broken glass that covered him. Stepping through the store's newest exit, he found Toomes waiting for him on the street holding the warlock's lost pistol.

"Now that wasn't very sporting at all, was it?" The mage-cum-banker-cum-robber baron wore his finest Sunday suit. The conservative look contrasting sharply with the gaudy display of rings and amulets he wore. To a normal human, the jewelry would merely constitute a poor fashion choice. To a man of magic, it was the equivalent of dressing yourself in an armory. "You hardly gave poor Terrance a chance. Not what I'd expect at all from one of the Council's righteous avengers."

The two mages circled each other. The warlock was weary. He was an agent of the Council's justice. Any mage who knew of the Council knew to fear the wrath of its warlocks. And every mage knew of the Council. This banker was far too arrogant for comfort.

"Interesting pistols, the enchantments are fascinating. Is it just golems it kills, or is it any supernatural creature? Doesn't really matter. What intrigues me is that you never seem to reload it. Unlimited bullets. That should be impossible. You can't get something for nothing. It's the first law of magic. So where do they come from I wonder?"

The warlock said nothing as the two mages continued to take each other's measure.

"A mystery for my idle hours perhaps." Toomes tossed the pistol behind him and continued to pontificate. "I suppose you're trying to work out why a mage of my talent would waste his time in a backwater frontier town such as this."

The warlock remained silent.

"No? Really? It's quite the captivating tale. It would be a shame for you to die without knowing why." Toomes stopped circling.

"You broke the Treaties. Ain't much else to say." The warlock planted his feet and began focusing his energies.

"I forgot how unimaginative you Council dogs can be. Very well, before we begin do you need to list the charges against me or some other such prattle?" The air crackled around the two men.

"You plan on coming peacefully?" In the distance, the warlock could hear the sound of thunder.

"Not hardly" Toomes face broke into a grin.

"Then I reckon there ain't much point." Power filled the mages. The world around them held its breath, fearful of what was about to be unleashed. It was time for the warlock to end this. "You done talking?"

"Quite." Fire flew from Toomes' right hand, no doubt powered by one of those rings he wore. The warlock was ready for the attack and conjured his shield. Raging red flames broke against smooth, rounded indigo.

With his free hand, the warlock threw lightning towards the corrupt mage. Three of Toomes' rings glowed and a shield of translucent green appeared, protecting the banker from the warlock's wrath.

Toomes' shield was holding while his free hand prepared a counter-attack. The warlock readied his own shield, knowing his survival depended on his ability to seamlessly switch between attack and defense.

The counter never came. Or rather it didn't come in the way the warlock anticipated. Instead of unleashing his gathered energies in a frontal attack, Toomes instead directed them towards the earth beneath him.

"*Golem Adscendi*" At Toomes' command six golems grew from the dirt road they stood upon. The creatures' creation was near instantaneous. When they were fully formed they rushed at the warlock.

"Fuck" The warlock swore. Toomes had outmaneuvered him. If he maintained his shield the golem would surround him and he'd be trapped. If he dropped the shield he'd be an easy target for anything Toomes wanted to throw at him.

One way he was certain to die. The other he was almost certain to die.

From that point of view, it was an easy choice to make.

He dropped his shield and drew his remaining pistol. Firing without aiming, his first shot took the closest golem to his left between the eyes. White flames engulfed it, turning the unloving thing to ash where it stood.

Sensing the golem on his right was too close for him to turn and get a shot off; the warlock instead ducked into the creature's lunging attack, flipping it up and over him.

The warlock came up out of his crouch ready for his next two foes. The closest golem led with a right hook. The sloppy attack was intercepted by the warlock's forearm. His arm twisted around the golem's, putting it in a secure hold. At the peak of the hold, when his gun hand came free again, he tossed his pistol into the air.

Applying a specific kind of pressure, the warlock wrenched the golem's arm from its socket. A human would have screamed, this creature merely blinked.

While the warlock dished out abuse to the golem on his left, his right hand caught his pistol at the apex of its flight and took aim.

Golem number four was six inches out from the barrel of his gun when the warlock pulled the trigger and blew the creature's face off.

The warlock did not wait to witness the tell-tale flames of the creature's doom. Instead, he pivoted and swept the legs out from under the golem who's arm he still held. The golem's back hit the ground hard, but not as hard as the warlock's knee slammed into the beast's trachea.

His pistol moved on instinct towards the golem he'd initially flipped over his back. He fired just as the creature found its feet again. The bullet burrowing into its forehead before exploding out of the back of its skull.

Still, in motion, the warlock rolled clear and came up in a crouch. A ball of lightning struck the golem he'd just been on top of. Toomes was not content to simply stand by and watch his creations do his dirty work.

Two golems remained on their feet. They charged him. The golem on his right led with a haymaker. The warlock waited until the last moment and stepped back. The punch hit nothing but empty air. The golem stumbled forward out of control.

A mass of heat and flame flew from Toomes' hand.

The warlock slipped his non-gun arm around the flailing golem's neck and yanked, positioning the creature's body between himself and the rogue mage's high-temperature attack.

Toomes' fireball struck the golem in the chest. Having no more need of the golem, the warlock put a bullet through its ears. He released his hold; the combustible corpse fell to the dirt.

His fingers danced as he called nature's raw power to himself. Ducking and spinning the warlock avoided a series of rapid-fire punches from the last golem standing. Letting his momentum carry him forward, he got behind the creature and put his pistol to the back of its head. He spoke a single word as he pulled the trigger.

"*Vis*"

The stored energies in his palm exploded from his hand towards Toomes. They traveled with the same velocity as the bullet that was simultaneously exiting the barrel of his pistol.

Toomes conjured a shield in time to survive the warlock's attack. The golem was not so resourceful.

The warlock sprinted towards Toomes, intending to press his advantage. Something grabbed at him, he tripped and fell flat on his face. He looked back and located the origin of his tumble. The final golem, wildly flailing at him with what remained of its broken body.

A quick shot and the final golem succumbed to the white flames. But the damage was done, the golems interference had cost the warlock the initiative.

Toomes unleashed a torrent of fire and lighting at the warlock. The energy smashed against his shield, forcing him to drop his pistol and hold on with both hands.

"Impressive." Toomes' condescension is what irked him more than anything.

The onslaught relented. In the space between the two foes, sparks of energy popped in and out of existence. The warlock and the renegade mage locked eyes.

"It's a shame I have to kill you." Toomes gestured to his overabundance of jewelry.

"The truth is without all this added help I wouldn't have a prayer against you. We both know that. We also know that a great magician is always prepared. You're good, warlock."

Toomes' hands moved.

"But not great."

The warlock conjured his shield. Ready for Toomes' attack.

Or at least he thought he was.

Pain exploded across the warlock's back and limbs. Hundreds of shards of glass flew past him. Dozens more embedded themselves in his flesh.

The warlock screamed.

Toomes did not relent, firing a blast of lightning into the warlock's chest. Electricity charged through his body, exploding every nerve until the whole of him went numb. Black spots filled his eyes. The warlock collapsed to a knee. His screaming stopped.

"I'm going to send your body back to your masters as a warning. They should know that the time of treaties is at an end. That the old ways are returning. They should know their loyal pets cannot protect them." Toomes readied a final blow as he spoke. The warlock's vision began to clear. Desperately he tried to harness enough energy for one more strike.

"Goodbye War_" The dark mage was interrupted by the sound of a pistol firing a single shot.

A look of surprise came over Toomes' face. His hands went to his chest, blood oozed from the newly formed hole they found there. Falling to his knees, Toomes began to cough. More blood trickling out the corners of his mouth. He attempted to speak, but nothing came out except the sound of a man choking on his own fate. Two more shots rang out. Toomes fell to the ground, convulsed, then was still.

Clint Rawls stood behind the body, smoke rising from the barrel of the warlock's discarded pistol.

"He killed my boy." A tear ran down the old man's face.

The warlock stood and wiped the blood from his face with his handkerchief. He walked over to the dead mage's body and removed the assorted jewelry from the corpse, stuffing it into his pockets.

"What- What are you doing?" Rawls asked, still gripping the warlock's pistol tightly in his hand.

"Magic. Can't leave it here." The warlock held out his hand. Rawls looked at it then looked up at the warlock confused.

"My pistol." The warlock gesture to the still smoking gun in the rancher's hand.

Rawls was genuinely surprised to see that he was holding the pistol. He quickly handed it over when prompted.

The warlock holstered the gun and issued a command. "Stay here."

He stepped into the bank. Rummaging through every drawer, cabinet, and safe in the building. Searching for any remaining traces of magic Toomes might have hidden, lest some sorry soul find something they shouldn't and forced him to make another trip to this hellhole of a town. There were a few pieces to be found but none of any significance. He doubted there would be.

When he reemerged a crowd had begun to gather in the streets. He could hear the familiar murmurs on their lips "Did he really…?", "…. Devil's work …", "Did you see…?".

It was time to leave before someone decided that he was the one who could give them answers. The warlock set a deliberate but quick pace towards his horse. Clint Rawls ran after him.

"Is that it then? Is it over?" asked the still trembling rancher.

"It's never over." Climbing into Agni's saddle, the warlock gave the grieving father one last tip of his hat before leaving the town of Oasis far behind him.

Remedial Spellcasting

Six-thirty. In the morning. On a fucking Saturday. Alexandra Maese most assuredly did not want to be where she currently was, topless in the parking lot of the Weatherbrooks' Academy of Magic and Sorcery. So why was her car currently resting on the curb of this most venerable institution? Well, when the headmaster catches you ditching a faculty luncheon to smoke an illicit substance of your own creation, you forfeit your right to a peaceful Saturday in bed and instead are conscripted to chaperon a group of magical hoodlums whose transgressions match or exceed your own.

And why was she topless? Because transmogrifying tap water into a deliciously warm French press at seventy miles per hour was easy, not spilling it when the asshole in front of you slams on their breaks for no fucking reason is impossible. Luckily, she had a spare blouse in her trunk. She kept a change of clothes in there in case she got lucky on a weeknight. After all, she couldn't show up to school wearing the same outfit two days in a row. That's how rumors got started.

The Weatherbrooks' Academy of Magic and Sorcery had been around since sixteen ninety-two when, fearing for their lives, its founders had bailed on Salem, Massachusetts and set up shop here in lower Manhattan. All in all, a pretty bright decision on their part.

Since its founding, the school had held a reputation as one of the premier secondary schools for magical education in North America. Graduate from Weatherbrooks' and a student had their pick of universities; Harvard, Yale, The London School of Magic. It was a serious school for serious students, as the headmaster liked to say, and thus definitely not a place for rumors.

Alex thought the headmaster was a bit of a prick.

A prick who, according to her contract, could fire her without cause at any time. Not for the first time Alex wondered why magicians were so anti-union.

Weatherbrooks' did have one thing going for it in Alex's opinion. Because magical talent was so rare to find and producing powerful mages was the basis of its entire reputation, the school did not hold up its nose when it came to admittance. Fully a third of the student body was there on scholarship.

Of course, another third of the student body was there because their mommy and daddy had bought their way in. Elitism and magic had always gone hand in hand. Bullying was a serious problem at the academy.

Disarming the school's alarms took Alex about five minutes, four minutes to dismantle the wards the night time rent-a-cop had left up and another thirty seconds to remember and then type in the five-digit code that deactivated the motion sensors.

The dull light of dawn diffused itself throughout the building's long hallways, giving everything a gray-tinged hue. Alex made her way towards the teacher's lounge.

It was a room she generally avoided, as it was often full of her fellow teachers gossiping and commiserating about students who were probably much more talented than they would ever be. Also, the coffee was terrible.

Terrible or not, Alex needed the caffeine infusion this morning and she was too lazy to summon up another cup. Conjuring a decent cup of coffee took a lot out of a girl. Ironically, without her morning joe, she just couldn't be bothered to exert the energy to whip up another perfect brew.

Demoralized by her own laziness, she poured the cold, disgusting remains of the previous day's black sludge down the sink and put on a fresh pot. While it heated up, she kept herself busy by reading the notification board.

Apparently, the women's basketball team was playing for the state championship later that day and the school's spell bowl squad had made it to regionals. So, that was nice. Also, it seemed Ms. Callow would be filing a harassment complaint with the school board if her lunch was stolen from the faculty refrigerator one more time.

If she had a better nose for magic, or really just a better nose, she would know that her sandwiches hadn't been taken at all; but had been rendered invisible by a rather mischievous spell. Alex didn't know who was responsible. Whoever it was, she appreciated their sense of humor.

When her coffee was ready she left the lounge behind and swung by her classroom to pick up some ungraded term papers. This way if the term papers were sub-par she could take out her frustrations on the students in detention and vice versa. Her therapist had told her to find a healthy output for her emotions. This system seemed like the perfect way to do that.

Papers in hand, Alex made her way to the designated detention room. A couple of students were already waiting for her when she arrived. One of them she recognized.

"Morning, Ms. Maese." came the greeting from a tall, lanky senior who'd previously taken her Ethical Use of Magic course.

"Good Morning, Mark. And what fresh rebellion brings you to my door today?" Alex asked. The young man smiled sheepishly.

"Mr. Ditzel was incorrectly describing the number of phases Thraxes predicted a population must go through before a mundane society can transition into a magical one. It was irritating, so I corrected him."

"And that scored you Saturday detention?" She queried incredulously.

"That, several off-color remarks about his intelligence, and a circular inquiry as to whether or not his mother had ever been intimate with a hippogriff" Mark admitted without any sign of embarrassment.

"Well, that would certainly do it." Alex nodded.

"I like to get my money's worth." The senior stated with a boyish grin.

"Don't we all." Alex had always pegged Mark as a smart and talented kid with a good head on his shoulders and a bit of a rebellious streak that was typical of being the smartest kid in his class. The rest of the faculty saw him as a miscreant and potential arsonist. Mark was one of the many reasons Alex thought her fellow teachers were idiots.

She turned his attention to the scrawny, pimply youth watching their exchange in stunned silence.

"What about you, kid? What are you in for?" The kid in question nearly peed himself when addressed.

"Nothing Ma'am." He squeaked.

"Ma'am? Really? Jesus. My name is Ms. Maese. I'm thirty-two. 'Ma'am' me again and I'll turn you into a hamster for the day. Got it?"

"Yes, Ma……Ms. Maese." The poor kid looked like his eyes were going to pop out of his head.

"Better. Now come on, out with it, what did you do that landed you in this very specific version of hell?" She asked again while fiddling with her keys to find the right one.

"A bully was trying to stuff me into a locker he had enchanted, I was trying to shut the door with a spell but instead it flew off and hit my arm then my arm hit his face. It was totally an accident. I didn't mean to bust his nose." Alex bit back a chuckle. Mark was grinning ear to ear.

"What's your name?" she asked the young pugilist.

"Felix." The nerdy freshman answered sheepishly.

"Okay Felix, if the story you're telling me is true, it sounds like self-defense. How did that get you a ticket to my door?" Right as she finished asking her question, Alex finally managed to get her key to work. Mark pulled open the heavy fire-proof door for her, but she did not go in right away. Instead, she waited for Felix's answer.

"His buddies lied and said I'd started the whole fight. The headmaster gave us both detention. That's him coming now." With a slight nod of his head, Felix nodded in the direction of his approaching harasser.

Alex turned to peer down the hall and sure enough, Donny Esser was there, his stride almost angry in how it aggressively closed the gap between them. Donny was one of those people whose faces appeared to be in a constant state of self-righteous rage. His bandaged nose only added to his sullen eyes and sneering smile. Alex didn't like to judge her students. Actually, that wasn't true at all, she loved to judge her students. But even if she was the sort of morally superior teacher who refused to judge her students, Donny Esser would still be an exception to that rule. That kid was an asshole.

Donny said nothing as he pushed past them and took a seat inside the classroom, but his glare never left poor Felix. The freshman kept his eyes on the floor and slide into the desk as far away from Donny as he could find. It was the smart thing to do, and the last thing Alex wanted to deal with was a fight breaking out on her watch, but a part of her wished the kid would show a little backbone and stand up for himself.

One by one the other students filed in and took their seats. They were possessed of a general air of apathy and antipathy that made Alex long for the fifth of bourbon tucked away in her filing cabinet.

When the clock struck seven she counted sixteen students in total, twelve boys and four girls. Made sense. It wasn't that boys were more prone to breaking the rules than girls were, it was that they were more prone to getting caught. Teenage girls were unnervingly good at covering their tracks. Alex should know. The number of felonies she committed as a young woman would have been enough to make sure she never saw the light of day. Instead, society put her in charge of molding young minds. Ain't that a bitch.

She took a look around the room, matching names to her attendance sheet. Alex found she recognized quite a few of the students, either from her own classes or from their reputations with other teachers. While the group consisted of a fairly standard mix of campus trouble-makers and ne'er-do-wells, there were a few surprises.

She was, for instance, curious as to what kind of trouble little miss perfect sophomore class president Sabrina Espinoza could have gotten into to land herself in Saturday detention.

According to the academic dean, Ms. Espinoza was the biggest kiss-ass, brown-noser he'd seen since an errant spell had literally turned every senior's nose brown on parent-teacher night a few years back.

There were some other intriguing names on the list as well. Two annoying senior cheerleaders she called Ashley One and Ashley Two (because calling them White Ashley and Black Ashley seemed a little racist, even if it was just in her head). Conspiracy Carlos, the junior who, amongst other things, was convinced magic was the result of aliens tampering with the human genome. And Molly Tanner, the school's resident hippie, moon-child vegan.

A mix of jocks, stoners, and pranksters rounded out the lot.

After she'd taken roll, Alex assumed her best authoritarian teacher voice and laid down the day's ground rules.

"Here's the deal. I don't particularly want to be here anymore than you do, but since we are here I don't think we need to make things any more difficult for ourselves than they have to be. So I'm going to sit at my desk and grade papers and you guys can feel free to do whatever you want to do, so long as you keep the noise level to a minimum." Alex finished then reconsidered her position before tacking on one more addendum. "Also, no spell casting. Last thing I need is to have to explain to the headmaster how one of you managed to inadvertently burn down the school because I wasn't paying attention."

Most of the class nodded vacantly before putting their heads down on their desk.

Most of the class.

Sabrina Espinoza, being oblivious to standard social cues, instead raised her hand emphatically. Alex was beginning to get the feeling this would be a tortuously long day.

"Yes, Ms. Espinoza. You have something to add?" Alex asked when it became apparent the sophomore would not be ignored.

"You're supposed to collect our wands and cellphones." Little miss brown-nose said as she lowered her hand.

"Seriously? You're the kid who reminds the teacher to assign homework aren't you." Alex responded with the well-practiced snark of a teacher who knew right where the line was.

"It's in the handbook." She insisted.

"Okay. You heard her. Wands and cell phones in the basket." There was a paper tray on the desk. Alex handed it to Mark, and the senior went around the room so she didn't have to.

Slowly and with a great deal of grumbling, the students banned possessions were collected and set on her desk. While Alex and Mark received a few glares but by and large what death stares there were seemed to be directed at Ms. Espinoza.

Alex would have put good money up that, come Monday, Sabrina would be the subject of more than a few hexes and jinxes.

For the next hour, Alex buried her head in her papers, with only the occasional upward glance from her grading to check on her delinquents. The time went by easily enough, she only needed to quiet the room down a couple of times.

About a third of the way through her stack, she felt a telltale shiver ran down her spine. A strange buzzing began to build in her ears and the hairs on the back of her neck stood straight up. The symptoms might have been shaken off by a layperson; but to a trained magician they were a flashing, neon sign that pointed to one thing: dark magic

Immediately she rose from her chair looking for the culprit. The sudden movement drew the attention of the students. All eyes turned to her. All, except the eyes of Mr. Donny Esser, which stayed glued firmly to the floor by his feet.

A shimmer of red light flickered, a deafening thunderclap exploded in the classroom.

Alex's hands covered her ears to minimal effect.

"Donny!!" she screamed over the eruption.

She was too late.

A pool of glowing, red energy replaced the linoleum floor beneath the junior.

Donny smiled smugly at his success, or at least he did in the five short seconds before a clawed hand reached up out of the portal and through his chest, creating an empty cavity where the sixteen-year old's heart had been moments before.

As if in slow motion, the boy's body tumbled down into the gateway to hell he had opened.

The some of the students gasped and screamed, while the others remained frozen in shock.

"GET BEHIND ME NOW!" The students did as they were told. The ones whose hearing had recovered did anyway. The rest followed when they saw the others moving.

Wand in hand, Alex concentrated her energy on closing the dimensional portal before the demon could fully emerge.

"SHIT! SHIT! FUCK! SHIT!" One of the secrets about magic: Incantations were less about the phrases used and more about the intention behind them. Having been raised an army brat, Alex had a soldier's knack for invective when faced with the chaos of combat. That didn't keep her from being an effective battle mage. Quite the contrary in fact.

Blue energy exploded out of her wand. It merged with the red pool of Donny's portal and the two energies quickly began to collapse in upon each other.

Somehow Alex knew it wouldn't be fast enough.

A dark shape shot out of the portal moments before it closed. Alex's eyes followed it. They did not like what they found.

Clinging to the ceiling was the creature that killed Donny, blood still dripping from its claws. Its eight red eyes were arranged in two vertical rows. Four crab-like legs skittered beneath it. Keeping its small body and massive head in balance. The beast had two muscular arms that ended in clawed three-fingered hands. It took a long, slow lick of its fingers before addressing them.

"Hello, Children. It will be my pleasure to eat you." It spoke in a gravelly bass. The demon smiled showing row after row of sharp teeth. Taken as a whole, the demon was really quite intimidating. Even by demon standards.

Alex was fairly confident they were fucked.

Still no point in rolling over and giving up. Alex had things to live for. Fried chicken taco shells. Johnny Walker Blue. Finding and seducing one of her doppelgangers from a parallel universe. And fuck this demon asshole if he thought she was just going to up and die before she found out who won this season of The Bachelorette.

Alex positioned herself between the creature and her students and issued the hell beast an ultimatum.

"Listen, dickweed. The magician who summoned you is dead. You have no business on this world. Leave now, peacefully, or else I'm gonna have to kick your ass back to whatever hell dimension you came from." The threat would have been more effective if Alex's voice didn't give off the idea she was about to pee herself.

The demon was unimpressed.

"Pathetic human, do you really believe you can stand against one of the Fallen? Who do you think you are?" It growled.

The sheer pretentiousness of the demon pissed off Alex enough to make her forget about her fear and put some steel back in her voice.

"I'm an underpaid, overworked sorceress with a big-ass wand and a lengthy history of anger management issues. You really want to test me, asshole?"

The demon blanched for a moment. Its eight eyes narrowed.

Alex could hear her heart beating in her chest. For a moment she could almost let herself believe the demon wasn't going to try and kill them all.

Then the creature opened up its mouth and let out a glass-shattering scream.

"RUN CHILDREN! RUN!" Alex shouted as the demon leaped towards her. *"CUSTODIO!"*

Once again a stream of blue energy shot out of her wand. This time the beam was less concentrated. Instead of flowing to a single point, it spread out. Forming a translucent but solid wall separating the demon from her and her fleeing students.

The demon struck the shield head first. The creature raged, pounding its clawed hands against the magical impediment. It buckled, but held firm.

In order to maintain the shield, she had to keep pouring energy into it. A spell of this magnitude was draining, and her magical batteries were depleting quickly.

She needed to make a move, now, before she emptied her tank.

While her right hand continued to pour energy into her hastily constructed translucent barrier, her left hand, unencumbered by a wand, began to gather together its own energies.

Strictly speaking, magicians didn't actually need wands to unleash their powers. Harness them and focus them yes, absolutely. Alex wouldn't be able to light a candle without her wand. But if all you wanted to do was unleash some serious chaos, raw magical energy would do just fine on its own.

The demon's howl became an unholy laugh as Alex's shield began to flicker and fade, unable to maintain itself under the creature's relentless assault.

"You only delay the inevitable human. It won't be long now. I think I will eat the younglings first, you can listen to their screams as I gnaw at their flesh." The demon teased.

"You want some? Get some!" She shouted in retort. The shield broke. Alex was ready.

A ball of energy flew from her hand, breaking apart into a thousand tinier balls like scattershot from a shotgun. Lightning filled the air. Desks and chairs began to float before exploding into a million shards of wood and steel. Pillars of fire and ice spontaneously appeared and disappeared, setting off the fire sprinklers and impaling those of the flying desks that had yet to combust on their own.

The beast threw its clawed hands up to shield its eyes.

Alex made a break for the door.

Behind her, the demon had recovered and begun to move.

The mirror by the door let her watch her doom race toward her, even as she rushed toward her escape.

With unnatural agility, the demon wove its way through the chaos. Closing in with every step. She could feel its presence in her bones. Its hot breath on her neck.

A few more steps and she'd be in the hall.

A few more steps and she'd be dead.

She cleared the threshold. With a flick of her wrist, Alex used her wand to slam the reinforced fire door in the beast's face.

It plowed right through, taking out the door and a good chunk of the wall with it.

The students stood at the end of the hall.

Some staring.

Some screaming.

None of them moving.

"DON'T JUST STAND THERE!!! RUN!!! GET TO THE TEACHERS LOUNGE!!!" Alex screamed.

She sprinted towards them, her feet barely touching the linoleum tile beneath her before they lifted off again.

Alex snuck a peek over her shoulder. The demon had shaken off its dramatic classroom exit and was now skittering after her.

Desperately she flicked her wand left and right behind her, ripping lockers off the walls as she passed them.

She'd hoped she'd get lucky and one would smack the eight-eyed bastard chasing her in his smug demon face.

But today was not a lucky kind of a day.

The lockers barely managed to slow her pursuer down. Instead, it leaped deftly from obstacle to obstacle.

She turned the corner.

Four of her male students were there waiting for her.

Mark, Carlos, and the two jock boys. Four half-trained magicians with a pair of wands between them. "We got you, Ms. Maese." One of the jocks, Jake, said in an attempt to reassure her.

Testosterone-fueled teenage idiots full of indoctrinated machismo.

It was this kind of dumbass bullshit that was going to them all killed.

If she had time to think of a plan, or if she hadn't just blown most of her magical wad back in the classroom, they might have stood a chance. Maybe.

But even with a big gulp's worth of adrenaline coursing through her system, she was coming to the end of her reserves. And in the precious half-second, it took Alex to stop her momentum and turn back towards the boys their time ran out.

The beast didn't round the corner as Alex had. Instead, it lunged forward, pivoted its body, and kicked; using the far wall to change its vector.

Jake was closest to the demon and so Jake died first. Blood spraying from his throat as the demon's claws found flesh.

On instinct, the boy's hands grasped at his neck. His dying mind forgetting that those hands were charged with unfocused magical energies. As soon as Jake's palm touched his throat his head exploded in a ball of white flame.

Charred pieces of brain and skull painted the walls.

The demon paused. Its eight red eyes locked on to Alex, boring a hole into her soul. Its mouth twisted into a sickening grin.

Alex wanted to be ill. There was a look of abject horror on her face and this bastard was savoring it. Taking it in like he was smelling the goddamned roses.

They stood like that for a second, frozen in a gory tableau.

The demon pounced, launching itself straight at Carlos.

Alex was ready.

A wave of invisible energy burst from her wand, striking Carlos and pushing him out of the way.

The demon's claws, looking to occupy the space where Carlos' heart had been, instead found only empty air.

"You Fucker! You killed Jake!" The other jock, CJ, screamed, running toward the beast as he did.

"Incendia!" The boy gestured with his wand and a stream of fire flew from the tip.

In one smooth motion, the demon dodged to its left then lunged forward. Its claws went right through CJ's stomach to the other side. Blood trickled out the corners of the boy's mouth as his intestines unfurled themselves on the linoleum floor.

Again, the beast locked eyes on Alex. But this time it did not smile. No, this time its mouth did something much more terrible.

It began to eat CJ while the boy was still alive.

Fury and horror welled up inside Alex. Vomit rose in her throat, but she had herself swallow it back down. Mark stood next to her, all color gone from his face.

Blood spurted everywhere. CJ's eyes were frozen in terror and pain as the last light left his eyes.

The demon was in a frenzy now. Its attention completely focused on its feast of flesh.

If they were going to do something it needed to be now.

"Mark, did you see what I did before, to Carlos?" The senior nodded weakly in affirmation, transfixed by the slaughter before him.

"Do you know that spell?" No response.

"MARK!! DO YOU KNOW THE SPELL?!?" She shook him until she broke through his daze.

"Yeah. Yeah, I know it." he finally responded.

"Get behind us." She pulled Carlos to his feet. The stunned sophomore was shaking but let himself be guided.

"When I say run, you run." She instructed him.

The beast had almost finished with its meal. Their window to act was closing.

"Together on three." She didn't wait for Mark to get his wand up before she began her count.

"One" Alex could feel the energy draining from her, she was like a car with an empty gas gauge trying to eke out the last few miles to the gas station.

"Two" A white ball of energy began to glow at the end of each of their wands. Pulsing in time with the beating of their hearts. Alex poured everything she had into that tiny white ball.

"*Three!*" Twin blasts of invisible force struck the demon central mass, sending the bastard flying through the air and down the hallway a good forty feet.

"Run!" She screamed.

This time when she turned she did not look back. There was no point. She wouldn't have been able to play a kid's birthday party with the magic she had left inside her.

The boys long, lanky legs kept them in front of Alex. If the demon was going to catch someone it was going to be her. And if it did it would find her a defenseless, easy kill.

Her legs pumped and for the thousandth time, she gave thanks that she'd worn flats today instead of heels.

At the end of the hall, she could see the rest of the students urging them forward.

"Inside! Now!" she shouted.

Carlos reached the door first, then Mark followed.

Alex had only a few steps to go. And she had no idea how close the demon was to tackling her and slicing her open.

One more step and she was there.

She dove through the doorway and Mark slammed it shut behind her.

"Now what do we do?" Mark asked.

All eyes were on Alex as she pushed herself to her feet. She was as scared as any of them. The difference was she was an adult and they were still just kids. Her kids. The first responsibility of any teacher was to keep your students alive. And she couldn't do that if she lost her head.

Alex allowed herself one deep breath. Then, in a clear, calm voice gave them their instructions.

"Barricade the door. Boys grab the couches, the cabinets, anything that's not nailed down and place it against those two doors." She barked, pointing to the entrances at either end of the room.

"Girls I need you to shut all the blinds and seal the air vents. Use the duct tape from the supply cabinet" Alex continued.

Most of the students did as they were instructed. A few were too shell-shocked to move.

"Somewhere around here is…" Frantically she ripped bulletin boards and inspirational cat posters off the walls. "Found it!" she shouted triumphantly.

Alex slammed her fist down against a big grey button with an ancient rune etched into it. The walls shimmered blue then returned to normal.

"What was that?" the question came from the freshman Felix.

"Every room in the school is equipped with a secret security ward. I just activated this one." They all looked at her with that stupid teenage look that said they had no clue what she was talking about, forcing her to explain what she didn't have time to explain. "Basically, I just turned the teachers' lounge into a magical panic room. It will give us the time we need to figure out a plan, but right now I need you to work."

The students did just that. While they were distracted Alex did a head count.

"Eleven." She'd started with sixteen. The demon had killed CJ, Jake, and Donny in front of her. That should leave her with thirteen. She was missing two.

"Where did those two stoner boys go?" Alex asked the group.

"Caleb and Bryce? When we got here they just kept running. They're still out there somewhere." Molly answered.

"We have to go after them." Mark urged her.

"There's no point. If they're not dead already they will be soon. Same with us if we go out on some half-cocked rescue mission." The children blanched at Alex's coldhearted assessment.

"We can't just leave them. You saw what that thing will do to them." Carlos puked at Mark's reminder of the carnage they'd just witnessed.

"Yes, I did. And you saw that I threw everything I had at it and it just kept coming. So, your plan is to wander out there with no defenses and no idea where it or they might be. I'm sorry but there is nothing we can do for them. Right now, my focus is on saving the lives of the people in this room." Alex's voice picked up steam as she spoke. By the time she was finished, she was shouting. Tears ran down the cheeks of most of the students.

Alex sat down in one of the rooms cheap plastic chairs. "Mark, can you grab me some water please?"

The senior did as she asked. Filling a blue coffee mug with water from the faucet and putting it in her outstretched hand.

"Anybody else?" He asked.

A few of the kids raised their hand or nodded numbly. Mark got them each a cup and then poured himself one. First rule of magic: remember to hydrate.

Alex waited until Mark was done, then she took a deep breath and tried again to explain their situation.

"I need you all to stay calm and listen to me carefully. I told you the school has certain protocols in place in case of emergencies. The ward on this room is just one of them. In the event of an interdimensional incursion, the school is put on a lockdown and a self-destruct timer is initiated." Alex's information sent a wave of panic through the students. They started talking all at once.

"Well, we're not going to use those right?" Mark asked

"Somebody's going to come and save us. They have to." Felix declared.

"Assholes. Fucking assholes covering their own asses." Carlos swore.

"We just have to shut them off. That's all." Sabrina asserted nervously.

"FOCUS" Alex stated forcefully, bringing the cacophony to a halt. "The measures are automatic. They were activated the second the portal opened, and that thing came through."

"What kind of asshole thought that up?" Carlos asked with righteous indignation.

"You go to school with almost a thousand hormone-driven, teenage wizards. Did you really think the school board wouldn't have contingencies in place?" Alex snapped.

Again she forced herself to modulate her tone before continuing.

"We have two options. Either we figure out a way to kill that thing, thus ending the incursion and the lockdown, or we find a way out of this magically-shielded building that was specifically designed not to allow any way out." As she spoke Alex saw her students' eyes gloss over with fear. She could tell that the reality of their situation wasn't registering with them but she wasn't sure how to make it any clearer without shouting 'we are all going to die' which would have the net effect of helping absolutely no one.

"Forget fighting that thing we have to get out of here." Sabrina was quite a bit ruder now that her life was in danger. Her terror would have been more enjoyable if Alex didn't share it.

"You're not hearing me. There is no way out. Not while that monster is on the loose. Not while….." Alex trailed off, distracted by something in Sabrina's eyes.

She could have sworn they'd just flashed red.

Mark said something but Alex missed it.

"I'm sorry?" she asked

"How long do we have left?" he repeated

"The timer is set for an hour." Alex looked at her watch. "I'd say that gives us about forty-five minutes."

"And then?" Carlos prodded.

"And then the magical equivalent of a tactical nuke goes off. We, along with every molecule of matter in this building, will cease to be." This revelation silenced the room. They sat there, stunned, absorbing the information.

"Forty-five minutes?" Mark asked.

"Yes, give or take." Alex said, keeping her voice calm.

"Then we'd better get to work. Tell us what to do."

The first thing to do was take an inventory of their supplies. Mark had managed to grab four wands from her desk during their frantic escape. One of which was out in the hallway lying next to CJ's corpse. They found another two spares in the supply closet. Added to Alex's wand that gave them six wands for twelve of them. They also found a stash of Mr. Pruett's special rejuvenation juice, which was as polite a euphemism as Alex could come up with when the students asked about it.

She assigned the wands to the upperclassmen and assigned each an underclassmen buddy. Since there was an odd number of students she paired herself with Felix.

"The Russians did this during World War II, if your partner falls you pick up their wand and keep fighting. Understood?" She explained as she partnered them off.

The group mumbled an affirmative. It was hard to tell which group looked more dispirited the upperclassmen who would be dead in this scenario or the freshman and the sophomores who would be forced to pry wands free from their classmates cold, dead hands.

"Good. Now I've given each of you a vial of Mr. Pruett's concoction. It will act as sort of an artificial booster. If you feel your magical energies running down, this will give you a supercharge. But be careful once it only works for a little bit and when it's gone, it's gone. You won't be able to summon up a spark for at least eight hours." The students, especially the girls, eyed the vials with a mixture of disgust and horror.

"Ms. Maese, due respect, but none of this is going to help us against that thing. We need a plan." Mark was right. Alex had been stalling. Hoping that some brilliant idea would come to her and she'd suddenly know how to fight the beast pounding on their door. But even if every one of the half-trained wizards in this room had been a hardened battle mage, she still would have no idea what to do next. She'd thrown every bit of magic she had at that thing and had barely knocked it off its feet.

"I think I have an idea." Carlos spoke up, absurdly raising his hand as if they were in class discussing the distinction between a curse and a hex.

"Oh, Conspiracy Carlos has an idea. This ought to be good." Ashley One said, rolling her eyes in the way only a teenage girl can manage.

"Maybe we are all being experimented on by a secret corporate cabal and all of this is really in our heads?" Ashley Two chimed in, the two girls giggling derisively.

Carlos wilted and fell silent.

Alex was pissed. They didn't have time for this penny ante, high school bullshit.

Every teacher has a voice they use when they want their students to know they're not fucking around. That voice was doubly effective when the person using it had the ability to turn you into a toad.

"Open your mouths again and I'll take away your wands. Do you understand me?" Alex warned in her "don't fuck with me" voice. For emphasis, she also threw in her "don't fuck with me" look which was as, if not more, intimidating than her "don't fuck with me" voice.

"Yes, Ms. Maese." The girls responded in unison.

Alex held her glare an extra second for emphasis before breaking her stare and turning her attention back to Carlos. "Go ahead, Carlos. What's your idea?"

"Well back when the school first started the school board and the headmaster still performed blood rites. They would sacrifice students to supercharge their own magic." Carlos began.

Alex was starting to regret her decision to indulge him. Still, she let him continue.

"In order to do that, they needed a way to get in and out of the school undetected. They built a secret passageway from the headmaster's office to the outside. I'd bet that its exempt from the school's lockdown procedure." When Carlos finished, there was a noticeable amount of grumbling amongst the students.

Alex couldn't blame them. Carlos was known to be a little off his rocker and seventeenth-century blood rites and secret passageways didn't exactly inspire confidence. Alex tried to let him down gently.

"Thank you, Carlos, for that information. But that's a big chance to take on an unconfirmed rumor. Let's see if we can't come up with a plan that's a bit more grounded in what we know for sure." She said trying to be nice, but very much regretting going to bat for the young man.

"I think Carlos is right." The voice was quiet and belonged to a rather unexpected source.

"Felix?" Alex was shocked that the freshman had spoken and doubly so that he seemed to be backing up Carlos' ridiculous theory. All eyes turned to Felix as he explained.

"Back during winter break my dad volunteered us to redo the school's IT systems. We networked the school office. When we tried to run fiber into the headmaster's office he seemed extremely nervous. I started to move around some furniture, he freaked out. Kicking us out as fast as he could while making some excuses about being a Luddite and it not really being worth our time to worry about his office." Felix looked around nervously unsure if he had just discovered the meaning of life or had simply shit his own bed. For her part, Alex wasn't completely sure what to make of the information either. She'd been hoping the freshman was going to have much more for her to go on.

"That's still not proof of a secret passageway." Alex voiced her skepticism.

"True. But it's the best chance we've got." Mark chimed in.

The kid was right. What did they have to lose? Stay here and they were going to end up demon food or magical craters. If the whole secret tunnel thing turned out to be bullshit at least they died trying to do something. Even a preposterous conspiracy theory is better than nothing at all. Alex had made her decision.

"All right. That's our move then. Boys, I hope your right" she announced to the group.

Every one of the students faces reacted differently to the decision. Fear, skepticism, relief, hope. Each of these could be inferred from the expressions in the room. With the notable exception of one particular student.

Sabrina's face was completely blank. The sophomore's eyes were glowing an eerie red, just as they had before, only this time it wasn't a momentary flash.

Sabrina's mouth opened but it was not her that began to speak.

"I was hoping one of you delicious fleshbags would show me a way out of here and now you have. I only wish you were going to live long enough to see your world run red with blood." The demon's deep, gravelly voice emanating from the sophomore's tiny body.

The Ashleys, who were standing closest to the now, apparently, demon-possessed Sabrina, began to scream.

A blunt pair of scissors forcefully stabbed into her jugular cut short Ashley Number One's wailing rather abruptly.

Whereas a wand through the eye briefly increased the volume of Ashley Two's lamentations before she too fell silent.

Alex raised her wand to defend herself and the children, but her reactions were too slow.

The demon-Sabrina hybrid lunged forward, knocking Alex's wand out of her hand and seizing her by the neck.

Supernaturally strong fingers tightened around Alex's throat, making it impossible for her to breath and raising her up off the ground. She struggled, kicking her legs and slamming her fists down against Sabrina's wrists, but it was to no avail. Her vision began to blur.

Alex gave up on trying to break Sabrina's grip at the wrist and instead hauled back and slugged her across the face. The blow barely registered. Again, Alex drew back and slammed her fist into her student's face. But even as blood flowed from her nose, the sophomore did not let go.

"*Incendia!*" One of the freshmen boys shouted. A thin line of fire sputtered from his wand. It struck Sabrina in the chest but managed to do little more than singe her shirt.

With seemingly no effort, the demon-possessed Sabrina threw Alex across the room. Alex collided with the bulletin board and fell in a slump to the floor.

Sabrina lunged at the freshman boy.

Again, he shouted *"Incendia!"* This time a solid spout of flame emerged from his wand.

Sabrina slid past the stream and grabbed hold of the boy's wand arm, directing it towards one of the other boys.

The other boy howled, his flesh consumed by unnatural fire.

As that boy burned alive, demon Sabrina ripped the first boy's wand arm from his body.

Arterial blood sprayed through the air.

Sabrina was not finished. In a wide arc, she swung the freshman boy's own severed limb at him, striking him across the face. The boy spun around at the force of it.

He tripped and fell forward, impaling his head on one of the room's rows of coat racks.

His body stopped twitching at about the same time the burning boy stopped screaming.

Wandless, concussed, and dizzy from oxygen deprivation, Alex could only watch as two more of her students met their brutal ends.

Mark was not so helpless. The senior stepped forward, wand raised and shouted something Alex's ringing ears couldn't quite decipher.

His wand glowed. A fraction of a second later Sabrina was lifted off her feet by an invisible blow. She was only down for a moment, recovering too quickly for Mark to press his advantage.

Sabrina snarled at them like a rabid animal. On all fours, she rushed forward, eyes still glowing red. Savagely she pulled the scissors free from the still bleeding jugular of her classmate as she passed.

It was only at the last moment it became clear that Molly, not Mark, was Sabrina's next target. She charged forward, scissors ready to pierce poor Molly's heart. Desperately Mark pushed Molly out of the way. Grabbing Sabrina's hands and attempting to hold her at bay.

Mark's hand, wet with blood, slipped. Sabrina brought the scissors down with a powerful stab. Inches from Mark's heart, she suddenly stopped.

In her moment of hesitation, Molly struck.

"*Frigia!*"

Sabrina's eyes rolled back into her head. Her body went limp and she fell to the floor. Unconscious and immobile.

"I don't get it, she could have killed me, but she didn't." Mark was shaking. An unconscious Sabrina lay at his feet, her hands still clutching the pair of bloody scissors.

"Not she, it. That wasn't Sabrina, it was the demon possessing Sabrina." Alex said, climbing to her feet. "And it didn't kill you for the same reason it didn't kill me."

"And that is?" wearily Mark stepped around the unconscious sophomore. His eyes never stopped watching her.

"The demon wants to escape. You notice it didn't kill anyone who had knowledge of the door." The thought didn't occur to Alex until she said it out loud, but it made perfect sense.

"I don't know anything about the door." Mark objected.

"No, but you're the most likely to take over as leader if something happens to me. Without the two of us, this group becomes unpredictable." Shell-shocked and rudderless would have been more accurate descriptors, but she wanted to be tactful. Teenager's feelings tended to bruise easily.

"Then why attack at all?" Carlos asked.

"To thin the herd. Make it easier to kill us once we opened the door for it." Molly answered, her wand hand still raised, expecting more trouble. Alex didn't add *and because it was having fun with us.*

"My guess is if Molly wouldn't have stopped it, it would have stopped itself after another kill or two." Alex felt guilty for being so detached. But she didn't know how else to be. If she gave into her feelings now they were all as good as dead.

The corpses of four of her students were scattered about the room. Their various individual pools of blood were beginning to meet in the center of the floor. Felix was being violently ill in one of the trash bins. The rest of the survivors looked like they might join him at any moment.

But, if they lived through this, there would be time to grieve later. Right now, if she wanted to get that chance she needed to remain dispassionate.

She owed it to her students to keep it together.

"We shouldn't go for the door." Mark said abruptly.

"We're going for the door." Alex countered calmly.

"We don't even know if the door exists. And even if it does exist what if that thing does get out. How many people will it kill before someone finally stops it? If we stay here at least we know it can't hurt anyone else." Mark stated his case coolly and rationally. His eyes still didn't leave Sabrina and the pair of scissors.

"I'm not staying here. Not now, not with them." Molly said, voice trembling, hand pointing the bodies on the floor.

"Listen to me. We have a chance at a way out and we're going to take it. Yes, it's a risk. But it's a risk I'm willing to take. You children are my responsibility and I am getting you out of here. Demon or no demon." Alex needed them to believe in her.

"But-" Mark started to respond but she cut him off.

"Mark that's the end of the discussion. I'm the adult, I make the decisions. And if it goes sideways that's on me as well. Understood?" Alex spoke gently but firmly.

"Yes, Ms. Maese." Mark acquiesced.

"Okay." Alex was relieved Mark didn't continue to argue his point. It was a good one, but Alex couldn't just sit there and condemn these children to death. Not if there was a chance they could get out alive.

That meant all the children, and unfortunately, one of them was now unconscious and would be for quite a while. It would be too long to wait for her to wake up. So they were going to have to carry her.

Alex instructed the two remaining boys to pick her up. And, after noticing the poor girl's shirt was ripped-slash-burnt in half a dozen places and her bra was showing, she felt the need to warn them that if they used this opportunity to cop a feel she would personally feed them both to the demon.

Their looks of terror satisfied her that they wouldn't try any funny business.

"Mark, you remember where the headmaster's office is?" Alex asked the senior, knowing full well the boy had spent half his high school career being sent to that office.

"Yeah, I think I remember." Mark replied, with a boyish grin. It was the first-time Alex had seen him smile since this whole nightmare had begun.

"Good. You take the lead and I'll guard the rear. Go slow and be careful." She instructed him.

The group moved as one unit, in a circular formation with Sabrina and the two boys carrying her in the center.

While the teacher's lounge was towards the back of the school's ground floor and a bit out of the way, the headmaster's office was connected to the school's main office which was located at the school's main entrance.

If you've ever worked at a school, this geography makes perfect sense. If you haven't, you're probably one of the reasons so many schools prefer to use such a floor plan.

On a normal day, it wouldn't take more than a few minutes to walk from one to the other, moving as they were it took them fifteen.

But just as Alex had suspected they would, they managed to reach their destination without incident.

The trouble would start when they found the door. If they found the door.

Alex instructed Carlos and Felix to take the rest of the group and search the headmaster's office while she and Mark took up defensive positions in the outer office.

Nervous energy filled her. She could hear the students ransacking the headmaster's office. Every second they failed to find the secret door her anxiety increased.

She could hear the sound of skittering legs against linoleum in the hallway. She knew the demon was out there, biding its time, waiting for them to open the door so it could attack and escape.

"What's taking so long?" she shouted behind her, never taking her eyes off the front doorway.

"We've taken everything off the walls" Carlos shouted back "We can't find it."

"Maybe it's not on a wall." Felix said. "Help me move this desk."

There was some grunting and the shuffling of feet, followed by a large thud then nothing.

"We found it." Felix shouted.

In the moments after Felix's words, three things happened almost simultaneously. Alex and Mark raised their wands and put an invisible wall between themselves and the rest of the office, the demon crashed through the office's front doors with a primal scream, and Alex poured five vials worth of Mr. Pruitt's special concoction down her throat.

"Go! Now!" Alex instructed the students.

Power coursed through her, all her weariness faded away. Aside from one very experimental night in college, she'd never felt anything like this. Her magical batteries were now supercharged.

Which was good because she doubted her shield would have held underneath the Demon's brutal assault without the extra juice she was pouring into it.

Suddenly the beast stopped, its arms dropped to its sides and all eight of its red eyes went dark.

"Ms. Maese!" Molly needn't have bothered. Alex knew what was coming even before she shouted her warning.

That anticipation bought her a precious few fractions of a second that may have saved her life. Alex turned to her left. Mark was there, running towards her with his eyes glowing red.

His hands reached for her throat. Alex grabbed hold of his wrists before he could succeed in strangling her, but she was forced to drop her wand and thus the shield.

Before, when the demon had possessed Sabrina, Alex hadn't understood what she was up against. Now she had data. The demon could only possess them one at a time, or they would all be in its thrall right now. And while a possessed person gained supernatural strength and speed, they didn't have access to their magic. What's more, their bodies may have been enhanced, but the demon still fought like it was in its own body when it controlled them. Making their attacks wild but predictable.

Alex's mother had been one of the best combat mages the United States

Army had ever seen, and if there was one thing the Lieutenant Colonel had taught her daughter it was that depending on your magic in combat was a good way to get yourself killed. It was why she had insisted Alex take self-defense classes as a kid and why Alex still took a kickboxing class at the local YMCA now that she was an adult. All of these skills became of use to her over the next sixty seconds.

First, she let Mark's momentum do the work for her, falling backward even as his demon-possessed body lunged forward. She kicked her leg into his gut and pushed, flipping Mark over her head and creating a bit of room for her to work with.

They both recovered into a crouch, with about ten feet of distance between them.

The demon-controlled Mark spoke in the same disconcerting voice demon-controlled Sabrina had used before.

"Why do you bother. You know you can't win. Make it easy on yourself and just give up. I promise I'll eat you fast. You'll hardly even scream." It cackled at her.

Alex responded to the demon's taunts with a burst of magical energies. Mark dodged them easily and the destructive forces instead turned the attendance secretary's desk into a crater.

That had been Alex's intention from the start. The demon's dodge put Mark's face on a collision course with Alex's foot as she spun and delivered a roundhouse kick right to the possessed senior's face.

Mark landed a few feet away. Alex prepared herself for another attack. She hated fighting one of her own, especially knowing he wasn't in control of his own actions. But every second they fought was another second she bought for the other children to escape.

The demon must have had the same thought because instead of attacking again it merely bent down to pick up something by Mark's feet. It was her wand.

Mark took the wand in his hand and, with only the slightest bit of pressure from his thumb, snapped it in two.

The glow in his eyes faded. Confusion replaced it.

"Ms. Maese?" his voice was normal, he was Mark again.

Alex fired off a blast of directed kinetic energy at the senior anyway.

The invisible blow struck him and pushed him backward. Right as the demon, returned to his own body, struck the air where Mark had just been.

But Alex was unaccustomed to casting spells with this much juice flowing through her and without her wand she couldn't regulate herself properly. Instead of merely pushing Mark out of the way, she sent him flying across the room, through the headmaster's door and careening into the far wall of the headmaster's office.

"Nice work Teach. That's okay. You're the one I really wanted to kill." The demon intoned gleefully.

"Funny I feel the same way about you." A blade of solid white energy emerged from Alex's right hand. It crackled with heat and power.

The two foes charged at each other, knowing this time that only one of them would walk away.

The demon pulled back its claws, ready to slice Alex to pieces. Instead, Alex went low, dropping to her knees and spinning around. Her blade sweeping towards the demon's legs.

Alex's attack found only air. The beast leaped clear, avoiding her blade. Which was fine by Alex, her attack had done its job, forcing the beast into the air where it couldn't dodge her next attack.

With her left hand, Alex made a pulling motion. The exterior wall of the headmaster's office came free and flew forward to meet the airborne demon at a ferocious speed.

Brick and mortar collided with demon flesh and fractured into a thousand pieces. Alex would have rather it was the beast's bones that had shattered. There was no time to linger on that thought.

The demon did its own remodeling, tearing up a chunk of floor and hurling it in Alex's direction. A blast of magical energy turned it to dust.

Using the dust cloud as cover, Alex pressed her attack.

Magical sword battled razor-sharp claws, producing smoke and sizzling flesh whenever the two touched.

Spin, slash, parry.

Spin, slash, parry.

The two combatants danced with deadly choreography.

Alex bled from a trio of cuts along her abdomen, while the demon's right shoulder smoked from the searing bite of her mystic blade.

Twice Alex attempted to finish the fight with a magical strike from her non-blade hand, but they were too close, and the demon was too quick for her blasts to hit anything but air.

Slowly but steadily she was losing ground. Defending rather than attacking, being forced back a half step at a time.

"Ms. Maese" Carlos shouted from somewhere behind her. "Everyone else is out but I can't lift Mark on my own."

Sweat trickled down Alex's forehead, partly from the heat of her own blade and partly from exertion. She countered the demon's stabbing claws and stepped back, creating a momentary lull in combat.

"Just go! I'll get Mark." She instructed the junior.

The Demon slashed down, Alex brought her blade up, and their dance began again.

Alex didn't know just how long she could keep this up. There were too many clocks counting down against her. The school imploding, Mr. Pruitt's special juice wearing off, or her luck could just plain run out.

She'd given Carlos enough time to get clear, it was time to grab Mark and make a run for it.

Alex stopped funneling power into her blade and it disappeared. The move surprised the demon. Expecting to meet the blade's resistance, the bastard was thrown off balance. Alex used the opening to focus her energies. Her hands came together and she unloaded, striking the beast with enough kinetic force to fell an elephant.

The demon was sent careening backward, like a bullet from a gun, and didn't stop till it had been blasted through the far wall and into the adjoining classroom.

Alex ran into the headmaster's office to where Mark still lay unmoving. With one hand, she projected a barrier between them and the demon, with the other hand she checked for Mark's pulse.

When she found it a torrent of relief flooded over her. Alex began to shake Mark. Violent jolts began to run down her arm, letting her now the beast was attacking her shied.

"Mark. I need you to wake up now." She lightly slapped his face. "Come on Mark. It's time to go. You've got to wake up for me."

She got no response. Alex placed a hand on his chest and focused. Energy poured through her and into him. Slowly, groggily, his eyes began to open. Like he was waking from a long slumber.

That last was a spell too far for Alex. Her supercharge was almost gone. In another minute, she'd be completely useless.

Her barrier went first. Unable to keep pouring power into it, Alex's shield shattered underneath the demon's mighty blows.

She turned to face the beast. Putting herself between it and the door. It skittered towards her with all its unnatural speed, it's glowing red eyes hellbent on eviscerating her and escaping into the world.

A giant ball of fire flew from Alex right palm, followed by a ball of lightning from her left hand, then a second ball of fire from her right. Each attack weaker than the one that came before.

It didn't matter.

Alex missed.

All three of her attacks missed.

The demon's claws came straight for her. There was no time to move out of the way, no time to summon up enough energy for another attack.

Suddenly Mark was there, standing between her and the demon.

Shock filled his eyes. He looked down. Alex's eyes followed his. The Demon's claws were sticking through his chest. Mark looked back up at her. He flashed his boyish grin one last time.

"Go." He said in a whisper, before giving Alex a shove.

She stumbled backward, through the open trapdoor.

"No!" she screamed. Her hands reached out for Mark.

The demon pulled his claws free. Mark dropped to his knees. Blood soaked his shirt. His grin was gone. As the demon moved past him Alex could see Mark mouthing something.

His wand glowed, the trapdoor slammed shut, and Alex fell.

She could feel gravity take hold of her, pulling her towards the inevitable. But the inevitable was not yet here and she had one thing left to do before it arrived.

Alex summoned all her remaining power. The temperature around her dropped drastically. Her hands glowed a translucent blue. With one last effort, she raised her palms and let loose.

Twin beams of energy burst towards the door.

A thin sheet of ice began to form. Spreading and hardening until it covered the entire ceiling and measured three feet thick.

Alex exhaled. There wasn't enough time for the demon to break through that before the school imploded. It was over.

But she'd been falling too long. When she hit bottom, she would die and there was nothing she could do about it.

She closed her eyes and prepared for the end.

A current of air rose to meet her, slowing her speed and arresting her descent.

The seemingly sentient wind pushed her upright and her feet touched down softly on the dirt floor. Carlos and Molly were there, the glowing tips of their wands fading back to normal.

"Where's Mark?" Molly asked.

"He's not coming." Alex said simply, her voice colder than intended. "We need to move. I don't know what will happen to this tunnel once the school implodes."

The two juniors nodded numbly. Together the three of them jogged the length of the passage. After a hundred yards or so they came to a rope ladder. It led up to a manhole cover at the edge of the school parking lot.

Felix and the rest of the surviving students were there when they exited, along with hundreds of emergency personnel, faculty, and concerned parents. The second they'd gone into lock-down the police would have been notified along with the headmaster and the school board president.

A paramedic rushed to her side, placing a blanket around her shoulders. He tried to steer her towards an ambulance, but she pushed him away.

Her eyes were transfixed on the school.

In a haze, she walked towards it. Voices shouted at her, asking her questions she didn't know yet how to answer.

She wondered if she had been wrong. Maybe Mark was still alive. Maybe there was more time than she thought. Maybe, with all these people, they might be able to go back in and rescue him.

There was a blinding flash of white accompanied by a deafening thunderclap.

When her vision and hearing returned to normal the school was gone.

No fire, no rubble, no remains.

No sign it had ever been there at all.

It was just gone.

Alex and the six surviving children spent the next several hours being tended to by paramedics and giving their statements to the police.

The headmaster and most of the school board hovered around, interjecting themselves into conversations to ensure that they bore no liability for the events that transpired or the lives that were lost.

They were covering their own asses. Alex knew that meant her ass was flapping in the wind. She didn't care. Maybe they were right. Another teacher might have gotten more of the kids out alive. Another teacher might have noticed what Danny was doing and put a stop to it before he ever opened that portal.

These were thoughts that would haunt Alex for the rest of her life.

Sabrina regained consciousness with no memory of murdering four of her fellow classmates. Her parents were screaming about lawsuits and prison terms.

Felix waved as his father put him in their pickup and drove away as fast as the cops would let him.

Molly broke off from her parents and gave Alex a fierce hug before being pulled away, tears running down her cheeks.

Carlos mouthed thank you before being put into an ambulance and taken to the hospital so his shoulder could be treated.

The other two, Alex still couldn't remember their names, didn't come near her. She watched them being talked to by a trauma counselor before losing track of where they'd gone. She never saw them again.

When the police had finished with her, the headmaster was waiting for her.

"Ms. Maese?" he said

"What?" Alex responded curtly

"You're fired." The headmaster's words should have hurt her, caused her to panic, made her angry. Should have made her feel something, anything; but all Alex felt was numb.

"Yeah? Well…… Bite me." Alex flipped him the bird, walked to her car, and drove home.

That night she took the longest shower of her life and wept.

She wept until the warm water turned cold and then she wept some more.

Class Dismissed

Intermezzo

I dropped my hand to the radio dial and flipped it off. Leaning forward in my seat, I attempted to make out the numbers on the houses as I drove by. It was dark out, the moonless night sky revealing nothing of the road ahead of me. Most of the streetlights that lined the way forward lay dormant. The few possessed of any life flickered, as if sending out an S.O.S. in Morse code. The surreal ambiance strained my eyes as I searched for my destination.

Up ahead was a collective of beaten up station wagons flanked by a group of Mercedes and BMWs. *This must be the place.* I chuckled to myself. Finding an open spot behind one of those Mercedes, I pulled in and parked.

When I opened the car door I could hear the faint sound of music calling to me. I stepped out of my car and into the misty night air. I took a deep breath, shut the door behind me, and headed towards the melody.

The night was chilly, but not uncomfortably so, and I could feel a tingle in the air; an anticipation of autumn rain.

I approached the house and found myself unprepared for what lay before me. On the lawn sat two gigantic fountains. Fully operational, the water flowed effortlessly from the mouths of cherubs to the marble basin beneath their wings. They were everything you could or would imagine them to be; forgotten Fellini set pieces helicoptered in from Rome. I crossed the front yard to the door; feeling almost guilty for not walking barefoot and allowing my toes the feel of the dewy, short-cut grass.

My knuckles rapped the smooth mahogany, announcing my arrival; but instead of someone coming to greet me, the door simply fell away, inviting me inside. I stepped into a small foyer connected to a long corridor.

The hallway was lit by three wall-mounted bulbs; yellow, red, and blue. Underneath each of these was a doorway. I stood there. unsure of what door to take; not wanting to head down the wrong path, when I heard the faint whisper of an overture to my left. I turned and faced the yellow door. It was glowing in tempo with the tune. Pushing down on the handle, I walked through the door.

I entered a fairly nondescript kitchen where two men were having a discussion. The first man wore a cowboy hat and had a long white beard. His outfit was something out of an old country western song, complete with denim jeans and dusty brown boots. The second man had his face painted white and wore a black-and-white-striped shirt and black leggings. I assumed that he was a mime, but then he looked at the Cowboy and said:

"Consciousness is the awareness of illusion."

The Cowboy lifted his gaze to meet the mime's eyes, shook his head ever so slightly and replied:

"Our consciousness is but an infinitesimal fraction of what is, what was, and what could be. It blinds us to the whole, to the deeper meaning in all things. Consciousness is the illusion of being aware."

It was the Mime's turn to shake his head in negation.

"We give meaning to the world. We are the mazes that we build. Our constructs are artificial, but our need for these constructs is pure truth. When we embrace what we make, we find that we make what we love."

The Cowboy pulled out a cigarette and a matchbox and eternity passed as he lit it and took a drag.

"Give thanks to the world and all things that inhabit it; for they are what we define ourselves against. What is light without dark, thought without form? If we are shapeless, then we are nothing. When we are separated, we are special. The world gives meaning to us."

In unison they turned to me, expecting me to speak. I started to say that I didn't understand but I found my tongue to be swollen and my mouth unable to move. The Cowboy and the Mime turned back to each other staring each other in the eye. They nodded to one another and again turned to me expecting me to participate. And again my body betrayed me, and I could form no sounds. One second passed, then another, and then another; until I realized that I could not differentiate between moments. No sooner had that thought formed in my mind, than the two turned back to each other.

"Thoughts give meaning to words. Words are empty sounds when we have no ideas to fill them. What is lost in translation from thought to word and back to thought? On the fringes of a concept, the angle of perceptions; what do we miss because the cacophony is too well defined?"

When the Mime finished he slowly lowered himself to the floor. Lying down, he put his hands underneath his head, rolled over, and went to sleep.

"Words focus and direct us. They link our thoughts to the whole. We share words in order to survive. We create words in order to thrive. Without our words, we are nothing, formless in the void. Words give meaning to thoughts."

The Cowboy dropped his cigarette to the floor and put it out with the toe of his boot. Just as the Mime had, he lowered himself to the kitchen tile. He laid himself out flat on his back, lowered his hat over his face, and began to snore. The snore was melodic and melted into the air. All at once I realized that it was not snoring at all. The music had returned.

I followed the ethereal notes into the next room, but as I crossed the threshold I was greeted with only the quiet dark. Suddenly on the ceiling appeared interwoven designs of red and blue light. A bright white strobe began revealing my surroundings snapshot by snapshot. The room held a couch, a chair, and a beanbag. Three men dressed in shirt and ties were seated on the couch. They were all wearing large black headphones and nodding in time with one another.

In the center of the room stood a woman with a mane of fiery red hair in a sequenced white evening gown, her arms covered in long, white gloves. Even without headphones, it appeared as though she could hear the rhythm that was so determined to elude me. She ripped off her gown only to reveal a tasteful white cocktail dress underneath. The strobe gained speed and the periods of light and dark grew shorter and more frantic. I noticed that on her right leg that the space between her tall white heels and the hem of her dress was covered with a series of interwoven flames drawn onto her flesh.

She began to dance seductively, her curves filling the vacuum of silence. The men showed no outward changes towards her and continued their wordless head bobbing. Her fingertips moved like magic in the spaces between light and dark. Ever so gently she removed the glove on her left hand, letting each inch of porcelain skin become its own revelation. Then, in a flash of the strobe, the glove was half way between her hand and the floor, caught trying to defy gravity. She repeated the ritual with her right hand. But here, again, where I anticipated the pureness of her flesh, I found instead that it was consumed by fire.

Now, her hands found the zipper that ran down the back of her dress, but having located it they stilled themselves; gathering energy like a snake coiling for a strike. The anticipation built. Light. Dark. Light. Dark. Light. Dark. The strobe becoming our shared heartbeats. It was then that I realized she knew I was there. That she was daring me to take control, to stop her or reveal her. I found myself unable to move, impotent against her power. Her fingers began their dance again, lowering the zipper as if disappointed that they were forced to do it themselves.

She stood there completely naked. Now I understood. The entire right side of her body was covered in flame. The tattoos seared into her, the fire alive in her skin. My eyes burned as I stared at the most beautiful creature I had ever seen. She turned her head over her shoulder and her emerald eyes burrowed right into my soul. I heard a creaking noise and knew that a door had been opened behind me.

"I Am Chaos. I am Fire."

The words left her lips like an explosion.

I stepped backwards and stumbled through the threshold. I watched the door close slowly, leaving me no retreat to where I'd been.

It was then I found myself under a naked sky, its stars bared to the world. A full moon hung high in the firmament. I didn't remember there being a moon out before. In truth, I could barely remember that there was a before. I stood and slowly turned, where I found a girl of no more than twelve years staring up at me.

"Are you ready?" she asked me, her excitement tangible.

"For what?" I asked, suddenly embarrassed by my ignorance.

"The Game silly" and with that, she was off like a shot. Racing through the garden on a snaking path I hadn't noticed until now. I followed, my fear of the unknown overruled by my fear of ignorance. I caught up with the girl in another clearing much like the first. But here there sat a round, stone table in the center large enough to sit eight. Six people had already taken their positions and in unison, they gestured for the girl and me to fill the remaining two seats.

I looked around the table and took stock of the company I was keeping. To my immediate left, sat a grinning man wearing a dark vest and suit slacks. His arms were covered in a plethora of wrist watches of all shapes and colors. Next to me, on my right, sat a frowning man with tears tattooed on his cheeks. He wore a tie of blood red in a tight knot around his neck strong enough to be hung by. The young girl I had followed sat directly across from me. To her right sat a woman too ancient for words and to her left was a woman in her middling years whose face was covered in tear-soaked mascara. The final two seats bracketed the middle of the table. In them sat a pair of androgynous twins. Their faces were calm, revealing but not betraying the secret of serenity.

The Seven spoke as one voice. "When do we begin?"

"When do we want to begin?" The whistle-like quality of a giddy tenor surfacing from the Grinning Man.

"Why do we want to begin?" emerged the too tired, high-pitched whine of the Tear Soaked Woman.

"Where are our beginnings?" The twins spoke in stereo. Their mouths moving, but the eerie empty sound coming at us from all sides with no discernible origin.

"What do we seek?" The Hung Man in a deep rumbling bass of regret.

"How do we choose?" Said the throaty, full-voiced alto of the Ancient Woman.

"Can we choose?" Came the haunted, disembodied call of the Twins.

"Is there a time to come?" the sweet voice of the Little Girl.

INTERMEZZO

The odd conversation paused.

There was a beat.

And then another beat.

Their collective sight came to rest on me.

"I don't understand." I looked around bewildered and found a white teacup filled with a red liquid on the table in front of me.

The seven at the table spoke as one: "Shall you drink?"

Suddenly terrified, I shook my head no.

"Shall you drink?" their voices again in unison, like a death by a thousand cuts.

Wildly now my head shook. I tried to get up and run but I could not move my body.

"Shall you drink?" It was a chant now, chilling and frightful. My hands moved the cup to my lips of their own accord. The red liquid filled my mouth. It tasted of blood. Try as I might I could not spit it out and was left with no recourse but to swallow.

"When do we live?" said the Grinning Man. I felt my body begin to warm.

"Why do we want to live?" the question from the sobbing soprano of the Tear Soaked Woman. I felt clammy and stuffy, like the air would suffocate me.

"Where can we find those that live?" The sound of the Twins crashing down around me and my feverish state.

"What do we remember?" The Hung Man, the base of a bottomless crescendo. The pressure continued to build inside of me.

"How do we forget?" spoke the husky smoke of the Ancient Woman. My body cried out, buried under a thousand burning coals of my minds creating.

"Can we have memories?" The Twins echoing the hopelessness in my soul. I feared that no relief was coming.

"Is there a place for me?" the Little Girl making the words drip with honey while rage and despair took hold of me.

"Who are you?" I screamed through my tears of pain.

"When do we end?" The seven as one.

Now there were cups in front of all of us. Mine was filled with a blue liquid this time. I drank it greedily, quenching an untold thirst. Relief flooded me and I was instantly at ease.

"We Shall Drink." I looked at the other cups and saw that the red liquid filled each to the brim.

"We shall drink." Drowsiness was creeping up on me.

"We shall drink." My eyes grew heavy. I laid my head down on the table.

"We Shall Drink." The image of the seven sipping from their cups was the last I had before drifting off to sleep.

When I awoke I found myself lying in the clearing the girl had brought me to, only now there was no stone table and I was alone. I stood and wiped the sleep from my eyes. I could hear my music again, its presence the strongest yet, almost palpable in the air. Following my ear, I made my own path through the trees and brush. The initial foliage gave way to my presence and I made my way through a wooded area towards the sanctified harmony.

After a short walk, I found my path blocked by a wall of rose bushes tall enough to dwarf a giant. Pink roses in full bloom could be seen for days and the scent they radiated was as sweet as love's first kiss. My heavenly song beckoned to me and I knew without any doubt that my answers would be found on the other side of this wall.

I paused, with only a second's hesitation, before I closed my eyes and plunged forward. Thorns pricked me all over my body, my clothing offering no protection. My eyes watered in pain and blood flowed freely from hundreds of tiny holes in my skin. Every step I took brought my song closer and my agony to new heights. I willed myself forward inch by flesh tearing inch. Until, finally, I pushed myself through to the other side.

It was wondrous. My song was here, a full orchestra making its presence known. The melody sweetened the air and the moonlight granted everything around me a magical radiance. A statuesque woman stood on a hardwood dance floor that was situated in front of the orchestra. Her ebony skin stood in stark contrast to the pastel yellow of her simple sundress. I moved towards her but fell to my knees, my wounds overwhelming me. I raised my head and she was there beside me with a small cup. She tilted my head back and poured its contents down my throat. I was filled with awe. Instead of blood, cool water began to flow from me and when all residue of my struggle had been washed away my wounds healed, and I was whole again. The goddess helped me to my feet and led me by the hand to the hardwood floor. The orchestra played on and we began to waltz. As one we moved, my hand melded to her hip, her eyes inside my mind. The world spun and we stepped out of it, leaving everything behind but the music.I don't know how long our dance went on for: seconds, hours, eons; but I know that I was content.

Fog rolled into this sacred place and its thickness began to coat us all. As the band began to fade, my song found its natural end. The fog drew ever closer and I felt the goddess withdrawal from my embrace. I moved to follow, now seeing no further than my own nose, but found only a white gate attached to a red fence. I stepped through the gate and there were the two Fellini fountains on the front lawn. Here the early morning sun was bursting through the foggy haze.

I let the warmth of our yellow star wash over me and walked to my car. A spontaneous smile appeared on my face and I turned the key in the ignition. As I pulled out into the morning mist I turned on my radio.

The Climb

The gentle sound of crashing waves eased Cass back into the waking world. Blinking her eyes into focus, she raised her hand to shield them from the bright, glorious light of the mid-day sun.

Before her lay a vast, unending ocean. A perfect picture of idyllic waves and cloudless sky that extended out to the horizon and beyond.

Pristine, white sand lay to either side of her, unsullied by the unfortunate developments collectively known as civilization.

Mahani, it was called by the locals. A secluded paradise in the South Pacific. Here there were no tourists, no vendors, no true natives to speak of. Just nature and those who sought to understand her.

To even reach the island Cassidy had been forced to charter a private boat. The price had not been cheap. The perseverance of Mahani's beauty was not an accident. The island was said to be home to evil spirits, a reputation enhanced by the high number of fatalities experienced by those intrepid souls who dared to explore her hidden magnificence. Many men had set foot on Mahani's shores, very few had returned to their families. Those that had did not speak of what they'd found. Cass allowed herself a tight-lipped smile. It was a good thing she wasn't a man.

Sitting up, she tied the loose strings of her white bikini top behind her neck and put on her sunglasses.

The beauty of this island may be unsurpassed, and its history may be shrouded in legend and folklore, but those were not the reasons she had come to Mahani.

Cassidy was one of The Touched. A rare line of humans who could see beyond the veil of this universe and alter reality itself.

Without proper training, she was a danger to herself and to the world around her. There was only one place for people like her to learn to control their gifts. Mahani.

Tomorrow she would begin her trek through the jungle to the center of the island, where she would ascend to the peak Lawu'Kala, the island's tallest mountain. There she hoped to find the ancient temple of her people and someone to teach her to control the awesome power she had inherited.

But that was tomorrow. Today she walked along the beach, letting the waves lap at her feet. Basking in the warm light of the life-giving sun.

Eventually, she found herself back at what amounted to the island's downtown. A dive shop, a boat rental hut, a bar-slash-restaurant, and a collection of small bungalows. It constituted the largest concentration of buildings on the island.

As far as Cassidy was aware, the bungalows housed only two occupants at the moment. Herself and her guide.

Cassidy found her guide at the bar, sipping a glass of Johnny Walker Black. Cass didn't know enough about whiskey to identify it by sight, but the half-empty bottle sitting next to the half-empty glass made the drink's designation easy enough to deduce.

"Ms. Clyne." Her guide raised the glass and gave Cass a nod as she approached.

"Mira, I've told you before, call me Cass." Her guide didn't answer, choosing instead to turn her half empty glass of whiskey into merely an empty glass.

Mira was as different from Cassidy as night was from day. Where Cassidy was tall and buxom with long blonde hair and pale, white skin; Mira was short and lean, with dark brown skin made even darker by the island sun, and raven black hair cropped short at the ears. It would have been easy to mistake the guide for a man, while Cassidy's curves marked her as a woman even in the most androgynous of outfits.

The two-piece string bikini she was wearing was hardly androgynous.

Mira's eyes took their time scanning her, lingering just a few seconds more than they should. It was enough to make Cassidy blush.

When Mira had finished her appraisal, she turned her attention back to her glass and spoke in a smoky alto while pouring herself a refill.

"I hope you have something more substantial than that to wear tomorrow."

Embarrassed, Cassidy pulled a sarong from her bag and tied it around her hips.

"I brought suitable hiking gear and I packed my bag exactly the way you instructed. I did my research before coming here. I'm not an idiot." For the second time in as many minutes, Cassidy felt her cheeks go red.

"I never said you were. But Lawu'Kala makes fools of even the most experienced climbers. She is not to be taken lightly." Mira emptied the glass again, her head giving a slight shake as she swallowed.

"She?" Cassidy asked.

"Anything that lovely and that lethal has to be a woman." Mira gulped down another glass of whiskey, her third since Cassidy had found her.

"That's an interesting point of view." Cassidy responded diplomatically, at a loss as to what other response she should offer.

"It's not a point of view. It's a fact. Only a woman could kill you and make you beg for more." Mira stood and leaned over the bar. Making sure to wriggle and give Cassidy a full view of her perfectly toned backside as she did.

She rummaged around a bit before finding what she wanted. The display was enough to make Cass' mind wander.

"Have you ever begged for more?"

"I'm sorry what?" Cassidy asked, forcing herself back to the here and now.

Her eyes met Mira's eyes, which gave every indication that her guide knew exactly where Cassidy's mind had gone.

"I said 'The path is dangerous and unpredictable. We leave at first light.'" Taking her bottle and her glass, Mira headed for the exit; brushing past Cassidy as she did. The touch sent shivers through Cass' body. "Sleep well Ms. Clyne, tomorrow will be the hardest day of your life."

Mira's advice proved hard to follow. Anxiousness filled Cassidy to the brim. She tossed and turned, unable to turn off the torrent of thoughts that were racing through her mind.

The humid, tropical air sat on her like a wet blanket, so much so that beads of moisture left trails all along her body. She lay there in nothing but her underwear, even the thin cotton sheet that had been provided for her proving too heavy an encumbrance in this heat.

Restless and annoyed she pushed herself out of bed. Maybe Mira had been on to something, if Cass had a bottle of whiskey in her right now she doubted she'd be pacing the floor of her tiny bungalow. She doubted she'd be anything other than catatonic.

She could feel her heartbeat speed up as her frustration and anxiety formed a tight knot in her chest. The bungalow began to shake, and strange colors filled her vision.

Cassidy forced herself to breathe. Deep, calming breaths. In and out. In and out. Breathing in the calm and breathing out the bad.

The room steadied and her vision returned to normal.

That was the problem with the Touched; lose your temper, have a panic attack, give in to your fear for even a moment and you could unravel all of reality without ever consciously deciding to do anything at all.

That was why she was here. It was her least bad option. And the last chance she had to avoid doing something even more drastic than traveling across the world to climb a deadly mountain.

Cassidy knew the consequences of failure. The consequences of losing control.

When the first hints of sunlight peeked over the horizon, Mira rapped sharply at her door. Cassidy opened it ready to depart.

"Trouble sleeping? You're going to regret that later. You should have knocked on my door. I could have shown you the secret to sleeping blissfully." Mira's eyes twinkled with mischief but her face was all business. "There's still time to call this whole thing off. No one is forcing you to do this. Once we get up there, in the thick of it, there are no guarantees. Even if we decide to turn back."

Cass grabbed her bag and hefted it onto her shoulders. She stepped out of her bungalow and took a deep breath of island air.

"I'm ready. Let's go." Cass said with all the courage she could muster.

"All right, it's your dime." Mira gave a shrug and started walking.

The small gathering of huts the locals called the village was empty as they passed through on their way inland. Whether the locals were already up and going about their daily routine or still in bed enjoying the lazy nature of island life, Cass could not say. What she did know was that no one cared enough to see the white girl march off to her doom.

It wasn't the emptiness of the village that bothered her, it was the eerie stillness. That kind of quite off-ness that one only felt in the overcast hours between night and day.

Cassidy found herself looking skyward to where Lawu'Kala touched the clouds. The massive mountain towered over the island. It was impossible to look inland and see anything else.

Lawu'Kala was actually a collection of three peaks clustered together at the center of the island. All toll, they represented nearly eighty percent of the Mahani's acreage, leaving only enough room for a thin ring of grassland and another thin ring of beaches on its perimeter. The peaks of Lawu'Kala were staggered in height and separated by more than a mile, but all three began as one singular sprawling mass of rock and trees before splitting off towards their own scenic glory. Because of this odd geographical feature, Lawu'Kala was littered with hidden valleys and rivers nested high above sea level, in the space between its rocky heights.

It wasn't more than twenty minutes into their journey when the open green with scattered trees morphed into dense foliage. Cassidy followed Mira who followed the path of least resistance; a trail so rarely traveled as to make the word trail a dubious claim.

The first thing Cass noticed upon entering the jungle was the sudden lack of sun. The dense canopy above them blocked off most direct sunlight to the jungle floor. It was by no means dark, but now everything was in the shade. She no longer had to deal with the direct heat of the sun bearing down on her.

The second thing she noticed was the noise. While the outer edges of the island were by no means silent, they did possess a quiet tranquility. Now that tranquility was gone, undone by a cacophony of shrieks, buzzes, and clicks. The sheer variety of sounds astounded her.

With Mira leading her on, Cass worked her way through the thick undergrowth; stopping occasionally to marvel at the alien world she now found herself in. Fantastically colored birds of paradise flew from tree to tree expanding their brilliant plumage and singing their hearts out in an attempt to attract a potential mate.

Ring-tailed lemurs took up residence in a collection of fig trees, playfully wrestling with each other while they partook of the tree's bountiful fruits.

When the lemurs discarded their half-eaten meals, the partially devoured figs dropped hundreds of feet to the ground below where eager insects swarmed to finish what the lemurs did not.

Canny lizards, camouflaged so well that Cass had to concentrate hard to see them at all, waited patiently nearby, turning the bug's fig feast into their last meal and satisfying their own hunger in the process.

A few hours in, they came to a small stream. Mira took off her backpack and said it was as good a spot as any to stop for lunch. Cass was relieved for the respite. The new sights and sounds had kept her distracted from her aching muscles, but the climb was a difficult one and her body was not accustomed to this kind of workout. Yoga and spin classes may keep her fit and healthy, but they could not compare to the rigors of a jungle ascent.

Exhausted, Cass pulled off her pack and took a seat on a fallen tree trunk next to the rushing water. Mira pulled a pair of sandwiches out of her own kit and handed one over to Cass.

"I hope you like peanut butter." the guide half-joked.

Cass did not. But she saw no point in saying so. Besides, she was hungry enough that the taste barely registered. What did register was the sticky, gooey feeling the sandwich left in her mouth.

Reaching for her canteen, Cass felt something crawling up her ankle. She looked down to see a centipede the length of her arm wrapping itself around her leg.

She screamed, the sudden fright causing her to fall off the log she'd been sitting on.

"Get it off me" she pleaded while kicking at the creepy creature with her other leg.

"Be still." Mira instructed before pulling out her machete from its resting place on her hip.

Cass froze, uncertain of what Mira had planned, but unwilling to lose a limb for lack of trust.

Slowly the guide lowered the machete toward the centipede's head. Placing it flat against Cass' leg, Mira coaxed the creature onto the blade then gently back to the ground, where it skittered off in search of more stable climbing posts.

"See, there, the little guy just thought you were interesting. Can't fault him for having good taste." Mira chuckled, returning her machete to its sheath.

Cass exhaled, realizing as she did that she had been holding her breath throughout the whole ordeal.

The afternoon only got worse from there. Stopping had allowed Cass' muscles the time to realize they were being overworked. Once the adrenaline spike from her insect encounter wore off, her legs began to burn, and the climb became a struggle.

Mira was far from sympathetic. She pushed Cass forward, allowing no more than one five-minute break per hour.

If that weren't bad enough, the wonder that had kept Cass' mind occupied that morning was gone. Replaced by a fear that every buzzing noise or leaf brushed past was some new creepy crawly slithering its way up her leg.

Just as the sun was receding over the horizon, they broke out from underneath the canopy and on to a cliff-face clearing created by a small clustering of lightning-felled trees.

The view was stunning. Hues of orange and purple melded together with white clouds and blue ocean to create the impression that Cass stood at the edge of the world. It was enough to make her forget about everything else. The centipede, her sore muscles, being one of the Touched. It all just faded away when presented with such supreme beauty.

Her state of serenity was undone by the sound of manic squealing issuing forth from the tangled vegetation behind her.

Mira stopped what she was doing and stepped towards her, a warning hand up with the other resting on the handle of her machete.

Out of the jungle burst a wild boar the size of a small sofa. Blood dripped from its tusks and from several cuts along its belly and hindquarters. The boar stumbled, squealing even louder as it did.

It stood back up and shook its head from side to side, a crazed look in its eyes.

Other boars emerged from the jungle, they too wore cuts along their torsos.

These new boars eyed the first boar warily and lacked its manic disposition.

The rabid boar lunged at them and they retreated. Again the creature stumbled and now the others rushed forward to attack.

Injured and out of its mind, the beast spun in circles. Lashing out wildly at threats real and imagined.

The other boars were stabbing at it with their tusks, forcing the wild, rabid beast back towards the edge of the cliff.

It squealed and tried to turn its own tusks back against its attackers, but the pack did not allow it any room in which to do so.

The mad boar went silent, then in one lethal lunge, launched itself off the side of the mountain to its certain death below.

Having succeeded in their quest to banish the rogue boar, the rest of the herd fled back into the jungle.

The horror of it all left Cass dumbfounded, only seconds after marveling at nature's beauty she had just witnessed its uncaring cruelty.

"It was infected." Mira spoke softly. "What they did, they did for the good of the herd."

Cass turned her head back to Mira, whose dark brown eyes contrasted sharply with the orange sky behind her.

The lithe guide continued to explain, though Cass was uncertain if she wanted to hear more.

"There is a fungus here, it infects the brains of certain animals. Driving them insane before it kills them and uses their bodies for food. If they had allowed her to remain, they would have all become infected. They had no other choice."

The truth of the words stung Cass more profoundly then they should have.

Mira said nothing more. Choosing instead to set up camp in silence.

Cass cast her eyes back to the last vestiges of the fading sun, not wanting the other woman to see the tears filling her eyes as twilight descended all around them.

Dinner was a pair of freeze-dried pouches of pad Thai. Mira talked about what they could expect on tomorrow's leg of their journey. Cass pretended to listen.

It was obvious to Mira that the incident with the boar had shaken Cass. And it was obvious to Cass that Mira was looking for some way to make her feel better. Neither woman was much accustomed to being vulnerable. Neither woman knew what it was they were supposed to say. So neither woman said anything.

Almost as soon as dinner was eaten and the camp was cleaned, Cass crawled into her tent and went to sleep. After the day she'd had it was not a difficult feat.

Sometime later the darkness of her dreams was interrupted by a guttural growl. She opened her eyes and slowly rolled over. There she saw a shadow in the moonlight cast against the fabric of her tent. An outline of a monster she had no earthly reference for.

She could hear it breathing. A rough snort on the intake of breath and a low, throaty rumble when it exhaled.

It sniffed at the tent, its massive snout pushing the fabric inward towards Cass' face.

Cassidy's heart started to race, her palms became slick with sweat. Her thoughts spiraled as she thought back to the horror of the boar and then further back to the night she first learned she was one of the Touched.

Her vision began to blur, and she could feel the earth start to rumble beneath her.

The beast roared, as it too sensed the mountain's trembling.

It raised itself up on its hind legs and let out a bone-chilling howl before running off back into the jungle night.

Cass tried to breathe, but she had forgotten how. Her heart was ready to burst from its chest.

Her head jerked up at the sound of her tent flap opening. Terror seized her, but also prevented her from moving or do anything to prevent this imminent intrusion.

The flap opened and Mira crawled in beside her.

The guide put her hand over Cass' mouth and a finger over her own lips to keep Cass from speaking.

"Are you okay?" She whispered softly in Cass' ear. The warmness of her breath gave Cass goosebumps.

"Yes." Cass responded, her voice trembling.

"Go to sleep. I'm here. Nothing's going to happen to you." Cass felt Mira's hands wrap around her and Cass allowed herself to be enveloped in the safeness of the other woman's arms.

When Cass awoke, Mira was gone. Panicking, she unzipped her tent flap and rushed to find her. In the process nearly falling into the small fire Mira had made to cook their morning meal.

"Breakfast?" Mira pointed to a trio of impaled lizards roasting over the open flames. "It's the most important meal of the day."

"No thanks." Cass said, staring as Mira bit into a lizard she'd already pulled off the flame.

"Are you sure?" She asked. "Lizard on a stick may not sound appetizing, but it's really not all that bad. Just a bit chewy maybe."

"I'll stick to granola bars." Cass didn't plan on ever trying lizard meat, no matter what assurances Mira gave her.

"Suit yourself." The guide shrugged and bit into her meal.

Cass tried not to look as she pulled her own breakfast out of her bag. The two sat in silence until finally, Cass had to ask the obvious question.

"What was that last night?"

"That was a Gourabora." Mira replied while wiping lizard juice off her chin.

"What the hell is a Gourabora?" Cass asked incredulously.

Mira took a deep breath and explained.

"When explorers first discovered Mahani, they found no indigenous people here. But they did find evidence that people had lived here before. Huts, tools, cave carvings all the signs that there had once been a thriving community here, with absolutely no indications as to what happened to them. The explorers wrote off the disappearance to some strange illness. Which would not have been all that uncommon at that time." Mira stood and put out the cooking fire while she kept talking. "They'd leave behind a small group of advanced settlers and return to their home island for more supplies and settlers. When the explorers returned they found that everyone they had left behind had vanished save one man, a scared mute. When asked what happened the mute led the others to a cave. This cave was full of carvings, but the mute pointed to one painting in particular. The figure of a massive beast unlike any creature yet known to them."

Mira's words hung in the air. Cass was entranced by her story.

"It was then the mute spoke the only word he was ever known to have uttered. 'Gourabora'." Mira continued. "The story repeated itself over the centuries. With new people discovering and settling the island only to disappear without a trace, and always there remained only one witness saying one word: 'Gourabora'. That is until the Touched built a temple here. And the entire cycle stopped. Finally making the island habitable for man."

"Why did it stop?" Cass asked.

"No one knows. Some say the Touched killed all the Gourabora, others say that the touched are the Gourabora, and some say it stopped simply because the Touched willed it to. Some of the neighboring islanders even believe that if you catch a Gourabora and eat it's still beating heart you will become one of the Touched yourself." Mira concluded her tale.

"And you think that thing we saw last night, that it was one of these Gourabora beasts?" The idea made Cass uncomfortable.

"It matched the description. I don't really know what else it could have been. Just because an animal has got a funky look and a creepy name doesn't mean we're going to suddenly disappear. But all legends have some foundation in reality, so it's probably best if we don't mess with that thing. Okay?" Mira warned.

"Yeah, okay." Cass agreed

She was still pondering the legend of the Gourabora when they resumed their ascent. The climb was becoming more difficult as they approached the point where the three peaks of Lawu'Kala separated out from their singular base. The foliage grew thicker, the incline grew steeper, and the light by which to see it all grew darker.

The total result of these difficulties was the slowing down of their pace to a snail's crawl. Which was fine by Cass, who was still feeling the effects of the previous day's climb. At one point, Cass' leg began to cramp. Mira poured a pouch full of small powder into her canteen and handed it to Cass.

"Drink." She said.

Cass tipped the canteen back and began to gulp down the water mixture. Mira put a hand on the canteen and pushed it down from vertical to horizontal.

"Slowly." The guide instructed.

While Cass sipped, Mira pulled out a small tube and squeezed a white cream onto her hands. She bent down and rubbed the cream on to Cass' legs. Making sure to cover every bare inch of skin.

Cass tried very hard to focus on the contents of her canteen and ignore the excitement of the smaller woman's hands massaging her thighs.

She felt a twinge of disappointment when Mira's hands stopped working their magic, but she realized that her cramp was gone.

"Better?" Mira asked, her dark eyes taking in Cass' pale skin.

Cass nodded.

"Good." Mira's eyes lingered for a moment then turned their attention back to the mountain. "Come on. We need to keep moving."

The rest of the morning passed without incident. Shortly after lunch they reached the plateau that connected the three peaks of Lawu'Kala. There the steep climb flattened out until there was no incline whatsoever. If not for the noticeable thinning of the air, you would almost think you were walking at sea level again.

A thick cloak of mist permeated the trees. And even more voices seemed to join the jungle din. All around Cass, life flourished in this isolated lost world.

The two women continued their trek into the jungle. To reach the highest peak they would need to cross nearly five miles of thick jungle before they could begin the most treacherous part of their ascent.

Sometime just before dark Cass noticed a sudden quieting of the background buzz she had become accustomed to. She listened but could hear no buzzing insects or chirping birds. It was as if the entire jungle had gone still.

Mira noticed it as well and signaled for her to stop.

Cass froze. The only sound she could hear was the pounding of her own heart.

A single, blood-curdling scream rang out with primal rage, shattering the disquiet calm.

It was answered by another chilling howl, and then another.

Soon, a whole chorus of angry screeches echoed through the air.

The screeches stopped abruptly and silence reigned again.

Then pandemonium.

Like furious demons. angry primates came pouring out of the trees.

There were two groups, one with black hair and the other with red.

They met in furious battle, clawing and biting at their foes with a manic viciousness that was terrifying to behold.

"Run!" Mira screamed, and Cass did exactly that.

It was impossible to break into a full-on sprint in the jungle, even on flat ground the aggregate volume of vegetation and debris made the terrain a treacherous foe. The best Cass could manage was a quick jog and she could only manage that by following the path of least resistance.

She made the mistake of looking back and tripped, tumbling head over heels through the underbrush. Her body was a mass of pain, cuts and scrapes covered her from head to toe.

Lying there she heard a dreadful screech. She looked up. One of the primates was rushing towards her, blind fury in its eyes.

Mira stepped into view. Slashing at the ape with her Machete, forcing it to reassess its attack.

"Go! Hide! I'll find you!" she screamed at Cass without taking her eyes off the beast.

Cass scrambled to her feet and kept running. Fear overruling the shame of leaving the other woman behind.

She kept running until she found a hollowed-out tree trunk big enough for her to hide in. Ignoring the myriad of insects that called the trunk home, Cass crawled inside and scrunched down.

The trunk was dark except for a single hole, no more than a few inches in diameter, through which Cass could look out and get a limited view of her surroundings.

Her breath was ragged, chest heaving from the exertion of running away. She concentrated on taking deliberate breaths and worked to slow her thundering heart.

She heard the screeching of apes coming closer and did her best to remain absolutely still, no easy task when faced with a bevy of cockroaches and beetles exploring your bare legs and arms.

As much as those bugs made her want to squirm, the terrible savagery of the apes far outstripped her gross-out reflex.

The screeching grew louder, and the apes came into view. There were four of them, three full-grown members of the red-haired tribe and a single infant belonging to the black-haired apes.

The infant was injured, badly limping but trying frantically to get away.

The larger apes circled the infant, toying with it while it cried out for help. With a silent signal, they descended on it in unison, brutally beating the young ape to death with their closed fists.

While the infant's body was still twitching, the red-haired apes passed it around; using their teeth to rip the flesh from its bones and devour its corpse.

Cass let out an involuntary gasp of revulsion at the horrifying sight.

The apes paused their abhorrent feast and looked around.

One of them spotted Cass' trunk. She stayed absolutely still but it didn't matter. The apes knew she was there.

The first ape let out a horrible screech and pointed, alerting the others to his discovery. They dropped the infant's carcass and rushed to the tree trunk where Cass still hid.

Wild screams filled Cass' ears, drowning out all other sounds. The apes began beating on the trunk, tearing at its bark trying to rip it open with their bare hands. One of the apes found the opening that had allowed Cass inside. It gnashed its teeth and reached its hand through the gap, clawing at Cass' ankle. Cass tried to kick at it but only succeeded in allowing the beast to seize her ankle.

Tears ran down her cheeks. Her heart beat wildly in her chest. Fear paralyzed her and Cass felt certain she was going to die just like the infant ape. Beaten then eaten.

The earth began to shake, and colors swirled in her vision. Suddenly the world became unsure of itself, time and space bending out of shape.

Then there came a mighty howl. The same howl she had heard in her tent the night before. The howl of the Gourabora.

The apes broke off their attack and redirected their manic rage towards the new threat.

Cass took deep breaths and forced herself to calm down.

She peeked through the small hole in the side of the trunk and marveled at what she saw there.

The Gourabora was the size of small car. It stood on hoofed hind legs while its front two muscular limbs looked more like the talons you would find on birds of prey than anything else. It had slimy, green skin like a frog's, with a ridged back, and long, spiked tail that split in two at the end. Its face was dominated by large tusks and a blunted snout that left little room for its beady black eyes or its small, floppy ears.

It was by no means a pretty creature. It was easy to understand why ignorant men would blame it for all the unexplained things that happened on this island.

Drowning in their blood lust the apes were not as impressed by the arrival as Cass was. They pounded their chests and let out a collection of piercing screams.

Again the Gourabora roared and the battle commenced.

Normally the apes would not have stood a chance against such a fearsome foe but they were smaller and nimbler than the Gourabora and they had numbers on their side.

They encircled the creature, trying to get it to expose its rear flank. This was a mistake as the Gourabora's tail proved more than capable of defending its flank.

The apes attacked and the Gourabora swung its tail with incredible velocity.

Cass scrambled free of her hiding place just at the Gourabora's tail hurled one of the attacking red-haired apes into it. The trunk split and splintered.

The remaining two apes beat their chests at the Gourabora, trying to intimidate it. But the mythical beast reared up on its rear legs and roared, doing some intimidating of its own.

Seeing that there would be no easy victory here the apes fled back towards the rest of their kind.

The Gourabora snorted with satisfaction at their retreat, returning its clawed front legs to the ground.

A pair of tiny whines emanated from the trees behind the Gourabora. It turned its head back towards the sounds and answered with a soft grunt.

Two tiny Gouraboras emerged from hiding places of their own. The two babies were hardly the size of a golden retriever. Playfully, they rubbed up against the leg of their mother, who nuzzled them back with her own massive snout.

"Cassidy!" The sound of Mira's voice spooked the young Gourabora. They ran off into the jungle to hide. Their mother eyed Cass one more time then raced off after her children.

"Cassidy, where are you?" Mira cried out.

"I'm here." She called back, pulling her gaze from where the Gourabora had retreated.

Mira emerged from behind a thick tangle of vines carrying both her own pack and Cass'.

"Are you hurt?" The concern in her eyes was plain to see. She had saved her life and now she was clearly worried about her. Cass thought it was incredibly sweet.

"No. I'm fine." She told her guide and protector.

"You're not fine. You're bleeding." Mira grabbed Cass' arm and pushed up her shirt sleeve.

Cass looked down to find that she was indeed bleeding.

Mira wiped away the blood with a piece of cloth torn from her shirt. When the area was clear she pulled a tiny squirt bottle from her pack. The clear liquid burned as it disinfected the cut.

"Shallow and thin. You got lucky. No stitches for you." Mira said with a faint smile.

Cass didn't feel lucky, but she relaxed as Mira's hand set down the disinfectant and picked up the white gauze.

Mira wrapped it round Cass' arm three times, then tied off the bandage. Her fingers lingered there.

The two women sat only inches apart from one another now.

Anticipation hung in the air. Anticipation and uncertainty. Cass' heart was pounding again. But not from fear this time. The concern in Mira's eyes had not gone away. Though now it was joined by something else, something primal. Cass could identify it because she could feel that same basic need building up inside herself as well.

Mira's fingers drifted down from Cassidy's arm to her bare thigh.

Shivers ran through Cassidy's entire body, trepidation filled her.

Mira closed her eyes and leaned forward. Cassidy did the same.

Their lips touched and then their mouths parted.

They kissed. A deep, sensual kiss that seemed to go on forever.

Mira pulled back, ending their kiss.

There was a pause.

An electric tingle lingered on Cassidy's lips. Her body yearned for Mira's. The two women stared into each other's eyes.

Then they kissed again. Their lips hungrily seeking out their opposing number.

Mira's hands began to roam Cassidy's body, caressing her curves, squeezing her round, pale flesh. Their lips parted only long enough to allow their shirts to pass over their heads. Mira's hand drifted south while Cassidy's hips bucked to meet it. Desperate to remove any barriers to Mira's touch, Cassidy squirmed to get free of her shorts. Then as she felt Mira's fingers within her, she squirmed for an entirely different reason.

Gently, Mira's hands guided Cassidy down to the jungle floor. Cassidy's back arched with pleasure as Mira's tongue worked its way down her body, teasing her flesh with its delicate wetness while searching for Cassidy's own wetness.

Finally, Mira's tongue found what it was looking for and Cassidy's screams of passion joined in with the other animal cries of the jungle.

In the morning when Cass opened her eyes she found that for once she had managed to wake up before Mira. Cass relished everything about the moment. From the feeling of their naked bodies pressed against each other to the look of simple serenity that Mira wore as she slept.

She laid there for a few minutes, savoring the brief reprieve.

The moment could not last forever though. Gently, she disentangled herself from Mira's sleeping form. Outside the tent, the world resumed. Beams of sunlight crept over the horizon while the colorful birds of the jungle welcomed the dawn with their beautiful song.

It suddenly dawned on Cass that she stank of sex and fear, covered in the sticky remains of the previous day's varied adventures.

Cass needed a shower, desperately.

She settled for a waterfall.

The cool, clear water felt exhilarating against her bare skin. She raised her hands to the sky and let the water pour over her face. With all the care of a sacred ritual, Cass cleansed herself of the dirt, grime, and sweat her body had accumulated over the past two days. It was good to feel clean again. She thought about sneaking back into the tent and getting dirty all over again just so she could relieve this feeling. Well, this and other feelings. The idea brought a smile to her face.

Her reverie was disturbed by the sound of approaching voices. Surprised by the sound of other humans in this remote wilderness and unprepared to have her naked form ogled by a group of strange men, Cass scrambled out of the pool and behind a nearby boulder.

"I can't believe we actually caught the thing." She heard one of the men say to the others. "Honest to god I thought it was nothing but a myth."

Cass peaked out from behind her rock to get a better look. Three men approached the far edge of the lagoon. Each of the men was dressed in loose cargo pants and a cut off t-shirt. Each of the men also carried a rifle over their shoulder.

The man who was talking bent down to fill a group of canteens with water from the lagoon.

"If you didn't think the Gourabora was real, why'd you sign up for this job in the first place?" one of the other men asked.

"Hey, a paycheck's a paycheck, you know what I'm saying. If you got the dough, I'm good to go. You want to spend your money hunting fairy tales that's your business. Me, I'm a scotch and cigars guy." The first man answered, handing back the now full canteen and exchanging it for an empty one.

"But we did find it." The third poacher added enthusiastically.

"Yes, we did. And with the bonus that bitch and her two kids are gonna earn us, I'm going to buy me whole lake full of the most expensive scotch I can find." The first man concluded.

Cass couldn't believe what she was hearing. These assholes had captured the Gourabora and her young and planned to sell them to the highest bidder.

She waited for the poachers to finish and leave then raced back to her camp. Mira was still in her tent where Cass had left her, blissfully asleep.

"Mira wake up. There are people here. Mira." Cass babbled excitedly as she shook her lover awake.

"Good morning." Mira said with a groggy smile, leaning up for a kiss.

"Mira, you have to get dressed. We're not alone out here" Cass frantically explained.

Mira's demeanor changed in an instant, the experienced guide taking note of the distress in Cass' voice and reacting accordingly.

"Tell me what's wrong" She said while hurriedly pulling on her clothes.

The whole story flowed out of Cass in a jumble; the waterfall, the poachers, their plans for the Gourabora. Even as she spoke, she knew she wasn't making much sense.

"Slow down." Mira said gently, slowing down her own routine once she realized they were in no immediate danger. "So these men don't know we're out here? They're just after the Gourabora?"

"We have to help them, Mira. You weren't there. You didn't see. She saved me. We have to protect her and her babies." Cass pleaded, tears running down her eyes.

Mira pulled her in close, embracing her as she sobbed.

"We will." She reassured Cass. "Don't worry we will."

In addition to being an experienced guide, Mira was an expert tracker. After Cass led her back to where she'd encountered the poachers, it took Mira not time at all to pick up their trail.

She followed their tracks to a small clearing not far from the waterfall. There they found a collection of tents arranged in a circle. At the center of the circle were two large cages. In one was the full-grown Gourabora, in the other were her two offspring.

Mira and Cass took cover behind a large fig tree. From their hiding spot, Cass could see the three men she'd seen earlier in the morning along with two more men. All five of the men were armed with pistols and rifles.

Cass felt a tap on her shoulder. She looked over to Mira who gestured for her to follow. They retreated well back from the poacher's camp, far enough that they could talk without being heard. Still, when Mira spoke she did so in a whisper.

"Cass, there are five armed men in that camp. I know I said we'd help, but I think this is more than we can take on. What happens when they start shooting?" The concern had returned to Mira's eyes.

"What happens to the Gourabora when we leave?" Cass asked her pleadingly.

"Do you want to die Cass? Because if we try to confront those men that's exactly what's going to happen." For the first time since Cass had met her, she could see that Mira was afraid.

Cass was silent for a moment, considering the problem. Too often over the last two days she'd let her fear control her. Really she'd been giving in to it ever since she'd discovered she was one of the Touched. It was about time she took control of her own mind.

She knew what the right thing to do was and she would be damned if she wasn't going to figure out some way to do it. But Mira was right, confronting the poachers head-on was suicide.

So what if they didn't confront them at all.

"We just need to distract them long enough to sneak past and open the cages. The Gourabora will take care of the rest." Cass was pretty sure she had a plan.

"I can get close enough to get the Gourabora out, but how are you going to distract them without getting yourself killed?" Mira asked.

"I can handle it." Cass insisted.

"How?" The concern in her voice was touching, but one night in the sack did not make Cass' life Mira's to protect.

"Do you trust me?" Cass asked her, reaching a hand up to Mira's face.

"Of course but-" Mira answered reflexively before Cass cut her off.

"Then trust me." She said, knowing that would end the debate.

Having decided on a course of action, they returned to the fig tree. Cass would remain hidden there while Mira stealthily moved herself into a position closer to the camp.

When Mira was in position she signaled Cass with an agreed upon bird call.

It was time for Cass to create her distraction.

She closed her eyes and pictured the camp in her mind. Then she thought about all of the horrible things that had happened over the last three days. She thought about the centipede wrapping itself around her leg, about the mad boar driven off a cliff by its own family. She thought about how frightened she'd been when the night the Gourabora first appeared.

Finally, she thought about the red-haired apes. How they'd beaten that poor little ape to death. How they'd passed around its corpse, feasting on its dead flesh. How they'd come after her next. The terror she'd felt as they tore at her hiding place, their hands clawing at her. The certain belief that she was going to be their next meal.

Cassidy let that fear wash over her. Her heart pounded in her chest, she could feel the adrenalin rushing through her.

The ground started to shake, and she opened her eyes. Colors swirled and reality began to bend. But this time instead of trying to calm herself, trying to stop her powers from manifesting, she embraced them.

The colors solidified into shapes. The shapes became living creatures of flesh and blood. All around the camp, animals were coming to life out of thin air. Centipedes and boars and apes filled the camp, confused by their miraculous creation and enraged by that confusion.

The poachers did not know how to react to this sudden change in their reality. After the screams and the shouting, they decided their best option was to open fire.

While the poachers waged war on their unexpected guests, Cass could see Mira infiltrate the camp. The tiny woman moved with speed and stealth, skillfully avoiding the gaze of the otherwise engaged poachers.

Mira reached the Gouraboras' cages unseen and began picking the lock that held the mother Gouraboras' cage shut.

As otherworldly as their sudden appearance made them seem, Cass' constructs were still flesh and blood. Once the element of surprise wore off the poacher's guns gave them a definitive advantage over their animal foes.

From there it took them no time all to bring the chaotic situation back under control. This meant Mira had run out of time.

Mira was still fiddling with the lock when one of the poachers Cass didn't recognize grabbed Mira from behind and threw her to the ground. The Gourabora roared in its cage. Mira tried to get away from the man but froze when he fired a shot at the empty ground next to her.

Two of the other men seized her by the arms and hauled her to her feet.

"Enough!" The lead poacher shouted at the jungle. "I know what you are, what you can do! Stop all this or I put a bullet in your friend here."

Mira struggled to free herself, but the two, burly men were simply too strong for the small, wiry woman.

Cass knew she didn't have a choice. Taking deep breaths she calmed herself. In her head, she pictured the camp how it was before she'd summoned her creations.

One by one, the wild animals that had overrun the camp disappeared back into whatever nothingness they had come from.

Cass opened her eyes and stepped out from behind the fig tree and into the clearing.

"I surrender. Don't hurt her." She said, making an extra effort to keep her voice calm and level.

The lead poacher motioned with his gun for her to move over towards Mira. Cass did as he instructed.

"You're one of the Touched." He said to her, once she'd reached Mira's side. "We've got ourselves a couple of Gourabora and one of the goddamned Touched boys."

The man leaned in and stuck his pistol right under Cass' chin, pushing her eyes up to look at his.

"Do you know how much a bitch like you can fetch on the open market?" He taunted.

Cass ignored the misogyny-laced taunt and instead focused her mind on the lock to the adult Gourabora's cage.

In her mind she saw it as unlocked, she knew it was unlocked.

The cage was unlocked.

There was a creaking sound of metal as the door to the Gourabora's cage swung open.

Like any mother having been forced to watch her children suffer but now free to do something about it, the Gourabora went on a rampage.

The lead poacher turned his head back at the beast's sudden howl. He turned completely around when he realized she was free and charging right for him.

"Oh shit." Was all the man could muster in the seconds before he was trampled to death by the legendary creature he had tried to cage.

Cass jumped out of the way of the raging Gourabora. The other poachers opened fire but not one of them hit their target.

There was the thundering crack of gunfire, then the most dreadful sound Cassidy had ever heard.

"Oh." Mira gasped.

Cass' head snapped to her lover. Mira's face wore a look of stunned surprise. She lowered a hand to her belly, where it found a sticky, red fluid flowing out of her. Her dark eyes turned to Cass, confusion and fear filling them.

"Mira!" Cass yelled, rushing to her side.

She got there just in time for Mira to fall into her arms.

The dark-skinned, dark-haired beauty tried to say something but choked on the words.

Her body gave one last shudder and the light left her eyes, leaving Cassidy with nothing but a blank stare.

Cassidy screamed. The deep, primal scream of love and loss.

The ground around her started to shake. The whole mountain, the whole island, trembled with her in her grief.

In an instant, the poachers were gone. Then the Gourabora and her young disappeared. Then the trees and the rocks and the beach and the ocean. All of reality was unraveling around her.

Cassidy screamed and everything went white.

****

The first thing Cassidy felt when she opened her eyes was the biting cold, the kind of cold that chilled you right down to the bone.

The second thing she felt was confusion. She was sitting cross-legged in a large stone room. Wires and cables covered the room like modern day vines. Flat-screen monitor displays were mounted along every wall. Neon lights gave the entire place a magenta hue.

Cassidy took a deep breath. In the middle of the far wall was a doorway. It opened and Cassidy got a glimpse of the world beyond the room. What she saw were snow-capped mountaintops. Her memories came flooding back to her.

A woman entered and closed the door behind her. The woman was older than Cassidy. Somewhere in her late forties. She looked young though, and she moved with confidence and grace. Her dark, taught skin was a contrast to Cassidy's pale softness.

"Do you remember where you are?" The woman asked her.

"Yes." Cassidy affirmed.

"Do you remember who I am?"

"Yes, Mistress Mira." She answered obediently

"You did better this time. Now let's try again."

Cassidy closed her eyes.

She could hear the far-off sound crashing waves as her mind gently faded to sleep.

No Refuge

Fire. Unnatural, unholy fire. Burning, consuming, killing. Laying claim to everything in its path. It raged around him. Taking his world and turning it to ash. His lungs burned. The tears in his eyes evaporated as quickly as they formed.

Screams filled the night. The sky was starless, but still the mercy of darkness was denied him. Denied him by the bright blazes that consumed his neighbor's homes.

His neighbors did not care about their burning homes. They did not care about anything anymore.

Their blood mixed with the dusty road to create a swamp of red-brown regret. Their bodies covered the landscape, contorted in every foul way imaginable.

Bolts of lightning crashed down around him. The product of a petulant God and the children he abandoned.

Every breath made the next that much harder to take. It was coming for him. Coming for his family.

A monster of the world's creating. A beast summoned from his own, personal hell.

It was coming to kill him. He wished he could let it.

That would be so much easier.

Fire and lightning. Blood and anger.

It was getting harder to breathe.

So impossibly hard to breathe.

He couldn't breathe.

Khalid awoke in a cold sweat, gasping for air, his heart pounding in his chest. Consciously he calmed himself; slowing his pulse with deep, deliberate breaths. He let his eyes scan the room reassuring himself that it was not on fire.

Moonlight filled the spacious bedroom, reflecting off the surface of the mirrored closet doors and illuminating the various pieces of cherry oak furniture that had come with the house. Everything was bigger here in America than it had been at home. Even the dresser drawers.

He looked over to the other side of the bed, where his wife lay undisturbed by his night terrors. That image, more than anything else, brought him back to the present.

Carefully, so as not to disturb his wife, he slipped off the covers and got out of bed. There was something especially soothing about the soft, fluffy carpet against his bare feet. It was just one of the many small ways in which his life had changed in the last year that continued to astound him.

This house held twice as many bedrooms as their previous home in Ryzal. There the children had been forced to share a bedroom. Here they had a room a piece and another just for their toys.

Khalid had never been a man of means. Not back in his homeland and certainly not here in this new world. But he had enough that he could provide for his family, enough his sons would never know the hunger he had as a boy. And now, God willing, they would also be safe from the horrors of war.

Peace and prosperity. The American Dream. His American Dream.

This train of thought put a melancholy smile on his face. He gave the state-of-the-art refrigerator an inspection and decided upon a piece of naan and a glass of milk for his midnight meal.

When he shut the refrigerator door he discovered he was not the only one experiencing a sleepless night.

"Hello there. And what are you doing out of bed?" He asked his diminutive company.

"I heard you, papa. I thought I'd make you not be alone." Jahmil was his youngest boy, just shy of his sixth birthday.

"Well, that's very thoughtful of you. But now is the time when young boys like you should be fast asleep." Khalid dropped to his knee and gave his son's belly a teasing tickle.

"I couldn't sleep, papa." Jahmil answered in their native Karziri.

"English, Jahmil." He reminded his son. "You must practice so that you can grow up like a true American."

"But we're not Americans papa, we're Ryzalis." Jahmil insisted in the way that almost six-year-olds do.

Khalid poured a second glass of milk and set it down on the table across from his own glass. He waited for Jahmil to get comfortable in his chair before answering.

"Here, we can be both," he explained. "That's the beauty of America. In this land, peoples from all over the world live together in peace. Here people celebrate what makes them different."

His son looked down at his now half-empty glass. Jahmil never wanted to look into Khalid's eyes when he thought what he was about to say would upset his father. Khalid hoped it was a habit his son would grow out of as he got older. A son should not be afraid to meet his father's eyes.

"People don't celebrate us." Jahmil said, finally sharing what was on his mind. "The kids at school look at us funny."

"That's because we're new. People don't like change. Once we've been here for a while and they get to know us they won't mind us so much." Jahmil still looked doubtful. Khalid tried a different tact. "Look at this beautiful home we have now, our nice car, all of your new toys. You like your toys don't you?"

"Yes, Papa" Jahmil replied dutifully.

"Well, all of that comes from Mr. Vernon. Out of the goodness of his heart, he gave your papa a job and put us in this house. Now if people really didn't want us here, why would he do all that?" Khalid asked his son.

Jahmil shrugged.

"He wouldn't." Khalid continued. "That just shows how wonderful America can be. But if we want to stay, we have to adapt to our new home. Which means, first and foremost, you must learn to speak fluent English."

Jahmil pondered his father's words. The pondering quickly became a yawn.

"Okay, that's enough for one night. Back to bed little one." Khalid picked the boy up in his arms and carried him back to his bedroom. Jahmil was asleep by the time Khalid set him back down.

* * *

Breakfast was on the table and the boys were dressed when Shadi woke him. When he complained about being allowed to sleep in, his wife dismissed his concerns as immaterial. She had decided he needed more sleep and so she had let him sleep. Khalid learned long ago that Shadi was not to be trifled with.

When all four of them were dressed and ready, they piled into their leased, American-made SUV. It was a company car and yet another perk of working for Mr. Vernon.

The local temple was within walking distance; but, like good Americans, they took the car anyway. It was quicker and, dressed as they were for services, it avoided any unfortunate misunderstandings.

Khalid pulled the car into the parking lot with only a few minutes to spare. To be late to Sunday services was a grievous affront to the Prophet, but he noticed his family was not the only one hustling to make it through the doors. Comfortable lives made for poor disciples.

Once inside, the men and the women separated. The boys, not yet of age, went with their mother and the other children.

Khalid removed his shoes and entered the sanctuary. There were waves and smiles all around as each man laid out their rugs on the dirt floor.

The indoor dirt floor was not the only unique feature of the room. Three pillars were placed equidistant from the walls and each other, forming an equilateral triangle in the middle of the room. As prescribed by the Rhametna; the space was empty save for the Aman, who would lead them in their prayers.

At precisely the strike of eight, the Aman took his place at the center of the triangle. Speaking Karziri, he began to pray.

"We give praise to Him

> *Creator and Provider*
> *Defender and Avenger*
> *He Who Is and Will Always Be"*

Khalid closed his eyes and focused on the Aman's words, repeating them back in unison with the rest of the congregation. His body moved with grace and fluidity. His muscles remembering without prompting his weekly ritual of almost twenty years.

> *"We offer you our Hearts*
> *So that you may make them whole.*
> *Grant us Courage in the Dark*
> *Love for those who seek to do us harm*
> *And a Passion to Serve your Will."*

Heat filled the room, but Khalid's hands remained cool. Flashes of light penetrated the dark cover of his eyelids. He knew all around him small sparks of fire were appearing in the palms of hands as together the congregation spoke the ancient words. Flame was the easiest of the three principal elements to master. Most here could summon it with ease. Khalid pushed the thought of others aside and focused on his own prayers.

> *"We offer you our Minds*
> *So that you may bestow upon them Your Truth*
> *Grant us Clarity in the Chaos*
> *The Wisdom to deal with that which vexes us*
> *And an Understanding of how to Serve your Will"*

The heat disappeared, replaced by a cool mist. Stray drops of moisture splashed against his skin. Around him, he heard the faint sound of water splattering against the dirt floor. Water was the second of the principle elements. It was harder to master than fire. Requiring a level of mental discipline from an apostle that most believers could only achieve under the controlled, guided meditation of an Aman.

> *"We offer you our Souls*
> *So that you may cleanse them of all shadow.*
> *Grant us Certainty in the Abyss*
> *The Steadfastness to abstain from that which tempts us*

And the Purity required to Serve your Will."

The mist dissipated and became…. nothing. Not one of the disciples here at the temple had mastered the third of the three principle elements: Air. In Ryzal, back before everything had gone so wrong, Khalid would have spoken these holy words and felt the wind in his hands. Embracing the very breath of life bestowed upon him by his creator. Now the words seemed empty, without meaning, bereft of their power. Just like Khalid.

"We give praise to Him
Creator and Provider
Defender and Avenger
He Who Is and Will Always Be"

When they were finished, they retired to the temple's sauna. Early believers had used sweat tents, but more modern times allowed for more comfortable surroundings. Even in Ryzal, his temple had a nice bathhouse attached to the rear of the building.

The purpose of the sauna was to sweat out the toxins of the outside world and purify believers. Allowing them to go forth into the world unencumbered by past mistakes, ready to follow the teachings of Elohim.

This was also a time for fellowship and the airing of grievances. For how can the believers stand together against the world if there if there is strife between them? And how can they be a family if they are strangers to one another?

The men spoke to each other in a combination of English and Karziri. Slipping between the two without much notice or thought. As was customary, they began by asking each other about their families.

"And the children?" Khalid asked his friend Hakeem.

"Healthy. Azra started her second year at the university. She has met a boy. And gotten a tattoo." Hakeem announced to the gathered worshipers.

"No!" Khalid gasped, he was not the only one.

"Yes! Banu nearly had a heart attack when she saw it. They were screaming at each other for hours." Hakeem continued, turning the story into a production replete with wild hand motions and shocked faces.

"What did you do?" one of the other men asked.

"What else could I do? I stayed silent and nodded my agreement. Then, once her mother had gone, I gave Azra a wad of money and told her to buy herself some new long sleeve shirts for when she comes to visit." Hakeem laughed at his own story. Others joined him. Those with daughters did not quite laugh as loud as those without.

"You are a pillar of wisdom!" One of the men proclaimed between chuckles.

"I am aren't I?" Hakeem agreed with a wide grin, which initiated another round of belly laughs.

"What was it of?" Khalid asked when the laughter subsided.

"What was it of?" Hakeem had laughed so hard he was wiping tears from his eyes.

"The tattoo." Khalid clarified. "What was it of?

"Oh," Hakeem still had a smile, but he grew a bit solemn when he answered "incredibly it was a verse from the Rhametna. Chapter eight, verse ten…"

"Be brave and defend your Brothers and Sisters. For they are your home, and it is in them that you must live." Khalid quoted.

"She said it was 'woke.'" Hakeem shrugged at the slang "I don't know what that means. But if it keeps her in the faith, I'm willing to go along with it."

From there, the conversation turned to the topic of Ryzal and what things from their native land they missed most.

"Back home, my wife used to make the most delicious hamakib you have ever tasted. It would fall off the bone and dance in your mouth. The flavor, oh the flavor was enough to make a man forget his aches and troubles. It was the closest to Elohim you could come in this life. Now?" Amir spat on the ground. "She swears it is the store bought baharat, but I think she is doing it on purpose. Punishing me for bringing her here."

"All hamakib is shit in America." Jalil was the oldest of them. And by far the most cantankerous. "But the ice cream. Thirty-one flavors. Who knew there could be such decadence without disobeying the words of the Prophet?"

"Apparently you did." Behnam reached over to rub the old man's robust belly. Laughter echoed off the linoleum tile, every man there sharing in the merriment. All save one.

"Not everyone has adjusted to our new lives as well as you Jalil." One of the congregants Khalid did not know spoke up from his place in the corner. "My Cousin Massoud took his family back to Ryzal. Just picked up one night and vanished."

"If they vanished, how do you know they went back to Ryzal?" Khalid asked.

The man just shrugged "They left a note"

"He's not the only one." Amir added "A man I work with at the shopping center, his name is Parviz, one day he just stopped coming in. After a week, I got worried. I went to his home, but no one was there. I asked his neighbors; they said a moving truck had come in the middle of the night and no one had seen him since."

"Did you talk to the police?" Jalil inquired.

"Why bother?" Amir threw his arms up in frustration "They would just label him a terrorist and throw me in a cell until I confessed I was one as well."

Soon all of them were sharing stories of friends of a friend or a relative's acquaintance who just upped and disappeared. Khalid sat and listened as the same story was repeated over and over.

It made no sense. Why would so many of their brothers abandon their new homes in such a fashion? To return to Ryzal? Their homeland had been beautiful once, the jewel of the desert. But now nothing remained save blood and ash. No sane man would return. Not if given a choice.

Something was very wrong. Khalid could feel it in his bones.

With the tone of their talks now soured, many of the men began to take their leave. Khalid waited for the initial rush to pass, then he too exited the sauna. He dressed and made his way to the parking lot. Distractedly, he said his goodbyes to his fellow disciples; his mind still fixated on the disturbing mystery of his vanishing brethren.

Those disquiet thoughts were forgotten at the sight of Shadi and his two boys waiting for him at the car.

"Who wants to go see a movie?" Khalid asked. Summoning a broad smile to his face.

"I do papa! I do!" Jahmil exclaimed. Hands raised high in the air.

Khalid bent down and took his youngest son in his arms. The boy was growing big. Soon he would be too big for Khalid to pick up. But he was not too big yet, so Khalid enjoyed the moment.

"Can we get ice cream too?" His other boy, Fadi, asked excitedly.

"I don't know can we mother?" Khalid asked his wife, whose face was scrunched up in mock disapproval.

"Oh yes. Leave it to mother to say no." Shadi said sternly. "*If* you behave during the movie, then *maybe* we'll get ice cream after."

"Yayy!!" Together Jahmil and Fadi let out a victorious cry. Khalid laughed and bounced the smaller victor in his arms while reaching out a hand to muss the hair of the other.

"You spoil them." His wife told him.

Khalid gave her a softer smile. A sadder one.

She was right.

But what else would she have him do?

* * *

On Monday, the family repeated the same morning routine. Only this time, instead of going to temple, Khalid dropped off Fadi and Jahmil at school before continuing on to his latest work site.

But there when he climbed out of his SUV, he was not met with words of greeting or waves of welcome. There, he was barely met with any acknowledgment at all. A few luke-warm nods and a few more distrustful glares.

Khalid did not mind. He was a stranger. Why should they welcome any more than they already had? Eventually, he would earn his place among them. Until that time he could endure a few unfriendly glances. His family was safe and prosperous in this new world. Faced with the alternatives, there were a great many things he could endure.

With that thought firmly entrenched in his mind, Khalid threw on his hard hat and orange vest and got to work.

His day went by quickly, as it often did. Most of his tasks could be completed in isolation. He didn't know if this was by design or not, but he liked the work. Back home he'd been a teacher, here that wasn't possible. So he put in a hard day's labor with his hands. Building homes for families so he could provide the same for his own. He found the symmetry most pleasing.

It was nearly time to clock out when he encountered something was off with his daily inventory. After double checking to make sure he wasn't just imagining the problem, Khalid decided that it was an issue best addressed by Mr. Vernon personally.

He finished up his other duties and made is way back towards Mr. Vernon's trailer at the edge of the site.

As he was walking, he passed a group of laborers who were enjoying their lunch break. Khalid had not learned all of their names yet, so he kept his eyes down and gave them a simple courtesy nod as he went by.

"Maybe Khalid here can tell us." On hearing his name. Khalid stopped and turned around. The men, there were five of them, formed a circle around Khalid so that he was surrounded. They were a fairly interchangeable bunch, with sun-burnt skin and tattoos of barbed wire and wolves on their bare arms. It was the reason Khalid hadn't managed to learn all their names yet, despite making a concerted effort to do so. The truth was all white people looked alike to him.

Still, he wanted to be accepted, so he smiled and politely asked "How can I be of service?"

The man who's spoken before shrugged "Well we just wondering. You Ryzali's are supposed to control all the elements right? Water, air, earth, all that stuff."

"Many members of the faith can, yes." Khalid confirmed

"So why is it you Noshaa are always burning shit to the ground? You think with all that power you'd be able to do more than just set fire to shit wouldn't you?" The men tightened their circle around Khalid.

"The Noshaa are fundamentalists. Extremists." Khalid tried to explain

"They bend the words of the Rhametna for their own purposes. They use fire because it is the easiest of the elements to summon. The one that requires the least amount of discipline and enlightenment. They do not follow the true faith."

"Well, as long as they don't follow the true faith that's not so bad. Is it fellas?" He looked around to the other men for agreement, most of them just snickered. Khalid grew nervous.

"But the thing is I think they do follow the true faith. Your little book says your all supposed to be soldiers in some big war right?"

"Yes, but..." Khalid tried to explain that the war was meant as a metaphor and that in that war they were charged with defending the innocent, but the head man cut him off.

"See Mickey's brother here got his leg burned off by one of you flamers. He was over there defending our freedoms from terrorists like you and your Noshaa pals. So we're over here thinking that maybe we owe your kind a little payback" He thrust his finger into Khalid's chest.

"Please, I have nothing to do with them. I am not a terrorist." Khalid tried to plead with them

The situation was about to escalate when their employer stepped out of his trailer office.

"Khalid, can you come in here a minute. I need to speak with you." Mr. Vernon shouted across the yard. Khalid tried to move through the men put still found his path blocked.

"Fred?" Mr. Vernon continued "Fred, what are you doing? Can't you see the man's trying to get past you? Well? What are you all lolly-gagging about for? We've got houses to build."

Reluctantly the men dispersed, muttering about next times and Khalid being lucky as they did.

Khalid moved quickly to get away from them.

Mr. Vernon stayed outside to watch until Khalid was safely in his trailer.

"Thank you, Mr. Vernon." Khalid said once they were inside.

"Those boys are just foolin'." Mr. Vernon assured him. "Don't you think nothing of it. Hard work like this, some men just need to blow off a little steam come the end of the day."

"I do not mean to be a problem. You have done so much for my family and me, I would hate to think that my presence causes trouble for you." Khalid knew that such men could be prone to take out their frustrations on Mr. Vernon or his business in an attempt to intimidate him. In that way, his new home and his old home were very similar.

"No trouble at all. And please, Khalid, you don't have to thank me every time you see me. It's my Christian duty to help those in need. And I always do my duty." Mr. Vernon let that be the last word on the matter, before returning to business. "Now you were coming to see me for a reason. What can I do for you?"

Khalid handed him the inventory sheet along with the invoice for the lumber they had bought for the job. After walking through what he had found Khalid summarized his conclusions. "You see, we've got two receipts but only the materials for one. So either we were double billed or….."

"Or someone is stealing lumber." Mr. Vernon finished for him. "Well, Khalid this is mighty fine work. Leave it with me and I'll get into it. My guess its just some kind of bookkeeping mistake, but if somebody is stealing you can bet your behind that I'm gonna get to the bottom of it."

Mr. Vernon patted Khalid on the shoulder and gave it a little squeeze.

"Yes sir, that's some mighty fine work. You just get on home to that lovely wife of yours and don't give it another thought."

Mr. Vernon's smile was as wide as the sky when he opened the door to show Khalid out. Khalid was smiling as well as he exited the trailer and headed for his car. Happy to be of some use to a man who had done so much for him.

* * *

It was coming for him. Coming for his family.
  Thunder boomed outside. The earth shook. The sky howled.
  It was coming to kill him. It was coming to kill his family.
  Fire filled his lungs.

Behind him, he heard crying. He turned to look. It was his son Jahmil.
The boy was frightened. The boy should be frightened.
He could feel it on the back of his neck. The shadow who had come to claim his boy.
He wished he could let it kill him. That would be so much easier.
It was almost upon him now. His soul burned as it approached.
But the rest of him felt cold. So very cold.

A throbbing pain filled Khalid's skull. His whole body was shivering. He opened his eyes and found himself laying on a dirt floor, completely naked. All around him was a wooden fence that stood nearly three times his own height.

Speakers mounted along the top of the fence blared a martial march. The severity of the percussion playing only adding to his pounding headache.

Mounted alongside the speakers were four television screens. One for every corner of the wooden pen Khalid now found himself in. At the moment the screens were displaying nothing but an American flag rustling in the wind.

Khalid pushed himself up off the dirt floor. He tried to cover himself for some semblance of modesty, but he was too cold and instead, he wrapped his arms around himself. It was not enough to stave off the chilly night air, but futile as it was he could not fight the instinct to rub his hands over his arms.

The sheer shock of waking up in such a state began to wear off and was replaced by an overwhelming sense of panic and confusion. His mind worked overtime, trying to remember how he had gotten here and just what and where exactly "here" was.

Once his brain started to process his surroundings properly, he realized that he knew this song. It had been playing on the chopper that had evacuated him and his family from Ryzal. He'd asked the soldier back then, what the piece of music was. He'd said it was called Semper Fidelis and was the official march of the United States Marine Corps.

What had sounded triumphant then, now terrified him in a way he hadn't felt since he had left the bloody civil war of his homeland behind.

The song ended abruptly. The waving flags on the television screens were replaced by a close up of a man wearing an Uncle Sam mask. An electronically distorted voice blared through the speakers.

"Hello, Khalid. You and your family have chosen to make yourselves at home here in the good ol' U. S. of A.. Like so many filthy immigrants before you, you've come to this country to leech off our resources. Taking jobs away from hard-working Americans and infecting this nation with your poisonous ideology. Refusing to assimilate yourself and putting the laws of your hateful, militant faith above our own sacred constitution. But living in America is a privilege. One you have to earn. And no longer will we, its faithful citizens, roll over to your fifth column of infiltrators and terrorists. We will fight for this nation. And if necessary we will kill for it. So consider this your Citizenship test Khalid. Pass and you get to live as a proud American. Fail and you die, a traitor to the grand ideals this country was founded upon. Follow my instructions precisely or you will be punished. And now we begin."

The screens reverted to a picture of an American flag blowing in the breeze. Khalid heard a creepy, creaking sound. The fence in front of him split in two and slowly swung open revealing another fenced in area behind it.

Seeing no other option put to push onward with this madman's game, Khalid stepped forward. Leaving the first room behind, while silently praying this was all just another nightmare.

The path was dim and narrow. The way ahead lit only by strings of Christmas lights hung along the top of the fence. The space was intensely claustrophobic. And he soon realized that the tall, wooden fences were slowly creeping inwards; imperceptibly narrowing over time until the path was so tight Khalid had to slide his body sideways to continue forward.

When he emerged from this cramped trail, Khalid stood in a small area almost identical to the space he had just come from. There were two notable differences. The first difference was the floor. Instead of dirt floors, the ground was now covered in small tiles made out of some kind of metal plating, and standing in front of the far fence across from where he entered was a flagpole with an American flag attached.

Tentatively, Khalid stepped off of the dirt floor and on to the metal plating. When nothing happened, he took a few more steps, then a few more. When he had reached the center of the room the video screens came to life. The man in the Uncle Sam mask was back.

"The American flag is the beating heart of this country. For centuries men have died for that flag. Sacrificing themselves, shedding their blood, so that we might be free. If you want to live in this country you have to prove that you respect the flag and the men and woman who died for it." Uncle Sam picked up the camera and the shot panned over to where a red dial was hooked to a circuit box of some kind. "The floor you're standing on is wired to conduct electricity. When I turn this dial I'll be cranking up the power and you'll begin to feel what I'm talking about. I'm going to play the Star-Spangled Banner for you. If you can stay standing on that central tile with your hand over your heart for the entire song then you'll live. If you are, as I suspect, too weak to respect our flag the way a patriot should respect it, if you drop to a knee or take your hand from your heart; then I will turn the dial all the way up and you will be flooded with one hundred thousand volts of electricity." His tormentor cackled "Good luck surviving a jolt like that. Now that you understand what's at stake, let's begin."

The screen went black. A brief pause, then the Star-Spangled Banner began to play over the speakers.

Khalid hurriedly put his hand over his heart and tried to keep himself perfectly still. Rage and humiliation boiled inside him but what else was he going to do.

There was no doubt in Khalid's mind that this maniac would follow through on his threats. If he died here, in this godforsaken place, who would be there to look after his family. He had no choice but to do as he was instructed and wait for an opportunity to escape presented itself.

As the anthem played, a painful tingle started to run through his body. His feet burned and he could feel his muscles spasm uncontrollably. Every hair on his humiliatingly naked body stood on end. He clenched his teeth, worried that he might bite off his own tongue as his pain increased.

His vision doubled, then quadrupled. Every part of him was in agony now. The song continued to play but Khalid could not hear it.

Keeping his hand over his heart was becoming nearly an impossible task. Still, by the grace of God, he managed to hold it there. His knees grew wobbly. He was certain he was about to fall down.

He was ready to give in. To end this eternal anguish. Tears streamed down his face as the anthem reached its crescendo.

Khalid held onto one thought.

God, please let me see my family again.

Without that thought, he almost certainly would have given in to the pain.

The anthem ended and the pain stopped.

Khalid collapsed to the metal floor beneath him. His body still spasming. His feet blackened and burned.

"Very good, Khalid." Uncle Sam reappeared on the television screens to congratulate him. "You managed to learn the first lesson to becoming an American. Respect the flag at all times. Time to move on to your next test."

The monitors went black and the fence behind the flag slid open to reveal yet another long, dark pathway.

Still sobbing on the metal floor, Khalid decided he was done with this farce. This monster was going to kill him no matter how Khalid performed in his tests.

Khalid closed his eyes and focused on his faith in God. He began reciting the ancient prayers. He waited for the sparks to form upon his fingertips so he could burn down these fences and escape, but none came. As he had for so many months now, the prophet had abandoned him. Khalid had no choice but to continue onward.

As difficult as that choice was to make, it was even more agonizing to follow through on. Khalid's body hurt all over, but the most intense part of that pain came from his feet. After two and a half minutes of having electrical current run through them, they were scorched from toe to heel with electrical burns.

Every step Khalid took sent pain running through his body. It took him a full minute before he could consider taking another.

He half limped, half crawled down the fenced path to the next of his tests, knowing that all the while the man in the Uncle Sam mask was watching him.

The excruciating journey brought him to yet another makeshift room where the sight of a chair and table sitting in the center of it initiated a flood of relief and gratitude within him. The thought of any respite from his current suffering filled him with primal joy, even if that relief was offered to him by the man who had inflicted the suffering in the first place.

Khalid crawled to the chair and waited for the television screens to come alive. He did not have to wait long.

"You passed the first test, Khalid." The disembodied digital voice began "But it's not enough just to love America. You have to understand America's history, what it stands for. I'm going to ask you three questions. Get them all wrong and you die. Answer just one correctly and you pass."

The voice paused, almost as if it was waiting for Khalid to thank it for its benevolence. Khalid said nothing.

"Place your hands inside the two boxes in front of you." The voice continued on, more agitated than before. "Non-compliance will result in your immediate execution as a suspected traitor to this great nation. Put your hands in the box Khalid or suffer the consequences."

Khalid did as he was told.

"First question. True or false: The United States was founded as a Christian nation." Uncle Sam asked.

Khalid did not know much about his new country, but he did know that the law of this land established the separation of church and state. A law which he wished his own country had put into place. This masked man had said that Khalid wanted to put his own religious laws above the constitution. The constitution was supreme. Knowing this Khalid gave his answer.

"False." he said with confidence.

There was a hissing noise from inside the right box. At first Khalid's hand just felt incredibly cold. But then it felt like the flesh was burning off his bones.

Khalid screamed.

Instinctively, he tried to pull his hand free, but the clamp was too tight.

Khalid could do nothing as the fingers on his right hand were separated from his body. No blood spurted from his severed digits, they were simply not there anymore. Frozen and shattered into a thousand tiny pieces of flesh and bone.

His captor cared not one bit about Khalid's distress.

"Wrong." Uncle Sam screamed at him through the screen "The Founding Fathers were all Christians and they specifically designed the Constitution around Christian ideas. You haven't been paying attention, Khalid. Just because you want to destroy our Christian heritage and replace it with your Satanic cult doesn't mean we're going to let you."

Uncle Sam took a deep breath and collected himself.

"Liquid nitrogen, Khalid. Not all that hard to come by. A penalty for your heretical lies, but it's possible you simply made a mistake. That you'd been ill-informed by the lefty-libtards who are trying to kill God in America one happy holiday at a time, so I'll give you another shot. Two even.Second question: What was the reason for the War between the States?"

"To end slavery" Khalid answered. Certain of the answer but unsure of his captor's expected response.

Khalid heard the hissing noise begin in the left box. He screamed, begged and pleaded with his captor to give him another chance. Uncle Sam watched quietly while Khalid lost the fingers on his left hand in the same gruesome manner he had lost the digits on his right.

"Incorrect, Khalid." The voice informed him "The war between the states was about northern jealousy over southern prosperity and the rights of the individual states to make their own laws as they best apply to their own sovereign citizens.

"Last chance. Get this last question right or face the consequences." The inference of more torture to come focused Khalid even as his body struggled to make sense of the pain it was enduring. "What is the only economic system that is compatible with the Christian Ideals upon which this nation was founded?"

"Capitalism." Khalid spoke the words tentatively. Certain he was wrong again and this time he would pay for it with his life.

"Correct!" Uncle Sam roared. "Capitalism reflects the teachings of the Gospel, which teaches us that God will reward the devotion and hard work of his followers with material wealth and punish the wicked with destitution. Prosperity is proof that you are following the teachings of our Savior, Jesus Christ. Congratulations Khalid, you survive and advance to the next round. Right this way."

Again the wooden wall in front of Khalid swung open and again Khalid struggled to advance down the path of pain that this Uncle Sam had laid out in front of him. His feet were still burned, and his naked body still shivered from the cold. Now he also struggled with the loss of all his fingers. He was in shock. His mind almost completely detached from his body. It took all of Khalid's will not to lay down and wait for death to claim him. There was no possibility that his body could endure any more trauma to its system. Khalid doubted that it would ever recover from the indignities it had suffered here already tonight.

Still though, he crawled his way forward. Clawing his body along the dirt path with his elbows until he reached the next room Uncle Sam's murder maze.

The next room was similar to the others. A dirt floor with no adornments only tall, wooden walls. Here though instead of a square, the room was a pentagon. With four walls angled to face Khalid instead of three.

On each wall was a plaque with a single engraved word and beneath the plaque was a large metal switch. From left to right the words read "Jews, Negros, Homosexuals, Mexicans".

As soon as Khalid pulled himself into the center of the room, Uncle Sam appeared on each of the rooms five screens.

"Khalid, tonight I've taught you about our flag and the history behind that flag. Now its time for you to learn about the pernicious threats to our way of life that are infiltrating and subverting American values every day."

"The first threat is the Jews. The International Jewry controls a vast array of financial institutions and secret societies they use to pull the strings of their puppet governments. Lead by the Rothschild family they lie in wait to establish their New World Order and bring about the end of days."

"The next threat is the Negro. The Negro is a naturally inferior creature to the white man. He must be kept in his place. If he is not. He becomes lethargic and troublesome. Left to their own devices the negro will not work, choosing instead to use drugs and abuse women. All the while, living off what they can beg and steal from the hard-working white man."

"Then there are the homosexuals. Cucks who are so cucked they fuck each other in violation of God's law. They undermine the fabric of society with their hedonism and their sinfulness. They destroy the basic family unit that God and this country's founders intended Americans to follow, leading us down a path of moral relativism that flouts the laws of nature. "

"Finally we have the Mexicans, who flock to this country to steal our jobs and undermine our culture. They refuse to assimilate. Are lazy and entitled. And breed like jackrabbits so they can take this country from us, not by force, but by demographics. One day we'll wake up and look around and see that these wetbacks and their anchor babies outnumber us and at that point, it will be too late to stop them."

"You've heard the case against each Khalid. Now you have to decide which of these nefarious forces poses the greatest risk to the American way of life. When you've got your answer, flip the switch of your chosen enemy."

Khalid wept. Listening to this insane psychopath's ramblings broke his heart. No one should be capable of this much hate. But the pain of his missing fingers left him no doubt of his captor's evil nature.

Not knowing what else to do and knowing that a wrong answer would probably mean his death, Khalid went with his best guess of what his captor wanted him to choose.

Slowly, painfully, he crawled across the floor on his belly to the plaque that said "Negro". Enduring the pain of standing he pushed himself off the ground and stood up on his burnt feet. Having no fingers with which to grip the switch, Khalid pushed it down with his forearm.

The wooden fence fell forward. Khalid had to scramble back to avoid being crushed by its massive weight.

Behind the fence was a glass box. A glass cage really. Inside the cage was a young African-American man; bound, arms and legs, to a metal chair. His mouth was gagged with an American flag held in place by a large quantity of duct tape.

His eyes went wide when he saw Khalid. He screamed and he wriggled, and he tried to break himself free of his bonds. But no matter how hard he struggled he could not break free.

Khalid hobbled forward. Ramming the glass with his arms and his shoulders he tried to break open the cage. Try as he might, he could not so much as crack it in his weakened state. Khalid abandoned that tactic and attempted kicking the glass in. The pain of that effort nearly caused him to lose consciousness. After a few minutes, Khalid slumped, exhausted from his efforts. Efforts that had accomplished nothing other than to smear his own blood all over the glass.

It was then, once Khalid had given up completely, that a yellow gas began to pour into the cage. Khalid watched the panic in the young man's eyes as the gas descended towards him.

The yellow substance touched his skin, and the poor man writhed in agony. His skin blistered and boiled. Slowly his skin became a gelatinous goo that dripped off his frame.

The young man, having no way to avoid inhaling the noxious gas, choked on the noxious fumes. His eyes bleeding then bulging, then finally exploding just as his face was melting off of his skull.

Khalid vomited. Unable to look away from the horror until the innocent young man in the cage was nothing but a skeleton.

Uncle Sam, silent this whole time, waited until Khalid stopped weeping to speak.

"Sorry, Khalid. Wrong again." The monster taunted him. "A good attempt though. The answer is E, all of the above." The other walls dropped away, revealing three more men trapped in glass boxes. Naked and strapped to chairs just as the first man had been.

They were gagged, but at the sight of Khalid, all three men struggled and forced out muffled cries for help. Just as the first man had. And, like him, they did not know that Khalid could do nothing to save them.

The yellow gas flowed forth from the vents to fill their cages and turn them into glass tombs. Khalid knew what was about to happen. Knew that he was impotent to stop it. But he could not bring himself to look away.

These men were about to be slaughtered like animals for the crime of being born. Slaughtered by a sub-human monster who wrapped up his bigotry and violence in a righteous ideology so that it might give him an excuse to fulfill his own base desires. They did not know it, but these men were martyrs for a better world. Khalid owed it to them to bear witness to their suffering.

Their deaths were not quick. Their deaths were not painless. One by one each succumbed and fell still.

Khalid wanted to scream. To rage against his tormentor. To stop him from hurting anyone else. To stop any of this happening ever again.

But he was too tired to scream. In too much pain to feel rage. Too numb to care about anyone or anything that wasn't him now. Khalid was ashamed that he did not feel more for those men. They were dead now and he was not. Damn him he was still alive.

A strange smell filled the air. Khalid's eyes grew heavy. As darkness claimed him he welcomed the terrible void with open arms.

* * *

Blood. So much Blood. The ground was covered in it.

His son, Jahmil, crouched behind him. He did not know where his wife and middle child were.

He hoped they had escaped from this madness. Escaped the fury and fire of the monsters who had come to kill them.

The door opened and a shadow stepped inside.

"Stay back" Khalid warned it.

Still the monster approached.

The red eyes of a demon bore down on him.

Pain. Anguish. Fear.

The shadowy figure's gaze made him feel all these things and more.

It strode forward. Its fists igniting in red-orange flames.

"Stop. Please. Don't do this." Khalid placed himself between the figure and his boy.

The figure stepped out of the shadow and into the light.

"Stop or what Papa? You would kill your firstborn son?. Murder him to save yourself?" *The question echoed in his mind. Its mockery broke his heart.*

"Please Naasik. We are your family." *Khalid pleaded with the monster who had consumed his son.*

It did not stop.

"The Noshaa are my family. You are heretics. And Heretics must be purged with the Flames of Elohim."

Naasik raised his hands. Fire raged around his fists.

Heat filled the room.

There was a flash of white-hot light.

When it was gone Naasik stood there; mouth agape, his hands extinguished.

A hole the size of Khalid's palm now existed where his son's heart should be.

As the light faded from the boy's eyes, Naasik looked at his father.

"You killed me, father. Why did you kill me?"

The sharp smell of ammonia jolted Khalid awake. His eyes were filled with tears, making his vision blurry. He could hear his heart thundering in his chest.

"Naasik" He whimpered. "My poor, sweet Naasik."

"Still not with us?" Khalid felt a sharp crack against his jaw. His eyes widened and he was back in reality. Reluctantly leaving his oldest boy behind. "There, that's better."

Uncle Sam's words were muffled beneath his plaster mask. He was here in the flesh now, dressed head to toe in the stars and stripes. In his hand he held a large revolver, waving it around as he spoke.

Khalid was sitting in a chair. His legs were tied to its legs and his hands were bound behind his back. He struggled against his restraints. It did him no good. They were far too tight to give him even a fighting chance.

Uncle Sam watched him as he wriggled. Khalid could sense the man's smug satisfaction at seeing him chafe at the ropes and get nowhere.

"No use struggling. I was an Eagle Scout. Not even the Good Lord himself could get out of those knots."

Work-lights on metal stands lit the makeshift enclosure. Behind Uncle Sam was a large curtain, emblazoned with the American flag.

"So far you've learned about our history, our flag, and the Christian nation for which it stands. And you've learned about those who would threaten this country. The kikes and the godless Commies who use the spics and the niggers to do their dirty work. Now it's time for you to learn the most important lesson of them all. That freedom isn't free. That it requires sacrifice. So I ask you Khalid: What is it you're prepared to sacrifice to defend the principals of this great nation."

The maniac pulled the curtain back to reveal Khalid's family. They were tied and bound as he was, with gags in their mouths.

Khalid could see the fear and confusion in his boys' eyes. Tears running down their cheeks, they looked to him to save them from whatever was about to happen.

In Shadi's eyes, he saw something different. Horror and desperation. She knew terrible things were about to happen to them but she would not, could not, give up hope that they might still save the children.

Hatred and rage burned in Khalid's chest. He would not let this broken world take yet another son from him.

"I asked you a question, Khalid." Uncle Sam was pacing back and forth between Khalid and his family. Waving his gun around while he spoke. "What are you willing to sacrifice to uphold this great nation?"

"Please, I don't understand." Khalid pleaded.

"Yes. you do!" Uncle Sam screamed from behind his mask. He grabbed Shadi by the throat and pressed the barrel of his gun against her temple. "It's simple. If your family wants to live in this great nation, then it must prove that it is willing to shed its blood for the privilege.

Uncle Sam let go of Shadi. She wept silently into her gag. Tears flowing down her cheeks.

"So choose. Your wife, your eldest son, or your baby boy? Who are you going to sacrifice for the American dream?" Their torturer circled around behind his hostages pointing the gun he held at the back of their heads as he called each member of Khalid's family out.

"Myself!" Khalid shouted through his tears "I choose myself!"

Uncle Sam turned and pointed the gun directly at Khalid's head.

"That is not one of your options." Uncle Sam dropped his arm, pressing the gun against Khalid's left kneecap. There was a loud pop and Khalid's vision went white. Pain flooded his brain.

Khalid prayed to Elohim to give him strength, to bestow upon him the power to save his family. He whispered the ancient words and concentrated on He Who Is and Ever Will Be.

"Oh no, you're not going to start summoning up any of that devil worshiping mumbo-jumbo. The devil won't save you today." Uncle Sam fired a single shot into Khalid's stomach. Blood flowed out of him, like water from a spout. The agony should have been unendurable, but with the grace of Elohim he bore it.

Uncle Sam bent down and placed the still hot muzzle of his gun against Khalid's injured knee. The flesh burned and blistered. Khalid screamed in anguish.

"You're not going to be with us very much longer. Choose one, right now, or I put a bullet in all three and let you bleed out on the floor together like the dogs you are."

Khalid ignored the searing pain in his gut and focused on his prayers. Sparks danced on the edge of his fingertips. His wrists burned as the ropes that bound him turned to ash.

"Fine. If you're unwilling to make the hard choices. Then you're not worthy to be an American. Say goodbye to your sand-witch wife."

Uncle Sam put his gun to the back of Shadi's head and pulled the trigger.

Khalid raised his hands to try and stop him. All he could manage was a few impotent sparks.

In a heartbeat, his beloved Shadi was gone. Replaced by a gushing mass of blood and bone.

The boys screamed into their gags. Their faces covered in their mother's blood.

"And now the children. Before they can grow up and breed. Tainting the rest of us with their impurity." Uncle Sam stepped away from Shadi's slumped over corpse and aimed his massive revolver at Fadi.

"Elohim give me strength." With one final breath, Khalid summoned all his will, all his rage, all his love and hurled it at the monster trying to take his children from him.

A cylinder of fire erupted from his palms. It crossed the room with holy fury, striking their tormentor in the chest and burning a hole through his torso.

The man stood still for a moment, then collapsed to the floor. The Uncle Sam mask he wore slipped off and dropped to the ground beside him.

Khalid did not see who was underneath the mask.

His vision was filled with a bright light.

Khalid was cold and the light was warm.

There was a figure basking in the light. Bathing in its glow.

The figure reached out his hand and Khalid knew who it was who had come for him.

"Come Papa. It's time to go home."

Khalid reached up a hand and joined his son in paradise.

Fight Night

Blood flowed freely from a cut just above his right eye. It mixed with his sweat and blurred his vision, forcing him to fight with one eye closed. His heart pounded in his chest. His side throbbed in pain with every inhale and exhale. At least one of his ribs was broken and the smart money was taking the over.

Mitch kept his hands up. Protecting himself from the steady, relentless pummeling of his foe's fists. He ducked underneath a right jab and drove his shoulder into the creature's midsection and took it to the ground. He could feel the demon's hot breath against his skin while they grappled for position.

Sweat flew from his forehead as he pressed his advantage, landing successive elbows, not with the methodical precision of a seasoned fighter, but with the wild abandon of a common street brawler. His recklessness let his foe establish a closed guard, taking control of Mitch's hips.

His mistake was compounded when the demon ducked one of his elbows and managed to get hold of Mitch's neck.

Black spots filled Mitch's vision as he began to lose consciousness. His right hand grabbed at the scaly, green arm around his neck while the left slammed violently against the ground. He heard the distant sound of a bell and the arm released him. Oxygen rushed into his lungs as he rolled away from his opponent. With each gasping breath, his brain got a little bit less fuzzy.

A man wearing white gloves began asking him questions. It was impossible to hear him over the roar of the crowd. It didn't matter. They were the same questions every fighter got asked after a choke out. And, like every other fighter, Mitch could answer them without actually hearing them being asked.

It was expected that he would play the dutiful loser, humbly standing there as the referee lifted the opposing fighter's arm in triumph. Whoever had thought it was appropriate to make a defeated man stand center ring in the shadow of his opponent's glory had clearly never been a fighter. But Mitch did as he was expected to, muttering words of insincere congratulations during a brief embrace with his most recent foe.

The fight had come down to Mitch's recklessness. He'd gone wild and lost track of the fight, allowing his opponent to the counter and score a submission. It was a mistake you'd see from a young fighter. At thirty-six, Mitch should know better than to leave himself open like that.

And he did. But if he was going to take a dive, he had to make it believable. And a has-been fighter making a rookie mistake just confirmed the crowd's built-in narrative, that he was a loser. And everyone knows that losers always find a way to lose.

Slowly he made his way back to the trainer's room. Fixed or not, a fight was a fight and that one had taken a lot out of him. Mitch grimaced as he unwrapped the tape from his knuckles. His hands had already begun to bruise. Going toe-to-toe with a demon was almost always harder on the fists than battling it out with a regular human opponent. By and large, demons had much tougher skin than your run of the mill human being. Some of them even had hides, those bastards were a bitch to fight.

The trainer's room looked slightly better than his high school locker room but smelled far worse. Trainer's room was also a bit of a misnomer in that there were no actual trainers. This was not that sophisticated of an operation.

Mitch's opponent was still out in the ring, basking in the glory of his victory. That was fine by Mitch, he hoped to be changed and out the door before he had to look at the smug son-of-a-bitch's face.

Grabbing a towel, he hit the showers. When he exited a few minutes later, a gray-skinned demon in a three-piece suit was waiting for him, flanked by a purple bruiser in a green tracksuit. The bruiser stood near enough a full head-and-a-half taller than the average person, with muscles to match even the most devoted gym rat. But out of the pair of demons who'd just dropped in to see him, he was not the one who intimidated Mitch.

"Good fight tonight Mitch. You put on a real show. Those idiots out there ate it up." The stout, well-dressed demon said with a jovial smile.

"Thanks, boss." The words made Mitch sick to his stomach, but this was the way the world worked, and virtue had never paid his rent.

Similar to most demons, Donospohaliel preferred not to be called by his full name. Instead, people around the city referred to him simply as The Don. The moniker had as much to do with shortening the demon's name as it did with providing an apt descriptor of his line of work.

The Don had his finger in every pie from North Beach to Excelsior. His primary income came from drug dealing and gun smuggling, but his passion was his bookmaking. After all what kind of demon didn't like a little bit of gambling. And while The Don would have a hard time getting Steph Curry to shave points or Belshire the Indomitable to shank a field goal without alerting the higher powers; he didn't have that hard of a time getting a fighter to throw a fight. Especially when that fighter was on a card The Don himself had put together.

Making a concerted effort not to show The Don any disrespect by turning his back to him, Mitch reached into his locker and pulled out his street clothes.

While Mitch dressed, The Don pulled a small envelope from inside his jacket pocket and handed it over to the fighter. Mitch knew better than to count the money in front of the mobster, but he also knew that the envelope was too thin to hold the amount he was promised.

"Boss…" Mitch started to speak

The Don turned back glaring daggers, his amicable disposition having disappeared, wondering if the loser fighter would be stupid enough to question his integrity.

"No disrespect Boss and I'm always happy to do what I'm told, but I was just wondering when I'd get an opportunity for a clean fight again. I've taken a lot of losses lately. It'd be nice to get a win." Mitch kept his tone as deferential as he could manage.

The Don shared a disbelieving grin with his muscle.

"Can you believe this guy. He thinks his loses are rigged but his wins are clean. Human arrogance never ceases to amaze me." The Don turned his attention back to Mitch. "Now you listen to me. You win when I say you win, and you lose when I say you lose. Not my fault you humans only put your money on your own kind. You'd think by this point you'd have learned which of our species is bigger, faster, and smarter."

Mitch nodded along with The Don's chastisement. It chaffed him but if he wanted to keep paying his bills it was a necessary display of humility.

"You're right Boss, I was out of line. Few too many hits to the head tonight. Please forget I said anything" It was tough for Mitch to keep the sarcasm out of his voice, but he managed.

Sufficiently placated, The Don was all smiles again.

"You're a smart fighter, Mitch. You always do what you're told. That means you've never had to find out what happens to dumb fighters who can't follow instructions. It'd break my heart if one of these nights you lost a few IQ points and needed to be re-educated." The Don put extra emphasis on that last word.

Having said all he intended to say, the demon crime boss exited with his entourage of one in tow.

When they were gone Mitch breathed a sigh of relief. Tough guy he may be, The Don was not the sort of demon he wanted to be pissing off. A smart man knew his limits. And as much as Mitch wanted another shot at being great, he wanted to stay breathing a whole lot more. In the end, that made the decision to keep taking dives an easy one.

He grabbed a towel and rubbed the sweat from his face. Five minutes with The Don had roughed Mitch up far more than his three rounds in the ring. He needed a drink.

* * *

Mitch had never been much for religion. Even before he'd found out about demons and their supernatural brethren, he'd been of the opinion that God was a bit of a prick. Nothing he'd seen in his life had yet to convince him to change that opinion. His mother, though, had been a devout Southern Baptist, and before she'd died they'd gone to church together every Sunday like clockwork.

By and large those Sunday sermons were nothing more than faded memories to Mitch, but one always stood out in his mind. "Purgatory is not a location" the preacher had said, "But rather it is a state of mind." His point had been that we must seek God's forgiveness, or we risk creating our own private, portable hells from which we can never escape. Mitch had taken from it that morality was fungible, and faith was just a way for people to avoid dealing with the consequences of their own bad behavior.

As for Purgatory not being a real location, Mitch had found out that was bullshit as well. Purgatory was the Tenderloin's premier dive bar for crooks, con-men, and other small-time losers; making it Mitch's go-to spot after a fight.

The bartender was a six-foot-two succubus by the name of Lily. Blue skin from head to toe and possessed of all the attributes a mortal man could desire; Lily kept a baseball bat behind the bar for any human or demon who let their lust get the better of them. If the bat wasn't enough to scare off the overly handsy, the jar of teeth next to it usually was.

"Mitch" she greeted him as he pushed in the swinging door and its accompanying wave of cigarette smoke.

"Lily" he returned the welcome with a nod, taking his regular seat at the end of the bar.

"Usual?" She asked, her hand already reaching for a bottle of his preferred brand of bourbon.

Mitch grunted an affirmative. With the amount of time he spent in his life getting punched in the jaw, talking wasn't something he was big on. That's why he liked coming to this dive. No one spoke to him. They just let him drink in peace. Lilly knew he'd had a fight tonight, but she knew better than to inquire how it went. Hell, maybe she didn't know better. Maybe she just didn't care enough. Either way suited Mitch just fine.

His usual was a highball of cheap bourbon with exactly three ice cubes. It wasn't the tastiest beverage in the world, but it got the job done. Who cared if it burned his throat on the way down, so long as it numbed everything else when it hit bottom.

The bar was quiet for a Friday night, but Purgatory was more of an after-hours spot and Mitch guessed its regular crowd was still out enjoying their various weekend hobbies. That was fine by Mitch. He preferred the quiet.

Unfortunately for him, it didn't last long. As the nearby bands and DJs finished their sets for the evening the crowd swelled. And as the crowd increased so did the decibel level. Mitch downed his third drink and had decided to cash out when a familiar hand squeezed his shoulder.

"Tough beat tonight Mitch. Let me by you a drink." Harry signaled Lily for a pair of shots and pulled up a stool.

When Mitch was first coming up the ranks, Harry had been his trainer. More than that, he'd taken him under his wing, shown a naïve, angry kid the way the world really worked.

Eventually, they'd both had to face the fact that Mitch was never going to be a real contender. Harry moved on to younger and hungrier fighters and Mitch stopped being particular about what kinds of cards he ended up on. There were no hard feelings, it was just business. But even when Harry had stopped training him he'd never stopped being in Mitch's corner. Anytime Mitch hit a rough patch Harry had been there with a place to crash and a hot meal. That made him family. Which was tough, because Harry was also a drunk and a degenerate gambler.

"I need you to do me a favor." The aged trainer jumped straight to the point.

"What kind of favor Harry?" Mitch reached for his wallet. The word favor coming out of Harry's mouth almost always involved an overdue debt to the wrong kind of people.

"I got a line on this young fighter, hear he's ready to step up to the big leagues and is looking for the trainer who's going to get him there. I've watched him in a couple of fights and the kid's good, but I want to get a second opinion, your opinion." Harry shared excitedly.

The request genuinely caught Mitch off guard.

"I'm flattered Harry but I doubt there's anything I'll see that you haven't already. There's got to be somebody else you can ask. One of your old crew from the gym maybe." Mitch didn't want to be rude to Harry, but scouting talent wasn't really his line.

Lily arrived with their shots. The pair paused and raised their glasses before throwing back two fingers worth of cheap, brown liquor. Harry's breath reeked of whiskey as he continued his pitch.

"C'mon Mitch. You know more about the fighting game than any trainer twice your age. And you're the only one I trust not to swipe the guy out from under me. Come look at the kid and tell me what you think. He ain't got your jaw, but he's got reach and a hell of a left hook."

Harry looked at him with pleading eyes and Mitch eventually gave in.

"All right Harry. When's this kid fight next?"

A beaming smile broke out on his old friend's face

"Tomorrow night at ten. I'll pick you up at nine. Thanks a lot, Mitch I appreciate it. Listen I got to go see a man about a thing. I'll pick you up tomorrow. Nine o'clock okay." Harry threw some cash on the bar and practically sprinted out the door.

"You know where he's going don't you?" The voice was almost enough to startle Mitch. Lilly didn't often engage in extraneous conversation behind the bar.

"None of my business." He answered.

"I thought he was your friend." She quipped.

"He is. But he's also a grown-ass man capable of making his own decisions. What's it to you anyways?" Harry didn't know what to make of Lilly's questions. It wasn't like her to get involved in her patron's lives.

"He tips well and doesn't try to grab my ass. Regulars like that are hard to come by." She shrugged.

"Harry can handle himself." Mitch assured her,

"If you say so." She turned back to serve an out of place hipster and Mitch watched her walk away before heading home for the night.

True to his word, Harry was honking his horn outside Mitch's Hunter's Point apartment at exactly eight fifty-nine. The entire drive to the Cow Palace all he did was yammer on and on about how good he thought this young blood was. After a while, it began to irritate Mitch. Harry had never gushed over him this way. Well if Harry was over-hyping this kid it was a good thing Mitch had agreed to check him out. He had a feeling he was going to be tossing some cold water on his friend's hopes.

Mitch was surprised to find that the fight was between two humans. Not that it was unheard of, there just were so few humans on the circuit these days it was rare to see. The kid's name was Eric Diaz. Harry was right about his age. According to the program he'd swiped at the gate the kid was twenty-three and already he held black-belts in jujitsu and taekwondo. His opponent was a guy Mitch knew. Terry "The Weed Wacker" Gardner. So-called because he kept whacking you until you were no longer standing. They'd tangled a few years ago when Gardner was coming up and Mitch spiraling downward. It was hard to say what kind of style changes a fighter might make three years on but when Mitch had faced him he'd been a beast of a striker though seriously lacking in his ground game.

Diaz-Gardener was listed as the third fight of the night. The first two were snoozers. A quartet of inexperienced grapplers paralyzed by their fear of giving the opposing fighter any kind of opening. This led to a pair of fights that featured a heavy number of tepid jabs and half-assed clinches.

It was a relief when Harry's new find finally stepped into the ring. The kid looked nervous, which was understandable, but if that feeling lasted past the first bell he was going to get his clock cleaned

The fight started out slow, each fighter feeling the other out for weaknesses. It was typical of fights at this level. The national guys had three or four months to prep for a specific opponent. An opponent whose previous fights it was easy to get recordings of. Here at the local level, you had a week or two at most to train between fights and sometimes you didn't know who you were taking on 'til the day of. And tape? Forget about it, more than half these fights were unsanctioned. Who records incriminating evidence of themselves?

The bell rang and the round ended without much excitement. Other than a heated exchange during the last moments before the bell, the round had been a bit of a dud.

That was not the case with the second round. Both fighters came out of his corner with murderous intent, spurred on by their trainers to take the fight to their opponent.

A rapid exchange of blows fueled the first minute. Each fighter ferociously attacking his foe's defenses. It was absolutely brutal.

Halfway through the round, it was clear to everyone that Gardner was fading. His punches were losing their conviction and Diaz had him on the ropes. Mitch was convinced he wouldn't make it out of the round.

Then suddenly Diaz let his guard slip. Gardner landed a clean hook with his right and Diaz staggered. Gardener followed with two quick jabs and Diaz dropped to the mat.

The crowd gasped in disbelief and even Gardner seemed shocked at his good fortune. He stood frozen for a second before following the younger fighter to the mat.

Gardener initiated a brutal ground and pound, landing blow after blow cleanly. Diaz wasn't even trying to defend himself anymore. Finally, mercifully, the official called it.

Harry screamed in disbelief. Him and most everybody else. The medical staff was already in the trying to treat Diaz, but he just waved them off.

The crowd wouldn't have been able to tell. Hell, most of the fighters and trainers in the room might not have noticed; but Mitch had thrown quite a few fights over the years, you might say he was an expert at it, and to him it was clear as day.

The kid had taken a dive. Which was a shame because he was going to win that fight easily. Harry was going to have to find a new golden boy, someone had already gotten their hooks into this one.

The ring cleared out and the various staff and officials began to reset the arena for the main event. A gargantuan demon named Halaphas was set to square off against "Hammering" Joe Johnson.

Mitch turned to Harry and began to offer his condolences about the Diaz kid, but Harry interrupted him.

"You don't understand. I was in so deep. But they said one wager and I could wipe the slate clean. The kid was the real deal. I'd been watching him for weeks. Why wouldn't I take that action?" Harry was rambling at the rate of a thousand words a minute. His eyes were full of fear.

"Harry, what are you talking about?" Mitch asked, bewildered by Harry's sudden mood swing.

"I put it all on the kid. I don't have anything left." Harry was about to have a panic attack. Gently, Mitch lead him out of the main hall to get some fresh air. The grizzled fighter was beginning to understand what was wrong with his friend.

"Harry," Mitch spoke deliberately "I need you to slow down and tell me everything. First of all, what exactly did you bet?"

"Everything I owed against my soul." Harry's shoulders slouched. The enormity of his situation finally sinking in as he spoke the words out loud.

"Dammit, Harry" Mitch sighed.

"The kid was a sure thing. You saw him fight. Just bad luck him going down like that." Harry insisted defensively.

"It wasn't bad luck. The kid took a dive, Harry. The fight was rigged." Mitch informed his mentor.

"Shit. Shit, shit, shit." Harry spit out the words as if he'd actually had a mouthful of shit. "You're sure?" Mitch nodded. "Shit. What am I going to do Mitch?"

"Calm down. Who's your bookie? I'll talk to him. See if we can't work something out." He doubted it. There wasn't anything more valuable than a human soul to a demon, but maybe they'd be able to figure something out.

The idea of making an idea brought some of the light back into Harry's eyes.

"Yeah. Yeah. That sounds good." Harry agreed excitedly "His name is Gaffeniel, goes by Gaffe. Squirrely little demon, green-skinned. Always wears an ugly ass fedora."

Mitch scanned the crowd. If this Gaffe was making book on these fights there was a chance he'd be here. He got lucky, across the arena making his way to the concession stand was a green-skinned demon wearing a powder blue fedora.

"That him?" Mitch pointed at his suspect.

"That's him." Harry confirmed.

Mitch and Harry hustled across the arena, pushing through the crowd of fans making their way to their seats for the main event.

They caught up with their demon as he entered the restroom.

Mitch followed him inside. A handful of stragglers were trying to finish their business before the next fight started.

"Everybody out." Mitch barked. When the restroom's occupants stared at him instead of moving he spun on his heel and kicked out one of the bathroom mirrors. "Now."

That seemed to give the assortment of humans and demons the motivation they needed to zip up their pants and get the hell out.

"Not you." Mitch grabbed the fedora-wearing demon as he too broke for the door. "Gaffe right? You made a deal with my friend here." Mitch gestured to Harry. "I'm here to renegotiate."

"Man, I knew you was a welcher. It's always the old ones. Well doesn't matter, not my problem anymore." Gaffe was a twitchy demon. His compound eyes made it hard to get a read on him.

"What do you mean it's not your problem anymore?"

"I mean it's not my problem anymore." The bookie responded with a bit too much attitude for Mitch's taste. He drew back a fist and pumped faked a jab in Gaffe's direction.

The skinny demon flinched at the prospect of Mitch's fist becoming more acquainted with his face. Mitch pressed the point.

"You may like repeating yourself." Lacing his words with menace, Mitch leaned in close to drive his words home. "I don't." Gaffe got the message.

"Okay man, no need to get violent. It means I sold you friend's marker for a nice sum and now I don't have to deal with his old ass trying to weasel his way out of paying." The bookie explained

"Sold it? Sold it to who?" Harry asked, panic in his voice.

"To the highest bidder. Who else?" Was the bookie's snarky reply

Mitch socked the obnoxious green-skinned little shit in the gut then slammed him against the wall.

"Alright, alright tough guy no need to get violent. I got a call before the fight even started. Said 'why take a risk' when I could make out like a champ before a punch was even thrown. Offered me a hefty sum right then and there for gramps' marker. So I took it. Nothing personal. Just business." Gaffe seemed to be the kind of guy who got cockier with each word that came out of his mouth. Mitch hated those types.

"Who? Who did you sell it to? I want a name." He shook the bookie bodily for added emphasis. And because it was satisfying to see Gaffe squirm.

"The Don okay. I sold it to the Don." Mitch loosened his grip on the weaselly bookie. It wasn't often Mitch found himself angry. Truly, righteously angry. That was how he felt right now.

"Kind of surprised the big boss was interested actually, but what The Don wants The Don gets." The demon called Gaffe just kept talking, oblivious to the change that had come over Mitch.

If The Don had called for Harry's marker before the fight, then he knew the fight was rigged. More than that he'd probably rigged it himself, just to get his hands-on Harry's soul.

"Fucking asshole!" Mitch shouted at no one in particular. Distracted, he let his grip loosen. Gaffe took the opportunity to wriggle free and bolt for the door.

"Mitch!" Harry exclaimed as his bookie pushed past him.

"Let him go. He can't help us anymore." Mitch went to the sink and splashed cold water on his face.

"So what do we do now?" Harry asked.

"We don't do anything. You go home and get some rest. I'm going to go pay a visit to The Don."

It was not a visit Mitch was looking forward to.

* * *

Agony was a good name for The Don's signature club. Located conveniently

FIGHT NIGHT

for the North Beach bros on the corner of Columbus and Broadway, the club was full of gentrifying tech assholes from Wisconsin and various other flyover states who thought the best way to be cool as adults was to emulate the asshole jocks who beat them up in high school.

Loud, incomprehensible electronic sounds bombarded the dance floor. Forcefully, Mitch pushed his way to the club's VIP area. Two impeccably dressed demons stepped between him and the velvet rope.

Mitch kept moving forward anyway. One of the bodyguards put his hand on Mitch. That was a mistake.

With his left hand, Mitch swept aside the demon's hand while a quick jab from his right hand broke the bastard's nose.

The other bodyguard took a wild swing. Mitch stepped back and let the arm go past him before grabbing it and forcing its owner to the ground, a strategic application of pressure and the arm came out of its socket. The demon howled in pain.

Broken nose demon had recovered and was now suitably pissed. He fired off a couple of punches that Mitch let land before countering with a three-hit combo. Jab-jab-uppercut and the demon was out cold. Teetering for a moment before tumbling over the velvet rope he had been protecting.

Club security arrived and took up positions between him and the exits. This fight would be five on one. Mitch had the advantage though, now that they knew what he was capable of he could see the hesitation in their eyes. If they didn't come at him all at once and were as poorly trained as the first two, he'd be just fine.

Someone loudly cleared his throat and Mitch turned to see The Don waving off the extra security.

"I think that's enough for now." The demon gestured for Mitch to join him. "Well, I guess I have to thank you for showing me how woefully inadequate my current security team is. You're a good earner for me and not prone to bouts of stupidity so I'm going to overlook this massive display of disrespect and ask you why you're here." The Don remained jovial, but in his eyes Mitch could see the anger of being shown up at his own club burning him up.

"Harry," Mitch said simply, taking a seat opposite The Don.

"Ah, come to clean up the old man's mess? Can't say I didn't see that coming. But I'm afraid there's no weaseling his way out of paying up this time. If the fool's going to put his soul up as collateral, he can't whine when I show up to collect. This is not the kind of wager you welch on. I have a contract."

The demon's tone fell somewhere on the scale between sympathetic and condescending. Mitch knew he was going to have to go big if he was going to get The Don's attention.

"No one is whining and no one's welching. I came with a counter-offer. One more bet double or nothing" The grey-skinned gangster's eyes went wide.

"I'm listening." The demon said, leaning forward to hear Mitch's proposal.

"You've got a card going next Friday. You're going to add on one more fight. I get in the ring with any fighter you want. I win, you wipe clean the slate. Harry keeps his soul and you leave us alone. Your fighter wins, you get my soul to go along with Harry's."

The demon contemplated the deal, you could almost see the wheels turning in his mind. For a species obsessed with temptation, they sure were terrible at resisting it. Apparently, The Don had never heard the phrase a soul in the hand is better than two in the pot.

"It's a deal." The demon's glee was written all over his face. "You've really done it this time Mitch. I think a few too many blows to the head may be affecting your judgment. Though I have to say I'm impressed by your loyalty."

"Eat shit." Mitch stood. "You knew this is what I'd do. Tell me did you plan to rig that fight from the start or did you do it just to get Harry and me on the hook?"

The Don shrugged. "Everybody needs a hobby. Now if you wouldn't mind I have actual business to attend to. Feel free to put a drink on my tab at the bar."

Two of The Don's security demons stepped forward. Mitch took the hint. After a long glare, he made his way out of the VIP area and towards the exit.

FIGHT NIGHT

A hand grabbed his elbow as he passed the bar. Mitch spun ready to fight whoever had made the mistake of putting hands on him.

"Woah, easy there champ." Mitch was surprised to find his favorite blue-skinned bartender starring back at him. Looking particularly striking in what must be her "going out" outfit.

"Lilly? What are you doing here?" The club was so loud Mitch had to shout the question at her.

"I know right? Not really my scene." she pointed at the bar where a statuesque green-skinned beauty was pouring drinks. "My old roommate is tending bar tonight, wanted me to come out for a drink."

"I was just…" Mitch started to explain but Lilly cut him off.

"Oh, I saw what you were 'just'. What are you thinking mixing it up with The Don? In his own place? You take one too many punches to the head?" Her words were ones of concern, her smile was one of mischievous encouragement.

"I'm really getting sick of people asking me that." Mitch complained. "No, I haven't. The Don and I had some business to work out. That's all."

"Does this have something to do with Harry." Lilly's intuition was always spot on. It was what made her a good bartender. Probably made her a hell of a succubus too.

But Harry's business wasn't Mitch's business to tell, no matter how good-looking the person asking happened to be.

"Sort of. Listen I really need to get out of here. Can we talk later?" Mitch was already moving away from

"Yeah you're right, this place is lame." She smiled seductively. Grabbing his hand she pulled him close and whispered in his ear.

"Buy a girl a coffee?"

The question threw Mitch a bit off balance for a moment.

"Sure," he said, agreeing out of sheer reflex.

"Good. I know just the place." She grabbed his hand and led him towards the door, Mitch didn't know if he was about to exit or enter a club called Agony.

201

* * *

Lilly insisted the coffee shop wasn't far, about halfway between the club and Coit Tower. It was a nice walk. Lilly talked about this bar or that restaurant as they passed. Apparently, she knew just about every bartender and server in the city.

It was nice to listen to her talk. Her words were melodic. Her voice was so easy to get lost in that Mitch had to be sure to focus on what she was actually saying rather than just get carried away by it.

By the time they arrived at 'the most-perfect little café ever' as Lilly called it, Mitch had completely forgotten about Harry and The Don.

Lilly got them a booth in the back while Mitch stood in line and ordered a pair of plain, black coffees. He felt the eyes of the hipster barista behind the counter judging him.

Mitch slide into the booth and handed his companion her beverage.

"Thanks, Champ." Lilly greeted him with a smile.

"My pleasure." He nodded back in return.

The two sat there in awkward silence.

"Is the booth okay?" Mitch asked with a nervousness that was unlike him.

"It's fine." She assured him.

"Are you sure? We could get a table. This can't be comfortable for your tail." Mitch was not normally one for babbling, stoic reserve was his default setting. But he was unaccustomed to flirting with a succubus, he was even more unaccustomed to drinking coffee with his bartender.

"Really Mitch I'm okay. You'd be surprised how flexible I can be." Her smile did more than hint at the double meaning of that remark.

They returned to their awkward silence.

Mitch sipped at his coffee and scanned the room with his eyes. He wondered if everyone else was having as bad a time at this as he was.

"So where were you when it happened?" Lilly blurted out to break the ice.

"When what happened?" Mitch replied confused.

"When what happened. When it happened. When we showed up on this plane of existence. 'Hell Day' as you humans like to call it." As far as icebreakers went it was a dozy and it threw Mitch for a loop for the second time tonight. Hell Day wasn't a subject people, humans or demons, particularly liked talking about. Not knowing what else to say he answered her.

"I was in Alabama. It was just after my eleventh birthday. We were on our way to church. A hell pit opened up right in the middle of Main Street. Scared the shit out of my parents. My sister and I just thought it was cool. Anyway, dad just swerved around it and kept driving straight on to the church. Figured we were headed there anyway and that was as good a place as any to hide out from demons. Seems most the rest of the town had the same thought. You know how bad it got in the south. Everyone convinced it was the apocalypse. Every preacher with a pulpit got his congregation riled up enough to go demon hunting. Things got ugly. Anyway long story short, I made it through all that and here I am now." Her look told him that she thought there was more to the story and she was right.

"What about you. What were you doing on Hell Day?" he turned the tables before she could ask any follow-up questions.

"Me?" she shrugged "I was having a threesome with Tango and Cash. Which was not nearly as exciting as it sounds. But a girl's got to make a living."

"How come you don't do that kind of work anymore?" Mitch asked.

"In hell there's only one kind of currency: souls. And there's only one way I know how to collect souls. I never enjoyed it." She blushed. "Okay, sometimes I enjoyed it. But it wasn't as if I had a choice. If I didn't meet my quota…." Her eyes went to some faraway place as her words trailed off. "Let's just say it would have been unpleasant."

Now that they'd open the faucet, their conversation flowed easily from one topic to the next. They talked for hours, only stopping when the hipster barista passive aggressively informed them he was closing up.

Outside on the street, they stood together watching their breath appear and disappear on the cool Pacific breeze as they tried to decide what came next.

"I should get going. I have to be up early to train." Early was an understatement. By going to bed at this hour, Mitch would be lucky if he got a cat nap in before his morning workout

"You know you may be the only first date I've ever had not to try to get into my pants on night one." She flashed him another one of her seductive smiles.

"Is that what we're calling this? A first date?" He asked.

"Maybe. We'll see how this fight of yours goes. So I guess you're right. You do need to train. I'd hate to think of that cute little ass of yours getting kicked on my account."

Mitch put his arm out to hail Lilly a cab. Neither he nor she said another word as they waited. Instead, they simply looked at each other. Each pair of eyes taking full inventory of what was before them.

One very long minute later, one pulled up to the curb. Mitch opened the door like the southern gentleman he was raised to be. Lilly leaned forward and kissed his cheek before climbing in.

As the cab drove away with the best part of his night, Mitch hailed a taxi of his own. The driver dropped him off at his door fifteen minutes later. The clock on the wall said two a.m., Mitch set his alarm for four thirty. In five days he would be in for the fight of his life. He needed to train. He could sleep when he was dead.

* * *

In a city awash with yoga studios and Pilate instructors, finding a gym that focused on fighters could be a trying endeavor. There were a few around the city, but not many, and most of them tended to be in the somewhat sketchier parts of town. Most of the more credible gyms were over in the East Bay, but Monument Gym had been representing Hunter's Point since before the Giants had come west and still housed some of the city's best fighters. Human or demon, if you wanted to hone your craft this was the spot to go. It had been Mitch's gym since he was a teenager.

When Mitch pulled up to it at five minutes after five, Harry was waiting outside holding a pair of coffees.

"Nice bike." He said.

"Thanks." Mitch answered dryly.

"I was being sarcastic." Harry handed over one of the coffees.

"I know." Mitch reached down to secure his bike lock.

"'You're late." Harry tapped at his wrist.

"I didn't realize we had an appointment." Mitch took a sip of his coffee and waited for Harry to explain why he was here.

"Listen, smart ass. Word gets around. I heard what you did last night. I should kick your ass myself. What the hell did you think you were doing challenging the Don like that?" Harry's voice grew louder and more forceful as his anger bubbled to the surface.

"I thought I was saving your ass" was Mitch's deadpan response.

"Goddammit, Mitch. Just once will you let me save my own ass. You had no right to go and put yourself out there like that." Harry had now transitioned from speaking loudly to full on shouting.

"You would have done the same for me." Mitch said at a volume much lower than Harry's.

"If you think for one second you're going to climb into that ring without me in your corner, then you're an even bigger idiot then I thought you were." The old man's tirade was beginning to lose its head of steam.

"I wouldn't have it any other way." Mitch agreed.

"Well then, what are we standing out here yammering about. Get your ass inside and let's get started." Harry folded his arms over his chest triumphantly and waited for Mitch pull open the gym door before entering.

The gym stank of stale sweat. The early morning sun fought to make itself known through dirt covered windows. Old bags hung from rusty chains against a background of vintage fight memorabilia from the forties and fifties. At five in the morning, most would expect a place like this to be empty. They would be wrong. Every station in the place held a fighter and his trainer. This was the time when contenders did their work. Mitch and Harry gave a nod and polite wave to Jerry, the gym's proprietor, then got to it.

The first hour was spent on stretching and drills; jump rope, shadow boxing, the speed bag, and so on. The next hour would be all about sparring. That meant Mitch and Harry first had to decide on a fight plan.

"Hard to train when we don't know which of The Don's meatheads I'll be squaring off against." Mitch kept his punches light, just enough to move the bag a little. He was more concerned with working on his timing at the moment. A week doesn't give you much time to build up muscle, but he could make some serious strides in the quick hands' department.

"Halaphas. It'll be Halaphas sure as shit." Harry held the bag as Mitch put his work in.

"It's not sure as anything, The Don has a half dozen guys that he thinks can kick my ass." Mitch replied between breaths.

"Maybe, but the Don doesn't fuck around. And there is no better 'I'm not fucking around' fighter than Halaphas. That red skinned bastard is twelve and oh with twelve knockouts. He's a monster. Literally. Trust me, I know The Don. And he's gonna put Halaphas in the ring with you. The expectation being you won't walk out of there with your head still attached to your body." Mitch still wasn't convinced, but if Harry was going to be in his corner for this fight he needed to trust him.

"Alright, it's Halaphas. So what do we do?" Mitch asked his trainer.

"He's a bruiser, but he's not slow. You're not going to be able to dance around him. He's got height, weight, and reach on you. You've got only one advantage, you're much better on the ground. So forget striking we are going to focus on takedowns and clinches. Hopefully, once you've got the bastard on the mat you can put him away."

With that decided, Mitch's training truly began in earnest.

For the next three days, Mitch did nothing but eat, sleep, and train. When he wasn't in the ring sparring, he was putting in his bag work. When he wasn't on the bag, he was in the weight room. When he wasn't in the weight room, he was working on his cardio. If he wasn't doing any of that, he was sleeping.

He'd put all thoughts of Lilly out of his mind. It wasn't that he hadn't had a good time with her, he had. There was simply too much riding on this fight to risk being distracted. And a gorgeous, six-foot-two-inch succubus was the definition of distracting.

That is, he had put her out of his mind until she called him up Wednesday night and asked him to come over to the bar.

As ordered he arrived at seven sharp, the bar was busy but not packed, the after-work regulars enjoying the tail-end of happy hour. Lilly was closing out her till and chatting with her relief when she spotted him pulling up a stool. She smiled and put up a finger to let him know she'd be a minute.

When she was ready she nodded her head towards the back door. Mitch got up and followed her. In all his years as a regular at Purgatory he'd never gone out this way.

They exited to a small hallway with a narrow staircase. Lilly locked the door behind them.

"Come on upstairs, I've got a pot roast in the oven." She said, gesturing for him to follow.

"You live on top of the bar?" Mitch asked skeptically, following Lilly up the stairs.

"I do." She turned her head over her shoulder and gave him a menacing look. "Is that a problem?"

"No. Just took me by surprise is all." Mitch noticed Lilly had a habit of doing that.

"The rent's cheap." She shrugged.

Her apartment was small, but that was true of most places in the city. It wasn't what he'd been expecting. Not that he really knew what he'd been expecting, whips and chains maybe. No, the place looked like any other hellacious tenderloin set up, old appliances, faded paint, and dirty windows. Dirty clothes and takeout boxes lay scattered about.

"Sorry about the mess. I don't get a lot of free time to clean up around here." Mitch thought messy was an understatement.

"Scotch?" She offered.

"No. Thanks. Just water is fine." Mitch didn't drink the week before a fight. Or at least that had been his rule back when he'd been trying to win those fights.

"Have it your way." She tossed him a plastic bottle out of the fridge before pouring herself two fingers of amber liquid from a decanter she kept in the corner. She cleared off a stack of bras from the couch and invited him to sit.

They made small talk while she pulled the pot roast out of the oven and made them plates. Lilly waited until he'd cleaned his plate and she'd served him seconds to come at him with the big questions.

"So why do you do it? Plenty of other ways to earn a living in this town. What is it that drives you to keep climbing into that ring?" It was a legitimate question. One he was asked often. Most of the time he gave the person who asked a bullshit answer about old dogs and new tricks and that he'd been a fighter too long to stop now. But Lily wasn't other people, she deserved better than bullshit. She deserved the truth.

"The other night you asked me where I was for Hell Day. I didn't tell you the whole story. After the demons came, my momma, well she lost it a bit. She got paranoid. Started sitting by the door with my daddy's shotgun, convinced demons were going to come and murder us in our sleep. One night my daddy and my sister came home late, he'd taken her out for an ice cream after her soccer match. My momma, she heard the door and she panicked. Unloaded with both barrels. She took Sarah's head off. Poor daddy just got gut shot. Bleed out holding my sister's headless corpse in his arms. When momma saw what she'd done she reloaded the shotgun, put the barrel under her chin, and pulled the trigger."

"Mitch..." tears rolled down Lilly's cheeks. She reached out, wrapping his hands in hers. Mitch kept going.

"After that, I was pretty much angry at the entire world all the time. Still am. But back then I didn't have control. Just another orphan lost in the system. I'd lash out at anyone or anything and I was only getting worse. Fights at school, stealing cars, destroying property. I was in and out of juvi 'til I was sixteen. That was when my latest set of foster parents kicked me out. I needed a change of scenery, so I went west, rode the rails, hitchhiked, took odd jobs in exchange for bus fare 'til I ended up here. When I got here I fell in with some street level brawlers. The ring was the only place I felt free. The one time I was giving a beating instead of taking one. Harry saw me in a street fight with a measly hundred-dollar purse and pulled me out of there and off the streets. He gave me a place to train. A place to sleep. He saved me. Path I was on, I would have been dead in a year, two tops. Instead, I learned how to harness my anger, how to control it. So why do I keep climbing into that ring? It's the only way I know how to stay alive."

She sat there looking at him. Saying nothing, simply staring into his eyes. Her hands cupped his cheeks and she leaned into him, pressing her body against his. Ever so slowly she tilted her head down to his.

Their lips met and the dam was broken. All of their pent-up passions burst out of them at once. Clothes ripped as they were savagely discarded on their way to the bedroom. Together their two bodies fell to the bed as one.

Afterwards, Lilly lit up a cigarette while Mitch put on his pants.

"I can stay. If you want." Mitch stated, thinking he should have said it before his shirt was halfway over his head.

"I'm a big girl Mitch." She took a long drag. "You've got a big week and you need your rest. I get it. I can promise you if you stay here rest will not be on the menu. Go home, get some sleep. Kick some ass."

He bent low and pressed his lips against hers. A soft, goodbye peck turned into a deep, passionate kiss. She was intoxicating. The favorite food of a starving man. It took all of his willpower to pull away.

"Goodnight Lilly." He said, not really wanting to go.

"Goodnight Mitch." She replied, not really wanting him to go.

Mitch went down the stairs and exited through another hallway that led away from the bar. When he hit the street he turned right towards his bus stop. It was a crisp San Francisco night. The cool air made him pull the hood of his sweatshirt up around his ears. Adjusting his own hoodie for comfort, Mitch walked down the street oblivious to the two similarly hooded men lumbering towards him.

The pair grabbed him and shoved him into a side alley where a third hood was waiting.

Slowly Mitch reached into his pocket and pulled out his wallet. "All I've got. Not much but you want anything more than that and we've got a problem."

Mitch scanned the alley. It was narrow. Too narrow for the three of them to come at him at once. That was a mistake. Three attackers would be too tough for just about any fighter to take on by themselves. But two was doable. Their choice of location had thrown away their biggest advantage.

"Oh, we're going to have a problem all right. Its time somebody taught you to stick to your own kind." One of them growled.

Mitch raised his eyebrow at that before offering the man a slight shrug of the shoulders. There wasn't anything to say. If the bigoted assholes wanted to fight, then they were going to fight and nothing Mitch said was going to put that genie back in the bottle. Better to get it over and done with.

He sprinted towards the lead hood. The two behind him broke after him, but they would have to wait a moment. One obstacle at a time.

When he got within a yard of the lead hood he pulled up and let his momentum power a chest-high front kick with his right foot. The lead hood retreated backwards and Mitch's kick found nothing but air. Which was fine. All he'd needed to do was create some distance between himself and his attackers.

He planted and spun, putting his left heel into the gut of the second hood who in turn stumble backwards into hood number three. The pair went to ground in a tangle, allowing Mitch's focus to return to their leader. The hood set himself in a fighting stance. He was close enough now that Mitch could see his eyes. The man's pupils were severely constricted.

Two realizations hit Mitch simultaneously. These guys were fighters. They were also junkies. Only the first revelation was relevant to his current circumstances. He could consider the second at some later point.

Mitch pushed forward, throwing a quick combination with the intent of ending things before the other two hoods could rejoin the fight.

It didn't work. Instead, Mitch's missed and caught a counter punch to the jaw. The hood followed up his counter with his own quick combo, forcing Mitch to retreat a few steps.

Mitch cocked his arm for a counter, but something grabbed hold of his bicep. He was out of time. The other two hoods had rejoined the fight.

He tried throwing back his elbow but there just wasn't enough torque there for him to do any damage with it. The third hood grabbed his free arm and delivered a kick to the back of his leg, forcing Mitch to his knees.

He was done for now and they all knew it. His three assailants went to work, beating on him with enough sustained rhythm that he couldn't recover enough to block or counter their blows.

Mitch's vision began to blur, and he felt certain he was about to be reunited with his family.

"Hey!" A heavenly voice screamed down at them from on high. All four brawlers looked skyward. Lilly was there, wings flapping, baseball bat in hand, floating ten feet off the ground.

She swooped towards Mitch's attackers and they fled, dropping Mitch's prone form to the watery asphalt. Lilly did not give chase, choosing instead to check on Mitch.

It was a gesture Mitch very much appreciated in the brief moments before he lost consciousness.

Mitch came to on something soft and pillowy. He had to blink a few times to get his eyes adjusted to the light.

"Hey, there champ. Welcome back." Lilly slid onto the bed next to him.

"How long was I out?" He asked, still feeling incredibly groggy.

"Not long. Just a few minutes. I flew you back up to mine as soon as I chased those assholes off." Lily's hands stroked his hair. Mitch thought his head was laying in her lap but he wasn't sure. Wherever he was it felt nice.

"Oh. Good" He mumbled his approval before slipping back into the darkness of sleep.

He came to again, this time in the middle of a conversation he didn't remember starting.

"Who were they?" Lily asked.

"Just some strung out junkies looking for my wallet." He muttered, not sure if it was true or not.

"Uh-huh. A couple of junkies with black belts? I saw the end of that fight. Strung out or not they were kicking your ass." Lilly was a smart woman. Mitch had clocked that back in the alley. But drifting in and out of consciousness made it hard to keep your conspiracy theories straight.

Mitch raised his head up off Lilly's lap. He was awake now and trying to stay that way. He definitely had a concussion and letting himself fade off back to dreamland would have been a very bad idea.

"Maybe I'm just not as good as you think I am." He quipped.

Lilly slapped him hard before lightly brushing her tongue against his lips. That certainly helped him with the 'stay awake' plan.

"First rule. If we're going to be together you don't lie to me. The Don sent them didn't he?"

"I don't know that for sure…" Mitch groaned as Lilly lifted his shirt over his head. "But yeah, that would be my guess."

"Well, then he made a serious mistake." She declared with fire in her voice.

"Oh yeah? What's that?" Mitch asked her.

"He shouldn't have messed with what's mine. Now he and I are going to have words." Lilly was teasing, but Mitch could see the worry on her face.

"Is that right?" He tried matching her playful nature, pretending that his ass wasn't hanging from the thinnest of limbs, but it was hard for him to reassure her when he wasn't all that sure to begin with.

"Mm-hmm" she kissed his forehead lightly. "Hang on I think I've got some icy-hot in the bathroom."

Mitch lay there and thought hard about his alleyway encounter. This wasn't the first time in his life that he'd been roughed up in an alley. Probably not even the seventh or eighth. Those beatings had a purpose. And the guys doing the beating had made sure he'd known what it was while they were railing on him. Mitch didn't buy the inter-species relationship hating crap. Bigots didn't usually have black belts. Of course, neither did junkies. There was only one place drugs and fighting crossed paths in this city and that was in The Don's orbit. This had been about softening him up. Making him fight at something less than one hundred percent. Judging by the way his ribs felt they'd accomplished their goals.

Mitch spent most of Thursday in Lily's bed recovering from the beatings he'd been taking all week. He made sure to leave in the afternoon while it was still light out and she was on her shift. It kept her from pushing him too hard to stay and let him be sure no one was waiting for him in another alley. Lilly was a great girl, but when a man's about to put his soul on the line it's better if he sleeps in his own bed the night before.

The night of the fight arrived just like any other Friday night. At quarter to six, Mitch sat staring at the clock on the stove while he forced the last of his carb loaded dinner into his mouth. At ten to six, he put his dirty dish in the sink. At five to six he double checked his gym bag and headed out the door.

The wind was crisp and cold. The usual kind of San Francisco chill. In the old days out at the 'Stick this kind of weather would have played hell with any ball popped up into the air. Now it just meant you saw hell walking the streets wrapped up in an extra thick coat. Most people figured the reason San Francisco was such a popular destination with demons was the city's history of accepting the weird as ordinary. A general belief that everyone has the right to let their freak flag fly.

Mitch thought the reason was a lot simpler than that. He figured it was the weather. After all, if you hate the heat but are biologically ill-equipped for the cold what better Goldilocks zone than San Francisco, a city built around being perpetually chill.

He rode MUNI down to the Tenderloin. Headphones on, music cranked all the way up, studiously ignoring the homeless man begging for change and the drunk teenagers puking in the back.

It was fight night. The most important fight of his life. Mitch couldn't allow himself any distractions.

That included Lily too. When he'd left her the night before he'd told her not to try to see him before the fight. That one way or another he'd see her when it was all over.

Harry was waiting for him in the trainer's room when he arrived. The old man had been pacing up a storm, clearly nervous about the fate of his eternal soul, but he sucked it up and put on his game face as soon as Mitch entered the room.

"Alright, Mitch? You ready for this?" The wizened old corner-man asked him in earnest.

"I'm good Harry. Let's do it." Mitch assured him. Banishing all thoughts and doubts from his mind.

"Okay then, put on your shorts and we'll get you warmed up." Harry clapped his hands together. It was go-time now. There was no room in that locker room for anything less than complete confidence in Mitch's ability to win this fight.

Mitch ran through his warm-up routine on automatic. While his muscles loosened and he worked up a sweat, his mind was running through a series of practice rounds. He pictured himself in the ring, establishing his fight plan and keeping the pressure on Halaphas.

So engrossed in his mental reps was Mitch, he didn't notice The Don arrive in the trainer's room.

"Wear yourself out all you like. Not gonna make one bit of difference tonight. Face it, Mitch. You're old, washed up. You've been tanking fights longer than you were ever winning them. Halaphas is going to eat you for dinner. And I don't mean metaphorically. Face it, you're a loser. You always have been. Why would tonight be any different?" The well-dressed demon mocked.

"Never had anything worth fighting for before now." Mitch answered simply.

"HA! Hahahaha! That's rich Mitch. Really. Great stuff. You've got a purpose, so all of a sudden you're going to stop being the failure you've spent your whole life training to be. Hand me a tissue, I'm watering up over here." The Don bellowed between maniacal laughs.

"What's the matter you so worried he's going to win you decided you needed to come back here and play head games." Harry said coming to Mitch's defense.

"Enjoy your last hour as free men you two. Eternal damnation is just three five-minute rounds away." With that last jab, The Don let them be.

Not long after The Don left them there was a knock on the door. The fight official stepped in.

"Gentlemen. It's time" was all he said.

"Okay. Let's go. Come on Mitch you got this. Just another fight. Your time to shine. Right now. Right here. Let's get after this."

Harry kept spouting hyped up clichés all the way down the hallway. Any other day of the week he'd call it out for the bullshit it was. But this was fight night. And Mitch needed every bit of adrenaline he could get.

The PA announcer introduced him and put on his walk-up music, Remember the Name by Fort Minor. A hard beat dropped, and Mitch stalked to the ring, head bobbing in rhythm with the music.

The official checked him out before he climbed into the ring. There Mitch was forced to wait for his opponent to go through the same ritual he had just completed. The demon's walk-up music was a bit more direct than Mitch's. Bodies by Sinner didn't exactly leave room for interpretation.

Halaphas stepped into the ring and the two fighters stared each other down. Mitch tried not to think how much larger the red-skinned brawler looked now that he could see him up close.

The official signaled for the two fighters to meet him center-ring.

"I want a good clean fight. No eye gouging, no low blows, no teleporting or summoning your opponent's body parts, no tails, no wings, or any of the other prohibited moves we went over in the locker room. Follow my instructions and protect yourselves at all times. Touch gloves and return to your corners. When you hear the bell, come out fighting."

The two fighters did as they were instructed, neither deciding to say a word to the other. There wasn't anything to say. They were about to spend the next fifteen minutes beating the life out of each other, but it wasn't personal. When you were a fighter that was just the way the world worked.

The bell rang and Halaphas came straight at him. There would be no feeling each other out phase of this fight, the demon was going to bring it from the very start. Mitch stood his ground. A trio of jabs came rushing towards his face in rapid succession. His hands absorbed most of the impact, his chin caught the rest.

Halaphas switched approaches, going low to deliver a fierce shin kick to Mitch's upper thigh. He tried to follow it with a second kick, but this time Mitch managed to get his leg up to block just in time.

The first few minutes of the first round went much like this opening exchange. Halaphas would push forward, aggressively attacking with a combination of jabs and hooks, while Mitch retreated, constantly backpedaling to avoid his opponents bulldozing fists. Occasionally, the demon would switch it up and put pressure on Mitch's legs with a series of quick kicks.

This line of attack had made Halaphas' fight plan clear as day. He meant to knock Mitch out and he meant to do it quickly.

Mitch was in trouble. He knew if the match kept going like this he'd lose. His thighs were already beginning to bruise. And despite spending almost the entire round throwing haymaker after haymaker Halaphas showed no signs of tiring.

Three rounds was too long to go standing up against this son of a bitch. Outclassed in both the reach and power departments, one wrong step would have him on the mat seeing stars. His only hope was to take this fight to the ground and score a submission.

The pair got tangled up and Mitch used the opportunity to land a couple of kidney shots before Halaphas pushed him off. Of course, that was assuming the big red bastard even had kidneys.

The demon grunted and came at Mitch with a cascade of jabs and shin kicks. Mitch kept his feet moving backwards as he ducked and deflected his opponent's massive fists.

Halaphas feinted with his left and Mitch fell for the fake out leaving himself open to the demon's right hook. The blow landed cleanly and Mitch's vision blurred. A deluge of jabs ravaged his face while he struggled to get his hands back up. He fell backwards and would have gone down if he hadn't been close enough to the cage to prop himself up.

Halaphas gave him no quarter. The demon just kept firing off jab after jab, his fist hammering away like the pistons of an engine, rhythmic and relentless.

Blood gushed from Mitch's nose. A cut opened up on his right cheek. He knew he had to defend himself, but his body refused to listen to his brain.

Unless a miracle happened he was done for and he knew it.

Just then the bell rang and saved his ass.

Halaphas scored one more jab to Mitch's gut before the official pulled him off. More than slightly dazed Mitch made his way back to his corner and took a seat. Harry handed him a water bottle and started spouting instructions while he pressed an ice pack against Mitch's chest. The ring designated cut man pushed cotton up his nose and against the cut on his cheek.

"What are you doing out there Mitch? You keep taking hits like that and they're going to have to scrap you off the mat. You've got to stay back, let him wear himself out with those big punches. Be patient then when he gets tired counter punch a bit before going for the takedown" the old trainer coached him.

The sound of the bell came far too quickly. Harry pushed Mitch's mouth guard back in and the fighter readied himself for another haymaker barrage.

The second round started much like the first, with Halaphas coming out strong. Again Mitch was forced to play defense, backpedaling to stay out of range from the demon's fearsome strikes. He did a better job of it this time, despite his early disorientation. Maybe it was his survival instinct kicking in, a primitive part of his brain screaming 'Holy Fuck no more of that'.

Whatever the reason he spent the first two minutes of the second round dancing around the ring, avoiding any direct confrontation with Halaphas. The crowd began to boo. They wanted to see some action. Mitch ignored them. They weren't the ones getting killed out here.

The spectators weren't the only ones growing restless, Halaphas' impatience was becoming more and more evident with each missed jab and dodged kick. Mitch continued to stay back and look for an opening to counter-attack.

That chance presented itself when Halaphas drifted too high with a spin kick. Mitch caught the kick and drove forward, taking Halaphas to the mat.

The crowd roared.

Mitch fired off a series of downward elbows to Halaphas' face. The first two landed cleanly, doing some serious damage. But the demon recovered quickly and got his hands up in time to defend the next three strikes Mitch attempted.

Halaphas began to kick upward defensively and Mitch was forced to back off or risk taking some serious damage of his own. The demon scrambled to his feet and Mitch knew he'd missed a golden opportunity.

Wearier than before the demon resumed his constant pressuring of Mitch's defenses. For his part, Mitch made a conscious effort to stand his ground.

A series of tentative jabs were exchanged as the two fighters reevaluated their respective fight strategies.

Halaphas fired off a three-punch combo.

Mitch countered with a spinning backhand.

He connected and the demon staggered.

The veteran fighter decided to push forward and keep the pressure on his red-skinned opponent. With a repeated Jab-Jab-Hook combination he chased the demon across the ring. Mitch could smell blood. A few more solid shots to the face and this fight would be over.

One of his punches went wide. Halaphas ducked and countered.

The demon's hook hit Mitch like a semi-truck. Mitch dropped to one knee before falling backwards. Desperately he flailed his legs and hands both to fend off any follow-up attack and to let the official know he was still conscious.

Still recovering from Mitch's brutal barrage, Halaphas' was slow to capitalize on this sudden reversal giving Mitch time to establish his guard.

His hands up Mitch deflected what he could of the demon's elbows. That was not much. Spots began to fill his vision as his head absorbed blow after blow.

For the second time that night he was saved by the bell.

Harry was waiting for him in the corner with a stool and a squirt bottle.

"Mitch." He spoke emphatically "Mitch you're down two rounds. You've got to knock him out if you want to win this thing. No more playing possum okay. You go out there and give it everything you've got."

The bell rang for the third round. Mitch could hear Harry shouting instructions at him, but at this point, his words amounted too little more than a buzzing in Mitch's ears. Halaphas lunged forward with a series

FIGHT NIGHT

of haymaker hooks, right then left then right again. Mitch stepped back, moving his head and letting his hands deflect the blows. As Halaphas came around with another left Mitch ducked. Exploding with his legs and arms, he lunged through his opponent's stomach and took him to the ground.

Halaphas kicked his legs, desperately trying to scramble clear of Mitch's hold. While the demon did this, it was all Mitch could do to hold on for his very life. He squeezed himself inside the demon's guard, relentlessly pressuring Halaphas' defense.

Slick with sweat and blood, they battled each other with their entire bodies. Each appendage worked to gain an advantage, savagely fighting to acquire for its owner some kind of leverage over his opponent.

A full minute it went on like this, an eternity in a bout of this nature, before Mitch finally managed to secure a dominant position. Straddling the demon and pinning its legs with his own body weight, Mitch began to throw down heavy blow after heavy blow with his fists. Unlike the last fight were he'd purposefully gone wild to give his opponent an opening here he kept himself under control. Here each blow was a deliberate, aimed attack designed to further wear down his foe.

For the first time in this fight, Halaphas was having to sit there and absorb punishment rather than dishing it out at will. Mitch made sure he took advantage of his superior position while still being cautious not to use up all of his energy.

Halaphas gave a head feint and Mitch went wide with one of his elbows. The demon grabbed hold of his arm and Mitch was forced to roll clear to avoid being caught in an armbar.

The two fighters got to their feet. For the second time, Mitch had allowed a solid ground position to be taken from him. His strategy of scoring a submission was not working. One way or another he had to find a way to knock this red-skinned bastard out if he wanted to keep his soul.

Halaphas was standing on the other side of the ring now. The demon knew he had this fight won. All he needed to do was survive to the bell. Mitch wasn't going to get any more openings. The only option he had left was to throw everything he had at his foe and pray he got lucky.

He took a breath.

Then another.

Then he charged.

Mitch screamed like a wild man as he roared across the ring.

Left hook. Right Hook. Left side kick. Spinning backhand.

Mitch flowed from one attack to another.

Using every bit of energy left in his tank and reserves he didn't know he possessed he unleashed a whirlwind of attacks against his foe.

Like a jackhammer he fired off jab after jab, pushing Halaphas against the cage, breaking through his fists and landing one strike after another.

The demon pushed Mitch off of him and retaliated with a quick combo to the face.

Mitch's vision blurred again. He stumbled backwards but managed to remain upright.

Halaphas came at him with a right hook. Mitch stepped back before stepping forward with a right hook of his own.

The demon's blow glanced off Mitch's chin while Mitch's fist connected squarely with the demon's nose.

Halaphas was staggered, blood flowed from a cut on his head down into his eye. Adrenaline surged through Mitch's body. He took a step back before charging forward. His legs pushed off the mat as he flew forward, arm cocked as far back as it would go.

Mitch's fist exploded forward, the full force of his body behind it. Time slowed. The distance between himself and Halaphas disappeared. The crowd held its collective breath.

Pain exploded up Mitch's arm as bone collided with bone, Halaphas' jaw giving way beneath the massive trauma of Mitch's superman punch.

The beast's head snapped backwards, his legs wobbled beneath him. Instinct made him flail his arms around but his wild, unconscious punches went wide.

Mitch pressed his advantage. Left, right, left. Mitch's fists were without mercy.

Halaphas' legs buckled.

FIGHT NIGHT

Time sped up again.

The demon fell.

The crowd roared.

Mitch's hands shot up to the sky and he let out a victorious scream. The ringside doctor rushed to Halaphas' side. Harry slipped under the ropes and wrapped Mitch in a massive bear hug. He could see Lily ringside shouting elatedly at his victory.

Sitting not too far from her The Don sat shaking his head dejectedly. The demon mob boss gave Mitch a good, long stare before angrily stalking towards the exit.

"You did it, kid. You saved me." Harry's words poured out between sobs.

Later that night, as Lily lay snuggled against his chest and he drifted off to sleep, Mitch smiled.

The Coming Flood

April 23rd, 1882

Tension gripped every muscle of young Lewis' body. His hands moved slowly, shaking slightly as they guided metal tongs towards their target, a bubbling flask of yellow-green liquid. White clouds of smoke spewed from the flask, fogging up Lewis' safety goggles and causing beads of sweat to form all along the ridge his forehead.

"Careful boy, I'm not entirely sure how volatile I made this batch. If you drop it they may find us at the center of a very large crater." His uncle cackled from underneath his bulky gas mask. "If they find us at all."

Not that long ago, mere months in fact, that kind of talk would have startled Lewis into dropping his temperamental cargo. Now, he took it all in stride. His uncle was a mad scientist. Almost blowing themselves into oblivion was an every-other-day kind of a thing around this house.

With great caution and as light a touch as he could manage, Lewis clamped the tongs around the neck of the flask and lifted it gently from the heat. He took a step back. Then, keeping his arms fully extended, he turned towards his uncle's workstation.

Lewis moved forward one deliberate step at a time. Eventually, after an overly agonizing seventeen steps, he reached the spot where Gideon was stirring a large cauldron of oozing pink gelatin.

Tilting his flask, Lewis poured his delicate parcel into the cauldron. Gideon continued to stir, mixing the yellow-green liquid into the pink gel. A noxious yellow smoke formed where the two substances merged.

GAROOOHHMMM, GAROOHHMMM

The bellowing, baritone mating call of a North American Chupacabra filled the house. Gideon's lab shook and Lewis nearly jumped out of his skin. He lost his tenuous grasp on the tongs and the half-full beaker fell to the floor, shattering into a hundred pieces.

Gideon and Lewis stared at the broken flask, then at each other. Both of them counting the seconds until the inevitable kaboom.

"Hmm. Not as potent as I thought it to be." His uncle shrugged before continuing on as if they hadn't just narrowly avoided meeting their maker. "Be a sport and get the door, will you Lewis. You know how I hate to be interrupted when I'm working."

"Uh-huh. No problem, Uncle Gideon." Lewis waved his hand at the Border collie hiding in the corner with its paws over its eyes. "C'mon Will. We've got a visitor."

Will barked excitedly at the idea, either the collie anticipated a thorough petting from the new visitor, or it understood the inherent dangers of remaining in the lab alone with Uncle Gideon. There was a high probability the dog had more good sense than any of the humans who shared his home.

Will trailed close behind Lewis as the young man removed his protective gear and climbed out of his uncle's lab. Which, in any other house, would have been called the cellar.

Lewis didn't mind these kinds of minor chores. His uncle was far too distracted to ever worry about something so trivial as answering the door, and they had yet to replace poor Mrs. Dunham since her grizzly demise this past Christmas Eve.

Finding a suitable housekeeper could be rather difficult in a house prone to chemical fires and demon attacks. To date, they'd been through seven, with the latest resigning her post in a huff after walking in on Antoine performing a blood ritual of some kind. Lewis didn't have all the specifics, but he'd overheard Antoine assuring Uncle Gideon that the whole thing had been one big misunderstanding and he'd only been using the chicken blood for a simple protection charm.

That wouldn't have been so bad if the woman hadn't come back with a priest intending to perform an exorcism. That intent was dispelled, along with the contents of the priest's bladder, at the appearance of Uncle Gideon in his dressing gown brandishing his twin silver-plated pistols.

Lewis was still smiling at the memory of the fleeing father when he opened the heavy oak door that was the houses front entrance. Standing there he found the most beautiful woman he had ever seen.

Now Lewis, being barely past the age of twelve and only just on the cusp of puberty, had a perception of the fairer sex that may have been prone to hyperbole at times. In this case, however, his assessment was not likely to garner an argument from anyone with even a basic level of visual acuity.

The woman at the door stood several inches taller than he. Her long auburn hair and alabaster skin providing a perfect frame for piercing eyes of sparkling blue. Her nose was small and delicate, and her smile was wide and comforting.

"Hello there. Is your father at home?" the woman asked with a voice as sweet as honey. Lewis could feel his heart thundering in his chest.

"My father's dead." He answered with an awkward bluntness. His lessons in tactfulness and charm well forgotten in a tidal wave of hormones.

"Oh, I'm dreadfully sorry." The woman blushed, her cheeks blooming with color. Lewis stood there, silently transfixed by the sight of her. "Could I speak to your mother then?" she tried again.

"I suppose, but you'll have to wait a while for a response." Lewis again responded honestly, oblivious to the true intent of her questions.

"And why is that?" The stranger inquired with polite befuddlement.

"Because she lives in San Francisco." Lewis stated simply.

"I see. Maybe I have the wrong address" She pulled a note out of her handbag, checking the address written upon it against the block letter numbers nailed to the front of the premises. "I'm looking for a Professor Giles. Professor Gideon Giles?"

"Oh, you want my uncle." A large explosion rocked the house, sending shivers through the old building's foundation. A pillar of black smoke came billowing up from the cellar door. "He's at home. Please come in." She nodded and stepped inside.

"May I take your coat?" Lewis asked, trying to remember all of his manners.

"I'm not wearing a coat." The visitor answered in a mild state of shock, her gaze firmly locked on the dark cloud quickly filling the hallway.

"Oh. Right. This way. You can wait in the study while I announce you." Lewis blushed. He too was becoming conscious of the discrepancy between his perceived reality, where he was being exceedingly polite and helpful, and actual reality, where he was being anything but.

Sheepishly he led his guest through the bowels of the house, not noticing how big her eyes got at the sight of some of the building's more eccentric trappings. He'd become accustomed to his uncle's collection of oddities. Strangers often found them more alarming.

They entered the study and Lewis was about to go looking his uncle when Gideon found them instead.

"I think the answer is more nitroglycerin less calcium carbide, maybe a dash of peppermint for flavor." Gideon strode into the room, oblivious to its extra occupant. He was quite a sight to behold. He still wore his bulky gas mask, which covered his whole face and garbled up much of what he was saying. His white lab apron was now black with soot and smoke, while one of the fingers of his thick, cowhide gloves was still slightly on fire. He put the finger out in a pitcher of lemonade Antoine had brought by for them earlier.

If their visitor's face had expressed shock at the minor explosion of a few moments ago, it was now dialed up to complete and utter disbelief.

Gideon removed his gas mask and brought his gloved, lemonade-soaked finger to his lips and gave it a lick.

"Lewis remind me to ask Antoine where he's getting his lemons from. This is undoubtedly the best batch of lemonade I've ever tasted. It's positively salacious."

"Uncle Gideon?" Lewis ventured tentatively.

"Yes, Lewis?" His uncle answered without looking up. "What is it? I'm right in the middle of perfecting this new compound. I think I might just be able to blow a hole in the fabric of the universe when I'm done. A truly exhilarating endeavor."

"We have company." Lewis persisted. "A lady to see you."

Suddenly aware that they had a guest, Gideon carefully removed his finger from his mouth.

"My apologies Miss…..?" His uncle looked at him expectantly. Lewis stood there, uncharacteristically oblivious to his uncle's social cues. Prompting Gideon to ask "Lewis, did you happen to ask the lady her name?"

"Oh." Lewis blushed. "I forgot. What's your name miss?"

"It's Dunham, Ms. Cassandra Dunham. I believe my mother was in your employ at the time of her passing." With that revelation, the mood of the room took a sharp turn.

Lewis felt like he'd been kicked in the chest by a mule. He could see the color drain from his uncle's face. Mrs. Dunham's death had been their fault. A combination of Lewis' carelessness and Gideon's arrogance.

Gideon, being possessed of far more life experience than Lewis and thus having had far more practice concealing his true feelings, was the first to break the silence. With great solemnity, he set down his gas mask and removed his lab apron. Underneath he wore a magenta vest and scarlet tie much more in keeping with the style of a modern gentleman. He took a deep breath then spoke the words he had been practicing for months.

"She was. And her loss is still felt deeply by every member of this house. You have my deepest condolences. Words cannot express my gratitude for the dedication and loyalty your mother showed me over the years. She ran this house with the precision of a finely tuned machine and the warmth of a roaring fire." His words were smooth, but his voice was tight. Lewis was too much in his own head to notice the difference in tone. Ms. Dunham, however, noticed the change with great interest.

She acknowledged Gideon's sympathies with the slightest of nods. Then turned her attention to the walls of books that surrounded her. Her fingers danced along leather-bound spines, their lazy motion making her movements seem almost lyrical in nature.

Lewis watched her, unable to look away. If he'd had eyes for anyone other than Ms. Dunham he'd have noticed that the same anticipation that had so entranced him was making his Uncle Gideon quite uncomfortable.

Ms. Dunham pulled a book from off the shelf and opened it. Perusing its pages with earnest intent.

"I was told that she was killed in some sort of animal attack?" she asked, without raising her head from the book she held.

"Yes, terrible. There was a rash of such attacks around town. Over Christmas no less. I believe there were five deaths at the time. Nasty business. We were all relieved when it was over." Gideon's response was too practiced, it had the rhythm of a well-worn refrain.

Ms. Dunham returned the thick text to its original perch. She moved along the wall, eyes scanning the various titles before selecting another.

"But they never caught the beast?" Her fingers scrolled through the table of contents.

"Not to my knowledge. No." Gideon's voice was growing harder by the question. He was unaccustomed to being on the defensive.

Ms. Dunham slammed the book shut with great veracity. Its pages filling the room with a substantial clap as the pages slammed together.

"Then how do you know that it's over?" Her eyes bore into Gideon now, burning with the fire of someone who knew they were being lied to.

"Well, there have been no more attacks since. One can only surmise that whatever kind of beast it was it suffered its own untimely demise." Gideon stood firm. Refusing to look away from Ms. Dunham's gaze.

The conversation was growing tenser by the moment. Lewis was unsure what to do. So, he did what most children do when two adults are fighting, he tried to pretend he was invisible.

"But you don't know with certainty?" Ms. Dunham asked curtly.

"I'm afraid I do not. Perhaps the police can...."

"And she was inside when it happened?" Gideon's rote deflection was interrupted by yet another pointed inquiry from Ms. Dunham. Refusing him the opportunity to gather any verbal velocity.

"Yes, she was baking bread. Like she did every morning. It's all in the official report. I'm sure the police would be more than accommodating if you wish to read it." Now Gideon tried pouring Ms. Dunham a glass of lemonade but she refused and continued on unabated.

"They were. But I'm afraid it raised more questions than answers. For instance, the police report said the animal killed her, then escaped out the front door. It makes no mention of how it got in to begin with." Lewis knew that he should be worried that Ms. Dunham was asking all the right questions but her tenacious questioning of Uncle Gideon served only to increase her esteem in his eyes.

"It doesn't?" For all his Uncle Gideon's intelligence and charisma, Lewis could tell he was unaccustomed to being interrogated in this way and if it continued much longer he would say something they would all regret.

"No, it doesn't. You wouldn't happen to know how a dangerous creature came to be in your home would you Professor Giles?" She asked her question while pointedly looking at the mounted head of a rather fierce looking Yeti.

"PROFESSOR?" A familiar, bellowing voice filled the house and cut off whatever response Gideon was about to offer. "PROFESSOR?"

"We're in the study, Antoine." Gideon shouted back, looking relieved to have an excuse to end his audience with Ms. Dunham early.

In just about any other part of the western world, a man of Antoine's skin color entering a white man's house unannounced would be cause for a hanging, if the man wasn't just shot on sight to begin with. But not here. Not this man and not this house. That was just another reason Lewis loved living with his uncle.

Antoine was his uncle's best friend. He was also a voodoo priest or "doctor" as he preferred to be called and was highly respected by both the black and white communities here in New Orleans. He was a man people came to with their problems when they had nowhere else to turn. And he, in turn, came to Lewis' uncle when he believed his own talents insufficient to the task.

Antoine had helped Gideon create his 'mirror' to other worlds and thus he too bore a portion of the responsibility for Ms. Dunham's mother's untimely demise.

Upon entering the study and seeing that they were not alone in the house

Antoine removed his hat and pulled himself up straight, making polite and perfuse pardons for the manner of his entrance.

"Antoine, may I introduce you to Ms. Cassandra Dunham, the only daughter of our recently departed Mrs. Dunham." With this pronouncement, Antoine's solemnity increased tenfold.

"You have my deepest sympathies. Your mother was a great woman." He took her hand in his and, making a deep bow, kissed it.

Ms. Dunham was for her part quite taken aback. Lewis doubted she'd ever encountered a man quite like Antoine. He hadn't. Not until he'd come to New Orleans.

Using the opening offered to him by Antoine's unusual entrance, Gideon began hurrying his unexpected visitor out the door.

"Well, Ms. Dunham it was certainly a pleasure to meet you. I'm sure if you still have questions concerning your mother's unfortunate passing the local police will be more than happy to provide you with whatever answers they have in their possession. I can only tell you again that you have our deepest sympathies for your loss and wish you the best of luck with your inquiries. Lewis, would you show our guest out please?"

Gideon's face froze in an accommodating smile that didn't quite touch his eyes. Ms. Dunham's mouth was open, attempting to form some sort of objection to her obvious dismissal but none came. Instead, she switched tactics mid-word.

"Thank you for your time Professor, I realize it must be valuable. Good day. I look forward to our next conversation." She turned abruptly and exited. Lewis scrambled to catch up.

He wished to attempt some conversation while he escorted her to the front door but could think of nothing that might break the woman out of the thoughts that seemed to have ensnared her.

It was fortunate for Lewis that his uncle's unusual residence was enough to jolt her free of her tangled thoughts. After bumping into a stuffed ridgeback elephant, Ms. Dunham went from ignoring her surrounding to examining them with a keen eye. This included Lewis.

"If I may ask, what is it your uncle is a professor of, precisely?" It was a common question in this house. Lewis was surprised it had taken her so long to ask.

"Oh, he teaches all sorts of things. This semester he's got two classes; Theories of Transdimensional Dynamics and Occultism in the Industrial Age." The words rolled off Lewis' tongue. He practiced them in the mirror every night so he could sound smart like his uncle.

"I don't believe I know of anyone teaching such varied and progressive subjects. Are his classes very popular with the students?" If Miss Dunham was impressed by Lewis' articulation abilities she didn't show it, rather she carried on with no more to do than if Lewis had said his uncle taught math. Her lack of astonishment disappointed Lewis.

"Not really. They never seem to know what he's talking about. I think that's the way he likes it." he shrugged.

"I notice he does a lot of hunting in his spare time." Miss Dunham observed, gesturing to the various stuffed heads in the hallway.

"You mean the specimens? I don't really know about those. I haven't lived here that long." Lewis paused. Emotions roiled around inside him. "You see my mother didn't want me getting in the way of finding a new husband and so she sent me down here to live with Uncle Gideon. And well the day I arrived was the day Mrs. Dunham, that is to say, your mother was killed. I didn't know her very long, but she was very nice to me. I'd guess she was a very nice mother too. You must miss her a great deal."

Lewis' did not know why, but his words seem to rattle Ms. Dunham more than any of the other things she'd witnessed so far. She took a moment to compose herself before answering him.

"I do. A great deal. Which is why I want to find out everything I can about how she died. Can you help me, Lewis? I think there is something your uncle isn't telling me." Her voice was sad and urgent. Lewis wanted to tell her everything, but shame kept his tongue from wagging.

"I'm sorry. It's like my uncle said. You'll have to ask the police." Lewis pulled open the door for her.

Before exiting she pulled out a tiny white card from her handbag and placed it in Lewis' shirt pocket.

"This is the hotel where I'm staying. I'd like it very much if you came 'round for supper while I'm here. I don't know anyone in town, and you'd be doing me a great favor by keeping me company." She bent down and placed a kiss on his forehead then walked out the door. Several minutes passed before Lewis' heart stopped trying to beat its way out of his chest.

When Lewis returned to the study he could hear his uncle and Antoine arguing in hushed tones. Quietly he put his ear up to the crack in the door, hoping to hear more.

"She came looking for the truth about her mother." Gideon said.

"And did ye give it te her?" Antoine asked.

"Did it sound as if I gave it to her?" was his uncle's predictably sarcastic reply.

"She deserves te know what happened." The voodoo priest insisted.

"And what exactly would I say? 'I regret to inform you that your mother was murdered by an intra-dimensional demon that got loose because I fiddled with primordial forces I did not truly understand. Terribly sorry. Of course, you'll have to keep this to yourself so we don't all end up in a sanitarium with electrical nodes attached to our temples.' You're a bright fellow Antoine, how do you see that conversation ending?" The speed and volume of Gideon's voice grew more manic as his rant gained steam. When he finished there was a long silence.

In a quiet, flat voice Antoine repeated himself. "She deserves te know."

"Yes, well, if you choose to assuage your conscience I'll not stop you. As for me, I'll be sticking to the official coroner's report. Which fastidiously avoids any mention of hell beasts. But Ms. Dunham was not what brought you to my home this morning." Uncomfortable with the conversation as it was currently constituted Gideon changed the subject.

"Dis morning I was visited by a Mrs. Sanders. She runs de Chinese mission." Antoine said flatly, clearly irritated and unsatisfied with the abrupt end to the previous topic.

"I'm aware of who she is. She's tried to have me fired from the university on moral grounds. Twice. Thinks my fields of study are a cover for converting my students to Satanism. Why would she come to you for help?" Gideon asked.

"A man showed up at de mission. Died in her arms. She wants my help te find out why." was Antoine's brief explanation.

"'She wants your help to find out why?' What about the police? There are still police in this city aren't there? Men in funny hats whose job it is to handle these sorts of things. Police. I keep using that word but between you and Ms. Dunham I'm beginning to think it doesn't mean what I think it means."quipped Gideon.

"A Chinese man wid no name? How hard da ye think the police are going te look professor?" Antoine asked rhetorically.

"Point taken." Gideon conceded. "I still don't see why it falls to us to pick up their slack."

"De spirits say dis be our responsibility. Dat if we do not intercede many will die." Antoine intoned in his very serious 'the spirits have spoken' voice. It was the voice he used when he wanted Gideon to do something but didn't want to fully explain why he wanted him to do it.

"You and your spirits. Fine, we'll look into it." Antoine smiled at Gideon's acquiescence. "Because you asked and because I'd rather not be home if Ms. Dunham comes back round. Not because I believe any of this is connected. I'll lay good odds this doesn't amount to anything more than a simple mugging."

"Lewis," His uncle raised his voice only slightly. "What have I told you about eavesdropping?"

"If I'm going to do it don't get caught." Lewis opened the door all the way and stepped into the study.

"Precisely." His uncle gave him a good long stare before impatiently asking "Well, what are you waiting for? Grab your gun and jacket, we're going out."

* * *

"And what, may I ask, is *he* doing here?" Mrs. Lena Saunders was a woman approaching but not quite having arrived at her middle years. Her severe demeanor gave her features a hardness that Lewis found off-putting. She very much reminded him of his mother.

On the carriage ride over Antoine had filled them in on her background.

Mrs. Saunders and her husband moved to New Orleans almost a full year ago, leaving their home in Boston to take up what they hoped would be more rewarding pursuits in the south. For Mr. Saunders that meant trying his hand at a variety of local industries. For Mrs. Saunders, it meant teaching English to newly arrived Chinese immigrants in order to acquaint them with the glory of their Lord and Savior Jesus Christ and the precepts and customs of His chosen nation the United States of America.

Her mission lay just off Tulane Avenue, between South Rampart and La Salle. Traditionally, this section of town was known for Elk Place, but now it was increasingly becoming known instead for her mission and the influx of Chinese residents and retailers it was attracting. A nascent New Orleans Chinatown.

If her beet red face was anything to go by, Mrs. Saunders was less the turn-the-other-cheek and more the fire-and-brimstone kind of Christian. And she was not overly fond of Uncle Gideon

"A pleasure to see you again as well, Mrs. Saunders." Gideon's smile was genuine even if his words were not.

"I ask'd him te join me. If der be somding evil afoot. Der be no better companion te have by yer side den Professor Giles." Antoine extended one of his meaty hands and slapped it down hard on Gideon's shoulder to reinforce his words.

"If there is something evil about, it is most likely *Professor* Giles is the cause." Mrs. Saunders eyes narrowed, reappraising Antoine in light of these new revelations about the company he keeps. Considering Antione was a practicing Voodoo priest and the woman a devout Christian, her opinion of Gideon must have been awfully low to be able to make Antoine the one who was guilty by association. The new verdict was not in their favor. Not even Will's puppy dog eyes could win her over. "I can see now it was a mistake to involve you Mr. Laveau. I will handle this matter on my own. Thank you for your time."

"Told you." Gideon said to Antoine with a shrug. "If the lady doesn't want our help. I see no reason not to let the proper authorities handle the matter."

"Please, Mrs. Saunders, der be danger in dis. It would be unwise te pursue dis yourself." Antoine warned.

"If it's so dangerous why did you bring a child?" This woman definitely reminded Lewis of his mother.

"How else do you expect him to learn basic investigative techniques?" Gideon countered quizzically.

Antoine turned sharply at Gideon.

"Professor, you are not helping. Perhaps it is best if you do not speak for a few minutes." Gideon rolled his eyes but did not say anything more.

"De boy can handle himself. Missus Saunders please, you came te me for help 'cause ye knew ye could not deal wid dis alone. Let us help. Tell us what has happened. I promise you we will do nothing dat will cause you te break faith wid your God." Antoine urged her.

"Very well." With a fair amount of reluctance, Mrs. Saunders returned to her seat. "Where would you like me to begin?"

"Just tell us yer story, as you remember it." Antoine said, gesturing for her to take a seat.

"All right. This all happened three days ago. The morning of the twentieth." Mrs. Saunders took a deep breath before continuing. "As per usual, I arrived at the mission before sunrise to ready it for morning prayers. I was sliding my key into the front door when I heard a rustle in the bushes. Startled, I dropped my keys. I called out but heard no answer. I assumed the noise to be nothing more than my imagination playing tricks on me, so I bent down to pick up my keys."

Mrs. Saunders paused and poured herself a glass of water before continuing.

"A hand touched my shoulder. Stepping out from the bushes came a rather depressing picture of a man. He was Chinese, but not anyone I recognized from the mission. His clothes were ragged and torn. He grabbed at my blouse and I backed away out of his reach. Then I noticed he was clutching at his right side. Blood was soaking through his shirt. Knowing then that the man needed my help I tried to keep him upright. He stumbled and fell, pulling me down with him." Mrs. Saunders took one more deep breath before concluding her story. "He asked me to help him."

"He spoke English?" Lewis spoke without thinking.

"No, I speak Mandarin. He asked me to help him and then he told me to beware." Mrs. Saunders elaborated.

"Beware of what?" Gideon chimed in from his perch in the doorway.

"Lóng de pú rén." She said.

"Lóng de pú rén? What does that mean?" Gideon was posing the question to himself more than anyone else.

"I do not know. But those were his last words, 'Lóng de pú rén.' I tried to coax more out of him, but it was no use, the poor man was already gone. I can only hope that he came to the mission because he had accepted the light of God into his life so that he may know peace in the next." Mrs. Saunders closed her eyes and bowed her head in a silent prayer.

Gideon made a snorting noise and covered his mouth with his hand. He played it off as a cough, but Lewis knew his uncle was choking down a chuckle.

"Is der any 'ting else you can tell us?" Antoine asked.

"Yes, there is one more thing." Mrs. Saunders reached into her handbag and pulled out a small piece of paper. "He was clenching this in his palm."

The paper was torn at the edges. Blood stained it obscuring some handwritten letters. But what could clearly be seen was a single Chinese character, made with a bold, black stamp.

Gideon looked to Antoine and back to the stamp.

"I suppose ye know who dis belongs te." Antoine seemed reticent to name the owner of the stamp.

"I do." Gideon agreed with equal reticence.

"Den I guess you know where we have te visit next." The pair rose from their chairs. Antoine offered a deep bow that met with Mrs. Saunders approval.

"We have enough te get started. Dank you, ma'am, for entrusting dis wid us. We will endeavor not te fail you in dis madder." Antoine assured the matronly woman before they rose to leave her.

***

Human beings are not, by nature, particularly moral creatures. Each one, no matter their station in life, is beset by certain desires and temptations that they find difficult to resist even under the best of circumstances. For some, their Achilles' heel may be no more than the consumption of one too many beignets. For others, their proclivities may be far more taboo.

It is inevitable then, that there will be those who seek to exploit those weaknesses for profit. The more people in a place, the more room for such leeches to grow and thrive. Because of this, it is a fact that most major metropolitan cities are possessed of a seedy underbelly. New Orleans was possessed of several.

Lewis was not a stranger to this fact. He was, however, a stranger to the world that fact described. It would be unfair to characterize his life to this point as easy or sheltered, but while Lewis had come face to face with darkness he'd never been past its edges. To understand these places, you had to live in them. The area of the city they were now entering was one of these places.

Being a port city, New Orleans had no shortage of docks. Some were bright and clean, where respectable folk boarded and departed from nice respectable riverboats. Other were commercial, where men toiled to load and unload richer men's cargo; a bit dirtier but still on the up and up. Then there where the dock that stank of piss and vomit. These were the docks for Coloreds and Orientals. Where the only white people you'd come across were crooks and addicts.

Lewis didn't much care for the segregated world he lived in. He was sure that when he grew up he would do something about it. But for the time being, he was twelve years old and the adults made the rules.

A few people greeted Antoine as they passed. Lewis smiled at those who did. They reacted to his smile with wary nods of their head. He and his Uncle Gideon stood out like a sore thumb here.

"You still haven't told me where we're going, Uncle Gideon." The question became more pressing the deeper they sojourned into unfamiliar terrain.

"We're going to see a man about a stamp." His uncle answered enigmatically. Lewis hated when he did that.

Will stayed close. Lewis had to be careful not to trip over the loyal collie. Men in ragged clothes sat propped against brick walls. Their faces black with dirt and grease. Some slept on their sides, using their rucksacks as pillows. Others stared blankly ahead, their minds somewhere else. Lewis knew the look well. It was the faraway look his mother got when she took in her vapors.

"Do ye dink it wise we brought de boy along? Dis be dangerous ground." Antoine asked after they stepped around one such man.

"He'll be fine. No better way to learn than through experience." Gideon crossed the street and approached a large warehouse. Its doors were rolled open and inside Lewis could see men moving large crates. The sign above the door said *Oriental Imports Ltd*. There were Chinese characters underneath the words that Lewis assumed meant the same thing. A large chain blocked off the warehouse. Hanging from the chain was a sign that said *Employees Only*.

His uncle stopped and bent down so that he and Lewis were at eye level. "Lewis, I need you to listen carefully. We are about to deal with some very dangerous people. What are our rules when we encounter individuals of ill-repute?"

"Don't speak unless its an emergency. Don't volunteer any information. And don't pull my gun unless I see you pull yours." Lewis responded with practiced precision.

"Very good." Gideon smiled with paternal pride. "You see Antoine, nothing to be worried about."

Antoine response to Gideon's gloating was nothing more than a raised eyebrow. "I dink you do not worry enough professor."

Lewis agreed with Antoine but kept the thought to himself. Gideon for his part took the comment in stride.

He smiled maniacally as he took in a full view of where they were standing. Lewis copied his uncle but did not understand why he found their surroundings so interesting.

"Now, I believe if we just step over here." Lewis' uncle raised his arms a did a little flourish, taking one very large step over the chain and into the restricted area.

The laborers froze where they stood. Abruptly another group of men appeared, stepping out of the shadows with their pistols drawn to surround them.

Antoine put his hand on his gun but did not draw it. Similarly, Will let out a low growl but did not bark. Their example and remembering the rules Gideon had drilled into him were the only things that kept Lewis from drawing his own pistol.

Gideon, as always, was both unsurprised and unperturbed by the men's sudden appearance. He had clearly been expecting their response.

"Yes, Professor Gideon Giles and company to see Mr. Wong please." He announced, pretending not to notice the guns pointed at his person.

"He's busy." One of the men responded. His accent was heavy. It was unclear if any of the other men even understood English.

"We'll wait." Gideon said with a smile.

"He's always busy." The head guard, Lewis decided guard was more polite a word than thug, did not budge. Neither did his men.

Uncle Gideon was undeterred. "Ah. Well, in that case, perhaps if you tell him this is in regard to his missing man, he may find a way to extricate himself from his present commitments"

One of the other guards said something to the head man in Chinese. The head guard barked something a waved his gun at Gideon.

Gideon made a production out of yawning.

Lewis tried to imitate his uncle.

Instead of yawning he ended up in a coughing fit.

There was some more arguing in Chinese. Eventually, the head man lowered his gun.

"Wait here" he said, before storming off in a huff.

They waited in silence. The other guards had not lowered their revolvers when the head man had.

Lewis used the opportunity to observe his surroundings, just as Uncle

Gideon had instructed him to do. The laborers had resumed their work. They looked almost as nervous as Lewis felt.

He tried to shift his posture to get a better look, but just then the head guard returned. He was followed by three more men. One in a well-tailored suit and two others flanking the well-dressed man.

"Mr. Wong, I presume." Gideon's smile had finally disappeared.

Mr. Wong was not a tall man. In truth, he stood only a few inches higher than Lewis. Neither was he possessed of much mass. His suit, while expensive and well-tailored, hung off him as if it sat on a wire hanger. Short and thin. No one would ever mistake him for the muscle of the operation.

No, the mistake they would make, the mistake Lewis bet many had made and not lived to regret, was to assume because of his diminutive stature Mr. Wong was frail. All it took was one look at his bodyguards was enough to dispel that notion. They were warier of the man they protected then of any potential harms that might come his way.

Mr. Wong acknowledged Gideon with a nod.

"I am familiar with Doctor Laveau. We are, after all, pillars of our respective communities. But you, I'm afraid, have not yet proven significant enough to warrant my interest."

"Well that's disappointing, here I thought I was the feature attraction of everyone's social calendar. Professor Gideon Giles, at your service." Gideon gave the man a slight bow. Deep enough to show respect, but not so deep as to be patronizing.

Mr. Wong's gaze took them all in. Weighing and assessing each member of their party in turn. Even Will.

"As interesting as it is to make your acquaintance Professor, I'm not sure what it is that has brought you here today." he said, his eyes coming back to Gideon.

"We've been asked to investigate a suspicious death. A man collapsed in front of the mission. He was badly beaten. He succumbed to his wounds before a doctor could be found." Gideon explained.

"A tragedy to be sure. The man's family has my sympathy. But I fail to see my connection to this matter." Having made his assessment of them, Mr.

Wong turned his focus back to his employees. He whispered instruction in Chinese to his security forces and began checking the manifests of the various shipping crates stacked up around them.

"The man was an Oriental. I thought it wise to approach you first before launching any other inquiries." Lewis could tell that Uncle Gideon was trying to be courteous. But it wasn't an area he had much practice in.

"Again, I fail to see the connection. Do you believe this man worked for me?" Wong replied, his eyes never looking up from the papers he was holding.

"I made an intuitive leap." Gideon's quip was enough to get Mr. Wong to focus his attention back on the professor.

"I would say your intuition needs work. None of my workers have gone missing and, unlike Dr. Laveau, I do not keep track of every member of the population who shares my skin tone." Mr. Wong's eyes held a tinge of menace in them. The man-made Lewis uncomfortable.

While Gideon and Mr. Wong traded verbal barbs something at the edge of his vision caught Lewis' eye. He turned his head, careful to avoid looking like anything more than a bored young man ready for the adults to be done talking.

Then he saw it again. A glimmer of green stone in the sunlight. And holding it was a woman who looked an awful lot like Ms. Dunham.

"I think in this case my intuition is doing just fine." Gideon's raised voice brought Lewis' attention back to the here and now.

"Is it really so hard to believe Mr. Giles, that I may not know every Chinaman who passes through this city?" Mr. Wong asked, his forbearance clearly deteriorating.

"I find it helpfully to overestimate people's capacities. It ensures I never underestimate them." Gideon met the old man's eyes. The two stared at each other, locked in a battle of wills.

"Not an unwise philosophy, but one that can result in great disappointment." Mr. Wong broke the gaze. "Much like the disappointment you're sure to be feeling in a few moments."

"And what is the source of my impending disillusionment?" Gideon asked, but Lewis had a pretty fair idea.

"Myself, when I tell you once and for all I have no knowledge concerning your deceased man and no further patience in standing here repeating myself." Mr. Wong gestured to his men. "So, I will bid you good day. Can you find your own way out or do you need my men to escort you to the street?"

"I'm sure we can find the way ourselves." Gideon raised his palms in surrender.

"I'm less sure." Mr. Wong's men grabbed them by the arms and hauled them outside. Dropping them on their rears when they let go. Will followed, barking his head off on behalf of his master.

"Dat could have gone better." Antoine said, pushing himself up with his staff.

Gideon jumped to his feet. Taking care to dust off his long coat.

"What are you complaining about? I think that went swimmingly."

* * *

"Well, Antoine?" Gideon asked as soon as they were clear of the docks.

"He's obviously hiding some 'ting." Antoine responded. "Why didn't ye ask him about de symbol?"

Gideon explained his thinking.

"No need to show our hand just yet. We asked our question and he gave us the answer he wanted us to believe. Whatever else he may appear to be, Wong is a dangerous man. Better to let him think we know less than we do. At least until we know who all the players are."

Antoine nodded. Lewis was glad all that made sense to somebody.

"Perhaps 'den a nice walk home?" Antoine suggested.

"Exactly what I was thinking."

They bypassed the for-hire carriages and made their way down St. Charles on foot. It was not a short walk by any reckoning. By the time they passed Tivoli Circle, only Will was still excited about the journey.

Gideon halted precipitously, raising his hand as a signal for Lewis and

Antoine to stop as well. Will turned back and let out a low growl.

"We're being followed." Gideon stated with confidence.

Antoine looked at him quizzically. "Aye. Miss Dunham has been following us for quite some time"

Gideon shook his head.

"No, that's not what I mean. Someone is following her, following us. They started shadowing us shortly after we left the docks." Gideon stopped and raised his voice loud enough to draw complaints from both sides of the street. "Ms. Dunham. I know you're out there. There is something I need to tell you about your mother's death."

Ms. Dunham stepped out from one of the various side streets that crossed St. Charles. She was dressed in the same outfit Lewis had seen her in that morning, with the notable addition of a jade pendant that seemed to shimmer in the moonlight.

"Professor Giles, what a coincidence, I was just returning to my evening accommodations." Ms. Dunham approached them with a forced air of casualness.

"We've no time for face-saving lies Ms. Dunham. We are all about to be in a great deal of danger." Gideon's warning fell on deaf ears. It was clear from the look on Ms. Dunham's face that she had already decided what she thought about Gideon Giles. And the first thing she thought was that he was not to be trusted.

"I'm certain I have no idea what you are talking about, but your brusque manner is really quite ungentlemanly." Ms. Dunham retorted choosing to ignore Uncle Gideon's accusations as well as his warning.

Five men dressed in all black stepped out of the shadows. They wore blue, dragon's head masks over their faces and in their hands, they held long wooden staffs with curved blades at the end.

"Lewis, at the ready." His uncle barked.

Lewis drew his pistol and stepped into the defensive line with Antoine and his uncle.

"Ms. Dunham if you would be so kind as to step behind me." Gideon made the request with little more urgency than if he had asked the woman to pass the sugar.

"If you think I'm simply going to…" She started to say before Lewis cut her off.

"Behind you Ms. Dunham." She turned and gasped at the sight of the masked men. Quickly she backpedaled away from the armed gang and towards Gideon.

He guided her behind their protective demarcation.

Will's growls grew louder.

The five men spread out, forming an attacking line to mach Gideon's defensive front.

"Who are they?" Ms. Dunham asked, voice trembling.

"That's a very good question. Perhaps we should ask them." In a calm, clear voice Gideon addressed the quintet of masked men. "Gentlemen, I'm afraid you've put quite a fright into my companions. If you wouldn't mind identifying yourselves, it would go a long way towards reducing tensions."

The men stood silent, the dark red eyes of their dragon masks staring at them with unblinking menace.

"I see. Well then, I suppose then the duty of introductions falls to me. Good sirs, my name is Professor Gideon Giles. I am a seeker of truth, not of quarrels. Fade back into the darkness from whence you came, and no blood need be shed. Persist and I give you my word as a scholar and a soldier, you will perish by my hand." Uncle Gideon warned.

The masked men continued their approach.

"Nice speech. Does that ever work?" Ms. Dunham asked.

"Not usually, no." Gideon shrugged.

As one, the men gave up their slow approach and surged forward. Two apiece rushed towards Antoine and Gideon, while the remaining assailant charged Lewis.

The man in black swayed as he ran, refusing to travel in a straight line.

Lewis aimed his pistol and fired.

He missed.

The man was almost on top of him now.

Will barked and jumped into the air, colliding with the man's ribs and knocking him off balance.

Lewis dodged to the left. The man's edged weapon cut through the fabric of his shirt but missed flesh. Looking down, Lewis was stunned by how close it had come to puncturing his innards. While he was staring down, the curved blade came swiping back towards him.

He fell to the ground and watched the blade cut through where he'd just been standing. His foe regained his footing and stood over Lewis.

Lewis fumbled for his pistol. All he felt in the dark was damp dirt.

The thug raised his weapon. Preparing to drop the blade into Lewis' skull.

Lewis' palm found iron and relief flooded through him. He raised his pistol and fired.

The gun barked.

There was a spark of brilliant white, Lewis' bullet bouncing off the dragon mask the man wore.

Lewis' assailant staggered back, dazed.

Will rejoined the battle, biting at the ankle of the man who threatened his master.

Lewis pulled the trigger on his pistol again.

The barrel clicked dry.

The masked man gathered himself again. Using the blunt end of his weapon, he struck Will in the head. The brave collie whimpered and fell silent.

Again, the masked man raised his blade over his head, preparing to deliver a fatal blow.

The blade gleamed in the moonlight. Lewis watched helplessly as it began moving forward, slicing towards his head with lethal intent.

Lewis closed his eyes and prayed.

Steel clanged against steel an inch above Lewis' face and he was saved.

Gideon stood above him. The hidden blade he kept up his sleeve now held securely in his palm, denying the masked man's curved blade its bloody satisfaction.

The professor flashed his nephew a manic grin.

"Lewis, you made two mistakes in this engagement." His uncle told him in his official teaching voice.

Gideon pushed up, spun, and slashed.

The man in black jumped backward, creating distance between himself and his new, more experienced foe.

"Can you tell me what they were?" Gideon asked, not taking his eyes off his opponent.

The masked man twirled his blade around his body. The blade gathered momentum as it danced through the air. Then, suddenly, the man extended the staff to its full reach, taking a horizontal swipe at Gideon's head.

Rather than retreat, Gideon moved forward, intercepting the staff well in front of its bladed end. There was a dull thud as its wooded shaft collided with Gideon's bony forearm.

Gideon slashed with his own blade. Cutting his opponent across the hand. The man made no sound and did not drop his weapon. Dark blood oozed from the wound.

"I forgot to keep track of how many shots I fired." Lewis answered his uncle's question, knowing it was one of what his uncle called the Fatal Mistakes.

The cultist did another three-hundred-and-sixty-degree turn, switching to a one-handed grip and further extending his blade's reach. This time he went low, directing his attack at Gideon's legs.

Gideon jumped back, clearing the attack with ease.

"And?" he prodded Lewis.

Gideon attempted to push forward, but the masked man's superior reach kept him at a distance.

"And I fell down?" Lewis said, more question than answer.

Three quick jabs from the pointy end of his adversary's staff left Gideon off-balance and out of position to press the attack.

"No, falling down isn't inherently bad." His uncle said, undaunted by his sudden disadvantage. The masked man charged furiously at Gideon. Slashing his blade from side to side. "Sometimes it can even work to your advantage."

Gideon leaned back, letting gravity do its work. The blade passed harmlessly above him. Lewis' uncle hit the ground and rolled.

When he came up again his dagger had already left his hand.

The six-inch steel blade sailed through the air. The man in the dragon masked turned, bringing his weapon around for another attack.

The dagger struck him square in the heart. The man dropped his weapon and clutched at the small hilt sticking out of his chest.

He made a strange coughing noise and fell to the ground. Dead.

"Aim for where they are going to be, not for where they are." Gideon pushed himself up from the ground. Calmly he walked over to his slain foe and retrieved his blade. He wiped the blood off on the man's black shirt then returned the dagger to its hidden, spring-loaded sheath.

Gideon walked over to Lewis, bending down and checking his nephew for injuries. He took extra note of the hole in Lewis' shirt.

"Cutting it a bit close, Lewis?" His uncle asked with a raised eyebrow.

Abruptly, Lewis remembered he hadn't been the only one fighting for his life.

"Will!" Lewis raced to his dog's side. Will was whimpering. There was a cut above his ear. Blood and dirt mixed together in his fur.

Lewis picked up his wounded pup and held him close.

"Professor!" Antoine shouted.

He knelt beside Ms. Dunham. Her dress was ripped and her hair disheveled. A dark red spot stained her right side and it was still spreading.

Gideon hurried to where she lay. He took one look at her before motioning to Antoine to pick her up.

"Back to the house. Quickly!"

Over Ms. Dunham's half-hearted objections, Antoine scooped up the young woman in his arms. Gideon kept his pistols out while the party set off at a brisk jog, leaving five corpses in their wake.

They reached their destination without incident.

Hurriedly Gideon opened the doors, then locked them again once they were all inside.

Lewis went about turning on the house lights, which was much easier at Uncle Gideon's house than in his old home. There he had needed to run around lighting lamps here he only needed to flick a few switches.

The modern lights came as quite a shock to Ms. Dunham.

"How? What?" She struggled against Antoine's massive frame. "Oh, put me down you oaf."

"Her mother's room please Antoine," Gideon instructed.

"Yes, professor." Antoine moved quickly but carefully towards the late Mrs. Dunham's room, studiously avoiding bumping her daughter's struggling form into any of the houses protruding oddities as he did.

"Antoine, I need a basin of warm water, towels, and my medical bag. Ms. Dunham I'm going to have to remove your blouse now so I can get to the wound." Uncle Gideon barked orders like the former combat medic that he was.

"You're not a real doctor." Ms. Dunham accused.

"The Union army would beg to differ. In my day, I have seen just about every battlefield injury there is to see and a few more besides. I can promise you I know what I am about. Now either do as I say and live or don't and die a slow, painful death from a very preventable bout of sepsis. The choice is yours, Ms. Dunham."

Ms. Dunham relented and let Gideon lift up her shift just as Antoine returned with the items Gideon had requested.

"How about we see what we can do for brave Will here." Antoine put his hand on Lewis' shoulder and led him out of the room, shutting the door behind them.

Antoine directed Lewis to one of the study's comfier chairs, then pulled out a stiff straight-backed chair for himself.

After a few reassuring words and belly rubs, Will stopped whimpering long enough for Antoine to sew up his wound.

When Antoine was done, Will jumped out of Lewis' arms and curled himself up in front of the fire. Antoine cleaned up and Lewis set himself down in one of his uncle's big fluffy chairs.

Lewis had almost nodded off to sleep when Gideon entered.

"Ms. Dunham?" he asked his uncle urgently.

"The cut wasn't too bad. I gave her a sedative and stitched her up. She'll have a scar but that's all." Gideon removed his gloves and gestured to where Will lay by the fire. "How's our other patient?"

"About de same. He should be back te his happy self in no time at all."

Gideon went to where his jacket and bag lay on the table. From his satchel, he pulled out one of the dragon masks their attackers had been wearing. "These are not the kind of trinkets you buy from the general store. Do you know anything about them, Antoine?"

The houngan picked up the mask and examined it from every angle before announcing his conclusion. "De Servants of de Dragon."

"Who?" Gideon asked. Lewis smiled. It was nice to be reminded sometimes that his uncle was not in fact omniscient.

"Dey be a cult of some kind. Der's not much ta be going on. Just rumors and whispers but dey call dem selves de Servants of de Dragon." Antoine frowned. Clearly, he was not encouraged by this latest development.

"Charming. What are they opium smugglers? Dealers? Suppliers? Or did they just think the word dragon sounded imposing?" Gideon was fiddling with the dragon mask now, even going so far as to try the thing on. Lewis thought his uncle looked ridiculous. But even in the light, looking absolutely absurd on Uncle Gideon's head, there was still something about the mask that made Lewis extremely uncomfortable.

"From what I know, dey be true believers. Immigrants mostly. Worshiping some god from de old country." There was a trace of sympathy and respect in Antoine's voice. It made sense, after all, he too was a practitioner and protector of a religion from a different land.

"Any connection to Wong?" Gideon asked after removing the dragon mask from his head.

"Outside de fact dey attacked us on de way back from his place. No, not dat I know of." Antoine shook his head. "I'm sorry professor, dat is all I know."

"No need to apologize. It's a good deal more than we had to go on this morning." Gideon folded his coat over his arm. "Nothing more we can do tonight. I think the best thing is to pay Mr. Wong another visit in the morning."

Antoine nodded his agreement while stifling a yawn.

"Antoine your usual room is ready for you if you wish to stay the night." Gideon offered.

"I dink dat would be wise, dank you." Antoine accepted without even a polite argument.

"Lewis up to bed. Big day tomorrow." Gideon had no idea how right he was.

***

April 24th, 1882

Lewis woke up to the sensation of Will's rough tongue licking his face. His beloved collie was in better spirits this morning. Though the bald patch behind his ear where Antoine had stitched up his cut, made him look more mangy-mutt than well-cared for pet. Lewis' own spirits sank a bit thinking back to all the times his pup had gotten injured protecting him.

The smell of bacon and eggs wafted up to his room from the kitchen.

"You up for some breakfast boy? Antoine's here." Lewis asked.

Will's tail wagged excitedly. He let out two sharp barks in reply. They were both in agreement breakfast was a much better meal when Antoine was there to cook it.

Lewis threw on his dressing gown and the pair hurried down the stairs.

When they entered the kitchen, they found Antoine and Gideon engaged in a heated discussion. What was more unfortunate, it was Gideon, not Antoine, who was manning the stove.

"You take too many risks. First de mother. Den you almost get de daughter killed last night." Antoine whisper-yelled.

"How was I supposed to know a bunch of dragon cultists were going to attack us? Also, I don't recall inviting her along in the first place." Gideon retorted.

"She was der because you wouldn't tell her de truth." Antoine insisted.

"Wouldn't tell me the truth about what." Ms. Dunham was standing directly behind Lewis in the doorway.

"About how much better your mother's cooking was than mine." Gideon turned his attention back to the stove, conveniently ignoring Ms. Dunham's glare. "But I'm afraid I'm all we've got these days. Ms. Dunham won't you take a seat. Eggs will be ready in a moment."

Lewis pulled out a chair for Ms. Dunham and waited patiently for her to give up her death stare and sit down.

Breakfast was a long, arduous affair, not least because of Uncle Gideon's terrible eggs. The entire meal was a series of questions posed by Ms. Dunham and vague non-specific answers given by Gideon. With Antoine and Lewis caught in the middle.

Tired of Ms. Dunham's relentless pursuit of satisfactory answers, Gideon stood up and grabbed his coat while his plate was still half full.

"Antoine, you'll stay behind to look after things while Lewis and I pay Mr. Wong another visit?" Gideon nodded his head towards Ms. Dunham in a gesture that was far less subtle than Lewis thought his uncle intended it to be.

"I am not a child. I do not need looking after and I do not need to be spoken about as if I am not in the room." Ms. Dunham objected.

"My apologies, Ms. Dunham. It's just, after last night and considering how we lost your mother, I think we're all a bit on edge. It would be a tragedy if something happened to you. Please, if for nothing else other than my peace of mind, will you remain here and rest until we are certain your wound will not become infected." Gideon held her gaze until she relented with a reluctant nod of acquiescence.

The room was quiet except for the sound of grease sizzling on the skillet. It was Antoine who finally broke the silence.

"Mrs. Saunders sent word she will be arriving at six o'clock for an update." Antoine informed them. Studiously avoiding any mention of murder or investigations of murders.

"Good. I'll trust you'll have everything ready when I return." Gideon said.

"It takes four. And Lewis is too young." Antoine replied.

"He's old enough." Gideon insisted

"Not for dis" Antoine stood firm. He seemed close to losing his patience. Which was something Lewis had yet to see the man do. "Dis is my world. Ye listen te what I say, Professor. I will not do dis wid the boy."

"I can help you." Ms. Dunham volunteered.

"There you go. With Mrs. Saunders that makes four." Gideon said cheerfully. Grabbing his coat and heading for the door. "Come along Lewis."

The last thing Lewis heard as the door slammed shut was Antoine grunting irritably.

It was a short trip to Mr. Wong's and Gideon used the carriage ride to outline a series of circumstances they could encounter and how he expected Lewis to conduct himself in each of these given scenarios.

Lewis nodded along attentively, doing his best to soak in his uncle's every word. Which was not easy, his uncle used a lot of words.

"Are you comfortable with the plan, Lewis?" Gideon asked when he was through.

"Yes, Uncle Gideon." Lewis reassured him.

"Good." His uncle grinned "Remember, a prepared mind is our only bulwark against the chaos of an uncertain world."

The dock was bustling with activity. Crates of all sizes were being moved speedily and silently by an army of Chinese laborers. There were other Chinese there as well. But Lewis could tell by their clothes and the way they held themselves that they were guards, not laborers. The guns they were carrying helped mark them apart too of course.

Mr. Wong spotted them as they approached, waving them over to where he was inspecting a collection of crates.

"Not even a full day since your last visit Professor. What is it I can do for you now?" There was no rudeness in Mr. Wong's voice. In fact, as far as Lewis could tell there was no emotion of any kind. Just a flat, tonally neutral acknowledgment of reality. That kind of disconnectedness made Lewis nervous.

If his uncle shared his discomfort, he did not let it show. "We have a few more questions we'd like to ask if you wouldn't mind."

"Of course. Anything to be of service. We'd better talk in my office." Mr. Wong nodded to his guards then motioned for Gideon and Lewis to follow him.

They worked their way through the busy warehouse, navigating around busy workers and crates of all sorts and sizes until they came to an enclosed office in the back corner of the warehouse. There was an armed man standing outside the office's entrance, as they approached he opened the door for them. Again, Wong motioned for his guests to follow.

Lewis was nervous but followed his uncle's lead, both figuratively and literally. When they were inside, the door slammed shut behind them. That was the cue for all of Mr. Wong's men to draw their pistols and point them at Lewis and Gideon's heads.

"I don't appreciate unwanted attention Professor. It's bad for business." Wong's tone had changed from pleasant to one of open hostility. Of course with this many guns pointed at them Lewis thought the hostility had already been implied.

"So is murder." Gideon replied flippantly, refusing to let their current circumstances dampen his spirits.

"Not as much as you might think." Wong motioned to his security personnel who then pushed Gideon and Lewis against the far wall. "If you thought bringing the boy would protect you, you made a severe miscalculation."

"My name is Lewis. And if you're going to kill me you could at least do me the common courtesy of addressing me directly." Lewis declared, imitating what he's heard Ms. Dunham tell his uncle earlier.

Gideon beamed at his nephew's insolence.

"You are correct. My apologies young man, for my rudeness." Lewis thought he could see a smile trying to break free on the old man's face. He paused for a moment, then seemed to come to a decision. "All right professor. You have one minute to convince me why I shouldn't kill you and young master Lewis where you stand."

"Two things," Gideon reached for his bag. Mr. Wong's men cocked their guns. "If I may?"

Mr. Wong raised a hand to calm his men before gesturing for Gideon to continue.

Gideon pulls out the piece of paper with Mr. Wong's stamp on it. "That's your mark, isn't it?"

"You know it is." The gangster confirmed.

"That was found in my dead man's hand." Gideon stated plainly. "Still want to claim he has nothing to do with you?"

"My dock master has been missing for a couple of days now." Wong confessed.

"His name?" Gideon asked impatiently.

"Jun Xu" Mr. Wong paused before continuing, "You said there were two things?"

Gideon reached into his bag and pulled out the dragon mask. "This belongs to..." he began.

"The Servants of the Dragon." Wong cut him off.

One of Wong's hired guns, the one who'd been in charge the last time they were at the warehouse, leaned over to one of his subordinates and whispered in his ear. Lewis couldn't make out what they were saying but he was pretty sure it was in Chinese anyway. Eavesdropping was a lot harder when you didn't know the language.

The subordinate exited the room in a hurry. While Uncle Gideon and Mr. Wong's attentions were still on the mask.

"Oh, so you're familiar with them then." Gideon spoke with manufactured surprise.

"Yes." Wong replied, refusing to rise to the bait.

"Well, that makes sense, since you sent five of them to kill me after we left here yesterday." There it was. Gideon's accusation had put all their cards on the table.

"Professor, if I'm understanding you correctly, your argument in favor of me not having you killed now is to accuse me of trying to have you killed last night?" Mr. Wong broke into a fit of laughter. "I believe I'm starting to like you."

"Are you saying you didn't try to have me killed last night?" Gideon asked incredulously.

"Don't be absurd." Wong's denial felt genuine Lewis, apparently, it rang true with his uncle as well.

"If not you, then who?" Gideon asked

Mr. Wong considered the question. His eyes went wide, and he reached for his gun.

Before his hand could find it, half his men had re-trained their guns on him.

Such a turn of events might have rattled a lesser man, it very much confused and terrified Lewis, but Mr. Wong was unflappable even in the face of this sudden change of circumstances.

"Mr. Li, you disappoint me. A man cannot serve two masters." the aged gangster addressed his chief of security.

"I serve one master and his time is near." Li replied. Gone was the cold security guard. What stood before them now was a wild-eyed fanatic.

"You dare betray me?" The first signs of anger crept into Wong's voice.

"I'm confused here." Gideon looked around the room. "He's the bad guy?"

"For months now I've known someone was using my operations to bring in ancient artifacts from our homeland. At first, I assumed someone was simply unloading them on the black market for extra cash. I was actually impressed, the plan showed initiative. I intended to find whoever it was and offer them a promotion. After I received my cut that is. But there were no artifacts being sold. Now I had a real mystery. So I set Mr. Li the task of finding out who was arrogant enough to be using my organization for their own ends." Wong explained to them.

"That was your mistake." Li taunted his former employer.

"Yes, it was." Wong admitted. "You betrayed me. How long have you been working for the Servants?"

"You cannot betray what you were never loyal to in the first place." Li asserted "I have always been loyal to the dragon. And now, old man, it is time for you to die."

"I assume you have a way out?" Wong was addressing Gideon now.

"Always. Why do you think I brought the kid?" With that predetermined phrase, Lewis reached into his pocket and pulled out a cylindrical canister. He gave the end a quick twist, then let it drop to the floor.

White smoke poured out of both ends, quickly filling the room and obscuring visibility. As soon as the canister left his hand Lewis dropped to a knee. Pulling his pistol from its holster with one hand and using the other to cover his mouth with a handkerchief.

The last thing Lewis saw before his vision filled with white was his uncle pushing Mr. Wong to the ground.

The room exploded with the sound of gunfire. Lewis could hear glass shatter and shouting in Chinese, but he couldn't even make out vague figures in the smoke. Which meant neither could whoever it was who was shooting.

Lewis didn't know if that was a good thing or a bad thing.

After what seemed an inordinately long period of fearing for his life, he heard the dry clicks of empty revolvers.

That sound was followed quickly by three distinct thuds.

"All right Lewis, you can turn it off now. Thank you." His uncle instructed. Lewis twisted the side of the cylinder and pulled. The white smoke ceased, and a whirring sound accompanied a sucking wind was initiated.

In less than a minute, the smoke was gone, and Lewis could see again.

Gideon waited impassively for the smoke to clear. A display of patience made doubly impressive by the alternating sounds of shots and screams coming from outside the office.

When the machine was finished with its work Gideon turned to Mr. Wong and addressed their current circumstances.

"Mr. Wong," Gideon said in a tone most congenial. "You'll be happy to know I no longer believe you to be responsible for our current quandaries."

"Delighted."

More gunfire.

"Get me out of here and I'll forget that you charged into my place of business on two separate occasions and insinuated I was a murderer." Wong offered from his hiding spot behind his desk.

"That seems fair." Gideon agreed before turning his attention back to his nephew. "Lewis, pistol at the ready. You have my permission to shoot anything or anyone that makes you even the least bit cross."

"Yes, sir." Lewis acknowledged. Succeeding at keeping his voice from trembling. He'd never been in a proper gun battle before. It was terrifying.

"Shall we?" Gideon asked Mr. Wong.

"After you." The older man insisted.

Together the trio exited Wong's office. Lewis thought he was prepared for what they found find. He had been incorrect.

Bedlam had come to the docks. All around them, men who had just ten minutes ago been working side by side now fought one another with animal ferocity. Laborers and security men alike had donned dragon masks and were using whatever weapon was at hand to slaughter their fellows.

As his Uncle had taught him, Lewis kept his head on a swivel. Ignorance of one's surrounding was the surest way to end up dead in a firefight.

Sure enough, a man in a Dragon masked noticed them exiting Wong's office. Raising a pipe high above his head, the cultist screamed and sprinted towards them.

Lewis raised his pistol and took a deep breath.

Two shots took the man in the chest, dropping him on the spot.

Lewis looked at the end of his pistol. He hadn't pulled the trigger. His uncle had beaten him to it.

"This way."

Gideon moved without hesitation and without mercy. He stalked through the chaos allowing nothing to break his stride. Every crack of his pistol had a purpose, no shot was wasted. It was as if the three of them were in a bubble and anytime someone approached the edge of that bubble, Gideon's bullets found their heart.

It wasn't triumphant or exciting. It was brutal and macabre.

Something happened then when Lewis looked at his uncle's face. The arrogant aloofness was gone. So too was the wry charm. Uncle Gideon wasn't calm so much as he was detached, untethered from human emotion.

Lewis had faced death on many occasions since coming to live with his uncle. And he had certainly been frightened; by demons and dragon cults, gunmen and mad experiments. But never in all that time had he ever been afraid of Uncle Gideon. What Lewis saw in Gideon's face at that moment shook him to his core.

His uncle had just killed more than a half-dozen men with less effort than he expended getting out of bed in the morning.

Gideon's pistols ran dry.

One man still stood between them and safety.

Gideon holstered his pistols and lowered himself into a fighting stance.

The final cultist pulled a gun from a hidden ankle holster and pointed it at Gideon. Lewis pulled his own pistol and tried to get a clear shot, but his Uncle was in the way.

Gideon rushed forward, closing the gap quickly, but not before the cultist pulled the trigger. The crack of the bullet leaving the chamber drowned out every other sound in the alley.

The bullet grazed Gideon but did nothing to slow him down.

He lunged forward, his hand striking the dragon cultist's wrist and forcing the masked man to drop his gun.

Gideon followed his disarming blow with a spin kick to the man's face, causing the cultist's mask to go flying off his head.

The cultist spun away from Gideon and re-positioned himself into a fighting stance. Gideon renewed his assault, but this time the cultist deflected Gideon's fists and countered with his own attacks to the professor's body.

Gideon did not like the way the fight was going and quickly re-calibrated, diving for the cultist's discarded weapon. Seeing what Gideon was up to the cultist also lunged for the gun.

The two men reached it at the same moment. They were wrestling for control of it when the gun went off.

The cultist grunted and slumped.

Gideon pushed the man away from him. No longer propped up, the man fell to the ground, damp, dark redness spreading across his shirt.

"Let's go." Gideon commanded. And they did. Leaving the unnamed cultist to bleed out in the dank alley.

When they reached the street. Mr. Wong did not so much as nod an acknowledgment before melding into the crowd. Lewis couldn't help but feel a little indignant at the gangster's complete lack of gratitude.

Gideon pulled his jacket over his holster so that his pistols were hidden from view. Lewis followed suit. Together, they pushed through the assembled mob of gawkers to the nearest taxi stand. Gideon handed over a tidy sum to skip the queue and they were off. Settling into their carriage ride just as mounted police begin to fill the streets.

Gideon was uncharacteristically quiet on their ride home. Whether it was a residual effect of what his uncle had unleashed during the battle at the docks or a growing frustration at being no closer to unraveling their mystery, Lewis could not be sure. And if he was honest with himself, it was not a question he wanted answered just yet. In any case, what they found upon arriving home was unlikely to raise Gideon's spirits.

Lewis could hear the shouting as soon as he opened the front door.

"Satan worship! Blasphemers!" Mrs. Saunders screamed.

"It's a completely respectable ceremony. Perfectly in line wit de teachings of de saints." Antoine replied indignantly.

"It's heathen poppycock and I'll have no part in it." Mrs. Saunders screeched back at him.

Lewis held the door open for his uncle, showing both good manners and the good sense to avoid being the first one into the house.

His uncle's raised eyebrow as he passed let Lewis know Gideon was well aware of his dual motivations. Still, Lewis trailed a few steps behind his Uncle, just to be safe.

When they reached the study, they found quite the quadrumvirate.

Antoine stood half-way up a ladder on the far side of the room, with a paintbrush and a bowl. Both of which Lewis suspected of being covered in animal blood. Mrs. Saunders stood next to the ladder; bible in one hand, silver cross in the other. Both items were being waved madly in the air, seemingly in some attempt to counteract whatever Mrs. Saunders imagined Antoine was summoning. Will barked madly at the woman and she occasionally pointed the cross in the pup's direction as well. And finally, poor Ms. Dunham was clinging desperately to Will's collar to keep the collie from mauling Mrs. Saunders.

Gideon entered the room and everything stopped, creating a frozen tableau of chaos. It was then Lewis realized what he and Uncle Gideon must look like themselves, having gone out this morning for a conversation and come back from a war zone.

"Antoine, I assume whatever that is will wash up, otherwise you're responsible for repainting." Antoine looked down at his bowl dubiously while Gideon continued "Ms. Dunham, you can let go of the dog. His master his here now, he won't be any more trouble."

"Will, here boy. Sit." Lewis called to his dog who came running to him, tail wagging, as soon as Ms. Dunham released him.

"Mrs. Saunders, I would remind you that you are a guest in this house and ask you to conduct yourself appropriately. I hardly think Jesus did much shouting in his day." Gideon concluded his tour around the room with a stern rebuke.

Mrs. Saunders bit back what Lewis could only assume was a nasty retort. Instead, she folded her arms, harrumphed, and plopped herself down in one of the room's plush chairs.

"Professor, you're hurt." Antoine said, pointing to the blood-soaked shirt sleeve of Gideon's right arm.

"Somebody shot him." Lewis stated with a shrug.

"Somebody what?" Ms. Dunham blurted.

"It's just a graze." Gideon insisted as the room began to fuss over him.

"Mr. Wong did this?" Antoine asked.

"No, quite the opposite. I got this saving Wong's life." Gideon answered with a smirk.

"Explain." Antoine demanded.

"The Servants don't work for Wong. Well, I mean they work for Wong. Worked for Wong. They just tried to kill him so let's assume their employment has been terminated." The smirk quickly faded as Gideon found himself trying to explain the mess they'd found themselves in.

"I don't follow," Mrs. Saunders said. From their blank looks neither did

Antoine or Ms. Dunham.

"Wong didn't know that some of his men were secretly Servants of the Dragon and when he figured it out, they tried to kill him and us." Lewis clarified for the room.

"Thank you, Lewis. Succinctly summarized." Gideon nodded approvingly at his nephew. Or at least started to before Ms. Dunham tried to examine his wound. "Oww."

"Roll up your sleeve." She commanded.

"I'm fine. Honestly, it's just a scratch." Gideon continued to insist, despite wincing every time Ms. Dunham's hands came near his arm.

"It seems, Professor Giles, that in your world violence and blood are rather mundane occurrences. But where I come from, when someone gets shot it's a matter of some concern." Ms. Dunham gave Gideon a look then that would have broken even the most stubborn of men, which Gideon was. Her glare was so powerful, even Will buried his face in his paws.

Reluctantly, Gideon did as he was instructed, unclasping his cuff links and rolling his shirt sleeve up to his elbow.

"Higher." Ms. Dunham commanded

"It won't go any higher." Gideon's forceful presence of only a minute ago was gone, now Lewis though his Uncle just sounded a bit whiny.

"Then it will have to come off." Ms. Dunham stated with the authority of a field medic.

Gideon balked at the suggestion. "You can't be serious."

"Off with it. Now hurry up." The young woman barked.

With some assistance, Gideon undid the buttons of his shirt. Underneath, his chest was a mixture of purple, blue, and red.

"I suppose these bruises are nothing to be worried about either." Ms. Dunham said with more than a fair bit of sarcasm.

Gideon shrugged off her concerns.

"Old hat. Probably not even from today." he assured her.

"You get into so many brawls you don't even remember which of your scrapes caused you grievous bodily harm?" Ms. Dunham cleaned the wound out with an unmarked disinfecting solution. Lewis guessed she wouldn't have been so confident if she'd known Gideon had created the compound himself.

"You weren't complaining last night." Gideon winced as the liquid poured over his wound.

"As I recall, I was only in danger because I was around you; so that hardly a point in your favor." Ms. Dunham retorted. "You really have no idea what caused all this damage?"

She began wrapping the wound with white gauze.

"Not the foggiest." Gideon lied.

"That one guy kicked you in the stomach a bunch, remember." Lewis chimed in. Relishing the opportunity to tease his uncle.

"Yes, Lewis, thank you I remember. It wasn't a bunch. It was twice." Gideon insisted, attempting to protect his pride. "He might have punched me in the kidneys a couple of times as well."

"Sounds like you're not a very good brawler Professor." Ms. Dunham chuckled "Perhaps you should take up a new hobby."

"How was I supposed to know he was trained in the martial arts?" Gideon waved his arms in frustration even as Ms. Dunham was attempting to tie off her wrap.

"He was a member of a secret Chinese cult." Ms. Dunham stated finally managing to complete her dressing of Gideon's wound.

"So? Should I assume every Chinaman I meet knows kung fu? That seems a rather parochial lens through which to view the world." Gideon reached over to grab his discarded shirt and started to get dressed.

"But they did all know kung fu." Lewis chimed in.

"A mere coincidence Lewis. Remember: correlation does not imply causation." Then, to ensure Lewis had taken the lesson to heart, he asked his nephew to repeat it.

"Correlation does not imply causation." Lewis said dutifully.

"The point is, whoever these Servants are, they're dangerous. And, if their willing to go toe to toe with a man like Mr. Wong, they must have an agenda. That's why we need to speak to the one person who knows something about this. The one person who has no reason to lie. Our victim. Jun Xu. Are we ready Antoine?"

"We are." The houngan confirmed. "If you'll all be seated around de table. Lewis, you and Will can sit over der. Try not ta move, if ye can manage."

"I don't know how much clearer I can make myself, I am a good Christian woman and I will not participate in unholy rituals or satanic summonings." Mrs. Saunders reiterated emphatically.

Ms. Dunham walked over to Mrs. Saunders and took her hand. "If it's all nothing but foolishness, what harm is there in indulging them. Maybe God put you here so you could bear witness."

Miraculously this seemed to calm Mrs. Saunders, who acquiesced to being seated between Gideon and Ms. Dunham.

"Lewis, de lights please."

Lewis lowered the lights as requested then took his seat in the corner. Will followed suit, circling the chair a few times before laying down beside it.

"Jun Xu, we who seek te avenge your death seek an audience. Appear before us oh restless spirit and speak wid us, so we may know how te bring your mortal business ta a close." Antoine intoned.

Lewis sat quietly and watched Antoine work. While he had certainly seen his fair share of the weird and unexplainable since moving in with his uncle, he'd yet to see Antoine commune with the dead. And unlike the two women in the room, Lewis was convinced the voodoo priest would succeed in summoning a deceased spirit.

His concerns were for how it would all go horribly wrong once Antoine did.

The flames flickered and turned an eerie blue. Wind filled the room, making a mess of anything not nailed to the floor. At the center of the table, the bowl of chicken blood began to boil. Red smoke billowed into the air. The smoke began to take shape, forming a human figure.

"Where am I?" a disembodied voice asked, fear and uncertainty coating every word.

"Do the spirits always speak English?" Mrs. Dunham asked incredulously, barely suppressing a snicker.

"De spirit speak so dat we may understand dem, da dead know no language." Antoine spoke in a quiet aside before turning back to address the ghost of Jun Xu. "Ye are in limbo, de place between what is and what may be."

The smoky apparition became more defined. It tilted its head and considered what Antoine had told him. "I died. I remember dying."

"We seek dose who killed you. We wish te know why you died." Antoine said firmly.

The smoke figure turned from Antoine and pointed right at Ms. Dunham.

"The amulet. They wanted the amulet." Jun Xu exclaimed.

"What amulet? Who wanted it?" Lewis could tell from his Uncle's frenetic tone he was not comfortable questioning the dead.

"The servants. They were smuggling in artifacts behind Mr. Wong's back. I caught them and they killed me." The spirit explained.

"We already know that" Gideon stated impatiently. "Why were they smuggling artifacts?"

"They were looking for links to the other side. They killed me." The apparition began to lose some of its form as it contemplated it mortal demise.

"Jun Xu." Antoine spoke the name with power, bringing the dead man's spirit back to the present. "Think back and remember. What are the Servants planning?"

The place where the apparition's eyes should be began to glow an intense red.

"To free their master. To summon Gong Gong." The spirit's voice grew deep and menacing. Almost rabid. Again it focused its attention on Ms. Dunham.

There was a loud crash somewhere else in the house. The ghost's ruby eyes snapped to the where the noise had come from.

"Be warned, they are here" And with that cryptic premonition, the smoky apparition dissolved into the air as if it had never been.

"Damn it all, I've been a fool. A damn fool. Antoine, lock it down. We've made a horrible mistake. And now I fear we've no time at all." Gideon lamented "Ladies, I do apologize; but I'm going to need you to stand in the middle of the room and remain absolutely still."

Antoine and Lewis gently coaxed the two women into the center of the room while Gideon reached for a long metal chain that hung from the ceiling next to the rooms main entrance.

When Gideon pulled on the chain a great many things happened at once.

Large metal locks slammed into place while steel doors dropped from the ceiling, reinforcing the large oak ones that had been quite sufficient in their own right.

The tops of the various reading desks and bookshelves slid open and revealed a cache of weapons that would make even an artillery sergeant blanch.

Gideon did not wait for the jigsaw armory to stop unfolding itself before he began distributing armaments.

"Who the devil are you people?" Ms. Dunham broke her silence, astonishment and bewilderment briefly overriding her other emotions.

Gideon was too busy loading various weapons with ammunition to answer her. After holstering a pair of modified colt revolver for himself, he tossed Antoine a pump action shotgun and a large, wooden rod. Lewis received a pistol and a hand full of smoke cylinders.

"What do I get?" Ms. Dunham asked, looking warily at her companions' armaments.

"That depends, what can you handle?" Gideon responded without looking up from his tasks.

"I'm a fair shot with a rifle." She responded.

"A rifle won't do, you'll never get a shot off in these close quarters" Gideon tossed her a blunderbuss. "Rock Salt rounds. Non-lethal, but its got enough punch to take down a Chilean were-bear."

"A what?" Ms. Dunham exclaimed. Lewis chuckled at her confusion. She clearly wasn't a student of cryptozoology. Living with Uncle Gideon you kind of had to be.

"It hits like a locomotive." Antoine clarified for her.

"Good enough." She examined the weapon skeptically before satisfying herself it would indeed be good enough for the job at hand.

Now properly armed, the group took up positions covering the two entrances, making sure not to impede each other's lines of fire.

A silence hung over them like a cloud. The anticipation of danger made them all shift uncomfortably in their stillness.

"How do we know anyone's out there at all." Mrs. Saunders asked, her fear giving way to skepticism and outrage. "On top of everything else you're all just paranoid."

Her words were punctuated with a large explosion. The wall between the two doorways became a pile of rubble in an instant.

Mrs. Saunders screamed. Not that anyone could hear her over the ringing in their ears. Lewis started shooting and Ms. Dunham followed suit. With reckless abandon, they fired wildly into the gaping hole that now existed in their defenses, hoping to hit whatever was about to come rushing through.

"Hold!" Gideon was shouting when Lewis' hearing reasserted itself. He followed his Uncle's instructions and held his fire. Ms. Dunham did the same.

The dust settled and the echoes of the explosion and ensuing gunfire faded until again there was only silence.

That's when they came.

In three groups of three, dragon-masked men dressed all in black came rushing through the newly formed opening shouting some indecipherable battle-cry.

"Fire!" Gideon screamed and Lewis did just that.

Gideon took the first two cultists with pistol shots to the heart before being overtaken. Unable to get a clear shot, he discarded his pistols in favor of his sword.

Antoine hit one of the invaders dead center with his first shotgun blast. Knocking the intruder back through the gap from whence he came. Hurriedly, he tried to reload, but the masked men were too fast and as a consequence, his second shot went wide.

He dropped the shotgun and swung his heavy rod at the second cultist. Whacking the cultist's head like a baseball. The blow corrected the cultist's momentum sending the now unconscious man tumbling into a bookshelf.

Ms. Dunham also did her part, perfectly timing the blast of her blunderbuss to knock one cultist back into another. But she underestimated the force of the recoil, causing her to drop her weapon and leaving her defenseless.

All of this Lewis saw out of his peripheral vision as he dealt with aggressors all his own. Lewis took careful aim at the oncoming cultists, clipping one in the leg and then another in the shoulder.

"Lewis, Now! Get the women out." His uncle shouted over the roar of the battle.

Out of his coat pocket Lewis pulled two of the smoke bombs his uncle had given him and activated them. The whirring of gears was followed by streams of white smoke. Lewis rolled the two cylinders in opposite directions, hoping to maximize their effectiveness. Before the smoke had fully distorted his vision he grabbed their two bewildered house guests by the hand and yanked them against the wall.

There he pulled down on the wall-mounted light. Here too, clockwork gears began to whir, but on a scale much larger than the intricate workings of his uncle's smoke cylinders.

The lower half of the wall slid away, revealing a metal chute a few feet in diameter.

The slide was built for one man to fit comfortably, two in a pinch. The three of them, though all smaller than a full-grown man individually, together made the space more than a little tight.

Not that Lewis minded. Being pushed up against Ms. Dunham in such a way almost made him forget they were fleeing for their lives.

As he was trained to do, Will remained behind to be their lookout.

They landed in a tangled heap of limbs after only a few seconds. Lewis extricated himself from the pile, then assisted Ms. Dunham and Mrs. Saunders' to their feet.

The escape chute had deposited them in Gideon's underground laboratory.

Mrs. Saunders had become unhinged. Ranting about demons and Satan worshipers and how they were all going to hell.

Ms. Dunham slapped her. Hard.

"Get yourself together woman, or you're going to get us all killed."

It was too late. Will came sliding out of the tunnel, barking his head off and landing on his backside. This was the collie's signal to his master that the intruders had heard Mrs. Saunders and they were coming.

"Ladies, if you'll just stand over there please." Lewis pointed to an out of the way corner of the lab.

Taking a deep breath Lewis cleared his mind and let his instincts and muscle memory take over. Moving without thinking, he grabbed a box of vials and beakers marked "In Case of Siege" and went to work, mixing together the vial's contents in the beakers the way he had drilled a hundred times.

Uncle Gideon had an odd definition of emergency preparedness.

When the first beaker turned green and was cold to the touch Lewis stopped stirring and poured the contents out in a puddle on the floor in front of the secret passage's exit. Being incredibly careful not to splash any on himself or Will.

Lewis took the second beaker and placed it on a Bunsen burner in the center of his uncle's workbench. He turned on the burner and cranked the flame all the way up, just as Uncle Gideon had trained him to do.

"What are you doing? Why are you fiddling with that right now? Those men are coming to kill us." Mrs. Saunders' hysteria was returning. Ms. Dunham was worried too, watching what he was doing with a mixture of panic, fear, and confusion; but she at least remained silent as he went about his business.

Lewis strode to the far wall and pulled down on the left tusk of the moose-pig head that had been mounted there for just such a situation.

There was a loud rumbling of gears and the solid brick wall beside him was revealed to be a facade. Behind that faced lay a small room housing a flight of stairs.

The mixture he had placed on the Bunsen burner had begun bubbling and Lewis knew they were running short of time.

He hurried Ms. Dunham and Mrs. Saunders into the secret room and up the hidden stairs. He reached for the second lever inside the secret room before realizing he had forgotten someone.

Will stood staring at the first secret passage, still on the lookout for the danger following them.

Lewis gave a whistle. "Here boy, come on, hurry."

Will turned and ran to his master. Lewis pulled the lever and closed the door behind them once his pup was safely through.

The last noise he heard before the secret door locked shut was the sound of men screaming. The intruders had discovered the acid bath he'd left them at the exit of the first passage. By the time they recovered they second beaker would be ready to do its work.

Lewis climbed the stars hastily and exited through the hatch at the top. He rolled free and the heavy hatch door slammed shut behind him. There was a loud boom, followed by a small, localized earthquake.

Lewis didn't need to see it to know that his Uncle's lab was little more than a crater at this point.

They were outside the house now, in the side yard. Lewis hoped they were free and clear now.

Those hopes were quickly dashed.

More black-clad, dragon-masked men were positioned on the roof of the house. They shouted at each other in Chinese and pointed to where Lewis and his party were standing.

"Run!" Lewis shouted, literally pushing Mrs. Saunders and Ms. Dunham into motion.

Lewis pulled his pistol and took aim over his shoulder at the shadowy figures. Remembering his Uncle's tutelage from the night before he made a conscious effort to anticipate the cultists' movements and aim where he thought they were going to be.

He pulled the trigger. The gun barked in his hand, the flash of the muzzle dazzling in the darkness. But if Lewis hit his target, he showed no signs of being wounded.

Again, Lewis took careful aim. Again, he missed.

Panicking as the trained killers descended towards them, Lewis fired haphazardly, running through his remaining ammunition without anything to show for their expenditure.

The men surrounded them. The dark red eyes of their dragon masks gleaming menacingly in the moonlight.

Mrs. Saunders said something breathless about the heavenly father before fainting.

Ms. Dunham caught the older woman as she fell and laid her gently on the ground.

Lewis pulled out his pocket knife. He knew he was over-matched. But if he could just hold them off long enough there was a chance Antoine or his uncle would arrive in time to save them.

Will bared his teeth and summoned up a fearsome growl. The faithful canine prepared to make a last stand protecting his master.

Lewis felt a crack on the back of his head followed by the sensation of falling.

Everything went black.

***

"Lewis!" Someone was calling his name. "Lewis! Wake Up!"

He awoke to find he was shaking, or more accurately he was being shaken by someone else. Lewis' vision was blurred and it took him a moment to blink himself back into full consciousness.

Uncle Gideon knelt over him. His hands cradling Lewis' head.

"What happened?" Lewis managed to ask through a hazy fog. "Ms. Dunham? Mrs. Saunders?"

"Mrs. Saunders is fine. Antoine is with her." Gideon reassured him.

"Ms. Dunham?" Lewis asked, fearing the worst. "They've taken her. Haven't they"

Feelings of regret and shame poured through him.

"Yes." his uncle replied.

"I'm sorry Uncle Gideon. I tried to stop them but there were too many."

Will barked to affirm his master's assertion.

"I know you did. It's not your fault. It's mine. I made a mistake. Another in a long line. But we'll get her back, Lewis. I promise." Gideon gripped him in a fierce embrace.

"Uncle Gideon why does this keep happening to us?" Lewis asked despondently.

"I don't know Lewis. I honestly don't know." Lewis' heart sank at his uncle's words.

**

April 25th, 1882

After a short discussion, Antoine and Gideon agreed that Mrs. Saunders was not in any immediate danger and her assistance would no longer be required. This came as a great relief to her and to Lewis, who shirtsleeve had become soaked with the woman's sobs.

Gently, Antoine took her arm in his and escorted her home.

Which left Gideon and Lewis to clean up.

There were still a few little fires burning here and there, and a myriad of holes pocketed the residence. Not to mention the assorted dragon-masked ninja corpses that lay strewn about the various rooms. Lewis supposed they were lucky no bodies had ended up on the front stoop.

All in all, it was a depressing sight. While Lewis had only lived in the house a few short months, he'd come to think of the eccentric mansion as home.

Unsure of what to do next, Lewis looked at his uncle for guidance. But Gideon was too busy mumbling angrily to himself to notice.

GAROOOHHMMM, GAROOHHMMM

For the second time in two days the sound nearly made Lewis jump out of his skin. It's one thing to hear a Chupacabra mating call during the course of a normal day, quite another to hear it in the middle of the night while standing in the fiery remains of your recently attacked home.

Uncle Gideon placed a hand on his shoulder and gave it a reassuring squeeze. "Let's see who it is, shall we?"

The large, oaken door lay in the hall; a pile of splinters and kindling. Still, their guest stood politely on the other side of the threshold. Honoring the metaphorical barrier, while the physical one lay in disrepair.

"Mr. Wong" Gideon pronounced curtly.

"Professor Giles" the diminutive man returned the greeting with a smile that didn't quite reach his eyes. "I understand you had some unwanted visitors this evening. I know how irritating such people can be".

"I'm sure you do. Especially since my visitors were in your employ until quite recently". Gideon didn't need to remind his visitor of that fact, but Lewis could tell he enjoyed doing it anyway.

"Yes, they were. In my employ but serving another master all the while. Disloyalty and deception. These are grievous sins and ones a man in my position cannot abide. So, it seems we find ourselves aggrieved by the same individuals. You are no doubt acquainted with the notion that the enemy of my enemy is my friend" Mr. Wong took a finger and ran it across the top of a broken cabinet then examined it for dust.

Uncle Gideon was not in any mood for the man's pretensions. "A woman is missing Mr. Wong. I don't have time for banter. If you have a proposal, make it".

"You have information about these Servants I lack. I have the men you need to make a rescue attempt even plausible. You tell me where and when to find my former employees so that I can sever our relationship permanently, and I will assist you in rescuing your woman". Wong offered.

Lewis stayed silent while his uncle contemplated Mr. Wong's offer. The two men stared at each other. Finally, Gideon acquiesced.

"What would you like to know?"

When Antoine returned from escorting Mrs. Saunders home, he was less than enthused to find Mr. Wong in the sitting room with a book in his hand. That negative enthusiasm level became a full fountain of disbelief and displeasure when he learned Gideon had cut a deal with the Chinese gangster.

But at his core, Antoine was a gentleman, and it would have been improper for him to criticize a guest in front of his face. So the big, behemoth of a man swallowed down his feelings and moved on. It was a display of self-control that Lewis was sure neither he nor his uncle would have been able to match.

The four of them got to work, scouring every book in Gideon's extensive library for any mention of Gong Gong.

Being the only one of the four not fluent in at least two languages, Lewis received the manuscripts written in, or translated into, English. Mr. Wong busied himself with the Mandarin and Cantonese texts while Antoine scoured the French and Latin manuscripts. Uncle Gideon got the 'dead languages no one has ever heard of' pile.

The room was silent save the sounds of pages turning and unhelpful tomes being tossed away in frustration. Lewis read until his eyes hurt, then he rubbed them and kept reading.

Eventually, the futility of it caused Gideon to crack.

"Such a ridiculous name for world-destroying beast from another dimension. Gong Gong? Sounds like a creature from a fairy tale." Gideon complained to the room in general.

"That's not far off. Accounts of Gong Gong are varied and conflicting but almost all of them associate the name with water, floods, and great destruction. Some say he is a man, some a monster, but in quite a few he takes the form of a dragon." Mr. Wong volunteered.

"That's wonderful, but we've yet to find anything about his cult of followers or how he could be summoned here to New Orleans." Gideon dumped the book in his lap on the floor and picked up another from the pile.

Lewis stifled a yawn and gave Will a gentle rub on the head before he too discarded his current text.

"I dink I have de answer we seek." Antoine stood excitedly, knocking over several piles of books. Without looking up, he took the text in his hand to the table in the center of the room. "According te dis text. In order te summon Gong Gong d'ell need te offer up a virgin sacrifice adorned wid de jade pendant of Gong Gong."

"Well, I didn't need to know about the virgin part but now we know why they wanted Ms. Dunham. Does it say when the ceremony must be held?" Gideon asked in earnest.

"A long strip of grass next ta de river, wid a raised wooden pier dat extends over de water from which dey are te offer up de virgin sacrifice." Antoine read.

"I own a property in the Bywater that meets that description" Mr. Wong said.

"That's the where, what about the when?" Gideon was pacing now.

"In de Golden Hour." Antoine translated.

"What does that mean?" Lewis asked

"It's the hour just before dawn." His uncle answered with enthusiasm. "Antoine?"

"Two hours 'till sun up". The voodoo doctor informed them after a brief think.

"That gives us an hour to stop them". Gideon did the math.

"I will tell my men" Mr. Wong left the room, leaving Antoine, Gideon, and Lewis alone for the first time in what felt like weeks.

"To recap, we are about to go try and rescue a woman who doesn't much like us from an unknown number of Chinese cultists who are attempting to summon their Dragon god through a rip in reality we helped make possible while assisted by a gangster and his heavily armed men, who will probably try to betray us at the first available opportunity." Uncle Gideon's summary was enough to get Lewis' heart pumping.

"You're saying we should bring de big guns?" Antoine asked.

"I'm saying we should bring all the guns" was Uncle Gideon response.

* * *

They found the Servants of the Dragon precisely where Mr. Wong thought they'd be; in the Bywater, on a long stretch of property he owned that was perfectly situated along the Mississippi River.

It was still dark, making it hard for Lewis to be sure of an accurate count, but it seemed to him there must be upwards of a hundred dragon-masked cultists gathered here.

Torches lined the gathering and an altar had been set up on the pier.

The Servants chanted rhythmically in Chinese, bowing towards the altar. On the altar, a select few cultists whose black robes were adorned with gold chains prepared an assortment of relics. In unison, they raised two hands towards the sky. They then took a knife in one hand and cut down the palm of their other hand, dripping blood off of the pier and into the waters of the Mississippi.

The chanting grew louder as the winds whirling around them began to pick up speed.

"We should strike while they are distracted." Mr. Wong urged. "We have the element of surprise, but they have numbers. If we don't act now we will lose our advantage."

"Not until we locate Ms. Dunham. If we move before we know where she is, they might kill her before we can find her." Gideon insisted.

The argument was interrupted by a blinding flash of light and a crack of thunder.

Blue sparks of electricity burst forth spontaneously from the air above the altar, crackling in every direction. Shapes and colors melded together to the point Lewis was no longer certain what was real and what was not. Time slowed and the world itself seemed to bend.

Lewis had seen something like this only twice before. The first time his uncle had been ripping a hole in the fabric of the universe in order to reach what lay beyond. The second time was because something had reached back.

Electricity and fire coalesced into a spinning funnel of blue-white energy. Primal roars of no discernible origin filled the night. Lewis was ready. Experience having taught him to cover his ears, lest the sound drive him mad. Wong's men had no such forewarning. They gnashed their teeth and clawed at their ears. Hoping to silence the howls of the damned.

The wind screeched and thunder bellowed while lighting rained down all around them.

There was a shudder.

Then the portal snapped into place.

"What is that?" Mr. Wong asked, his voice betraying emotion for the first time since Lewis encountered him.

"Goddammit." Gideon cursed. "They're actually going to do it. Those idiots are going to summon a goddamn dragon."

"You can't be serious." Mr. Wong said. But he seemed more skeptical of his own words than what the portal meant for their chances.

"We cannot wait any longer professor. Its Ms. Dunham's life weighed against all dos who will die if dey succeed." Antoine insisted.

"You're right. We go now." Gideon agreed.

"Wait." Lewis saw figures coming out of the warehouse. Two figures pulling a third towards the altar. "Look, over there."

His uncle pointed his spyglass where Lewis was pointing. "It's Ms. Dunham. They've got here dressed up like a sacrifice."

"What do we do?" Lewis asked, watching anxiously as the cultists tied Ms. Dunham to a wooden pole at the center of their altar.

"Okay, everyone listen closely." Gideon motioned for the others to lean in. "Lewis, I want you to stay close to me. Antoine and I will hold the altar while you untie Ms. Dunham." Gideon turned to Mr. Wong. "If you and your men would be so kind as to provide us with some covering fire while we make our move…..?"

"We will do our part." Mr. Wong stated plainly.

Gideon looked them each in the eye for one final confirmation before nodding in satisfaction. "On my signal, then."

"Uncle Gideon, what is the signal?" Lewis asked, concerned he had missed something in his uncle's short speech.

"Oh, I think that will be fairly obvious." Gideon replied, wearing the devilish grin he so often wore when he was about to blow something up.

Mr. Wong retreated to his men, issuing orders and positioning his forces. He spoke quietly and in Chinese. Lewis realized that their entire plan rested on the hope that Wong would not betray them. It was not the kind of revelation that brought Lewis any sort of piece of mind.

Gideon, Anthony, and Lewis crawled on their bellies to a spot just beyond the range of the light from the first sentry's lamp. Will, completely unnecessarily, imitated his master and also crawled along on his belly, pulling himself forward along the grass with his paws. If not for the mortal peril, it would have been adorable.

When everyone was in position, Gideon pulled two glass jars from his pockets. A length of rope extended from each one. Using a bit of flint, Gideon set each of those bits of rope alight before hurling them towards the cultists' ceremony.

They exploded within seconds of each other. The rhythmic chants of the cultists were replaced by fire and screams.

Gideon had not undersold his "know it when you see it" signal and Mr. Wong's men did not hesitate to take advantage of the confusion Gideon's homemade explosives had wrought.

The sound of rifles filled the night. Men in dragon masks ran from the flames only to be felled by bullets of unknown origin.

Fire, chaos, and death. Those were the only things that any of them knew now.

Antoine stood up from their hiding place and began a slow, methodical march forward. He held his pump action rifle at his shoulder. Every shot was followed by a cranking motion, as the spent cartridge fell through the air to the bloody earth and was replaced by a new death bringer.

Gideon, by contrast, took the lead. Manically firing on the run. The flashes of his twin pistols dancing like fireflies at midnight.

Lewis and Will stayed between the two men. The battle-hardened canine pointing out potential threats with a bark and Lewis neutralizing those threats with his father's Colt revolver.

Unlike the last two times he'd faced the dragon masked fiends, this time Lewis did not miss. Before he had been afraid and panicked. The black-clad warriors had possessed a mythic quality and that had made him doubt his training. Made him doubt himself.

But this time was different. The Dragon cultists had lost their mystique.

They didn't look so impressive running away from the chaos Lewis had helped bring to them.

Besides which Lewis was battling alongside a Voodoo priest who communed with the dead and a demon-fighting mad scientist. They didn't make them anymore mythic than that.

Eventually, their party reached the altar. Leaving the bodies of almost a dozen Servants in their wake.

Antoine and Will took up a defensive position at the base of the altar, while Lewis and Gideon climbed the rickety wooden stairs to where Ms. Dunham was restrained.

The three Dragon priests were there waiting for them there.

Gideon put two bullets apiece in the two closest priests. The men fell into the Mississippi, clutching at their chests.

"Lewis, If you please." Gideon said, not taking his eyes off the head priest for even a moment.

Lewis holstered his pistol and pulled out his pocket knife.

He hustled over to a sobbing Ms. Dunham and began to cut through her bonds.

"Just stay still, I'll have you out in a second." Lewis said. Then, sensing she could use some further reassurance he added "It's going to be okay, We're here now."

Even as he said that, an otherworldly howl cut through the air. The winds began to swirl and Lewis' hair stood up on end.

The head priest removed his mask, revealing a rather irate Mr. Li. The former head of security turned dragon worshiper reached into his cloak and pulled out a curved sword.

Lewis' uncle said nothing, he simply pointed his pistols at Mr. Li and pulled the triggers.

Click. Click.

Click. Click.

Gideon's pistols were dry.

"I really need to invent a gun with more bullets." He muttered to no one in particular, holstering his pistols. "I suppose we'll have to settle this in the gentlemanly fashion then."

Gideon pulled his saber from its scabbard.

The two blades were as different as the two men who wielded them. Gideon's blade was straight and skinny. The battle sword of an officer in the Union Army. Mr. Li's blade was wide and curved, a relic of ancient Chinese glory.

Mr. Li gave his own sword a little flourish, baiting Uncle Gideon into making the first move.

Gideon complied, the soldier-scholar lunging forward with his saber.

Mr. Li deflected the attack with a swift swipe. Spinning his sword back over his head, he slashed down violently.

Gideon leaned back, narrowly avoiding being sliced in half. He brought his sword around and down, pushing Li's blade into the wooden deck beneath them.

Gideon fired an elbow into Li's face, breaking the larger man's nose with the blow.

Spinning to his right, Gideon came at Li with a downward slash.

Li parried and countered with a swipe at Gideon's torso.

Stepping backward, Gideon intercepted and deflected the attack.

Li let the force of Gideon's deflection carry him into a spin.

Gideon stepped forward with a lunge but his blade found only empty air.

Li exited his spin and took another swipe at Gideon's torso, this time his attack drew blood.

Gideon retreated, a hand instinctively checking the wound along his side. Lewis saw no signs of the red dampness of blood spreading across Gideon's shirt and concluded his Uncle had suffered worse.

Again the two men squared up, each waiting for the other to make the first move.

Li charged, bringing his sword down with a fearsome swing. Gideon took a step back, intercepting Li's blade with his own.

Li pressed the attack. Each swing of his blade forcing Gideon further back towards the edge of the altar.

On his fourth parry, Gideon stood his ground. Li's blade pressed down against the professor's, the two men's faces only inches apart from each other.

Gideon planted a boot against Li's chest and gave a mighty kick. The dragon priest stumbled backward, losing his footing and tumbling to the ground.

Now it was Gideon's turn to press his advantage.

At the last possible moment, Li raised his blade, deflecting what most certainly would have been a fatal blow.

The deflection left Gideon off-balance, unable to follow-up his attack with another.

Li swiped wildly at Gideon's legs, forcing Gideon to jump back to avoid Li's curved blade.

The attack missed but served its purpose, creating enough distance between the two foes to allow Li the time he needed to recover.

Li pushed himself to his feet and returned to a fighting stance.

The two combatants circled each other warily. Above them, electricity crackled and lightning filled the sky. Beneath them the mighty Mississippi raged, its waters violently crashing against the pier.

Again Li attacked, putting his full power behind an overhead strike. Gideon stepped back and raised his own sword to intercept.

Li surged forward, whirling his blade around and coming in for another overhead attack.

This time instead of blocking and retreating, Gideon stepped forward to intercept the blade. Now within arm's reach, he extended his off-hand towards Li's chest and flicked his wrist.

Gideon's hidden blade plunged into Mr. Li's chest, piercing the zealot's heart.

"Tā láile" the words passed from his lips like a prayer.

In one smooth motion, Gideon pulled his sword free and sliced through Li's neck; severing his head from his body.

The priest's decapitated corpse fell to the ground, twitching and convulsing.

His lifeless head rolled towards Lewis and came to a stop at his feet. Lewis could not help but look down. Mr. Li was staring back at him, his eyes frozen in a state of reverent glee.

Lewis had to force himself to look away.

"That phrase he said. At the end before he…. you know. What did it mean?" Lewis asked his uncle.

"I'm not sure, but I think it was something along the lines of 'You're too late.'"

The portal shook and shimmered. Lightning danced across the clouds followed by the kind of deep rumbling thunder you feel in your bones. The kind that makes you think the sky is exploding.

A terrible roar filled the night and Lewis knew that Li had been right. They were too late.

Its snout emerged first. Each pointed tooth twice as large as Lewis. Its nostrils flared, taking in the unfamiliar smells of a new world.

Next came angry, red eyes. Hate and rage centered around a tiny black speck. Its vertical eyelids blinked rapidly, dazzled by the bright blue electric light of the portal.

Along the back of its neck ran pointed blue spines connected by translucent green skin. The rest of its body was covered in scales that were the same dark shade of blueish-green as the river. They overlapped to form a kind of thick armor.

Its massive talons dug into the mud around them, the beast struggling to drag its leviathan frame into our dimension.

Lewis pulled Ms. Dunham down a fraction of a second before the dragon's fearsome snout snapped shut around the sacrificial post.

The creature managed to pull itself far enough into our dimension and that's when it truly became dangerous.

With one flap of its vast, bat-like wings it knocked every human in the vicinity to the ground.

Lewis felt as if he was being physically beaten by the immense force of the wind created when the beast began flapping in earnest.

Uncle Gideon grabbed him by the arm and pulled him clear while Antoine did the same for Ms. Dunham. They cleared the sacrificial altar just as it was smashed to splinters by the beast's mammoth tail. End to end, the beast was the length of a city block at least; with a torso the size of an ocean liner.

The dragon took flight and at last Gong Gong was loose.

The remaining servants sent up cries of adulation at the horrible magnificence of their god.

"Well, that's going to be a problem." Gideon said looking skyward.

Lightning flashed. Thunder crashed. And Gong Gong roared.

The dragon god flew higher and higher until it reached the center of the storm.

Then, pulling in its immense wings for a dive, Gong Gong descended towards his followers.

Cries of adulation quickly turned into screams of terror as Gong Gong's talons shredded through the flesh of worshiper and apostate alike.

His fearsome jaws skimmed the ground for human snacks as fleeing victims were impaled upon his mighty fangs.

Gideon, Antoine, and a handful of Wong's men stood their ground; only to watch every bullet they fired bounce off the beast's scaly armor.

"Retreat!" Gideon shouted, Antoine pulling him just clear of the dragon's reach. The men they were with were not so fortunate.

While the dragon gained altitude for another pass, Gideon lead them back to where Mr. Wong had taken cover.

"This is beyond my resources." Mr. Wong stated flatly. "Any ideas, professor?"

It was rare that Lewis saw a look of genuine astonishment cross his Uncle's face. He'd barely batted an eye when a giant dragon had emerged from an otherworldly portal only minutes before. But Wong's offer to help clearly caught Gideon by surprise now.

"You're going to stay and fight? Not much profit in noble last stands." Gideon pointed out to the gangster.

"Quite the contrary. It is my understanding from the folk tales of my homeland that dragons are generally bad for business." Mr. Wong smirked at the notion he acted out of anything other than his own self-interest.

"Bullets just bounce off it." Lewis stated helplessly.

"I doubt blades will be of much use." Antoine added.

"That leaves explosives" Gideon concluded with a deadly gleam in his eyes. He looked up at the dragon circling over their heads then back to the gathered party. "I have a plan, but I will need some bait."

Gideon issued his instructions with a quickness and clarity that would have been the envy of any battlefield commander.

Lewis could not help but feel uncomfortable standing around idly listening to his uncle give orders while all around them men were screaming as ate them alive. He knew in his head it was what he must do; but in his heart, it felt off not immediately racing in to offer assistance.

When Gideon had finished, they set about their respective assignments.

Mr. Wong gathered his remaining men together and organized them into a one long line facing the river and the dragon above it.

Antoine worked his way across the pier to where the portal still shimmered and pulsed. He took cover behind a large stack of crates. When the rest of them made their move it would be his job to close the portal.

Lewis and Will were assigned lookout duty. It was their job to make sure none of the Servants of the Dragon tried any funny business while everyone else had their back turned fighting the actual dragon.

Most of the Servants were dead, dying, or fleeing from the terrible, man-eating wrath of their messiah. Lewis knew that his uncle had assigned him the task to keep him out of harm's way and, for once, Lewis didn't mind being coddled. Fighting a dragon was all well and good when playing make-believe, but in real life, it was a terribly frightening, gory affair. The idea that he might end up as one of the mauled, twitching, half-dead bodies that littered the field around him was enough to make Lewis shake.

Still, his Uncle hadn't said stay over there out of the way. His uncle had told him to keep watch. Lewis had been assigned a job and he intended to do it right. He drew his pistol from its holster and let his eyes scan the battlefield. He quickly realized that when a giant dragon is flapping its wings in the sky above it's very hard to concentrate on anything else.

Lewis could see everyone getting into position. At his uncle's signal, they put Gideon's plan into action.

It started with Ms. Dunham screaming nonsense and waving her pendant about, the jade jewel reflecting the white lightning that danced among the clouds.

The pendant also caught the attention of Gong Gong, who abandoned his random marauding to investigate the gem.

Ms. Dunham ran from the pier, holding the pendant high in the air so as to keep the attention of the dragon.

Soon she reached the line formed by Wong's soldiers.

Wong's men stood fast, firing shot after shot as the dragon circled back around. The bullets couldn't penetrate Gong Gong's scale plating, but that was okay. They weren't meant to.

They were just meant to get the beast's attention. And in that endeavor, they were most successful.

Gong Gong roared and dove towards his attackers.

"Retreat!" Gideon yelled. With Mr. Wong repeating the order in Mandarin.

The men broke formation and ran towards Uncle Gideon, who was waiting for his own part to play in the action.

Everything was going to plan.

Until next to Lewis, Will began to bark.

The sound drove the dragon into a frenzy. Gong Gong changed direction and headed for the Border collie, whose response was to bark even more fiercely.

Lewis froze. Nothing in his training had prepared him to fight a dragon. Nothing in anyone's training ever prepares them to fight a dragon.

Will continued to bark wildly.

Gong Gong dove towards them with incredible speed. Its massive jaws opened wide. Lewis brought his pistol level and pulled the trigger six times, emptying the chamber.

His bullets bounced off the beast's leathery hide. Lewis could smell the creature's foul breath now. He had only seconds before Gong Gong's teeth ripped him apart.

The dragon wasn't the only figure racing towards him. Sprinting out from underneath Gong Gong's massive shadow towards Lewis was his uncle.

Gideon tackled him at full speed, knocking the wind out of Lewis. As the professor took his nephew to the ground, he threw a small pack over his shoulder.

The dragon narrowly missed his prey but swallowed Gideon's package. Roaring with anger, Gong Gong flew upwards. Gaining altitude for another pass.

Lewis lay on his back watching the beast climb toward the heavens, the air trembling with every flap of its enormous wings.

The Dragon turned its attention back towards them and began another dive.

It opened its mouth to let out another roar, but this time something different happened.

It made a horrible choking noise. The dragon pulled out of its dive and tried to scratch at its throat with its front claws.

There was an enormous boom.

A bright flash filled the sky and Lewis was forced to cover his eyes.

When his eyes readjusted, Gong Gong was still there, only now he was without his head.

"Yes! Woo!!!!" He cried with sheer exhilaration.

Lewis' joy was short-lived, however, as gravity presented them with an entirely new problem.

A giant, headless, dragon carcass plummeting back towards the earth at a startling rate of speed.

"Get down!" Gideon screamed in warning.

For the second time in less than a minute, Lewis found himself lying flat on the ground with his uncle laying on top of him.

Gong Gong's decapitated corpse exploded on impact. Bone and leathery skin shattered and fragmented into a million tiny pieces of shrapnel. Lewis watched as a piece of splintered rib ripped a hole in the heart of one of the fleeing cultists.

The rest of the beast became little more than gelatinous goo. A mixture of meat, fat, and bodily fluids pulverized together as it crashed into the earth.

Gideon pushed himself to his feet and made an attempt at wiping off the mud that covered him from head to toe.

"It's like I always say, 'No problem is so big that it cannot be solved with an equally large explosive device.'" He quoted himself with an ear to ear grin. Lewis took Gideon's hand and his uncle pulled him to his feet.

Lewis was shivering violently, a common occurrence when one is cold, wet, and standing in ankle-deep in dead dragon.

Blood mixed with mud everywhere he looked. Half-eaten, disemboweled bodies covered the ground. Which corpses were cultists and which were muscle for Mr. Wong, Lewis could not tell.

Antoine, exhausted and leaning on his staff, checked to see if any of the men were still alive. When he found there was no breath left in their body he said a brief prayer for the dead and moved on to the next. If they were breathing, Antoine would offer assistance. At least, that's what Lewis thought he would do. If he had found someone still breathing.

Ms. Dunham took great care not to look down at the carnage. Stepping carefully, she made her way to them, staying far enough away as to avoid getting Gong Gong on her shoes.

Lewis felt his uncle's hand on his shoulder. Gently, Gideon guided him out of the knee-deep gruesome gunk and over to Ms. Dunham.

She was shivering just like Lewis. Her eyes were red, but her face was composed. She'd been crying but didn't want anyone to know it.

An urge came over Lewis. He ran to her and, completely ignoring that he was covered in gore and grim, wrapped his arms around her in a fearsome hug.

To Lewis' surprise, after a moment she returned the hug. Putting her arms around him and squeezing tight.

Mr. Wong interrupted the embrace with a sharp cough.

"My apologies for disturbing you during such a tender moment. But being as though this dragon is on my property, I claim its remains as my rightful salvage" Wong's remaining men surrounded them, pistols at the ready. "Unless there are any objections?"

Lewis watched his uncle's hand drift towards his holster before Gideon decided against it, instead raising both palms in surrender. "I take it, Mr. Wong, that our détente is now at an end?"

"It is indeed Professor. I thank you for your assistance in this matter. If you ever set foot on one of my properties again I will have you shot on site." Mr. Wong's tone left no doubt he was sincere in his threat. Gideon did not allow the sudden reversal to bother him.

"Well, then we'd best be off. No point standing around in soggy socks now is there." Gideon said to no one in particular. "Mr. Wong."

Gideon tipped his hat to the gangster and the party took their leave.

Mr. Wong held his stare until they were all the way off his property. His men went to work without a word. Tending to their wounded, disposing of the dead, and pulling a large tarp over the still smoldering corpse of Gong Gong.

Rain continued to fall, but lighter now. Before the storm raged at them and the water it poured down had been a punishment. Now the clouds sprinkled them with a light drizzle, almost a cleansing mist. At least that's how Lewis chose to view it.

Will rubbed against his leg and gave a little whine. The poor dog was soaked to the bone, his fur a wet, matted mess. Lewis bent down and took the pup in his arms.

The party was of a mixed mood. Uncle Gideon was manic with triumph, adrenaline still coursing through his system. Ms. Dunham was still in shock, relieved but quietly trying to work through the strange and terrifying events of the past two days. And Antoine was brooding, about what Lewis did not know.

For Lewis' part, he was just tired. Tired and relieved that they were all still alive. He'd lost too many people in his young life. He was not sure he could take losing another.

Emerging from the docks, Lewis expected there to be a large crowd waiting for them. Anxious for information about what had just transpired. There had, after all, been a dragon flying over the Mississippi only minutes ago.

Instead, they found the streets deserted. With almost a foot of water on the ground. It seemed as a result of the more tangible peril of storms and flooding holding their focus, no one had noticed the more otherworldly menace that had threatened their existence.

"I don't think we're going to have much luck hiring a cab." Uncle Gideon said, trying desperately to keep the water out of his boots.

"Wait here." Antoine responded, before sloshing his way down the street.

The rest of them watched him go. When he disappeared into a double shotgun home down the street, they shifted their gaze to each other. It was more than a little uncomfortable. The rising water level didn't help.

"I'm sure he won't be a moment." Gideon announced awkwardly.

"Is this how my mother died? On one of your fantastic adventures?" Ms. Dunham asked abruptly.

"Not quite. But close enough, in that I shoulder the blame for her death." Gideon finally confessed. Lewis felt shame and relief at his uncle's admission.

"Did she know about you and your work?" Ms. Dunham pressed her inquiry.

"Yes." Gideon answered plainly.

"And she stayed in your employ anyway." It was easy to tell that she had her doubts about that.

"For almost fifteen years. She was an integral member of my house. Of my family." Gideon choked up a little as he said the words.

Ms. Dunham stood there staring at Gideon. Then her eyes moved to Lewis. Unable to face her gaze, Lewis lowered his head.

"Okay then." Was all she said.

Antoine re-emerged from the shotgun home, a moment later a carriage came around from the back of the house and Antoine climbed in.

They waited in silence. No one wanting to be the first to speak. Until suddenly Gideon did something unexpected.

"Ms. Dunham, it was my hope, now that you have a deeper understanding of this household's special needs, that you might decide to take your mother's place and stay on with us." As much as his uncle's offer surprised Lewis, it seemed to surprise Ms. Dunham even more.

"To be clear, after a week in which I have been lied to, kidnapped, nearly drowned and come face to face with both a secret underground cult and the Dragon God they worship; rather than run screaming all the way back to Connecticut, it is your wish that I become your housekeeper?" she asked with palpable incredulity.

"That is about the size and shape of it, yes." Gideon affirmed with a solemn nod.

"I want double what my mother was making." She demanded.

"Done." Gideon agreed without hesitation.

"Then Professor Giles, for the time being at least, it seems you have a new woman of the house." Ms. Dunaham stuck out her hand to make the agreement official.

Lewis shouted "Hurray" while Will added his own sharp bark of approval.

"Did I miss some'ding?" Antoine asked stepping down from the driver's perch and opening the carriage door.

"Ms. Dunham has agreed to stay." Lewis answered with great enthusiasm.

"A most excellent outcome. It warms my heart te have you join our merry little band." Antoine assisted Ms. Dunham into the carriage. "Gideon, a word please."

Antoine pulled Gideon a few steps from the carriage. Ms. Dunham was now talking away. Lewis let Will out of his hands to distract her. The collie jumped into her lap for a thorough petting. Lewis concentrated on what his Uncle and Antoine were discussing.

"…..you saw de portal. You know what dis means." Antoine warned.

"The barrier is weakening. Our world is becoming vulnerable to incursion. This was only the beginning." Gideon stated simply

"Because of us, Professor. Dis be on us." Antoine's voice was tight and full of shame.

"You don't know that." Gideon argued emphatically. The two men stared at each other for a long moment. Gideon was the first to look away. He took a deep breath before meeting his friend's eyes again. "Either way you're right. It's up to us to fix it."

"And if we can't?" Antoine asked in a fearful whisper.

Ms. Dunham, Will still happily wagging his tail in her lap, leaned out to interrupt their conversation before Gideon could answer.

"Come on gentlemen. I'm not getting any drier. We'd best get home so I can fix dinner. I assume chicken and biscuits will be to everyone's satisfaction?"

"Yes please!" Lewis exclaimed.

"Most excellent, thank you, Ms. Dunham. I find myself astonishingly famished after our latest adventure." Gideon said, climbing into the carriage.

"Dat seems te happen every time we fight a demon." Antoine grinned.

"Correlation does not imply causation." Lewis stated studiously, garnering a hearty laugh from them all as together they began the short ride home.

But even as he laughed, Antoine's last question lingered in Lewis' thoughts.

Professor Gideon Giles will return in
Murder in the Marigny

II

Lagniappe

The War of Eight

(An excerpt from G. R. Linden's debut novel *The Seeker*)

"Tell us a story, Alistair."

Raph wasn't sure what had compelled him to make that particular request, but it seemed normal for a boy's godfather to tell him a story around a campfire and Raph was a fan of anything that seemed the slightest bit normal at the moment.

"Yeah Alistair, tell us a story. Please?" Billy took up the call timidly.

"I would be honored to hear a story from the Fox's own lips." Alistair harrumphed and broke out in a smirk at that last remark. But Raph knew that Lux had hit a soft spot by playing to Alistair's ego so Raph followed suit.

"C'mon Alistair, you always tell the best stories."

"Tell us a story about Avalon. It'll be educational and fun." Leave it to Billy to try and use the word educational to win someone over. Alistair might have had the same thought because his smirk had become a full-blown grin now.

"All right, All right. Settle in and I'll tell you a story." He waited for the boys to get comfortable on their bedrolls and a suitable quiet to fall upon them before he started, in a solemn baritone, to tell his tale:

"A long time ago, before you and me, before Arthur and the Grail, before civilization had even begun on Avalon or Earth, came eight men and women of enormous wisdom and understanding. There was Tarth who put his faith in an ordered universe. Tarth's closest companion was the maverick

Zha who believed that the universe's true beauty lay in its fundamental randomness. There were Lani and Aman who believed the universe was balanced between the forces of the feminine and the masculine. There was level-headed visionary Jer, who believed anything possible through science and technology. His opposite was the oldest and most beautiful among them, Terra, who believed that everything they had discovered was a gift from a living, conscious universe and should be treated with the appropriate reverence. The youngest of the collective was Gias, a devout seeker of truth who was second in wisdom only to their leader Galed. Galed who saw all of these fragmented philosophies and brought them together in common purpose.

They were a group as devoted to each other as they were to the pursuit of knowledge. And that pursuit took them to a radical discovery. They discovered that they could bend reality to their will and by doing so could open portals to other worlds. Worlds where different choices had been made, where humanity had taken another path, where the laws of nature as they knew them did not apply. This revelation was beyond any of their wildest dreams. Together they decided to explore these other worlds, learning all they could, cataloging their discoveries for future generations. And so the eight became the first Travelers; men and women capable of moving between worlds, hopping from one reality to the next. Whether they were truly the first to discover this power or simply the first amongst those worlds reachable by us I cannot say. I doubt even they knew in truth.

So they traveled, encountering every imaginable type of civilization as they did. Societies devoted to law and order. Societies both matriarchal and patriarchal. Some devoted to science and the pursuit of the rational and some steeped in faith and myth giving honor to the mystic. Some completely devoid of structure altogether. Most of the worlds they encountered were primitive compared to their own. Their inhabitants struggling to comprehend the visitors from another world. Some called them gods, others devils. Over time a few of the eight grew arrogant, believing themselves superior to the worlds they visited. There was talk that they should take a more active role in guiding these worlds towards a more civilized future. But just what the nature of this direction should be, quickly became a matter of contention amongst them. Rifts began to form. Differences became disagreements. Disagreements became rivalries. Rivalries became open hostility. The eight shattered. Abandoning the path that they had agreed upon; they sought out worlds to influence and shape, places where they could consolidate their power and plot against the others. All in the name of the greater good.

Only Gias and Galed stayed true to their original goals. They continued to Travel. Searching for truth and understanding in the worlds that they saw. Ignorant of how far their brethren had fallen. Until one day, the pair came to a world incredibly similar to one they had visited before. So much so that Gias was incredulous as to the assertions that this was not, in fact, the same world. He demanded to be brought a child named Olvir, whom he had befriended on their previous visit, only to be told that the child had died some time ago. Drowned in a river.

It seems that their visit to the first world had been the cause of some excitement and so the children of the village had forgone their usual trip to the river that day to see the strangers from another world. But on this new world, they had never come. So Olvir had no reason not to go to the river that day. He had slipped, hit his head on a rock, and fallen beneath the current.

Despair came over Gias. He had spent all this time, searched all these worlds for universal truth. For some deeper understanding of infinity. Finally, he had found it and he did not like what he saw. He went to Galed and told him of his epiphany. That any moment of joy creates an infinite tree of despair. That choice is an illusion we give ourselves. That we are just part of the universe's fractal geometry. That we are here not because we choose to be, but because we must be in order to account for this particular set of probabilities. Galed tried to calm his friend. If every choice is accounted for, he said, if all possible outcomes exist then that means that our choices are all that matters. We are the sum of a unique set of outcomes and no other version of us exists that is exactly like we are in this moment. That makes us special. It means we get to strive to be our best. Always knowing in the process we vindicate all the versions of ourselves who made lesser choices.

But Gias refused to see the universe the way Galed did. Worse he realized that his mentor had possessed this knowledge all along and not shared it with him. So he ran. To the farthest stretches of what the eight had explored together and beyond. He sought isolation to think on what he had discovered. He found it, on a desolate world useful only as a junction to other realities.

Galed wished to follow him. To counsel Gias and help him process the enormity of the knowledge he had gained. But he had ignored the rest of the eight too long, hoping that they would realize their follies and make amends when finally faced with the reality of what they were doing. But an open war was now being raged amongst the other six. The destinies of many worlds were being subjugated to the whims of his former friends. Galed knew he must make a choice. And so Galed went to war."

Alistair stopped there and reached for his canteen. Raph could feel the silence gripping him. Pulling at him but he dared not move for fear of breaking the atmosphere of anticipation that had settled over them all. Alistair took two long swigs of water looked each of them in the eyes then continued on.

"It was a fearsome struggle that would go on for centuries. The others had secured strongholds, raised armies, and designed weapons. Whole worlds worshiped them as gods. But there was a reason Galed had been their leader, had been called the wisest of them all. He understood the secret to Bending, the term they had come to use for their manipulation of reality. We are all connected and collectively we shape the reality that we see around us. While the others sought to impose their will upon the universe, Galed simply understood it for what it was. And in doing so had access to power beyond anything the others could imagine. Still, he was one man against a thousand worlds and he could not fix the damage that had been done overnight. Slowly and methodically he conquered world after world only to set them free. Allowed once again to pursue their own destinies, they rallied behind Galed. Perhaps if the six had combined their forces they might have stopped him, but at this point, the only thing they hated more than Galed was each other.

As Galed planned for a major offensive against Tarth and Jer, the last two significant threats to the free worlds, word reached him that Gias had finally reemerged, the final force in what would become known as the War of Eight or the Infinity War. Where the others conquered, ruled, influenced; Gias and his servants only destroyed. He laid waste to every world he touched leaving nothing, not even ruin, behind him.

Now here is where what is known and what is believed begin to blur together. Some say that Galed's spies came to him having discovered Gias' plot, others hold that the universe itself cried out to Galed for assistance, while still others believe that so great was Galed's wisdom that he needed no signs, no warning as to Gias' intent. He simply knew what his friend would try to do. Whatever the source of the knowledge, Galed knew that Gias sought the end of everything and that only he could stop him. Abandoning all other plans, he made haste for where it seemed Gias was headed, a lifeless world of storms and desert that they had visited long ago. From here Gias intended to end all suffering the only way he knew how, by ending reality itself.

Galed met his protégé in epic battle. The universes trembled as they fought. Bursts of power and destruction rippling outwards. Whole worlds extinguished, gone as if they had never been. Gias finding power in his madness, Galed in his acceptance. Both drawing upon a view of infinity that no mortal had ever glimpsed before. Finally, Galed found his opening and struck a fatal blow at the cost of his own life. The others knew what had happened. They knew that their arrogance and stubbornness had almost lead to the end of existence itself. Their pride would not let them admit that they were wrong, but they were no longer absolutely certain that they were right either. And so an uneasy peace fell upon them. No accord was struck, no treaties signed, but no more battles were fought. Galed's sacrifice had brought the Infinity War to a close. Thus ends the tale of the eight. The story of a man who understood and a man who didn't."

Alistair finished with a flourish. Billy and Lux broke out in quiet applause, faces beaming with delight. Raph sat quietly meeting Alistair's eyes. It was an excellent story and the telling of it had been phenomenal but Raph doubted that Alistair had selected this tale at random. He'd wanted them to hear it. It was related to what they were up against.

"Alistair, how was Gias going to destroy all reality? Your story didn't tell us." Alistair smiled and shrugged at Raph's question.

"I don't know. The stories don't say. It has been the subject of scholarly debate for millennia. Perhaps Gias took the secret to his grave. Perhaps he didn't. Let us hope that we do not find the answer in our lifetime."

Something about the way Alistair said that last sentence made sure that Raph did not sleep well that night.

Time to Dance

"Yes, I have killed. But what man here hasn't? I killed to protect my family, to protect my property, and to revenge myself against those who have done me wrong. I see no wrong, no evil in what I have done. Who are you to condemn me, you who would have acted no differently? This is not the end. There will be blood now. It drenches your hands not mine. I go to Mother with my soul clean. May you be damned for your foolishness and your pride."

And with that John Parker Willis was hung from his neck until he was dead.

Twenty years. That was how long it had been. Twenty years since The Cleansing. Twenty years since her mother had held her tight as she watched her father murdered in the name of justice. Twenty years since they were forced to flee the colony in the middle of night. Twenty years of doing whatever it took to put food on the table. Twenty years since she swore her revenge.

"Kat?" The voice jolted her back to reality. Frank and the gang were staring at her, waiting for the go ahead. The night was clear, the air crisp. The hum of the hover-train could be heard in the distance. It was time.

"Alright boys we do this quick and clean. Remember no bodies, no bounty. But if it comes down to some lout kin-shafter or you, burn 'em." Her voice was cold, confident. It held command, just like her daddy's. "Let's roll out."

"You heard her you soft- skinned dome dwellers! Move!" The roar came from Frank, doing his duty as her second. It was unnecessary; the gang was already in motion. Ted and Keena were off in the skimmer with the EMP prepped and ready. Taleed took to the tree tops with his scope to provide cover in case any colonials decided to play hero. He was trustworthy for a blue skin, even if Frank disagreed with her. Frank and Jer had their burners out, charged and glowing with their lethal light; ready to watch her back. She kicked her repulsorbike into gear and engaged the throttle. Ten seconds later she was in the canyon, ridding her dual pump Bardium charged motor at a hundred and sixty LPH on an intercept vector with the hovertrain.

Kat could feel the adrenaline pump through her body as she careened toward her target. The anticipation of the job, the thrill of the wind in her hair, the ever-present risk that this was the night she would be called to Mother's Bosom; they all served to heighten her senses and hone her mind. She received the double click on her com unit, the skimmer was in position. Thirty seconds to intercept.

"Time to Dance."

The words were a whisper on her lips.

The EMP exploded on schedule and the hovertrain's signature hum died with it. The safety foam fired as per standard emergency protocols and absorbed the punishment physics would have wished extracted. Even so the crash was fairly impressive, the mile-long train burrowing itself into the clay it had refused to touch only seconds earlier. She made an abrupt turn stop when she came to the fifth car from the end. Frank and Jer followed suit. "Start the clock." She hollered over the idle of the engine. "Four minutes starting now." Was the response from Frank as Jer unstrapped their equipment from the bikes.

Kat pulled the grappling hook out of her bag and scored a clean shot at the roof. Frank nodded to her; the laser cutter was good to go. She anchored the grappling line and the trio began their ascent. The foam had finally hardened now, making the climb easier than she had planned for. Once they reached the roof they moved quickly to get the laser cutter in place. Ninety seconds since the EMP went off. On schedule. Good. She slipped on her harness and narrowly avoided the sting of the laser as she dove headfirst through the newly formed hole. She felt the pull of gravity as the floor rushed to meet her. The harness snapped her momentum back as she was left suspended inches above the floor. She slipped out of the harness and got her bearings. The room was dimly lit by emergency glow rods. The room was full of safety deposit boxes using genetic key locks. Her information had been good. She snapped her own glow rod into action and searched for box three-twenty-three. Middle row, easier than opening a door. She pulled the spray pack out of her bag and sloshed her own version of the foam in the locking mechanisms across the whole middle row of boxes. This derivation of the foam was just a tad more explosive. She attached a small electric detonator and walked to the other side of the room.

The blast was small, controlled, and effective. She secured the contents of three-twenty-three in a special segmented pocket in her bag and went about cleaning out the other boxes. She moved methodically checking each for valuables but where an amateur would discard documents for gold and jewels; Kat took special care to secure them. On this planet information paid good money, besides you can't burn jewels. One box in particular caught her eye; in it was a stack of papers. The envelope on top was sealed with the mark of the Chairman of the Colonial Authority.

Her comm beeped loudly in her ear, one minute till the colonial militia joined the party. "Move it Kat!" came the shout from Frank. She secured the rest of the loot and slipped back into her harness. No sooner did she give the rope a tug than she was whipped upward and unceremoniously dumped onto the roof of the train. She felt pain and knew she would regret that later but pushed through and hurried to the edge of the car.

"Graceful." Jer teased, a grin plastered across his face.

A dull roar made itself known just as their comms blared a thundering alarm.

"Later." Was her only response.

Kat could make out a battle platform moving their way. Fast, but not fast enough. The repulsor-bikes escorting it on the other hand were going to be a problem.

"Need a lift?" Keena's sultry voice announced the solution. Ted maneuvered the skimmer into position and with a running start. Kat, Frank, and Jer all made it safely on board. As soon as they touched the deck, the skimmer was off; trying to put some space between themselves and their pursuers. This next trick would help with that.

Kat waited for just the right moment to triple click her comm. A blast of black muck shot into the air originating from the repulsor-bikes they'd left behind. As a reward for her good timing, only two of their half dozen pursuers emerged. That number didn't last long as Taled got into the action. The lead rider took a shot to the head and his now unmanned bike swerved right into the last thing between them and a clean getaway.

"Sometimes I love that magnificent blue skinned devil!" Frank had a tendency to forget his prejudices in the heat of a job.

Later when they'd made it back to the safe house without incident, Kat dumped the loot on the table so everyone could be present to check the haul. While the others sorted through the various items she had nabbed from the deposit boxes she pulled the envelope with the Chairman's seal on it out of her pack. She slipped her blade slowly out of her belt and very carefully broke the seal. That offense alone was punishable by death. She removed the letter inside and read it carefully, taking in each word. They struck her like so many lashes of a katari. Her hands trembled as she folded the letter up and returned it to the envelope.

They were all looking at her now, concerned for their leader, weary of what could possibly have this effect on her. "Kat?" Frank spoke; it was always Frank who spoke. "Kat what is it?"

The words burned her throat as they emerged. They were words of doom. Worlds would burn, innocents would die. But finally she had her chance. Finally she could avenge her father. *Time to Dance.* "The letter gives instructions for preparations to be made. The Tribunal is coming. The Cleansing is returning."

To be continued in...
The Tribunal

Selected Six-Word Stories

1. Empty bottle. Drove home. So sorry.
2. Damn cuffs. Next time, no elephant.
3. Yes, I set the timer. …..Chinese?
4. He promised they'd be tasteful.
5. Mrs. Thomas Garret? We're sorry Ma'am.
6. New door. This time it's bulletproof.
7. Two Kids. Wife. Husband. Murder-Suicide.
8. Love at first sight. Then divorce.
9. Long story short. Went camping. Bear.
10. Vending machines kill seven people annually.
11. National tragedy. Two-for-one caskets.
12. Honey, you should call your doctor.
13. Needed: Maid/cook for elderly widower.
14. Fifty years. Four kids. One Marriage.
15. Car. House. Job. Ramen for one.
16. Two goals to Nil. Bangin' Result.
17. Mom's cancer has come back again.
18. And that's why escalators aren't toys.
19. The sun rose. Then it set.
20. I asked. She slapped me. Twice.

Selected Playlists

A Time for Reflections
1. *House of the Rising Sun* by The Animals
2. *Steampunk Revolution* by Abney Park
3. *Weird Science* by Oingo Boingo
4. *Reflektor* by Arcade Fire
5. *I Want You (She's So Heavy)* by Halestorm
6. *The Lion, The Beast, The Beat* by Grace Potter and the Nocturnals
7. *Steam Powered (feat. Jon Clark)* by Professor Elemental

Where Have All My Heroes Gone
1. *Are you Going to Be My Girl* by Jet
2. *Cherry Bomb* by The Runaways
3. *One Way or Another* by Blondie
4. *I Can't Get You Off My Mind* by Miss Li
5. *Don't Let Me Be Misunderstood* by Nina Simone
6. *Good Intent* by Kimbra
7. *Barracuda* by Heart
8. *White Rabbit* by Jefferson Airplane
9. *Mad World* by Jasmine Thompson

SELECTED PLAYLISTS

Where Have All My Heroes Gone (Cont.)
10. *Bring Me to Life* by Evanescence
11. *Cold Hard Bitch* by Jet
12. *Holding Out for a Hero* by Bonnie Tyler

Oasis
1. *God's Gonna Cut You Down* by Kevin Lovatt
2. *No Place to Hide* by Jace Everett
3. *Black* by Kari Kimmel
4. *Season of the Witch* by Donovan
5. *Rain in The Valley* by The Steel Wheels
6. *Lift Your Head Weary Sinner (Chains)* by Crowder
7. *I'm a Wanted Man* by Royal Deluxe
8. *Blood on My Name* by The Brothers Bright
9. *Nothing but The Water* by Grace Potter and The Nocturnals

Remedial Spellcasting
1. *Trouble* in Mind by Larkin Poe
2. *Raise Hell* by Dorothy
3. *The Kid's Aren't Alright* by The Offspring
4. *Paranoid* by Black Sabbath
5. *Kids in the Dark* by All Time Low
6. *Demon* by Kandle
7. *Toxic* by Britney Spears
8. *Dead Hearts* by Stars
9. *Radioactive* by Within Temptation
10. *Black Sheep* by Gin Wigmore
11. *Mad World (Feat. Michael Andrews)* by Gary Jules

Intermezzo
1. *The Big Dream* by David Lynch
2. *All Shook Up* by Avila
3. *Bang Bang (My Baby Shot Me Down)* by Nancy Sinatra
4. *At Last* by Etta James
5. *Last Call* by David Lynch

The Climb
1. *Over the Rainbow* by Israel Kamakawiwo'ole
2. *Make Me Feel Better* by Alex Adair
3. *Walking Through the Jungle* by Sounds of The Deep Forest
4. *Attack of the Natives* by Dominik Morgenroth and Daniel Pharos
5. *Go Like Time Around An Arrow (feat. Circle Percussion) Part 3 Onwards to Meridian* by Niels van der Leest
6. *Wicked Games* by Parra for Cuva, Anna Naklab
7. *50 Ways to Leave Your Lover* by G. Love & Special Sauce

No Refuge
1. *Arsonist's Lullaby* by Hozier
2. *Arise and Shine* by Barry Segal and Batya Segal
3. *Praise the Lord* by Daniel Kopp and Sarah Liberman
4. *American Crazy* by Brothers Osborne
5. *Semper Fidelis* by John Phillip Sousa and the United States Marine Corp Band
6. *The Star-Spangled Banner* by John Stafford Smith and The Mormon Tabernacle Choir
7. *You're a Grand Old Flag* by George Cohan, Lowell Graham and the United States Air Force Concert Band
8. *Battle Hymn of the Republic (arr. K. Miller)* by William Steffe, Ken Miller, United States Air Force Academy Cadets
9. *This Land is Your Land* by Sam Hunt
10. *The Star-Spangled Banner* by Chase Holfelder

SELECTED PLAYLISTS

Fight Night
1. *Bulls on Parade* by Rage Against the Machine
2. *The Devil You Know* by JJ Grey and Mofro
3. *Enter Sandman* by Metallica
4. *Blow Up* by Curbi
5. *You're the One That I Want* by Angus and Julia Stone
6. *The Distance* by Cake
7. *Wicked Game* by Phillip Phillips
8. *Rage and Romance* by Bressie
9. *Fire* by Barnes Courtney
10. *Bodies* by Drowning Pool
11. *Remember the Name (feat. Styles of Beyond)* by Fort Minor

The Coming Flood
1. *Weird Science* by Oingo Boingo
2. *Trust* by Bitter Ruin
3. *Bones* by MS MR
4. *Building Steam* by Abney Park
5. *The Wondersmith and His Sons* by Astonautalis
6. *Victorian Vigilante* by Abney Park
7. *Eli's Coming* by Three Dog Night
8. *Splendid* by Professor Elemental
9. *Short Change Hero* by The Heavy
10. *Lady in Waiting (feat. Unwoman)* by Escape the Clouds
11. *Bogeyman* by Johnny Hollow
12. *Kiss with A Fist* by Florence + The Machine
13. *Written in The Water* Gin Wigmore
14. *Sinnerman* by Nina Simone
15. *Immigrant Song* by Led Zeppelin
16. *Firepower* by Judas Priest
17. *Wash Me in The Water* by Jamie N Commons

Milton Keynes UK
Ingram Content Group UK Ltd.
UKHW050831250324
439991UK00001B/322